THE
RECRUIT

ALAN DREW

CORVUS

First published in Great Britain in 2022 by Corvus, an imprint of
Atlantic Books Ltd. This paperback edition published in 2023 by Corvus.

10 9 8 7 6 5 4 3 2

A CIP catalogue record for this book is available from the British Library.

ISBN: 978 1 78649 374 3

Printed and bound by CPI Group (UK) Ltd, Croydon, CR0 4YY

Corvus
An imprint of Atlantic Books Ltd
Ormond House
26–27 Boswell Street
London
WC1N 3JZ

www.atlantic-books.co.uk

MIX
Paper | Supporting
responsible forestry
FSC
www.fsc.org
FSC® C171272

THE
RECRUIT

1985

The Ten Lost Tribes

The shades on the windows of the Citation II jet had been sealed shut. He knew enough not to try to open them. Until they held dominion over the state and federal governments, until they were on the edge of The Tribulation, the culmination of their work, secrecy was essential. He ran his finger along the caulking that glued the edge of the shade to the interior panel of the plane, the summer sun illuminating the opaque plastic. He knew, of course, as they all did, the location of many of the churches around the country, but a few of them, the last strongholds for when the war broke out, were kept off the map. Everyone knew these strongholds existed, but they were like mythical places, like the Nine Worlds of Norse mythology, and you never saw them until you were ordained.

Still, guessing the cruising speed of the plane, around 374 knots, he could calculate that they were about four hundred miles into the flight. Since the sun was on his right, he figured they were flying northeast, probably crossing over the Great Basin. He had flown his own four-seater prop plane out to the high Mojave Desert this morning—nothing like this plane, nothing like the small fleet of private jets The Reverend owned—and landed at an airstrip grated out of a dried-up lake bed. The name of the airstrip didn't matter—it was best the name remain unsaid. What mattered was its location—more than one hundred miles east of Los Angeles and far enough away from Edwards Air Force Base to go unwatched. The strip had no control tower and it lay beneath controlled airspace, so no one would know he had landed there. More important, no one would know that one of The Reverend's Citation IIs had touched down, either. He'd left his Comanche tied to the desert floor and waited in the morning heat until the wheels of the private jet touched the lake bed, the engines kicking up a stream of rock dust as they screamed the plane to a stop.

He was the only one on this flight. There was no stewardess, just a pilot and a copilot locked away in the cockpit, and this month's America's Divine Promise Ministries magazine sitting on the fold-down table in front of him. The Reverend's face filled the cover. Dressed in a deep-blue suit, shelves of books behind him, he smiled out of the frame as though you were the only person who existed in the world. That was The Reverend's power—his smile, the cobalt eyes that seemed to look straight through your chest and into your beating heart. He had this power on printed paper, wielded it from the television screen, and today, Richard Potter Wales would discover if the man had that power in person.

Wales had captured The Reverend's interest with a proposal concerning a system of bulletin boards that could be accessed anywhere in the world through the new personal computers. That was one of the reasons Wales would be ordained today, given the distinction of "reverend." But there was really only one: *The* Reverend. He was the man Wales wanted to impress and, when the time was right, one day be; The Reverend was the man they all wanted to be. He was the model for them all, the lowercase *r* in their titles both aspirational and a reminder of their place. They had been—all these groups all over the country—frustrated and lost in the wilderness of a dying culture, sitting alone in desert compounds, hiding in remote mountain valleys, watching as post-civil-rights liberalism destroyed America. But The Reverend would lead them out of the wilderness to reclaim what had been stolen from them, to destroy what had poisoned the culture.

An hour and ten minutes later, the engines of the jet wound down and the plane banked into a descent. Doing the calculation in his head, Wales knew approximately where they were, but he tried to keep it quiet to himself. Some things really weren't supposed to be known until it was time.

On the ground, the copilot opened the fuselage door and Wales stepped out into the light. Northern Utah, he guessed, or southern Idaho. They were on a sagebrush plain, the horizon darkened with humps of mountains. Nothing but empty land surrounded the airstrip, but, maybe a mile away, he could see rows of suburban-style homes, construction cranes, and a congregation of light poles that suggested athletic fields. The airstrip was adjacent to the church, a white single-story rectangle surrounded by neatly cut shrubs. The church was the center of an asphalt parking lot, and at the entrance to the lot, running along the edge of a newly paved service road, a large cross punctured the desert sky. A sign next to the cross read CHURCH OF JESUS CHRIST CHRISTIAN. Everything looked brand new, much of the money to build this church coming from The Reverend's Divine Promise Ministries. Promise had many connotations—theological, financial, and fraternal; once The Reverend sent you money, you were empowered but also bound.

On Sundays this lot would be full, the sanctuary filled with parishioners' voices flatly singing hymns. The power of the place was its normalcy, Wales knew, the way it felt like any other rural church filled with God-fearing white Americans— outside of the airstrip, of course.

Wales's own church, in the California foothills of the Sierras, was filled with average people—truck drivers, schoolteachers, small-business owners, clerks at the local grocery store—who weren't *in* the Identity Movement but were open to a more subtle version of the ideology. No Two-Seed Theory, no discussion of "mud people," but they were more than receptive to fury over the welfare state, rage about inner-city waste and violent minorities. Subtlety, that was the key, quiet indulgence of parishioners' fears. Identity wasn't the Klan with their silly hoods and their burning torches. Identity was The Reverend in his suburban Fort Worth mega-church, with its gospel choir and arena-sized audiences. The Identity Movement was America's Divine Promise's syndicated television broadcast, with its smiling gospel choir, and The Reverend's assurance that God wanted his *chosen* people to be wealthy. *Send your donations now and God will reward you tenfold!* What was it like, Wales thought, to have that kind of power, to compel people from all over the country to send you money, to convince people you were a conduit to God? How could he learn to be this kind of man?

As he descended the boarding stairs, Wales saw a man in a dark three-piece suit striding across the tarmac toward the plane.

"Brother Wales," reverend Klein said as Wales stepped onto the tarmac.

They embraced. Wales had never met Elias Girnt Klein, but he'd read some of his sermons in his *Liberty Front* magazine, a monthly pamphlet Klein distributed to a list of subscribers. It was Klein's sermons, Wales knew, that got The Reverend's attention. But Wales had proposed something much bigger than typed-up sermons on cheap paper; what he'd proposed to The Reverend was visionary, something that would make those pamphlets look like minor dispatches from the Dark Ages.

"He hasn't arrived yet," Klein said. "Please, let's greet the others."

Inside the church, women were setting up a potluck in the back of the sanctuary. Crock-Pots of meat and bean stews, hot-plates of hot dogs, potato salad. Huckleberry pie. The men were gathered near the pulpit. It looked like a business meeting, the other reverends dressed in dark suits, too, their hair combed and sprayed, a wafting of cologne. Behind them, on the pulpit, was a baptismal tub, and above the tub hung a flag with the blue shield and the cross and crown. It looked like any other denomination's crest—the Methodist cross and fire, the Holy See's crown and keys—except for the wolfsangel, the ancient German runic symbol, slicing the center of the cross.

"Brother Wales," one of the men said, and then they were surrounding him, shaking his hand: reverend Jordan of Mason, Ohio; reverend Perry of Levittown, Pennsylvania; reverend Gaetz of Alpine, Utah; reverend Barr of Paradise Valley, Arizona; and a half dozen more. Each of them wore a heavy ring on his right ring finger, the metal slapping Wales's knuckles as they shook. He'd never met the men, but he knew of them through their loose network of rural churches—even before The Reverend pulled them into his ministry. All of them felt they were on the edge of some important moment with the end of the twentieth century, the millennium, just fifteen years away.

"He just landed," a woman said from the back of the sanctuary.

All the men turned toward the wide windows facing the airstrip and watched The Reverend's jet streak across the tarmac.

Three minutes later, a young man in a charcoal fitted suit strode into the sanctuary. "The Reverend is on a tight schedule," he said. He wore a skinny black tie with a white straight-edge handkerchief, his green eyes flashing behind clear-rimmed glasses. There was something vaguely European about the look, something that whispered *aristocrat*. The young man strode up to the pulpit and started wiping the podium down with a cloth. Three men in black suits came through the back door of the sanctuary and frisked each of the reverends. Through the window, Wales watched as The Reverend walked down the steps of the plane and strode across the tarmac, all alone, Ray-Ban sunglasses obscuring his eyes, his jaw tight like he was grinding his teeth. Wales noted the look, a look of power and control he wished to emulate.

But when The Reverend walked through the back door, his glasses were folded into his coat pocket, and he threw the room that smile that electrified television screens.

"Mr. Wales," he said, striding between the pews toward him, both his hands outstretched. He took Wales's hands in his and held them like they were precious things. "My brother in Christ, it's so good to meet you in person." The Reverend's blue eyes radiated warmth and love, but more than that, his whole demeanor expressed control. Wales realized then that everything about his entrance was choreographed—the young man in the slick suit, the pseudo–Secret Service toughs, his lonely stride across the tarmac as though he were an iconic American hero in a Hollywood film: All of it was a part of The Reverend's show.

"This way," the young man in the charcoal suit said, his arm outstretched toward a back room.

"Please," The Reverend said, his hand on Wales's shoulder now. "Let's have a moment of fellowship."

They retreated to reverend Klein's office, where the young man in the charcoal suit had pulled together two green arm-chairs. The Reverend motioned for Wales to sit. He did but The Reverend walked around the small room and lifted something off a shelf behind reverend Klein's desk, weighed it in his hand, and then joined Wales on the chair across from him.

He opened his hand to Wales, a ceramic broken sun cross sitting in his palm.

"You know what this is, yes?"

Did The Reverend think he was an idiot? Of course he knew. "The symbol of the Thule Society. Adopted later by the Nation-alist Socialist German Workers' Party."

"This is *not* what we are," The Reverend said, a slash of anger

in his voice. "We have an image to uphold. Do you understand?" The Reverend looked at Wales hard.

"I understand." Of course, the swastika was too obvious,
even a subtle one like the broken sun cross. Klein was stupid
for keeping it around.

The Reverend held his eyes a moment longer and then
smiled. "Good." He pocketed the trinket, sat back in his chair,
and crossed his legs. He was all calm and pleasantness again.
"You've done well with the radio broadcasts."

Wales's radio sermons, broadcast out of tiny rural stations,
were what had initially caught The Reverend's attention. Small
donations to fund Wales's outreach occasionally arrived at his
church's PO box from Promise14Ministries, LLC—the company through which The Reverend quietly financed projects
that he felt served the movement. Just a check slipped into a
tri-folded piece of blank white paper.

"Not as well as you," Wales said.

The Reverend smiled, as though almost susceptible to flat-
tery. "You've inspired people."

Wales nodded. *Inspired.* Yes. You didn't have to kill; you could
inspire others to kill on your behalf. He knew The Reverend
was speaking about recent events in Nebraska and Colorado.
Events so distant to Wales, his hands were clean of them—
except for the killers' manifestos, except that they had used
excerpts from Wales's sermons. An unfortunate fact that left
Wales vulnerable, and The Reverend did not like vulnerability.

"You know you'll need to go into hiding?"

"Of course." They both knew the FBI was working those
cases, sniffing around for a larger conspiracy.

"We'll help facilitate that."

Wales nodded a thank-you.

"And"—The Reverend hesitated a moment—"you know
what you'll need to do if you get caught?"

Wales's stomach lurched, even though he expected the question and knew how he'd answer.

"I do."

The Reverend stared at him, searching for any weakness in his eyes. Then he leaned back in his chair, wiped his hand across his lap once as though brushing away crumbs. "Now your idea. You say it runs through computers and telephone lines? Lines law enforcement can't tap?"

"Yes," Wales said, sitting forward to explain. "It uses what they call a modem, a secure line that can only be accessed with pass codes."

In the spring, Wales had won an audience with one of The Reverend's representatives at the Aryan Nation World Congress in Idaho. He'd typed out a comprehensive plan, a list of materials to be acquired, potential for growth, initial invest-ment needed. He had handed it to the man in the small chapel on the Aryan Nation's compound. A month later the represen-tative contacted Wales with detailed plans for today's meeting.

"The FBI, other law enforcement might be able to find the bulletin board," Wales explained, "but they wouldn't be able to access it without those pass codes. Even if they did, no one would use their own names. They'd use handles like truck drivers do on CB radio. Everything would be anonymous—no names, no addresses, no way to trace."

"There'll be no mention of me, my ministries," The Rever-end said. "No ties to me."

"No."

"You say we can reach thousands."

"Maybe tens of thousands," Wales said. Truth be told, he didn't know the potential for this internet technology, but it seemed plausible—eventually. "Most important, it's interac-tive, connective. Not one-way communication, not like televi-sion."

The Reverend narrowed his eyes, as though the truth about the limitations of television was a personal offense.

"Anyone who has a computer in their home could access it,"

Wales went on. "A young man in Pennsylvania could communicate with other young men in Oregon and Missouri. It would be like all of us, every one of us around the country, the world, meeting in the same room—without the police knowing it even existed."

Wales knew he didn't need to oversell it; everything he needed to say had been clearly laid out in his written proposal. He could guess the equations The Reverend was making by the look on his face—the sharing of information, the dissemination of documents, the recruitment possibilities, the organizing opportunities, the potential, too, for a quickly mobilized army. Both decentralized and centralized at the same time.

"Good," The Reverend finally said, touching his shoulder, a reminder, it seemed, that it was his hand that could both save and destroy him. "Very good."

Back in the sanctuary the men formed a circle around Wales while The Reverend preached about Jacob fighting the angel at Peniel, about the Ten Lost Tribes, about how they came out of Israel and escaped over the Caucasus Mountains through the Black Sea to Arzareth and established Europe. He reminded everyone that they, white people, were the true Israelites. He recited Genesis 1:28 and sounded near to tears when he spoke about Christian stewardship of the land, about the divine duty of Adamic peoples to hasten The Tribulation, the war to rid the unclean from the nation.

"Do you swear to secure the future of this nation for our Adamic children?" he asked.

A few hands fell on Wales's shoulder now. His head was bowed and his eyes closed, but he knew he was the center of a spoke of arms that formed a wheel of defenders of the faith.

"I do," Wales said.

"Do you recognize the government of this great country to be in the hands of the satanic offspring of Eve and the Serpent?"

"I do."

"Do you swear to work to create an Edenic Adamic Israelite Colony in this nation?"

"I do."

"Do you commit yourself to hastening The Tribulation, to set the table for the return of our Christ?"

"I do."

Then it was over. The Reverend, taking Wales's hand in his, slipped a ring on his right ring finger: the red background, the blue shield and white cross. While the reverends congratulated him, Wales watched as The Reverend guided Klein back to the office. When Klein returned to the group, his face was bleached white. That stupid sun cross, Wales thought, making note of reverend Klein's foolishness. Still, Klein invited everyone to the potluck, tried to play the gracious host. Five minutes later, Wales took measure of The Reverend as he strode across the tarmac toward the jet—the man's broad shoulders, the perfectly fitted suit, that movie-star jaw. Yes, a show, but an effective one. As the others filled their plates, Wales stayed by the window and watched the choreography—The Reverend ducking into the fuselage of the plane, followed by his assistant and the three bodyguards, all of them glancing around as though expecting an assassination attempt—until the jet banked into the desert sky, a spark of light fading into the distance.

Soon, Wales was ushered onto the jet that had flown him here, after a hasty sampling of pulled pork and huckleberry pie. On the seat next to his sat a small briefcase. He didn't have to open it; he knew what was inside.

1987
PART ONE

Chapter One

Detective Benjamin Wade was parked in the emergency lane of the Lucky's parking lot at Alta Plaza, admiring the sight of the snow-covered Santa Ana Mountains shouldering out of storm clouds. It had snowed overnight down here, too, on the flats of Rancho Santa Elena, and shoppers, pushing their carts toward the entrance to the store, gawked at the rare spectacle of it. He was stealing a fifteen-minute lunch in his idling unmarked cruiser to put away an "animal style" In-N-Out burger, keeping an eye on the Salvation Army Santa who was pocketing change when no one was looking. He was just about to walk over there to introduce himself to St. Nick when the Code 3 hot response squawked in over the scanner. *Child in distress*, Marsha Lynn, the daytime dispatcher called over the radio, *19734 Jupiter Street, California Homes. Mother on-site.*

Ten minutes earlier, Ben had called to check in with his ex-wife, Rachel, on the cruiser's Motorola cellphone during her planning period at the high school where she taught English literature. Yes, he was getting Emma from school today. No, the pediatrician's appointment wasn't until *next* Tuesday. Yes, she'd pick up Emma out at his place at 4:30. He'd put in a call to Natasha—his girlfriend, he guessed, though that made it sound trivial—up at the county coroner, but according to Mendenhall, the chief medical examiner, Natasha was still out on the scene. Her pager had buzzed at 5:43 this morning, and he'd watched from his bed as she dressed in the dark, off to face the dead. He knew what they'd be talking about tonight.

Ben listened to the scanner now, waiting to see who would pick up the call. The Portrero Station EMTs were already working a three-car fatal on the Santa Ana Freeway, and the Trabuco Station was five miles away. The address was just a few blocks from where Ben sat in the strip mall, so he crumpled up the rest of the burger, jerked the cruiser into gear, and jetted out of the parking lot. The thieving Santa Claus would have to wait.

He was there in two minutes, parking the nose of the cruiser on the sidewalk in front of a single-story ranch home. The mother stood outside on the snow-splattered grass, a child, maybe three years old, twisted in her arms. "Oh, God," she was saying—he could hear her even before he threw open the door. "Oh, God. What's wrong? What's wrong, baby?" The terror streaked across her face jacked Ben up, his adrenaline suddenly pumping.

"Please," she said as Ben ran to her. "Please, he's not breathing."

Foam bubbled from the boy's lips, and blood, streaming from his nose, streaked his cheek.

"I don't know what's wrong," she said. "I don't know what happened."

Ben pressed his fingers to the boy's neck, trying to find a pulse in the carotid artery. Nothing. Shit.

"How long's he been like this?"

"I don't know. He was watching TV. I was in the kitchen."

He pushed up the boy's Sesame Street shirt, Cookie Monster munching chocolate chip, and laid his hand on the boy's belly.

"Please, let me have him," Ben said, pulling the boy from his mother's grasp, which sent her into a new round of wails.

He laid the boy down in the snow-wet grass, cradling the back of the boy's neck with his left palm and pressing his right hand on the child's thin sternum. With the heel of his hand, Ben pumped the sternum, foam frothing in the boy's open mouth, and pressed again. *Come on, kid. Come on.* He pumped again and again, the bone flexing beneath his hand, the boy's body limp in the grass.

A black-and-white swerved on scene, the bar lights throwing red and blue against the boy's white cheek. Using three fingers, Ben scooped the foam from the boy's mouth and flicked it onto the grass. He pinched the boy's nose shut and placed his mouth over the kid's lips, breathing his air into the child's body. The foam tasted syrupy-sweet metallic-bitter, Ben's tongue burning numb with it. *Come on, come on.* He broke the suction around the boy's mouth and took a surfer's breath, pulled in all the cold air like he was about to dive beneath a fifteen-foot crusher, and thrust his air into the boy. The child's chest heaved and he spit foamy breath across Ben's cheek.

"Oh, God. Thank you. Thank you."

Then the kid was coughing, his chest convulsing with oxygen.

"Where're the EMTs?" Ben yelled at the uniforms standing dumbly on the edge of the scene.

One of the cops ran to his cruiser, called in an ETA. "Junipero and Serrano."

"Shit." Ben lifted the coughing kid into his arms. "Get in the car," he said to the mother. Hoag Hospital was three-quarters of a mile away; he could be there in a minute. It'd be ten, maybe fifteen before the EMTs arrived, assessed the situation, and got the boy into emergency. The mother jumped into the passenger seat and Ben laid the boy on her lap—his blue eyes wide with fear now, the blood still running from his nose. Ben peeled the cruiser out of the driveway, and then gunned it out of the housing tract down El Rancho Road.

Hitting sixty, he called in to Hoag emergency. "Driving in a code pink," he said to the nurse on the line. "ETA one minute."

At the hospital, two nurses were waiting, a stretcher between them. Ben laid it out for one of the nurses as they ran the boy inside—unresponsive upon arrival, foaming mouth, bloody nose, CPR.

"How long in asystolic arrest?" one of the nurses said, two fingers on the boy's wrist as they ran through the sliding front doors of the hospital. "With no heartbeat? How long?"

"Not sure," he said. "At least a few seconds."

And then they were through the hallway and banging open the doors to the resuscitation room, the boy, wailing now, lifted out of the stretcher and laid out on the bed, an oxygen mask slipped over his mouth. A half dozen nurses and doctors crowded Ben out, a rush of scrubs, and the boy's mother crying *Is he going to be okay? Will he be all right?*

Ben stumbled out of the trauma room then, back into the waiting area. His tongue felt like a scrap of alloy, his mouth, too, like tinfoil lined the skin. He found a bathroom and locked himself inside, twisted on the faucet, and bent to slurp the water from the spigot, desperate to get the bitter taste out of his mouth.

————

It had been snowing when Natasha Betencourt arrived on the Huntington Beach scene. Not thick flakes like the ones falling in the San Gabriel Mountains, but hard pebbles that needled her cheeks. She was on her knees at the edge of a swimming pool, a warm fog of condensation rising from the heated water. The body was floating on its back, the man's eyes stunned wide open, staring blind at the white sky swirling above him.

"They usually bob facedown," the detective said, standing next to her.

"The skimmer's got him," Natasha said. The dead man's right hand was caught in the weir, holding the body in place;

jammed up with his fingers, the bucket was making a sucking noise.

"Right," the detective said. "But if he drowned in the pool, he'd still be doing a dead man's float." He held his right hand out to his side, mimicking the dead body, and spun his shoulders a bit, as though trying to imagine a scenario in which the body would somersault onto its back.

"Guess you've ruled out a midnight swimming accident then," Natasha said.

"I haven't ruled anything out."

She'd worked with Detective Joseph Vanek briefly on a case a few years back, '81 or '82, when she was learning the ropes as a brand-new medical examiner. During autopsy, she had found blood in the mouth of the female victim that wasn't her own and suggested to the detective that the woman had bitten her killer, perhaps in some kind of struggle. That led to a FedEx delivery man, whose route included the woman's suburban home, with bites on his right hand and wrist. Blood samples matched, and the killer confessed. A few days later, Vanek had sent her a thank-you note—a simple card with his name embossed on the front and his elegant handwriting on the back. Beyond that, she didn't know much about Vanek, but rumor back then had it that he'd been a homicide detective in South Central LA, working the crack cocaine wars before leaving the LAPD for the Huntington Beach job.

When she had arrived just after dawn, she had found the detective right here, in a fog of steam next to the pool, leaning on a black umbrella and talking scenarios out loud to himself. Now he tapped the aluminum tip of the umbrella against the cement pool edge, as though putting a quiet exclamation mark on an important thought.

"Real fancy, this one," Vanek said, "silk pajamas, slippers."

The dead man's wet pajamas clung to his body—little embroidered palm trees dotting the material, gold buttons down the shirt front, a rich, satiny look to the material. A button was

missing, just below the sternum, the man's white belly showing through. One slipper was dangling from his left foot, the
other spinning circles at the south end of the pool.

"His sandals are cheap," she said. "Like something you buy
in those tourist traps in the Garment District."

Vanek got down on his haunches to gaze at the rogue slipper.
"You've got an eye for cheap."

"Living on the county's dime."

He chuckled.

"Strange," he said, "to couple silk pajamas with those plastic
slippers."

She'd need to get her kit out of the van, start taking pics. She
stood now and glanced across the yard. A couple of cops stood
sentinel at the backyard gate. Through the haze of steam, she
could see the strand of raked beach beyond the fence and two
empty lifeguard stands facing a storm-churned Pacific.

It had been a pretty ride from Ben's place over to the Orange
County coroner to get her official Ford. Stoplights blinked
through the white haze of snow; the rising sun split a break in
the storm and lit up the hillsides, freshly glowing white. She
preferred a cold Southern California, and a dusting of snow—
well, not quite snow, but cold-clumped powdered sugar—was
such a rarity that it felt like a second Christmas. It made the
city quiet, as though the whole basin took a deep breath and
held it. She liked pause, the stillness in held breath. Now the
snow was turning into the lesser joy of rain. When people
woke, they'd never know the basin had briefly gone Wisconsin.
She sometimes thought about all the wonders people missed
while sleeping—and all the ugliness.

Detective Vanek popped open the umbrella and held it over
her head.

"Knew it would turn to rain once the sun came up," he said.
"Beautiful, though, that snow, wasn't it?"

"I'd say he's been dead at least three hours," she said, sticking to business. "Got rigor mortis in the arms and hands."

"Half-gone glass of red wine on the kitchen island," Vanek said. "Unless this guy's a real late-night drinker, I'm thinking longer than three."

"It's a damn big house." A beachfront three-story modern, glass from patio to rooftop. Definitely not working for the county.

"Got it all to himself," Vanek said. "At least until a few hours ago."

"Maid called it in?" Natasha could see her through the sliding glass door, sitting on a couch, shaking her head and talking it out with another detective.

"Said she was bringing him his morning espresso."

"Breakfast in bed," she said. "Lives of the rich and famous."

"When you're in real estate," Vanek said, "you get a maid to bring you whatever you want. Walter Brennan's his name. He's a player in the redevelopment of the waterfront."

"Maybe someone likes the waterfront the way it is."

"Maybe."

The rain was falling hard now, drops pelting the deceased's forehead and cheeks, pinging on the pool water. A wisp of smoke, she noticed now, rose from a firepit about fifty yards down the beach.

"Is there a lock on the backyard gate?"

"Nope," he said. "Would like to talk to whoever was bonfiring it out there last night."

"Good luck with that," she said. "Live in a house like this, giving a middle finger to the public beach, you invite antagonism."

Vanek nodded. "No sign of break-in. But look at this."

She followed him around the pool. He awkwardly held the umbrella behind him to keep her dry, the shoulders of his suit darkening from the rain. She couldn't tell if he was being kind or condescending or both. In a way she preferred open antagonism to subtle disdain. It was 1987, more than twenty years since NOW was founded, and most cops' fragile little egos couldn't handle a woman with brains on the scene. Would be happy to let her type up their reports, she was certain of that. Ben, though, was different from most cops; he respected her frontal lobe.

At the skimmer, Vanek bent down and pulled off the cap. Looked like a severed hand down there in the bucket.

"The pinkie finger's broken," she said. It cut a strange angle from the palm.

"Exactly."

Gashes slashed his knuckles. "You got a few punches in, huh?" she said to the body.

Closer to his face, she could see a contusion bruising the hairline.

"Blow to the temple," she said. "Punched, maybe fell, could have struck it against the side of the pool."

"I hear Mendenhall is running for chief again," Vanek said.

Chief medical examiner—her boss.

"That's what he tells me."

Something floated up from the bottom of the bucket then, spun a little red circle, swirled down beneath the hand, and then squiggled back up again. A thread, ox-blood red, the filter spinning it in circles.

"That's a shame," Vanek said. "Might be time for some new blood."

"Detective, this is a lovely conversation, but if you want to be useful get my kit out of the van and grab a vial."

"Here," he said, handing her the umbrella. And then she watched him stride out across the patio, already soaking wet from the rain and getting wetter.

———

Ben was parked outside the boy's house, the wet grass still matted where he'd laid the kid in the snow just an hour before. His gums still tingled, but the taste was mostly gone now, just a slight tinge of metal.

He'd left the hospital five minutes before, kicked out of emergency by the charge nurse. After the boy had stabilized, he'd been trying to interview the mother bedside. He'd felt like an A-grade asshole doing it—she was still frazzled, gutted by fear, and the boy lay there asleep, attached to the beeping EKG—but sympathy was no excuse not to do his job.

The mother said that she and Stephen had taken a walk in the snow that morning, looking for Duke, their dog, who sometimes jumped the fence and roamed the neighborhood. They didn't find the dog, but he usually came back in a few hours, so she wasn't too worried about it. Back at the house, she let the boy play in the backyard. They threw a couple of snowballs at each other. Then she gave him a morning bath and fed him Eggo waffles with maple syrup. They'd watched *Sesame Street* together.

Then the charge nurse had shut the interview down, an imposing six-foot-tall blonde who boxed him out and ordered him into the waiting room. "This is an emergency room, Detective," she said. "*Not* an interrogation room." He gave the nurse his card then, asked her to call him once the toxicology reports came in, and drove back over to California Homes to the kid's house to look around.

The front door was still cracked open, the television in the living room echoing the theme song for *Reading Rainbow.* An island separated the kitchen from the living room; an open jar of Jif with a knife stabbed in it, along with two toasted wheat bread slices, sat on the white Formica top. At his height, Ben could see most of the carpeted floor in front of the television. He crouched, trying to get down to the mother's level—he figured she was about five foot four. Sure, the boy could have been sitting on the carpet in front of the television, quietly going into seizure, and she wouldn't have been able to see him. He checked the cabinets—didn't matter how many public service announcements the county dashed across the television screen, kids still got into the Drano, sucked down diluted bleach. A blue plastic childproof fastener clasped closed the cabinet beneath the sink. He yanked open the other cabinets— stainless-steel pots and pans, green Tupperware containers, a mixer and measuring cups.

He scoped out the rest of the house—cleaning supplies in both bathrooms locked in cabinets above the toilets, a half bottle of Bacardi, a fifth of Cuervo, and a little bowl filled with cocktail umbrellas on the top shelf of a den built-in. He stuck his nose under the beds, in the closets, took a look at the garage, too—gas cans, two-cycle engine oil, fertilizer spray cans neatly stacked on shelves too high for little hands. Didn't seem like a social services call, from the look of things. But the look of things sometimes lied.

We threw snowballs at each other, he remembered the mother saying.

There was no dog in the backyard, but a couple of mounds of shit browning the snow attested to Duke's existence. Tiptoeing around the dog shit, he swept melting snow away with his loafers, looking for mushrooms in the grass, maybe. But no, the taste had been something chemical, something manufactured. Some kind of poison. He kicked a handball against the picket fence, toed a couple of peaches fallen from a small tree, walked the flower boxes along the property line. And then he saw it: a patch of electric green in the snow, right next to two tiny boot marks pressed into the wet grass.

———

Detective Vanek got the big house on the beach and she got the body.

Natasha was following the ambulance now up the elevated interchange to the 22 freeway. It was nearly 1:30 in the afternoon and the storm was clearing out, the sky a scrubbed-clean blue to reveal the basin, from the LA skyline to the sloping hill of Palos Verdes.

Beautiful, though, that snow, wasn't it? she remembered the detective saying.

Yes, she should have said. She could have taken a moment to acknowledge that fleeting beauty when invited. She thought maybe Vanek had been flirting with her—that black umbrella held above her head—but now she thought he was just being human—humane.

She took it in now, the distant skyline, such a rarity to not be fogged over with leaded smog. She thought about the dead man covered in the bed of the truck up ahead. It was a morning he would not see. It was an obvious thing, but she thought about that a lot—all the things the dead never got to see again. How they were both physically here and lost to the world.

It took another seven minutes to get to County, down into the guts of the basin now—the concrete, the telephone poles, the graffiti and gutter trash. At the delivery bay, she guided the stainless-steel gurney through the automatic doors and into the chilled building. The body was shrouded in a sheet stamped with OC CORONER, as though the county claimed ownership. With the murdered, it sort of did—at least it had a lease on them.

"No," she could hear Mendenhall saying. "Descendants want the organs placed back inside the body. Read the paperwork."

The *chief* medical examiner was barking orders to Jerry Horowitz, the diener, who was sewing up the chest cavity of a cadaver. Jerry, who assisted with most of the autopsies, held a needle and thread in his gloved hands and squinted at the clipboard on the wall.

"No one can read your handwriting," Natasha said, finding a toe tag.

Dr. Calvin Mendenhall, as Detective Vanek had said, was running again for county coroner, putting a hold on Natasha's ambitions. This, even though he did less and less work, turning most of the below-the-radar cases over to her—the prostitutes in alleys, the drug overdoses, the suicides—and keeping the newsworthy cases for himself. The last, a murder-suicide of a prominent entertainment lawyer and his wife, made the front pages of both *The Orange County Register* and the *Los Angeles Times,* not to mention *Variety* and *Orange Coast Magazine.* The case was straightforward, the file practically stamped before they even pulled the sheet back to expose the gunshot wounds, but Mendenhall had stood at the press podium in front of the deceased's house, the palm trees waving above the gleaming waters of Newport Bay, and acted the conquering scientist. She had stood off to the side, out of camera focus, and suppressed a disdainful laugh as he read off dramatic-sounding medical minutiae that could be summarized, in plain English, as: Blew a hole in her chest and then blew a hole in his head, both died. Mendenhall's whole thing boiled down to *Elect me, elect me, elect me,* and everyone standing around him knew it—from the mayor to the detectives on the case to the news cameramen zooming in on Mendenhall's bloated face.

"What've we got?" Mendenhall said now, his back turned to her, washing his hands in the basin.

"Drowned in his pajamas," she said.

"Ocean, lake, or pool?"

"Pool," she said. "Beaten, too, by the look of things."

"Location?"

"Huntington Beach."

"Surf City USA, dude!" Horowitz said, bent over the body.

"West of Beach Boulevard?" Mendenhall said, drying his hands now. "Or east?"

West meant money, which meant priority, which usually meant Mendenhall's case.

"West," she said.

"Beachfront or in the grid?"

"Modernist at the number fifteen lifeguard station."

"Let me take a look." He pulled back the sheet and the body stared up at them. "Nice pajamas."

"I was on the scene," she said, which should have made it her case.

Mendenhall glanced at her, smiled, and turned around.

"Move that homeless out of four to the back of the line," he said. "And put Mr. Pajamas in there."

"I did the grunt work on this."

"And don't forget I gave you a chance," he said, "when no one else would hire a woman."

Yes, and he never let her forget it. Worse, he used it during elections. *Look how progressive I am!*

"And your boyfriend called," Mendenhall said, throwing open his office door. "Again."

She shook her head and wheeled the body down the hallway to the cold lockers in the morgue. She pulled out the homeless in 4, slipped Pajamas into the newly empty locker, and then wheeled the homeless down to number 27. She could think of two bodies immediately that deserved to be pushed back behind the homeless, the genius who drank a pint of vodka and played Russian Roulette to impress his equally drunken friends, and the heroin OD. But both of those cases made the news—the RR because it was sensationally stupid and the OD because it was a state senator's kid.

Back at her desk, she filled out the paperwork and started filing the bags of evidence from the scene this morning—the man's slippers, the red thread, the button from the pajamas. A couple of hours earlier, a uniform had tried to get the button off the bottom of the pool with the skimming net, but it just kept sliding along the cement floor. Finally, Detective Vanek took off his coat and lowered himself into the water. He could have made the uniform do it, but there he was swimming past the body to the deep end to pinch the button off the bottom.

"I was already wet," he had said when he climbed out of the pool and handed her the button.

She smiled now, recalling his drenched slacks and dress shirt, his tie pasted to his chest. She looked at the button and the thread for a minute, thinking, before she placed them in the file. If Brennan didn't drown in the pool, he was dead when he hit the water. She'd have to check to see if there was any water in his lungs, but she couldn't perform the autopsy until next of kin was notified, a job left to Detective Vanek.

It was a quarter to four. It was Tuesday, fiesta night over at Ben's. She'd been on the clock since 5:13 A.M. She got into her 280Z and drove home, the snowy San Gabriels rising above the Los Angeles Basin like a mini Antarctica. She spent twenty-five minutes in the shower, washing the smell of County off her skin, then slipped into her favorite jeans and a blouse, the one with the scoop neck that Ben said he loved on her. She checked herself in the mirror; she thought she looked pretty damn good.

Chapter Two

"What's wrong?" Emma said, when Ben found her in the courtyard of the high school, rushing her way to class. "Something happen to Mom?"

"Nothing. No."

"Grandma?"

"Probably watching *Magnum P.I.*" They'd recently put his mother in a nursing home, after she'd gone missing and had been found a half mile from her apartment, barefoot and in pajamas, squeezing avocados in the produce section of Lucky's.

"Hell's freezing over," he said. "Let's get up in the hills."

And by 3:10, he and his daughter were up on the horses, climbing Quail Hill into Bommer Canyon, the snow-sprinkled wilderness spilling toward a shockingly cerulean Pacific.

An hour earlier, he'd run the evidence bag full of neon-green slush down to Dr. Norris Lofland in the new "crime lab" and asked for a rush on toxicology. Then he typed up the report on one of the new Macintosh computers and sat at his metal desk, thinking about the boy laid out in the grass, his own fingers pumping the tiny chest, the soft bones bending like wet tree branches. That conjured the ghost of Ariel Ramirez again, the thirteen-year-old gang-banger who died in his arms nearly eight years before—one of the crimes that never left him. Ben had been working street gangs in North Hollywood, the kid, a Loco, shot on his bike. There was nothing to do, the kid was pumping a stream of blood down the gutter, his eyes already going glassy; so Ben untangled the boy from the bike and held him in the street, the kid's eyes searching Ben's for some kind of answer. That was the start of the end for him in LA, sick of watching teenagers blow holes in other teenagers. Two years later, Ben got the job in Santa Elena and they moved south. He hadn't realized then that he'd take the feelings about those lost kids with him.

He had picked up Emma at 2:17, the high school usually not letting kids out until 3:30. But who the hell cared? That was a perk of this job, one of the reasons to leave LA and move down to the master-planned paradise of Rancho Santa Elena. To save his marriage. (Fail.) To spend more time with his daughter. (Moderate success.) To be a present father and not the ghost parent he'd been in LA. A kid had nearly died in his arms today, and snow in SoCal was a pretty damn good excuse to miss sixth-period Latin, if you asked him.

"The hills look like the backs of albino porpoises," Emma said now, her free right hand making diving motions in the air.

"Yeah," he said, cocking his head to see what she saw. "Their backs breaking the surface of the water."

He knew that Emma had never seen snow before, except maybe on television or in the movies. She'd seen it from afar, sure, on the winter San Gabriel Mountains, but she'd never stepped foot in it, never tasted it on her tongue. The horses had never seen snow before, either. When he first walked Tin Man out of the barn, the horse had danced a bit, unsure about the cold stuff sticking to his hooves and fetlocks. Gus, Emma's gelding, plowed his nose down in it, pushed it around with his lips, and then seemed to accept this new strange world. Now they blew clouds of breath into the air, and Tin Man occasionally huffed and shook his head. Tin Man, these days, protested most things that didn't involve his stall and a bucket of oats.

"So you dragged me out of sixth period, just to show me snow?" She eyed him from atop her horse with that X-ray-vision look she'd inherited from her mother.

"Aren't I a great dad?"

She frowned at him. "You're a terrible liar, that's what you are."

She was right. He was a terrible liar—at least when it came to his daughter. But what was he going to say to her, *Sometimes, sweetheart, I get scared and you're the one that keeps me sane?* Yeah, sure, hit her with that.

The first time Ben had seen snow, his father, one of the last cowboys before the ranch became part of the town of Rancho Santa Elena, had taken him for a ride through Modjeska Canyon and then five thousand feet up to the top of Saddleback Mountain. They'd made a fire, squeezed into his father's old army sleeping bags, and watched the sun set over the basin until the city lights pulsed into the night sky. His father had built a world of wonders for him up in those hills, and he was damned if he was going to miss the opportunity to do the same for his daughter.

Now they were coming up on the old oak sentinel above Crystal Cove. They tied the horses to the trunk and sat in a snowless patch beneath the tree and ate a couple of avocado sandwiches Ben had picked up at the Rancho Deli.

"You know," Emma said, "you don't have to be all Mr.-Tough-Guy cop all the time."

He was gathering melting snow in his hands. It was almost hot now, as though the universe remembered that this was a desert.

"You can talk to me, you know," she said. "It's not like I'm ten."

The snow was baseball-sized in his hands now. The older she got, the more she wanted to know about his job. She knew that his silences—from on-the-job PTSD, if you asked the police psychologist—all the time he had spent at his desk in the barn, working cases late at night when he should have been sitting at the dinner table talking out the banal details of the day, had killed the marriage, at least in part. The other part, his secrecy about the abuse he suffered as a kid at the hands of a swim coach, blew up last year, too, when his investigation into a high school kid's death led straight to Coach Lewis Wakeland and forced Ben into a public reckoning with his past. It had been a very public scandal—the beloved coach arrested on child sexual abuse charges. So, it seemed, his daughter had decided silence was the enemy.

"Got a call on this boy today," he said. "He was sick."

"Did he die?"

Ben shook his head. "Almost."

She eyed him, trying to decide, it seemed, how much more he wanted to say. "And so you wanted to see your daughter," she said finally, nodding, flashing him her I'm-sixteen-and-have-the-world-figured-out smile. "Makes sense. It's sweet, really."

Ben tossed the snowball at her, bull's-eyeing her in the stomach. She jumped up, scooped snow into her palm, and pressed together a snowball so quickly he had no time to spin away from her shot.

"All right, all right," he said, slush running into his shirt. "You win."

She wiped off her hands and sat back down.

"You know, Mom's going to be pissed you took me out of school early."

"Yeah," he said. Rachel, the high school English teacher, would see it as an affront to the profession and to education in general. "Let's keep it between us, huh?"

"You know she'll find out somehow. She always does."

He smiled. He admired Rachel for it, the way she always knew. Always knowing was a form of love. It hadn't worked out between them, but the feeling was still there. Well, some of the feeling, anyway. Now there was Natasha, and he felt pretty damn lucky to have her in his life.

"Worth it, though, don't you think?"

Both of them took in the panorama, snowy wilderness all the way from Laguna to Newport Harbor.

"Totally worth it," Emma said, smiling, "except for the loss of trust and the sense of mutual parental cooperation."

———

They rode the horses down to the beach in silence, crossed PCH, and sat in the saddle and watched the surfers, in neoprene wet suits, ride long rights down the coastline. Ben was a body surfer and when he wasn't riding waves he liked watching them, liked the idea that energy had driven a swell across the Pacific to crash on this shore. By the time they climbed the ridges back home, the snow was gone, and when they reached the house Ben was presented with an even rarer event: Rachel, his ex-wife, and Natasha both standing in front of the house, talking it up like old friends.

"Your lady friend is here," Emma said to him, disdain in her voice.

"Try to be nice."

"I try every time," she said, turning Gus toward the barn.

"You know," Rachel said when he got close, "the school calls when there's an unexcused absence."

He hadn't figured on that. He had gotten his daughter and left, forgot to check in with admin.

"You didn't tell attendance, Dad?" Emma said, tugging Gus to a stop. "Now I'm screwed. Miss Brown won't let me make up work if it's unexcused."

"This kid could use a day off," he said, pointedly, as he climbed off Tin Man.

He stepped past Rachel and walked over to place a kiss on Tash's cheek. Emma muttered something that sounded like *Oh,*

God, and spun around to take Gus back to the barn. Ben felt cornered, for some reason. Rachel and Natasha had met before, of course, but he'd always been around to play host. As far as he knew, they didn't get together for coffee.

"Excuse me," Natasha said, "I'm going to step inside. Nice to see you, Rachel." And then suddenly he was alone with his ex in front of the house they used to share.

Rachel's arms were crossed. "It snowed, I know. I get it," she said. "But let me know, *please,* when you make these decisions. I want us on the same page about Em."

"Sure," he said. He knew she was jealous. He'd suffered through meeting a couple of her boyfriends, so a little turnabout felt pretty good.

"You know," Rachel said, "I like Natasha."

Wave that feeling goodbye.

"Yeah, I like her, too."

"She's . . ." A little smile on her face, that dimple of hers killing him a little. "No nonsense. Down to earth."

"Very," he said, turning to walk Tin Man up to the barn.

———

"You just had to try to make Rachel feel jealous, didn't you?" Natasha said as soon as Emma and Rachel left. "You think women can't see right through that?"

She was standing by the back window, arms crossed across her chest, a wry smile on her face that said: *I got your number.* She was five foot two—she would say five three—but she was no one to mess with; it was one of the things that turned him on about her. Behind Natasha, Rachel's Buick, with Emma strapped inside, kicked up dust down the driveway.

He shrugged.

"That dramatic stepping in front of her," she said, laughing a little, "like you were a star in your own soap opera."

"I was just glad to see you." He grabbed two Coors out of the fridge. He popped the top on both and handed her one. "Been a long day."

"Benjamin Wade," she said, "don't throw me the been-a-long-day line."

"All right, maybe I *was* trying to make Rachel jealous." She knew that his feelings about his ex were complicated. Didn't change how he felt about Natasha. Of course, that might be easier for him to accept than for her. His marriage was over and here he was with Natasha—and he was pretty damn happy about it. Might even say he loved it. "But I didn't think about it that way. I just sort of wanted to show off."

"Don't try to charm me, either," she said. "It's not your métier."

He laughed. "My what?"

"Means you're not good at it, at charm."

"I'm good at tamales, though," he said. "And, man, I love that shirt on you."

She smiled, the light in her green eyes sparkling. "You think I'm that easy, do you?"

"I think you're the toughest damn thing I ever met."

She looked at him sideways, an eyebrow raised. "Get me a real drink. It's been a long day for me, too."

She turned around to face the hills, and he found the Dewar's in the cabinet above the sink. He poured her two fingers over ice and a couple for himself, too, and then wrapped his right arm around her shoulders as he handed her the highball. She smelled of disinfectant and Chanel No. 5, the scent of her washing County off her skin.

"Your case first," he said, hands hooking the ridges of her hips now.

"Rich man, some real estate guy, floating on his back in his pool," she said. "In his pajamas."

Evening debriefings with Rachel in LA had always been unequal—her pain-in-the-ass schoolkids versus his murdered boys. No matter how stressful her job was—and it was stressful, he knew—his stories always won, even after they moved to Santa Elena. It was like playing with a loaded deck, and Rachel, after a few years, began to resent the cards he always threw at her. With Natasha it was like an I'll-show-you-mine-if-you-show-me-yours kind of deal.

"Floating on his back?"

"Yeah, a real mystery," she said. "Doesn't matter, Mendenhall's taking it."

"Mendenhall needs to retire to Oregon."

She lifted her glass in a mock toast.

"What about yours?"

"CPR'd a toddler."

"Oh, no." Her hand was on his now. "Did the kid make it?"

"Yeah," he said. "Got into some poison, I think."

"God." She knew what it meant when it came to kids. Whenever she had to autopsy a child—an occurrence frequent enough to make you hate the world, if you let yourself—he poured her drinks in silence, fed her in silence, let her take a bath in silence, until she was ready to form words again. Some things really couldn't be talked out.

"A few moments there, though," he said, shaking his head, "I thought . . ." He cleared his throat and let it go.

"You win," she said. Then she poured the remainder of her whiskey glass into his. "And to the winner goes the spoils." She came around the counter, got on her tiptoes to open the liquor cupboard, poured herself a fresh one *without* ice, and winked. "You know I like it neat," she said, raising the glass. "So, Wolfgang Puck." She put her left hand on his belt now, a rush of blood firing his body. "What're you cooking up?"

"Pork with jalapeño, red rice, a little corn salad."

He'd gone shopping yesterday, spent a little cash. Natasha had Wednesday and Thursday off, Emma would be with Rachel on Thursday, his open cases were pretty minor, so Ben and Natasha had planned a mini midweek vacation. An intimate dinner party tonight, maybe a few hours in bed tomorrow morning, a trip to the beach to ride a few waves, a dinner at Surf & Sand in Laguna Thursday evening. Who knew? A couple of open days and the possibilities seemed endless.

"Got a good wine, too. Sonoma Valley Cab."

"You slip into that apron," she said, nodding to the baby-blue tie-around she'd bought him as a joke hanging from a hook on the wall, "and I'll sit and watch."

She hoisted herself onto a counter stool, a smile on her face now. It was one of her favorite places, he knew, perched at the kitchen island watching him cook. Natasha was an order-out kind of girl, but Ben liked to work the flames—especially for her. It'd become a sort of foreplay with groceries. He threw some cherry tomatoes on the cutting board, sharpened the knife, and then raised his glass to her.

"To working on my métier, my charm."

She cocked an eyebrow at him, they both took a sip, and then Ben set the glass on the counter, ready to slice into the tomatoes.

"What's that?" Natasha said, nodding at the glass.

Ben glanced down at the highball, a puff of red floating in the whiskey.

"Ben, you're bleeding."

Chapter Three

Bao Phan's right shoulder cramped like knotted wire, and the scar—where shrapnel from the crashing South Vietnamese helicopter had sliced into his right arm—itched to a burn. Maybe, after more than twelve years, there was still a little American-forged steel lodged in the soft tissue above his elbow. When it flared, like it did last night, he had the dreams, the ones that woke him in the middle of the night, as though the scar itself were the repository of his ugliest recollections. Last night it was the burning jungle, the hopea tree tops white-hot with napalm phosphorescence, and the egret—the one flying toward him where he lay fallen on the road—struggling to keep flight, the tips of its right wing feathers alight. And then there was the helicopter, always the helicopter.

Something else was wrong this morning, though. Maybe it was the unusual cold, the desert air thin and sharp feeling. Maybe it was the residue from a night of drinking and playing cards. The empty bottle of Hennessy still sat on the folding table he'd erected last night near the basa fish aquarium. Bao, his brother, Danh, Giang Dieu, and Trai Ngo had played rounds of Tiến lên until nearly midnight—telling old stories between rounds, but also talking strategy for Danh's run for councilman, for which Bao was an unofficial campaign manager. He could tell his brother was drunk when Danh kept slapping Bao on his back, repeating, "I'll be the first Vietnamese councilman in Santa Elena"—laughing now—"*if* I remember to file the paperwork." Which Danh had not. Bao had filed it for him just an hour before the deadline. Still, Danh was a success story, having made a small fortune manufacturing parts for the airline industry. Danh was lucky, too; last night he had scored a dragon and a half dragon both, clearing the table twice of a stack of bills.

In his grocery store, Bao pulled up the shades on the windows to the crack of 5:00 A.M. light. He liked this time of the morning, before his wife and daughter came to join him at the register, before his customers, many of them refugees from the American War, stumbled in looking for jasmine tea or a bottle of ruou rice whiskey to burn away the Southern California day. The very early morning was his, not a small thing to say when you've lost everything once; not a small thing to treasure an hour and a half alone in your grocery store, a business you built up from a small fruit stand selling imported durian and star fruit and the bitter melons you couldn't get anywhere else in Orange County.

After rolling up the shades, opening the windows to the empty parking lot, Bao pulled the register money from the safe in the office. There was a gun in the safe, too, an old Smith & Wesson Model 60, which he had bought at a pawnshop and had kept beneath the counter at the old store in Westminster's Little Saigon. But since they had moved to Santa Elena, the gun stayed locked in the safe. There weren't any gangs here, extorting money from shopkeepers. In Santa Elena, everything was neat and clean, a cop for every five residents, it seemed.

He slid the cash into the register and sat on his stool, chewing a Winchell's maple bar, washing the sweet dough down with black coffee. "That American coffee is weak," Ai, his wife, would say. But he liked the coffee, liked the convenience of it: Walk into the store and it was there waiting for you on a hot-plate. He liked his morning ritual, too, the grocery to himself, the hum of the fluorescent lights and aquarium filters, his pencil sketching in the white paper with his drawings. Today he sketched the long shape of a mourning dove he had found roosting in the backyard plum tree yesterday morning.

Usually, he could get lost in drawing, but this morning the memory of the helicopter twelve years ago kept pressing on his mind. Thirteen people had been crammed into the Huey's hold that April 30, 1975, so packed in that his brother, Danh, a colonel in the suddenly nonexistent South Vietnamese army, had to dangle his legs over the open side door. Danh's shirt was ripped open by the wind, exposing a gash across his chest. Bao had no idea how Danh had been wounded, but Saigon had been chaos, especially after the bombing of the airport, and who knew what he and the pilot had had to do to steal the helicopter? (Danh had never told him and Bao didn't ask.) It was difficult enough to think about the people they left behind.

The helicopter had landed in the rice field behind Bao's home, and their neighbors had come running. The helicopter was already overloaded, and they had no choice but to leave those people behind, but the sight of his neighbors standing in the field, their bodies buffeted by rotor wash, still haunted Bao. What happened to them? Labor camps? Killed? The world was not fair, that was true.

He had clung to his daughter, Linh, just ten at the time, as the helicopter lifted off, terrified Linh would be tornadoed out into the air. The fingernails of her left hand dug into his wrist as the helicopter pitched away from the land. If he looked now, the crescent-shaped scars were still there, faded yet indelible. Ai, his wife, had buried her head in his shoulder, her eyes clamped shut. She had never flown before and the machine frightened her—the booming thwap of the rotors, the shuddering metal walls, the general violence of flight.

As the helicopter pushed out over the South China Sea, Linh had let go of his wrist, pulled his pen from his shirt pocket, and started writing across the palm of her hand. He had nothing but the clothes he was wearing, a sketchbook filled with his bird drawings, two 1,000-đồng notes, his ID, and this pen, which had been clipped to his shirt pocket, when they got the call from his brother, telling him to be ready to go. Moments before, Linh had tried to yell something in his ear, and even then, with her hot breath against his cheek, he couldn't hear the words.

She held her left palm open to him. *Mình sẽ đáp xuống đâu* was etched into her skin. *Where are we going to land?*

Bao took the pen and wrote in blue ink across the lines of her palm, *On a big American ship.*

She read it and then looked up at him, her brown eyes searching his for fear. He hid it far down in his gut, though it thrashed around and clawed at his chest. There weren't any ships out here, not any he could see, just whitecapping waves, rising as though to slap the helicopter out of the sky. But soon there was another helicopter, to their left, and then another, a smaller insect-like thing pushing low across the waterline.

Danh leaned into the air and pointed to something Bao could just now make out—a smattering of ships, a few dots bobbing on the water, the American fleet. Bao pointed the ships out to Linh, to calm her, but her eyes popped and she scribbled across her hand.

Too small, the words read.

They will get bigger, he wrote back.

As their helicopter descended, Bao held his daughter's other hand across his lap and drew a crane on her skin, the bird's wings spread across the heel of her palm, its neck and beak stretched to the base of her index finger, its long legs etched into the veins on her wrist. She watched him draw, her body sagging against him, the helicopter dropping through the gray sky. He glanced out the open door and there was the ship, an arrow of gunmetal bobbing in the sea. A helicopter, like the one they were in now, floated upside down in the water and his hand shook when he saw the crashed machine. Linh glanced up at him, but then he drew a splattering of poop dropping from the rear end of the crane and she laughed. Out of the corner of his eye he watched the landing pad, no larger than a postage stamp five minutes ago, grow to fill his vision. An American soldier stood in the bull's-eye of the X, waving his arms to the pilot, as though his arms alone would catch the helicopter and set it down safely.

The helicopter spun above the landing pad, the soldier ducking away as the skids descended toward contact. Then the fuselage shuddered and sheared metal tore into the hold of the Huey. Bao enveloped Linh in his arms and something hot stabbed his shoulder, fire burning the muscle. Linh thrashed in his arms, and when she snapped her head around to face him, her mouth gaped in a soundless scream, blood was blotting out her left eye.

A knock now on the front door made Bao jump.

Jian Wei, a Taiwanese regular at the grocery, waved from behind the window.

"Since when are you up this early?" Bao said when he opened the door.

"My wife sent me," Jian said. "She needs coix seeds for congee. Apparently, it's an emergency."

Bao found the coix seeds in aisle two. Jian paid for the seeds, slipped the packet into his pocket, and then grabbed one of Ai's homemade rice cakes, a conspiratorial look on his face. Bao just smiled and raised his hand, and Jian, despite the congee emergency, sat down on the plastic chair next to the register, unwrapped the cake, and started talking about the new Korean market across town. It was huge, he said. Had its own "café." Bao returned to his stool and listened, rubbing out the knot of his right shoulder. Jian just wanted to talk, that was the real reason he was here. Asians gathered at the store—not just Vietnamese, but Chinese, Hmong, and Indonesians, too. The market smelled like places they knew—the sour of fish sauce, the salt of dried shrimp, the vinegar of fermented tofu. The smells brought you home, Bao knew.

Something suddenly crashed in the alleyway behind the grocery. Through the open back door, Bao saw shapes slink in the shadows—dogs, raccoons, maybe.

"You have to keep a lid on the cans," Jian said.

"I do," Bao said, irritated. He didn't like to be told how to do things.

Bao grabbed a broom and stalked down the hallway and out the back door. Something seemed to be grunting on the other side of the trash cans. He smelled something, too, a scent that left a mineral tinge on the back of his tongue. He flipped on the security light and the alleyway erupted into movement. A trash can spilled at his feet and he jumped backward, smashing the broomstick through the back window of the shop. Quái! Three overexposed forms—coyotes, he could see now—tore at something, a body, clumped in one of the parking spaces. The body was the size of a child, and his heart leapt with fear. He lunged at the coyotes, swinging the broomstick at them, yelling to make them scatter, until finally they streaked down the alley toward the strawberry field beyond.

He crept closer, terrified at what he might find. It was a dog, he realized with relief. Its throat cut open, the open hole of its larynx gaping black at him. Standing over the animal now, he noticed something else: a piece of paper pinned to one of the dog's ears. He reached down, pulled the paper toward him. His heart lurched when he read the ugly English words. He ripped the paper from the dog's ear then, stuffed it in his pants pocket, and stumbled back to the grocery, trying to get his breath.

The phone next to the bed startled Ben awake. He slapped his hand across the bedside table in the dark, hoping to grab the receiver before it woke Natasha.

"This better be good," he croaked into the receiver. Ben looked at the clock, 5:57 A.M. They hadn't hit the sheets until nearly 1:30, after a run to emergency, after the on-call doctor suspected Ben had ingested some kind of anticoagulant, and after a wait at Sav-on for the prescribed precautionary vitamin K that would help his body coagulate again.

"You said to call you if anything came up with a dog." It was Ken Brady, the night desk sergeant. "Well, we got a dead pooch."

Ben glanced next to him, expecting to see Natasha's curled back, but she was gone, the covers neatly pulled to the edge of the bed.

"And this dog, it seems, did not die of natural causes," Ken Brady said.

"Animal cruelty deal?" Ben's mind flashed back to the electric-green slush in the backyard yesterday.

"Don't know."

Ben was up now, phone cradled to his ear, slipping on the jeans—minus his boxer shorts—he had left in a pile of clothes on the floor last night. He searched around for his T-shirt. It had gone AWOL along with the boxers. It was still cold this morning, a wet Pacific chill in the air. He found his sweatshirt hanging on the back of the door and slipped it on.

"Two black-and-whites already on it," Ken was saying, "but they called in for a detective. Seems whatever fate befell this mutt is above their pay grade."

"Address?"

He wrote it down and stumbled into the living room, where he found Natasha sitting in the blue morning light at the table next to the window. Her hands were clasped around a coffee mug, her bare feet propped on the chair opposite her. For a moment he admired her stillness—her shoulders pressed against the chair back, her chin cocked in the air as though challenging the new day. She stretched when she saw him, her lithe body backlit through his Viper Fins T-shirt by the early-morning light. First mystery of the day solved.

"What's wrong?" he said.

"What's wrong?" Natasha said. "You were poisoned. I couldn't sleep."

Sometime in the night, he had been vaguely aware that she was awake, sitting in the chair in the corner of the room, keeping vigil over him. He had let her, and, to be honest, kind of liked it. Out in the field, you had to act the stoic tough-shit cop. It got tiring, and he didn't want to play with her, didn't want to pretend he didn't love her and love her attention.

"I'm fine. But it's nice that you care."

Ben bent down to kiss her and she stopped him, pulled down his bottom lip to check his gums.

"You're not bleeding to death?"

"Not at the moment." She kissed him then, her lips tasting of coffee and toothpaste, a lived-in flavor he loved.

She was wearing his boxer shorts, too, he noticed. Mystery number two solved. She was tiny in his clothes, and she had tied the end of the shirt so that it clung to her stomach, revealing a sliver of skin between her belly and her hips. He touched her there and the warmth of her skin, her body slipped into his underclothes, just about made him call in and resign. Why was a woman dressed in your own threads so damn sexy?

"I'm guessing that call wasn't about the dry cleaning?" she said.

"Dead dog," he said, wrenching his mind out of the bedroom. Shitty way to start their mini vacation. But what were they going to do, lounge in bed with mimosas? No, they'd start talking cases—Ben's perps that got away, her Joes and Janes buried now in unnamed plots. They weren't Club Med people; they lived on a different frequency. "Might be something with this poisoned kid. Mother said their dog was missing."

He kissed her again, a long one that caused her to lift her body out of the chair a bit to meet him. Then he left her there by the window, the morning light cutting canyons out of the hills, and walked into the bedroom to change into something a bit more professional.

"I'll cancel brunch," she said. "And the whale-watching cruise."

———

The dog had been dumped in the alleyway, a small puddle of blood leaking toward the gutter. But there was a more pressing concern at the moment: the shopkeeper.

"He's inside," Officer Meyer said, a uniform who was the first to arrive on scene. "When we got here, he was locked inside with another Asian man, holding a revolver."

"Standoff?" Ben said.

"The other guy was a buddy of his," Meyer said, shaking his head. "We asked the guy to leave. He's over there with Bremer giving a statement."

Ben glanced across the street, to the parking lot where another uniform was interviewing a man, taking notes on a pocket-sized notepad.

"But the owner was worked up, waving that gun around," Meyer said. "Thought we'd let him chill out first."

Ben got down on his haunches, tugged at the dog's muzzle, its slit throat yawning open. A bloody notch marked one of the ears, like the skin had been ripped away.

"Yeah," Ben said. "I see why."

There were three units on-site, two uniforms pacing the alley with the dog, two stationed out in front of the grocery, and one at each end of the strip mall. A few gawkers crowded the crime scene tape, a couple sipping coffee from Styrofoam cups as though this was some form of morning entertainment.

Ben watched the man through the back door's broken glass, pacing the floor of the grocery, a revolver clutched in his right hand. Ben didn't want him startled. So he walked around to the front of the building, shook hands with the two uniforms, and tapped the glass door with his badge.

"I'm Detective Wade," he called. The man wore khakis and a white button-down. Two pens clipped to his shirt pocket. The revolver, a Smith & Wesson 60, was still dangling in his right hand, but his left hand was shoved down in his pants pocket. Made Ben nervous, not being able to see that hand. "Mind if I come in?"

The man eyed him a moment through the glass, unlocked the door, and cracked it open for him.

"I'd be more comfortable," Ben said, "if you put the revolver on the counter."

"It's mine, I have a permit."

"Look, I've been shot before." Ben pointed to his left shoulder. "Makes me jumpy when someone pulls a gun, especially when there's a bunch of cops around packing their own metal. Nerves and guns are a bad deal, you know what I mean?"

The man glanced at Ben's shoulder, then set the revolver on the cashier's table, barrel pointed at them. He lit a cigarette then with his right hand, the left still shoved in his pants pocket like he was protecting something.

"I appreciate it," Ben said, his heart slowing to 4/4. "Nice place." Clean white linoleum, walls the green of a forest canopy, rows of neatly stacked shelves, bright bins of fruit. A framed map of Southeast Asia hung on a wall above a freezer. "How long you been open?"

"Year and a half."

Funny. Ben'd never noticed the store before.

"Where you from?"

"Here."

"Before that," Ben said. "Vietnam, I'm guessing, but where?"

The man narrowed his eyes, blew smoke. "Does that matter?"

"No," Ben said. It might, if the grocery was targeted.

"My Tho."

"Near Saigon," Ben said, nodding.

"You were there?" the man asked.

"I was in college." He felt guilty about that, still, but he had been glad he didn't have to go. "Know some guys, though. It was hard on them."

"Yes," the man said. "Was hard on everyone."

The man perched on a stool near the cash register. A good sign, sitting down. Ben kept an eye on that left hand, though. Behind him, pinned to the wall, were dozens of pen-and-ink drawings of birds—a red-tailed hawk, a mourning dove, a California quail.

"Your sketches?" Ben asked.

Some of the hard-on detectives came in all business, hammering who-what-where questions as though they could bludgeon their way to an arrest. Sometimes, Ben knew, you just had to talk with people. The normal everyday bullshit, restore a little order.

The man nodded. "I'm—I was an art teacher. In Saigon."

"They're real nice," he said, nodding. Damn good, actually, realistic but stylized, too.

"But here," the man said, holding his hand up to the shelves lined with goods, "I'm groceries."

Ben couldn't tell how he felt about it, just a statement of fact.

"Look," Ben said. "We're going to have to talk this out. So can we get you something?"

The man stared at him a moment, as though he didn't trust the offer. Then he reached over the counter, picked up a Winchell's coffee cup, and shook it.

"Another one of these," he said. "No sugar."

Ben sent a uniform across the street to Winchell's for two cups of joe and some donut holes. He slid a plastic chair across the linoleum, sat down across from the man, propped his legal pad on his knee, and asked his name. Bao Phan. Ben wrote it down—*Bow Fan*. The man glanced at Ben's legal pad and then looked away.

"I'm going to call a friend to take a look at the dog while we talk. She's a medical examiner. She'll be able to tell us a lot I can only guess at."

Bao lit another cigarette, nodded, and blew the smoke to the fluorescents.

"One more thing, sir," Ben said. "I need to ask what you've got in your left hand."

The man's face blanched, as though remembering something. He pulled his hand out slowly. The most he could have in there was a small knife, maybe one of the pens he used for his drawings. He opened his fingers and unfolded a three-inch sheet of paper. Scrawled in red ink: *KILL 'EM ALL!*

———

Ben called Natasha at her Garden Grove apartment at 7:15.

"You're kidding me, right?"

"I'm not."

An hour earlier, she'd filled up a coffee mug at his place and drove the empty pre-rush-hour morning freeway back to her apartment in a sort of relieved daze. The man had been poisoned, he'd been bleeding from the gums, and he had somehow thought he could skip medical treatment last night. "I hate docs," he'd complained as she drove him to the emergency room. My lord, what was it with men and their crazy fear of doctors? She'd sat up most of the night, watching him snore the stars away like he didn't have a worry in the world. She'd never been terrified of losing someone until she met Ben—and there were any number of ways a cop could lose his life daily, though poisoning hadn't been on her list of possible dangers. Why hadn't she fallen for an accountant?

Now she sat on the edge of her bed, wrapped in a towel post-shower, Fleetwood Mac's "Rhiannon" playing on her stereo, and listened to Ben.

"It's a dead dog," she said.

"Murdered dog. Nearly took the head off. But there's more to it than that. I need you down here."

He always seemed to need her now—personally and professionally. She was glad about it, but sometime in the middle of last night, as she sat there watching him sleep, she thought, *This is the only place I want to be.* It felt so right, it was like she'd banged some emotional gong inside herself and this morning she needed to get home to her apartment, at least for a few minutes, to remind herself that there had been a time when she needed no one.

"I gotta get dressed," she said.

"Good idea," he said, and hung up.

———

She got to the coroner's office in fifteen minutes, and within twenty she was in her official Ford, riding the shoulder past lines of traffic on the 405. When she got on scene, Ben grabbed her elbow to push her past the tape.

"Professional mode, Detective," she said.

"Right, sorry," he said, shoving his hand back into his coat pocket.

Ben hadn't been exaggerating, the dog's head was nearly sawed off. Some kind of Labrador mix—a good pet, probably. She knelt down and stared at the misshapen O of the exposed trachea. There were lacerations on the haunches and belly area where the white viscera of intestine poked through the skin.

"Turkey vultures?" she said, pointing at the wound.

"Coyotes," Ben said. "The owner says he chased them off."

"Cannibals."

There wasn't enough blood, maybe six to eight ounces puddled beneath the dog's neck. A bit of froth colored the dog's muzzle. The trachea gash was jagged, not a knife wound, not some spontaneous cruelty, but a deliberately brutal act.

Ben was down on his haunches, staring at the dog. "No tags, but I'm betting this is that boy's dog, Duke."

There was a jagged notch ripped out of one of the dog's ears. "What's this?" she said, mostly to herself.

Ben handed her a ziplock bag with a piece of paper inside. She turned it over in her hand until she could read the words. *KILL 'EM ALL!* She winced at the ugliness of it.

"This doesn't look like Magic Marker," she said, looking at the red letters, clotted with bits of viscera. A large staple was pinned to one side of the paper.

"Thinking it's the dog's blood."

"Did one of these damn street cops rip it from the body?" No way Ben would defile a crime scene like that. But uniforms pulled all kinds of dumb moves that made her job difficult.

"Owner did," Ben said. "Said he didn't want his wife and daughter to see it."

Understandable, but now his prints would be on the paper, making it harder to identify the perpetrators, if they were stupid enough to leave any prints.

"Did the shop owner give you anything else?" she said.

"Opened the store like usual, heard something outside, found the dog. Says it's not his. Says, too, nothing like this has happened before."

Doubtful, she thought. She had seen this kind of thing near Little Saigon in Westminster, up in northern Orange County, hateful words spray-painted on cement walls. She had volunteered years ago down at Camp Pendleton, when the refugees had been flown in after the fall of Saigon. Now she sometimes stopped in at a Little Saigon storefront for pho. She liked the place, liked the teenage boy who served the steaming bowls of soup, liked the way he chuckled whenever she came through the door as though he was pleasantly surprised each time. But she'd bent over bodies in Little Saigon, too; boys killed in drive-by shootings, a prostitute dropped in an alleyway. Still, when she thought of Little Saigon, she thought of the soup and the boy who served it, the way he retreated to a table by the kitchen while she ate to play his handheld Mattel football game, shaking his fist in silent triumph when he scored. It mattered what you chose to remember about a place, about people.

"It's not a knife wound," she said.

She slipped on her gloves and pressed on the dog's muzzle. The nose was still wet; she could feel it through the latex. The neck wound gaped open, the edges serrated and jagged with flesh and hair.

"It's too jagged. A knife would cut clean." She took a picture of the wound, serrated, points of white flesh. "Who beheads a dog?"

"Someone who'd write that note, I guess."

She got down on her elbows again with the Polaroid to take another close-up of the exposed trachea. No maggots, no beetles, but the dog had been dumped in an asphalt alleyway so that didn't mean much. A necklace of ants sucked at the puddle of blood, which had started to congeal.

"It wasn't killed here," she said.

"Not enough blood?"

"You got it. They must have drained him somewhere else. I'm thinking it's only been here for two or three hours, at most."

"Shopkeeper got here at five A.M.," Ben said. "My guess they've had an eye on him then, knew when he'd be alone."

"Hand me one of those," Natasha said, pointing to the glass vials in her kit.

"So they drove it here," Ben was saying, mostly to himself, talking it out. She watched him step backward from the dog, his right foot sweeping across the pavement.

Pickup truck, she thought. They'd transport the dog in the bed.

"Truck bed," he said to himself. "No one's stuffing a bleeding dog in the trunk of their car."

She smiled to herself and worked her fingers down the dog's haunches. They would have dragged it out of the bed by the paws. She ran her fingers down to the legs and pulled some hair from the hocks just above a paw. Were these people smart enough to wear gloves? She'd read in the *Journal of Forensic Sciences* last year about DNA testing. Evidence had been tested in England already. Since then she kept vials of things that could one day be tested—vaginal swabs of dead women who had been raped, spilled blood, hair, even scraps of half-eaten food. There were too many unsolved cases, too many open files that haunted her. One day she'd go back through them, test them all, heat up cold cases.

"Here they are," Ben said, five feet from the dog. "Tire prints. Tread picked up some blood."

He asked to borrow the camera and took a couple of shots of the tread.

"Has to be at least two people," Natasha said.

"I'm guessing three," Ben said. "Two to dump the dog and one waiting in the idling truck."

"Two's company, three's an accessory." She yanked another tuft of hair from the left front paw and slipped it into the vial.

———

At 7:58, the shopkeeper's wife arrived on scene. Ben watched them through the broken window while they talked. Bao placed his hand on his wife's cheek, as though to reassure her, but she kept talking, as though pleading with him. If her fear was an indication, something like this *had* happened before.

Ben had canvassed a couple of waitresses and a cook at an early-morning diner two stores down, talked up a couple of the overnight stock boys smoking cigarettes in the docking bay of the Lucky's a few doors down. Nothing. The stock boys had been inside, loading up the cereal aisle with Wheaties boxes. The waitresses, brewing Folgers. The cook, whisking up scrambled eggs. The other shop owners were just arriving, rolling in at a decent hour with coffee and croissants, tea and plastic tubs of yogurt.

Ben gave Bao and his wife a minute and then stepped back inside the shop, intent on interviewing her. A young woman pushed open the front door then, a backpack slung over her shoulder. She grabbed Bao's hand and then touched his shoulder before turning to Ben.

"Where is it?" she said.

"Detective Wade," he said, offering her his card. "You are?"

"Linh," she said. "Their daughter."

"Your real name?" Ben said. "Your Vietnamese name?"

She drilled him with her eyes. A pale scar slashed through her left eyebrow, a jagged blotch from some long-healed wound.

"Linh," she said. "Linh Phan."

Lynn. He wrote it down on his legal pad.

"*L I N H,*" she said, glancing at his pad. "And Phan is with a *ph.*"

He erased it and rewrote her name.

"Where's the dog?" she said again.

"Out back."

She brushed past him, not even bothering to take the backpack off. He hooked her elbow before she got out the back door.

"Don't touch me," she said.

He let go.

"You can look," he said, pointing to the trickle of blood pooling at the edge of the back door. "But if you want us to catch who did this, I need you to stay right here."

She swiped loose hair behind her ear and nodded, staring at the dog's body. Natasha had her back to them, taking pictures with the Polaroid.

"There should be more blood," the daughter said.

Natasha turned around, glanced up at the girl.

"Right," Ben said, surprise in his voice.

"I used to be pre-med," she explained to Ben.

"UC?"

She nodded.

"Used to be?"

"I'm comparative lit now," she said, glancing past Ben toward her parents, who were now standing in the hallway. "Useless, I know."

"Yeah, well, my daughter says she wants to be an art major," Ben said. "Anything like this happen before?" He didn't believe the grocer, something in his eyes when Ben had asked the question, the way he wanted to hide the ugly note from his family.

"Like this?" she said, staring at the dog. "No."

"Other things?"

She turned and flashed her eyes at him. "What do you think?"

Natasha was standing now, a strange look on her face.

"Linh?" Natasha said. "Linh, is that you?"

"Miss Betencourt?"

Natasha dropped the camera on top of her kit and rushed around the body, her face suddenly glowing. "It is you."

"I can't believe it," Linh said.

Natasha stripped off her gloves and cradled Linh's hands in hers. "Look at you," Natasha said. "You're a woman." She held Linh's hands with both of hers, a look in her eyes Ben had never seen before. She pulled one hand away and gestured at herself, apologizing for her scrubs. "My God, Linh, I wish I could hug you."

Then Natasha took off her scrubs, and Linh and Natasha were embracing after all.

Bao and his wife recognized Natasha, too, and the four of them retreated inside the grocery, huddling together like long-lost intimates. Natasha didn't introduce Ben, didn't even look his way. She kept looking at Linh, an uncomplicated joy flashing across her face. Ben sidled in on the edge of their circle and caught bits of what they were saying—the Camp Pendleton tent cities of refugees a dozen years ago in '75, the Phans getting a sponsor, something about a grocery in Westminster.

"I'm so sorry about this," Natasha said.

"We have insurance," Bao said. "The window can be fixed."

"Yes," Natasha said, nodding, "the glass can be fixed." She said it as a confirmation, but Ben could hear her other thoughts.

Mrs. Phan said something in Vietnamese.

"She says, we're sorry we lost track of you," Linh translated.

Ben had known Natasha for over six years now, since she was a rookie medical examiner, and he'd never heard anything about Natasha and refugee families at Camp Pendleton, nothing about a girl named Linh. We all had our secrets and that was fine, but from their reactions to each other this felt like a pretty significant omission.

"No," Natasha said. "*I lost you.*"

The mother smiled, clasped her arms around her waist, and bowed twice. Then Bao was grabbing a chair for Natasha and the mother was rushing behind the counter to boil water for tea, and Natasha seemed so taken it looked like she was actually going to accept the invitation and sit down.

"Doctor?" Ben said.

"Oh." Natasha glanced at him and smiled, touched his elbow and pulled him closer. "This is Benj—" She fumbled for a moment. "Detective Benjamin Wade."

They'd already met, of course, but now he was shaking their hands and the line between personal and professional was suddenly blurred.

"These are old friends," Natasha said, her hand on the back of Linh's arm now, like she couldn't help but touch her.

"Nice to meet you folks," Ben said.

They stood there awkwardly for a moment. Ben didn't want to break this up, but it *was* a crime scene.

"Doctor," Ben said now. "Maybe we should wrap things up?"

"Yes, Detective," she said, smiling apologetically toward the family. "Of course."

Ben had a whole lot of questions, but this wasn't the time. For now, they walked back out into the alleyway, the sun shining down on the sliver of asphalt and the dead dog. He got one of the uniforms to cordon off the back door with yellow crime scene tape.

Chapter Four

Jacob Clay had found the box in the garage when he was thirteen, a little over a year ago. Back then, the pictures inside had frightened him. Photos of a severed leg, a close-up of a popped-open head, brains splattered like oatmeal across the dry ground. He had closed the box then, raced inside to play Atari. But the box was alive after that, something breathing in the garage. It took two days to get up the courage, but he returned and found more pictures—a charred body next to a smoldering hut, three corpses draped over one another in a shallow ditch, Polaroid after Polaroid of flesh that had once been living people.

There were pictures of his dad, too, a kid in camouflage, standing on the axle of a 105 howitzer. His old man didn't talk much about the war, but Jacob knew he'd been in artillery. It took Jacob a few weeks of looking at the pictures to realize that his father had been chronicling the killing he'd done in the war as a nineteen-year-old soldier. Bullets didn't split bodies apart, even M60 bullets; that kind of shit could only be done by artillery. That realization, for some reason, made Jacob less afraid of the pictures. Killing was an ordinary thing done by ordinary men, and one of those ordinary men sat down with Jacob every night to eat supper, a man who always said Please and Thank you when the plates were passed around—except, of course, when he was having one of his "rememberings."

But there was another box deeper into the pile, the one he was now excavating from behind the shell of the old Firebird his father was supposedly restoring. It was 3:30 in the afternoon, and his parents were still at their insurance office, State Farm, down in Corona del Mar, and wouldn't be back until at least 5:45, later if there was traffic. He was just home from school, where he'd gotten the math test back. He'd stared at the grade that afternoon as everyone went to lunch, a big red *D–* scrawled across his name. *Dumb shit,* he'd said to himself. He'd studied with his father every night last week, Monday to Thursday, for that test. *You're a dumb shit.*

The box hidden on a back shelf was heavy with loose metal pieces. "Math's dumb," he said to himself. But he thought, *No, you're dumb, dumbass.* He unfolded the flaps of the box, and inside was the treasure: dusty M60 bullets, M1 carbine bullets— unused and discarded, like little brass missiles, or metal lipstick shafts, or, and he smiled at this one, like tiny dildos. He'd just learned that these existed in the world—his friend down the street, Michael Rowan, had told him—and their existence was exciting and disgusting. He grabbed one of the M1 bullets and carefully tightened it into the vise grip on his father's workbench until it pointed toward the ceiling, a tiny rocket about to be launched. *You're going to blow your dumbass head off one of these days,* Michael had said over the summer when Jacob showed him. Whatever, Jacob knew enough not to lean over the bullet.

Using needle-nose pliers, he pried the bullet head away from the casing until he found the prize: gunpowder. He poured the powder into a Tupperware container, and found the white PVC pipe left over from when his father installed the automatic sprinkler system. He sawed off a three-inch length and sandpapered the rough edges. You had to have a tight seal. He'd read about this in *Soldier of Fortune* magazine, which he picked up at El Rancho Books and News, on the rack right next to the *Playboys*. He capped one end of the pipe with a disk of PVC, glue-gunned it shut, drilled an eighth-inch-size hole in the top of the PVC, and poured the powder in the open end of the pipe, the graphite gas smell of it chalking his nose. He packed the powder tight and shoved a few thumbtacks inside. He capped the pipe, hot-gluing it shut, and threaded the cannon fuse—bought from Sears with his allowance money—through the eighth-inch hole and glued around the edges to seal it tight, too.

Excitement swelled in him—the weight of it in his hand, the feeling of potential destruction.

He cleaned up the evidence, putting everything back as he found it, and went out back into the late-afternoon sun. The backyard was a square of Bermuda grass with a six-foot wooden privacy fence. Slanted rooftops of the neighbors' houses rose around the fence, but you couldn't see any windows, no back doors. People liked their privacy here, liked to be left alone. Swaying on a telephone line high above the yard were three brown birds, turning their heads at him, watching him.

He dropped the pipe bomb in the dirt next to the back fence and fished the lighter out of his pocket. The fuse was short, maybe too short, but that made it more exciting. The first bomb took two minutes to go off, and he had crouched behind the trash can for what seemed like eternity until it blew. The next one was around a minute and a half. The third one just fizzled out. The last one he made, a couple of weeks ago when Sherri, the girl he asked to the fall dance, said no, blew in twenty-three seconds. But even that seemed too long. He wanted to dive out of the way as though artillery fire was coming in hot. He lit the fuse now, turned to run, and the plastic boomed, something piercing the back of his neck as he dove into the grass.

He lay there for a minute, imagining his body ripped apart like the ones in the photographs. Imagined his mother and father coming home to find him legless, his right arm blown to the side of the yard, his head rolled to the back-door steps. *Oh, my son! Oh, no, Jacob, my son, my son!* He lay there, watching the startled birds scattered above the telephone wire. He touched the back of his neck. No blood. He listened for sirens, imagined an army of police breaking down his fence, guns drawn. But all he heard was the ringing in his ears, and then one by one the birds returned to the telephone wire, tilting their little heads to eye him curiously.

"You dead?"

Jacob sat up. Ian Rowan, Michael's big brother, was standing there on the grass.

"No."

"The gate was open," Ian said, jerking his thumb in the direction of the fence.

The gate hadn't been open. Jacob had checked to make sure it was closed before lighting the fuse. Maybe Ian had meant it wasn't locked.

Ian bent down and picked up a shard of PVC. His tank top was streaked with sweat, the veins in his arms like blue rivers just beneath the skin. The Rowans had a bench press on their driveway, and it seemed to Jacob that Ian spent most of his time there, on his back, lifting impossible amounts of weight.

"That was bigger than your last one," Ian said.

"You heard the others?"

"Yeah," Ian said, chuckling. "I heard the others." He examined what was left of the bomb, a sly smile on his face. He shook the pipe and a tack tumbled out. "Thumbtacks, huh? You put nails in there, you could do some real damage."

"You gonna call the cops?"

Ian looked at him like he had X-ray vision. He slipped both hands into his jeans pockets, the bomb shard still fisted in his left hand. Jacob wanted it back, but Ian was twentysomething, a man, and he couldn't think of a way to say so that wouldn't sound like a challenge.

"Nah," Ian said. "I'm not going to call the cops. But we should talk sometime, all right?"

"Sure," Jacob said.

"Watch out, Jake," Ian said, pointing at something behind Jacob. "Gonna blow the doors off your own house if you're not careful."

Jacob turned to see what Ian was pointing at: the cracked sliding glass back door, pocked where a tack had exploded the glass, sending fissured cracks all the way to the aluminum frame.

———

Jacob locked himself upstairs in his bedroom until his parents got home, psyching himself up for another beating. He heard the car pull into the driveway, the doors closing, thump thump, and then the heavy footsteps of his parents as they walked into the kitchen.

"Jacob, sweetie," his mother's hushed voice called. "Supper."

Halfway down the stairs, he stopped and listened to them argue in the kitchen. He couldn't tell what they were bitching about, but did it really matter? They argued a lot, like every day it seemed. He was hungry and nothing killed his appetite like an argument over dinner.

"They didn't give us mashed potatoes," his father said, a bag crinkling. Kentucky Fried Chicken; Jacob could smell the grease. "You always need to check. How many times do I need to tell you?"

"Lucas," his mother said. "It's just mashed potatoes."

"I work too damn hard for this."

"Oh, just you? *You* work so hard?"

He heard the clip-clop of heels coming across the linoleum, the sound of maternal fury.

"Jacob," his mother yelled toward the stairs. He tried to play it like he wasn't just standing there listening to them focus all their anger with each other on a mashed-up vegetable.

"Jaco—oh, there you are."

She was in the foyer, dressed in a plaid skirt and high heels, an avocado blouse with a water stain on it. Suddenly all smiles, like some switch had been turned on that said, *Activate bullshit smile.*

"Day okay?" she said.

"It was a day."

"Be positive, please."

Yes, be fucking positive, always. Had to act like the sun showered glitter on the world.

"All good," he said.

She searched his eyes for confirmation. He had to lie when he felt like shit or other questions followed. *What's wrong, Jacob? Tell me everything's okay. Oh, that's not so bad, Jacob.*

His father was standing at the kitchen counter, both hands propped on the edge as though he was being held up by it. A bad sign. In front of him on the counter was the bucket of KFC. Jacob glanced at the sliding glass door. From here you could barely make out the crack, just a faint gray line upsetting the clean glass.

"Hey, big man," his father said, forcing a smile. "We don't have any mashed potatoes. Sorry about that."

His mother exhaled a sigh of barely contained fury.

"It's okay. I like the biscuits better, anyway."

His father smiled again, like Jacob had relieved him of some terrible disappointment. Then his mother, who had been standing still on the edge of the kitchen, started clacking plates out of the cupboards. Jacob was already fucking tired of peacemaking and the night had just begun. They plopped greasy chicken on their plates, squeezed honey onto soggy biscuits. His father turned on the television, the evening news with Tom Brokaw, and they all sat at the table, Jacob trying to block his father's view of the sliding glass door, and got down to the business of eating sinewy drumsticks.

On TV, Brokaw was saying something about President Reagan and weapons being sold to Iran to help fund some group in Central America. His father watched the screen, the sockets of his eyes like carved half circles. He wasn't even very old, thirty-six, but he looked like a man who had been hollowed out.

"I don't understand this Arab thing," his mother said, shaking her head. "What does Iran have to do with Nicaragua?"

"It's about hostages," his father said. "About trying to get Americans home. And they're Iranian, not Arab."

His mother scowled and bit off a piece of biscuit. The television switched to the image of a soldier, answering questions fired at him from a bunch of old men in suits. His mother glanced at the screen and then at his father and then she reached for her glass of Blue Nun—a glass when she got home, a glass over dinner, a glass at bedtime, a glass with her Wheaties, for all Jacob knew.

"Your father sold a big policy today," his mother said. "Who was it, Lucas?"

His dad plopped chicken and biscuits on his plate, but his eyes were drilled to the television.

"Gabe Washburn."

Who the fuck was Gabe Washburn?

"A policy on his big yacht," she said, triumphantly. His mother acted like he was a god or something. "Maybe he'll invite us to one of his movie premieres."

"I never talked to the man, just sold it through his assistant."

"Still . . ." his mother said, trailing off.

Sunlight angled through the window. A prism of light cast a quivering rainbow across the carpeted floor. He didn't dare turn to look at the crack. He dove into his meal, all of his attention focused on the strips of meat clinging to the bone.

"Did you get your test back?" his mother asked.

Jacob glanced at his father, who didn't even look his way.

"No," he said. "Miss Barrow wasn't at school today." A lie. "There was a sub. Some of the kids are saying she might have cancer." Another lie. Still his father stared at the television, his eyes reflecting little blue screens. He could tell them Miss Barrow spontaneously combusted and his dad wouldn't give a shit.

"That's terrible," his mother said. "We'll have to pray for her."

She leaned back, grabbed a pack of menthols sitting on the table, and lit one up. Apparently she'd pray later. His parents were Mormon or they used to be Mormon or at least they were from Utah and had Mormons in their family. Mormon or not, they smoked and drank, gulped coffee like water.

"What's that?" his mother said.

As the sun set, the prism of light had slid across the table and settled, vibrating slightly, on the chest of his father's shirt. Jacob played lies in his head—someone tried to break into the house, Michael Rowan and he were playing catch and the ball hit the window.

"There's a rainbow on your chest."

His dad looked down his nose to see it wavering on his polo shirt. His eyes followed the moted ray of light to the sparkling fissure cut across the plane of glass. He got up then, pushed behind Jacob, and ran his fingers along the edge of the crack. Jacob could feel the heat rise in his father, he swore he could, his skin like burning coffee and cigarette smoke, a smoldering man.

"At least a hundred and fifty dollars," he said, still running his finger across the edge of it.

"It was like that when I got home," Jacob said.

His father's hand was now on the back of Jacob's neck, the palm hot like he'd just pulled it out of an oven.

"When you got home?" his father said.

"I swear."

The last time his dad had clocked him it was like his head exploded, the world gone white until shapes reassembled his vision. His father cried afterward, which was worse than the slap; it was his fault his dad had to hit him. Didn't he know his father was fucked up? Couldn't he be a better kid? His father had given him aspirin and then he sat in bed with Jacob and told him a story about the pig he raised when he was a kid in Hurricane, Utah. About the day his father took it to the butcher. About the pounds of meat iced in the freezer the next day. The story terrified Jacob, and after his father left he lay awake in bed until the first light colored the morning sky.

"Luke," his mother said. "It's just glass."

The hands that had pulled firing lanyards to shoot shells into jungle villages clamped his neck and Jacob hoped for the cuff across the head. It would be over then, the judgment swift and painful, but over.

Then the phone rang, a shrill metal zing that echoed from the kitchen. His father let go and strode across the room to answer. "Yes," he said into the receiver and then he turned his back and said something Jacob couldn't hear. His mother glared at his father's back, the cigarette between her fingers burning the filter now.

"Jake," he said. "I need to take this in the office. Hang the phone up, will you?"

Jacob pushed himself up from the table, his legs like water. Through the receiver, he could hear the soft exhalations of the person on the other end of the line until his father picked up and said, "Got it."

Jacob hung up and sat back down at the table. Tom Brokaw was saying something about a balloon flying across the Atlantic Ocean. They ate in silence, his mother staring at the picked bones of fried chicken, until his father reappeared. His hair was combed and he smelled like Old Spice.

"Got a claim I have to deal with," he said, walking across the room now to pick up his briefcase.

"Now?" his mother said, a knife in her voice.

"A break-in." He kissed his mother's forehead. "Over at La Bonita Plaza."

"La Bonita," her mother said to herself.

He touched Jacob on the top of the head. "Don't worry about the glass," he said, like some new soul had filled the vessel that was his father. "We can fix it."

When his dad fired up the Oldsmobile, his mother lit another menthol and glared at the front door. "Take care of the dishes, please," she said, standing up. "I'm going to go get comfortable."

———

The police had finally left Bao's grocery in the late afternoon, nearly a whole day of business lost. They took their evidence, asked their questions, scooped the dog's body off the ground and drove it away in an ambulance. But they didn't clean the dried blood slicking the cement, and they didn't fix the broken glass. Bao was in the alley now, hosing down the blood. His wife and daughter were inside, packing produce in the walk-in for the night. The water frothed pink and leaked toward a drain that would carry the mixture into the Pacific Ocean.

People still stood at the crime scene tape, watching him like a zoo animal—kids on BMX bikes and skateboards, adults on their way to Lucky's. He pressed his eyes to the diluted blood rivering toward the drain, but he could feel them watching him. *This kind of thing didn't happen until they showed up,* he'd heard a white woman say in Little Saigon once, when graffiti defiled a cinder-block wall. Her logic was solid, inarguable, really, and he knew some of these people must feel the same way.

"You wanna smoke?"

Mr. Lucas Clay, his insurance agent, straddled the line of

water, the filter end of a cigarette peeking out from his extended fist.

"I do," Bao said, taking the cigarette and leaning toward the Zippo flame Lucas offered.

"They left a dog, huh?"

Bao hadn't called Mr. Clay, not yet. He wasn't in a talking mood, and he didn't want to ask for help from anyone, insurance or not, especially from a veteran of the American War. *Yeah,* Mr. Clay had said when they first met. *I was in 'Nam. I liked you people. Not the Cong, but you people. Tough bastards. Same people,* Bao had said in response, *different politics.* Bao had even felt a shade of embarrassment seeing Miss Natasha today; it made him feel like a child who needed to be cared for. He still remembered the helplessness he felt at Camp Pendleton, until Natasha got her family's church to sponsor them. Out of the camp, he could care for himself, take care of his family—and he had made a pretty good life out of things. But he'd never forget that feeling of helplessness, of his life not being his own, when they were sleeping beneath canvas tents, lining up to have food placed in their hands.

"They throw a rock?" Mr. Clay said, nodding toward the window.

"No," Bao said. "The coyotes surprised me. I jumped and hit it with my broomstick."

Mr. Clay glanced at him, taking a drag on the cigarette. "I imagine that would make me jump, too."

Mr. Clay scraped his scuffed leather shoes over the shards now. He was a thin man, his shoulders like bamboo poles, his arms, covered by the sleeves of his button-down shirt, like willowy branches.

"We won't tell anyone that part."

Mr. Clay glanced through the broken window into the shop. Beyond him, Bao could see his daughter at the register, standing on her toes, slipping cigarette cartons into the sales case.

"Any damage to the inside?" Mr. Clay said, still staring through the broken glass.

"No." If you didn't count his trembling wife, his infuriated daughter. Insurance only cared about property damage. America, Bao sometimes thought, only cared about property damage, too.

"Well, that's something to be thankful for, anyway," Mr. Clay said. He always took his time, like he was typing out a script in his head he would soon read out loud.

Someone made a barking sound from the end of the alley.

"Hey," Mr. Clay said, spinning on his heels. "Get the hell out of here."

Bao glanced toward the street and saw three boys, two with shaved heads. The third, a strip of hair down the center of his scalp, barked again. The boys laughed, a couple of bystanders did, too. He tried to memorize the boys' faces, in case they came around the store. He didn't know what he would do if they did, but he wanted to know who they were, wanted to be able to recognize them.

Mr. Clay started toward them. "Go. Now."

Bao, embarrassed, turned to sweep up a few glass shards. Then Mr. Clay was back, running his right hand through his thick hair, as though to gather himself. "Three sixty," he said. Mr. Clay jostled loose the remaining shards of glass in the doorframe and dropped them on the cement. "Three hundred and sixty dollars. You got your deductible, but that's on me this time."

"No," Bao said. "We'll pay the deductible."

No gifts. No handouts.

"We can talk about that later," Mr. Clay said, glancing back to the crime scene tape.

"No." Why this insistence on charity? "We *will* pay."

Clay turned back to Bao and smiled, his eyes a furious blue, as though he was embarrassed by the world.

"Let me give you a hand with that," he said, gesturing toward the cut of plywood Bao had dragged across La Bonita Street from the hardware store.

It was awkward to lift, so Bao accepted the offer. Together they lifted the square of wood, and just before they positioned it in place Bao saw his daughter glance their way. The look on her face—something about it, he didn't know—hovered in his mind as he drove the nails into the doorframe.

Ten minutes later, after Mr. Clay had left with a gift of star fruit carefully wrapped by Ai in the front page of *The Orange County Register*, Linh grabbed her backpack and said something about a study group on a writer named Morrison. When Bao opened the register to count the day's take, two opened cartons of Marlboro Reds sat on the counter, the packs left unstocked.

————

In his bedroom, Jacob changed into his black jeans and black sweatshirt; he found the calico blue bandanna in his sock drawer—his ninja suit, he called it. The one he had worn when he blew up an outdoor lunch table at El Camino Elementary one November night. The one he was wearing when the police strafed a spotlight across the shrubs to look for him.

This had happened before, a mysterious phone call, his father's urgent need to leave the house, his mother locked in the bedroom—and then the silence, the fucking stupid silence. Something was going on. His was a house of unanswered questions. Well, he wasn't getting sucked into the void tonight, no fucking way.

In the garage, he found two premade pipe bombs he'd duct-taped to the back of the shelving unit; he stuffed them into his backpack. Then he was out the door, racing his BMX bike toward La Bonita Plaza. It was mostly dark now, just a glass-clean blue fading over the Pacific. At the shopping center, he rode up and down the sidewalk in front of the stores, swerving around shoppers, hopping the leash of a dog strapped to a bike rack. Nothing. Everything looked perfect, no breaks, no cops, no asshole father. He sat for a few minutes in front of Lucky's when he heard someone say, "Dead dog, dude."

It was a couple of football dicks from school, Thomas Dietwaller and Brady Ryan.

"Yeah, man," Brady said to Dietwaller. "Left it in the alley. Completely decapitated the dog."

Jacob rolled behind them, standing up on the pedals to balance the bike.

"Dude!" Dietwaller spun around. "Get off my ass, faggot." He sprang for the handlebars, but Jacob wheelied into a bunny hop and pedaled into the parking lot.

Jacob cut across the parking lot, hopped an island, and then saw the yellow crime scene tape. That was cool, like a cop show or something. He tossed his bike into the grass, bent under the tape, and walked the alleyway until he saw the plywood nailed to the window frame. There was a smaller window next to the broken one that opened into the shop. Inside there was some Chinese dude, running a feather duster over shelves of goods. Jacob watched him, wondering if his father was inside, but then the man switched off the lights and the alleyway went pitch black.

Jacob's bike was gone when he got back. He spun around looking and saw Dietwaller and Brady pushing it up the hill that led into the park. Assholes. Assholes just because they could, because they lifted weights and played football, because they screwed cheerleaders. Jacob stalked them, keeping his distance, Dietwaller's hands on the handlebars, Ryan's cupping the seat, a trophy for the popular kids. The assholes passed the water tower slide, passed the community center playground sandbox that stray cats took shits in. Diet and Ryan were almost to the end of the path, and it was do or die.

If they beat him up here, there'd be witnesses. In the green-belt, they could stomp on his head for ten minutes and no one would notice.

He made a break for them. "Give me my bike."

"Your bike?" Dietwaller said, a shit-eating grin on his face. Brady laughing. "Your name on it?"

No, his name wasn't on it. There was a registration serial number on the neck of the bike, a requirement of all new bikes in Rancho Santa Elena. But numbers only meant something to the police. "Give me my bike now."

"Well," Dietwaller said in an exaggerated lawyerly voice, "we haven't established if this is, in fact, your bike."

There was no point talking to these fuckers. Jacob reached his left hand into his backpack now, his fingers searching around for one of the bombs. The matches were in his sweat-shirt pocket. Some people understood only one thing, espe-cially dumb-shit football players. The bomb was nestled in the palm of his left hand now, the book of matches pinched be-tween the fingers of his right.

But then he saw something. A face, the profile of a man sit-ting on a bench beneath one of the streetlamps. It was his fa-ther, his long arm rested across the back of the bench. Next to him, Jacob realized, was a woman, her head pillowed by his father's shoulder.

"He's gifting us the bike," Dietwaller said, Brady popping him with his shoulder as they passed.

But Jacob just stood there, watching his father and this woman. They were lit by a flickering streetlamp. His father's arm was draped over the woman's shoulders, her body resting against his chest as though she knew his body well. She was Chinese, he thought. She was talking to his father, her hands moving in gestures of frustration, and his father nodded as she spoke, his head tipped toward her as though to listen closely. They didn't fit together, not at all; they belonged to differ-ent worlds, different time–space continuums. But his father looked, Jacob didn't know . . . he looked concerned—that was it—like he really cared. When his father leaned forward and kissed her on the lips, all the unanswered questions had one answer, and Jacob found the pipe bomb and the matches ready in his hands.

Chapter Five

"I thought you were taking a *mental health break*," Mendenhall said when she arrived at County with the dog that evening. He was sitting at his metal desk, smoking a cigarette, reading the sports section of the *Los Angeles Times*.

"Something came in."

Mendenhall was going to give her hell about the dog. She knew the *chief* medical examiner wouldn't deign to look at the body of a dead dog, much less investigate. He'd leave it to the cops. But she didn't give a damn. There was something about this that was eating at her, and also it was an attack on the Phans, a family she had felt close to once.

"What've we got?" He turned the page, a preview section of Sunday's Rams game.

"Dog," she said.

"Dog?" Mendenhall crumpled the paper closed and looked at her.

Here it comes. "Throat slit," she said, trying to get ahead of him. "Dumped behind a Vietnamese grocery in Santa Elena, a note pinned—"

"Let me have a look," he said, snubbing out his cigarette with surprising urgency.

She led him to the loading dock, where the ambulance workers had left the corpse. Mendenhall pulled aside the sheet, narrowed his eyes, and bent over the dog's sawed-open throat. "A Labrador-shepherd mix," he said. He ran his hand down the back of the dog, touching the hind legs. "Was a beautiful animal. Well taken care of."

Mendenhall was quiet a few moments. In the six years she'd worked with him, six years of opening up murder victims, accident victims, overdosed celebrities, she'd never seen him look this upset. She'd come to think Mendenhall was alexithymic. It was the perfect disorder for a coroner, someone who can't feel emotions, but here he was going misty over a dog. She remembered him yesterday, concerned only with who was the wealthiest dead body.

"I despise people who hurt animals," he said, running his fingers through the long coat of the animal. "The worst of the worst." Then he grabbed the gurney himself and wheeled it inside the examination room, and Natasha followed.

———

At the station, a couple of cops had left a missing dog flyer on Ben's station desk, a cut-and-paste deal, a picture of a collie. A caption made out of clipped magazine letters read: HELP! FIND TOTO'S KILLER! Yeah, he got it. They thought his dog investigation was kid stuff. *Very funny,* Ben thought to himself, paper in his hands. *Really hilarious.*

Marco Girardi and Vince Sessions, a new guy straight out of the Academy of Criminal Investigation, hunched conspicuously over the paperwork on their desks, like two middle school kids trying to hide their glee. Since Vince had joined the department, he'd hauled in half the skateboarding population of Santa Elena, calling them "pot-smoking hippies." He wore latex gloves when making arrests because you never knew what kind of diseases "these people" were carrying. Some guys got into police business because they wanted to serve, recognized that there was often genuine human sadness at the heart of most crime. Other guys got into the business because they hated people and they wanted a daily opportunity to exercise their disdain. Vince Sessions, Ben had decided, was the latter kind of cop.

Ben balled up the flyer and lobbed it across the room, where it careened off Sessions's desk.

"This is Lassie, geniuses," he said, and Marco and Vince broke into laughter.

They'd just stepped out of evening roll call with Lieutenant Hernandez, the day shift turning over to night. Carolina McGrath, Santa Elena's first female detective, was working an investment fraud case, a crime as Rancho Santa Elena as 5 Series BMWs. Vincent and Marco were trying to hook Lieutenant Hernandez on a cocaine-smuggling narrative that had plot holes the size of semi-trucks—the kilos coming in through tunnels underneath the border, the mules hauling it in on four-by-fours through the Santa Ana Mountains, the illegals running distribution through legitimate orange-packing companies as fronts. Vince wanted the lieutenant to sign off on an undercover operation—fake IDs, cash to front as big-time buyers, wires, all the investigative toys Vince's adolescent mind could conjure.

"Did you say the dog's neck was sawed?" Lieutenant Hernandez had said, cutting Vince off mid-sentence.

Vince dropped his gold pen on the table in front of him. A Montblanc, probably a gift from his parents for graduating from detective academy.

"We're talking about a dog, Lieutenant," Sessions said.

Hernandez glanced at the detective and then chose to ignore him.

"Doesn't sound like a kid's prank," Hernandez said.

"Maybe not," Ben said, although he'd seen enough of what some kids could do. The drive-bys in North Hollywood. The "good" kids of Santa Elena beating an old Mexican woman in La Bonita Park.

"Vietnamese grocery?" Hernandez said.

"The alleyway behind it," Ben said.

Hernandez was quiet, his chin pushed down against his chest the way he did when he was chewing on something. He shook his head now but didn't illuminate them with his thoughts.

"Keep me in the loop," Hernandez said.

Back at his desk, Ben checked his answering machine— a message from a woman who'd had her Mercedes stolen last week, wondering why they hadn't found the sedan. "It's in Tijuana, sweetheart," he said to himself while listening to her whine on. A call from a Daniel Driggs, Esq., wanting to interview him about a hit-and-run Ben had handled a few months back. All of that could wait.

He pulled the file on the dog and found the pictures from yesterday, slipping the least graphic shot inside his coat pocket. On the way out, Sessions was still bitching about the meeting.

"You know what I don't get?" Ben said, pausing in front of Vince's desk. "If the drug cartel can dig a tunnel beneath the most surveilled border in the country, why would they run product through illegals?"

"'Cause wetbacks are dispensable."

"Nah," Ben said. He suspected Vince liked his theory because it would give him license to harass migrant workers. "They wouldn't want immigration sniffing around their operation—even if they paid a few officials off. They'd have professionals, dudes in for life. You're looking for suits, not orange pickers."

"Woof, woof," Vince said.

———

"Stephen, this is the man that helped us," the boy's mother said in a singsongy voice. "Say thank you."

Ben got down on one knee in the Connollys' living room and the little boy hugged him. "Thank you," the boy said, his breath warm against Ben's neck.

The hospital had released the boy that afternoon, after twenty-four hours of observation. Ben had seen so many boys killed, it was hard not to think of them while this child embraced him. Stephen let go then, toddled over to a pile of Legos, and continued building a multicolored wall, three bricks tall and going on a fourth.

"We're indebted to you," the boy's father said, handing Ben an envelope.

"That's unnecessary, Mr. Connolly," Ben said, waving it off.

"Without you," Mrs. Connolly said, her voice breaking a little, "we're planning a funeral today."

Mr. Connolly touched his wife's shoulder, Stephen glancing up at his parents before his mother caught herself and smiled at him. Ben reluctantly slipped the card into his coat pocket. He'd read it alone, when he didn't have to pretend to be the hero.

"Maybe we can talk in another room a minute?"

They led him into the kitchen, the smell of burning grounds from the Mr. Coffee, Mrs. Connolly sitting at the island countertop, her frosted hair done up in Farrah feathers. Behind them the late-morning news flashed mugshots of two South Central Crips, a South LA gang, wanted in a drive-by.

"You said your dog was missing," Ben said. He pulled the crime scene Polaroid he'd gotten out of evidence from his other coat pocket and slid it onto the counter. "Is this Duke?"

A dam of emotion broke from Mrs. Connolly, her hand pressed against her mouth.

"I'm sorry," Ben said.

"Coyotes get him?" Mr. Connolly asked, picking the picture up and holding it close to his nose like he was nearsighted.

"No," Ben said. Then he told them—the slit neck, found behind the Vietnamese grocery.

"Jesus Christ," Mr. Connolly said.

"You all set out any rat poison?" Ben asked.

"No," Mr. Connolly said. "We don't have a rat problem."

"Is that what made Stevie sick?" Mrs. Connolly said.

"I believe so," Ben said. "Just waiting on toxicology."

"They say they eat them," Mrs. Connolly said then, tears streaking her face.

"Excuse me?" Ben said.

"They eat dogs," she said. "The Orientals."

————

"The dog didn't bleed out on-site?" Mendenhall said. "It was transported and dumped?"

"Right," Natasha said. "Had to have been drained somewhere else."

Mendenhall was up to his forearm in the incision, rooting around in the gastric sac, emptying out the contents of the dog's stomach—blood and grass, bits of a chew toy littering the stainless-steel autopsy sink.

"I'm guessing it was the neck wound that caused death," she said.

He arched an eyebrow at her sarcasm. "Be damn hard to hold down a dog this size and saw it to death."

He had a point.

"When I was a kid," he said, "we had this border collie, Lucky—"

"Lucky?"

"Yes, Lucky," he said. "Like we were lucky to have her. She was the sweetest dog, but she liked to chase jackrabbits. See, that's what border collies do, they chase things, round 'em up. So she goes running off one day and doesn't come back. My dad and I go looking for her, calling her name down the street, checking with neighbors, until it dawns on us that she might have run into the orange grove across from the housing tract."

He pulled out a few bits of undigested muck and threw it in the sink—some dog food pellets, slivers of undigested bone, a streak of greenish-pink slush.

Sometimes Mendenhall liked to work in reverse order, from the least plausible cause of death to the most. *Minimizes embarrassing surprises*, he liked to say. Occasionally he was proven right—the heroin-induced pulmonary edema, not the stab wound; the black widow bite that killed the boy, not child neglect and starvation. That one made her angry. A neglected child would have been saved with antivenin, if taken to the hospital.

"We get four rows in and we find Lucky, shot full of buckshot. Those goddamned Santa Elena ranch hands had used her for target practice. I loved that dog," Mendenhall said. "My dad sent in a formal complaint to the Santa Elena Company. Went down to the offices. The company settled it with a fifty-dollar check. Fifty bucks for my dog. I'm still furious at my dad about that—and he's been in the ground ten years."

His hand and wrist still digging around. "Hmm," he said, and then plopped something down on the table, a slab of undigested steak.

"This dog was living the high life," she said.

Mendenhall grabbed the scalpel and sliced open the chunk.

"Look at that," he said, pinching something between his forefinger and thumb.

A green pellet, no bigger than a piece of rock candy.

"Rat poison," she said. She thought of Ben's bleeding gums.

"Some asshole really hates dogs," Mendenhall said, slicing into the meat again, another green pellet lodged in the sinews. "That would have been fatal, at least eventually." There was a question in his voice, though he wouldn't dare actually ask her for her help. "Be no need for a saw."

"For theater," Natasha said. "They sawed the neck to scare the hell out of someone."

———

They were locked inside his dad's Olds in the parking lot, the bomb sitting on the dashboard like a useless turd.

"Where'd you get this?"

Five minutes before, Jacob had meant to light the bomb, had imagined throwing it at his father and that woman, but instead he just stepped out of the shadows, the bomb clasped in his right hand, the unlit matches in his left, and yelled like some stupid little kid, "Leave my dad alone." They had both startled, the woman jumping up from the bench, a look of terror flashing across her face. His father had stood slowly, squeezed the Chinese woman's hand, and said, "Go home." She glanced at Jacob, fear firing her eyes, and then his father said something in Chinese to her. For a moment his father was a complete stranger to Jacob, like the words in his mouth transformed his DNA or something.

The girl turned then and jogged into the darkness of the park.

"Give it to me," his dad said. And Jacob, feeling like some programmed robot, handed over the bomb and matches.

Now the heat from the vents blew against his face, making it hard to breathe.

"You made it," his father said, looking at the bomb on the dashboard, the PVC pipe, the glued edges, the one-inch fuse. He picked the bomb up, weighed it in his hand, and then rolled it into the defrosting vent up against the windshield. "The broken glass door," his father said, putting one and one together. Then he yanked the car into gear and slipped into the stream of evening traffic on El Rancho Road.

"That was a business meeting," his father said. An explosion of light as he matched up a cigarette. "Someone vandalized her shop. She was upset. She needed someone to talk to."

"You're a liar," Jacob said.

"Sometimes my job demands I do more than write a check," he said, an edge coming into his voice. "Insurance is more than money. Insurance is helping people. You understand what I'm saying?"

"Kissing her? That's the kind of help you mean?"

Squirming in his seat, his father glanced at the bomb on the dashboard. He was driving excruciatingly slowly now, Jacob's side of the car floating into the bike lane.

"I can't believe the things people do to each other," his father said, as though to the universe.

Maybe it was the shifting of light, from streetlight to darkness and back again, but the character of his dad's face changed—his mouth tugged into a tight grimace, his eyes hollowed out like he was watching a movie inside of himself. Jacob used to think of his father as being like the Incredible Hulk— mild-mannered Bruce Banner one moment and the green monster the next—but that was stupid. He was just sick. Jacob's hand was on the door handle now. He'd jump out of the car, take a twenty-five-mile-per-hour roll to the curb, and make a run for it. Someone honked and swerved around them, and then his dad was making a right turn into California Homes. They passed the Meyers' place, then Gina's, the girl he had a crush on, and then Michael's house with his brother Ian outside lifting weights on the driveway. And then they were home.

His father parked the car and yanked open the garage door. There he found the boxes—the one with the bullets, the one with the pictures. He found the PVC pipe and glue gun, and tossed them in the trash. "Going to blow us up," he was saying now, and Jacob knew he was lost in a remembering. Jacob stood there watching him, stupidly paralyzed by his dad's fit. His dad shook the pictures from the boxes, Polaroid after Polaroid of dead bodies flying into the trash can like paper throwing stars. "They just keep coming, they never sto—"

Then Jacob ducked, the metal rake swishing above his head.

His father had lunged for the instrument so quickly, Jacob hadn't seen it until it nearly impaled him. He bolted then around the front of the house, yanking open the wooden fence to the backyard, his father on his heels, yelling obscenities. Jacob zoomed around the back of the house, past his mother's bedroom window with the drawn curtains, down the side of the house back into the front yard. His dad was still on his tail, the rake raised above his head like a baseball bat, when someone streaked across the grass. Jacob heard a thud and when he spun around Ian Rowan was pinning his father to the grass.

"Grab the rake," Ian said.

Jacob scrambled to his father's hands and pried the instrument from his fingers.

"Mr. Lucas," Ian said. "Stop. What you're chasing isn't real."

His dad's eyes widened, as though the actual world had just reassembled itself.

"What did I do?" he said, blinking water from his eyes. "What did I . . . ?"

"Get over to my garage," Ian said to Jacob.

Across the street, Jacob found his friend Michael standing in the driveway, watching the scene. Michael grabbed his hand and pulled Jacob inside the garage, where the two of them sat down on the ratty couch and watched Ian talk to his father on the front-yard grass.

"Man, Jake," Michael said. "Your dad is fucked up."

Not always, Jacob wanted to say, *not always, but . . .*

"Yeah," he said, watching Ian walk his father back into the house like an invalid. "Yeah, he's fucked up."

"Superwarfarin," Natasha said, sitting on a barstool at Ben's kitchen counter. "That's what poisoned you."

"Rat poison."

She nodded and told him about the poisoned steak undigested inside the dog's stomach.

"So someone throws the poisoned meat over the fence," Ben said, "the dog eats the steak, the kid eats the tainted snow."

"The upside," she said, pointing to a box of donuts on the kitchen counter. "With that blood thinner in your veins, you can eat all the donuts you want."

She picked up a glazed one and took a bite.

The Connollys had given him a gift certificate to Winchell's, that's what was in the card. Twenty dollars. So, what the hell, on the way back from the station he picked up a box. On TV cops were always on the chase, in public opinion they were always at the donut shop, in real life they were often filing reports.

Ben was standing over a skillet, spraying ground beef with lime juice. He glanced at the dining room table. Lance, Emma's boyfriend, sat next to her, stroking the back of her head while she tried to explain an algebra problem. "Lance," he heard Emma say, "stop that and pay attention to this." She sounded like her mother. "You can't fail this class again."

After picking up the donuts, Ben had driven over to the high school and picked them both up. Rachel had a faculty meeting followed by the spring-semester back-to-school night, so Ben had taken a night off from detective work. Lance had never been in the cruiser before. *This is so radical, man,* he'd said. And Ben had fielded questions all the way home from the kid. *How's the scanner work? What's a 10-13? Dude, that's a shotgun!* Emma had smiled listening to him, also slightly annoyed, it seemed. There was something genuinely doltish about Lance that Ben had come to appreciate, like he was too dumb to imagine hurting someone, and that kind of stupidity was fine with Ben. Nice and stupid was a whole lot better, when it came to his daughter, than mean and smart.

At the house, Lance was all distraction. He'd brought Emma one of his mixed tapes, and he kept rewinding moments in songs, imploring Emma to listen. "Check out this guitar solo" or "I thought of you when I heard this line" and Emma would stop her math, rest her cheek on her hand, and smile politely.

The kid fawned over her: getting her a glass of water (*Ice? No ice?*), wrapping a blanket around her shoulders when she said she was cold, watching her lips move when she talked about isosceles triangles. *Geez, man*, Ben thought. *Get a backbone.*

"Ben," Natasha said now. "When they start killing animals . . ."

"I know." Yeah, he'd read the Kellert and Felthous report in '85, linking childhood animal cruelty to future mass murderers. Read the Macdonald report, too, years ago in detective academy—the triad of teenage behaviors: bed-wetting, fire-setting, animal torture. "You're assuming the people who poisoned the dog are the same people who dumped it."

"Too coincidental otherwise," she said. "Doesn't make a whole lot of sense, though."

Right, didn't make much sense, if it had been planned out. Poison the dog, collect it from the backyard, slice its throat, drain and dump it. Too elaborate, too many possibilities for failure. None of this made much sense, something he'd spent another fifteen minutes with the Connollys trying to explain. It didn't make sense, if the Phans were going to eat the dog, to poison it, to leave it bleeding in the gutter outside of the grocery. Made even less sense to call the cops. But Mrs. Connolly wasn't having it. *This kind of thing didn't happen until they got here,* she said. *This used to be a nice place.* And what did you say to that? Something about that comment set him to thinking about Coach Lewis Wakeland preying on boys he coached. When the story went public, some nice people in this nice place blamed the boys—said they just wanted to take the coach down, some said they were gay and must have wanted it. It was taking some people a long time to see around the image the coach projected: the paternal mentor, coaching kids to have self-discipline and high moral character. Bad people could look innocent, could use their power in sick ways. Ben left the Connollys' place feeling pissed off, a feeling that was only now beginning to wear off.

"Whoever did this," Natasha said, "they'll do it again. Or worse."

With Natasha, pleasure and work often intermingled. He could talk a crime scene with her, like playing misconduct chess, and be dying to get her in the bedroom before you could say "motive." But he wasn't crazy about talking out cases in earshot of Emma. First, it wasn't very professional. Second, he wanted his daughter to believe she lived in a safe world, as much as he could manage it. Impossible, sure, and she was too smart to buy the lie entirely, but he was going to try so long as she spent half her life under his roof.

"What's the deal with the Phans?" he asked then. "It was like a family reunion today."

She let out a deep breath. "Back in '75, I volunteered down at Pendleton."

"When all the refugees were flying into El Toro marine base," Ben said, nodding.

"My parents' parish organized visits to the camps. A lot of churches volunteered to help the marines, who were overwhelmed. I mean, there were almost twenty thousand people in that camp. We helped serve food, dropped off boxes of clothes, looked for sponsors so they could transition into housing, get jobs."

She paused a moment.

"One day, I was serving spaghetti in the kitchen when this little girl came down the line with her family. You should have seen her, Ben. She was so small, rail-thin—I mean, they'd spent months sleeping outside in a camp in Guam and then here, eating soup-kitchen food—and she wore this sun hat pulled low over her eyes—maybe to hide the scar, I don't know. I'd learned a few Vietnamese words and when I said to her, *Xin chao,* she pulled the hat from her forehead and proudly said, *Hello!* like she was saying two can play at that game."

He warmed up the tortillas, watching her closely.

"As soon as I saw her . . . I don't know, I had this feeling."

She looked down at the counter a moment. "Then the Phans got sponsors, left the camp. Bao got a job and an apartment in Westminster." She shrugged. "And after a while I lost touch."

She looked at him, a pool of sadness in her eyes he wanted to kiss away.

"What feeling do you mean?"

"It's hard to explain."

Ben watched her a moment and then set the steaming plate of meat on the table.

"Em, set the table, sweetheart."

"Just a second," Emma said.

"I got it, sir," Lance said, jumping up from the table. The kid found the place settings and then started rummaging in the utensil drawer like he lived here.

"You sit down. You're a guest," Ben said. "Emma."

The boy sat. Emma huffed out of her chair and huffed over to the plate of tortillas and huffed back to the table to sit.

They sat down, a table full of taco fixin's—meat, pico de gallo, hunks of avocado, crema, slices of limes, red onions, radishes, a damn fine fiesta, if you asked him. Body surfing and tacos, that's the retirement he wanted.

But some thrashing music was squealing out of his hi-fi.

"What's this?" Ben said.

"The Circle Jerks," Emma said. "Rodney Bingenheimer on KROQ was playing them the other day."

Natasha flashed him a wry smile, but nothing on Emma's face betrayed an understanding of the band's name.

"Something's wrong with the ears of this generation," he said.

"You're old," Emma said. "And you're a musical fascist."

"Fair enough." And to prove her point, Ben stood, turned off the cassette, and cued up some vinyl Teddy Pendergrass.

"There," he said, sitting back down. "Music."

Emma rolled her eyes and placed a couple of radish slices on her taco. "Someone poisoned that dog?"

So she did listen.

"Seems so," Ben said.

"Kids were talking about it at school," she said. "They said it was beheaded."

"Dude!" Lance said, his mouth full of taco. "That's sick."

"It wasn't beheaded," Natasha said.

"This girl, Mai," Emma said, "she started crying at the beginning of English class when Randy Ross and David Grassley were talking about it. Mrs. Lowell let her go to the counselors'. Some of the kids aren't so nice, you know." Emma shook her head. "I mean, not everyone, but enough."

Lance nodded and then pulled his eyes into slits.

"Lance," Emma said, popping him in the shoulder. "Don't."

Lance threw all his energy into devouring a second taco.

"You said they flew into the marine base?" Emma said, looking at Natasha.

Note to self: Kids are always listening.

"They did," Natasha said. "On chartered Pan Am flights."

"That's five minutes away," Emma said, her uneaten taco clasped in her hand. "How come I've never heard about this? I mean, we had a whole unit on the Vietnam War last quarter and nothing."

"Yeah, dude," Lance said, mouth full of tortilla. "Like the runway's right over there."

Ben didn't have an answer for that, why that part of the history wouldn't be told in schools.

———

That night, after Ai fell asleep, Bao escaped to the kitchen and poured himself a Chivas Regal, one of those American things he liked. Well, Scottish, but he'd discovered it here and that forever made it American in his mind. He snuck into the living room, unlocked the front door—he always thought a child should come home to an unlocked door. Opening the curtains, he perched himself on the couch, waiting for the cast of light from his daughter's headlights. He realized now that he had no idea where Linh was tonight. No name, no address for the book discussion. Nothing. In the chaos of the day, he'd forgotten his duty as a father.

After the detectives left the store this afternoon, his brother had called Bao and asked him to attend the community meeting tonight at Heritage Park Public Library, across the park from the high school. The library, they had discovered, was infrequently used by the white people of Santa Elena. Here at the library they could speak Vietnamese with only an occasional raised eyebrow. Here their kids could gather to do homework while the parents were at work. The group of men had been small at first, a sort of informal city commissioners meeting to discuss the concerns the actual city commissioners didn't consider—where to find importers for Three Crabs fish sauce, how to avoid fines for fishing perch in city lakes, how to get permits for restaurants, the ins and outs of zoning laws—but since the harassments had started, the group had grown larger, a smattering of Chinese and Korean among them now.

People had been angry tonight, sharing stories, one after another, of recent hostile incidents—the graffiti spray-painted on the Korean Barbecue, the rock thrown through the front window of the Imperial House, the insults hurled from car windows, the abuse their kids suffered at school. Besides Danh, Giang and Trai were both there, too, Trai looking like the cognac from last night's card game had gotten the better of him—something that made Bao smile. They weren't the young men who could drink until dawn anymore, though they still sometimes tried.

"And now this," Xuan Than had said. "Beheading a dog—"

"The throat was slit," Bao said. "That was all."

"Does it matter?" Danh said.

It was a good question. What degree of ugly action tipped it into something dangerous? Graffiti bothered Bao, of course. An occasional *Go back home!* yelled from a passing car roiled his stomach, but what would have become of him if he'd not escaped Saigon? Whipping? Severed hands? A shallow grave? Safety was relative, and occasional abuse was a light weight to bear compared with political persecution.

"Tell them what else," Danh said.

Bao had told Danh about the note when he had called earlier, something he regretted now.

"They left a message," Bao said.

"What did it say?" Giang asked.

Bao paused a moment. "Kill them all."

The men erupted, the refugees from the war remembering that some of the American soldiers scrawled that phrase across their helmets, some of the others wore sewn-on patches with those words on their uniforms. The heated voices in this room made Bao nervous. These men, himself included, wanted respect, not tolerance. Worse, some of the men were taking these indignities as an affront to their masculinity. Men who had been soldiers, like his brother, forced to wait tables when he first arrived. Lawyers packing grocery crates. Doctors driving cabs. Once a man felt stripped of his masculinity, he felt compelled to act—and not with his mind, with his fists, with a weapon.

"Stop," Bao said. "There're many good people here." He thought of Miss Natasha, of her kindness in the refugee camp down at the Camp Pendleton military base a dozen years ago, of Mr. Keane, the businessman who took them in and gave them jobs when they arrived. "Don't forget them because of the ignorant ones."

"That's unfair," Danh said. "You can't ask us to weigh basic decency against open hostility."

Danh had a point, Bao knew it.

Just last week, Bao had stopped into Pacific Hardware to buy flathead screws to bolt a bookshelf to their living room wall, and the shopkeeper asked him to repeat his words four times. Finally, making him draw what he wanted on a piece of paper. "I can't understand you people," he'd said, shaking his head. By the time Bao got home, his suppressed anger had so exhausted him he didn't bother with the bookshelf. It still stood there in the living room, unbolted to the wall.

"Think about all we've built here," Bao said. "Think about what we're building." He raised his hand toward his brother. "And now we might have a voice in the local government. You, Danh. If we cause trouble because of a few bad people, they'll all blame us."

"Don't be naïve, Bao," Danh said. "If we want respect, we have to stand up for ourselves and tell them, *Enough.*"

Ngây thơ. Naïve. After the meeting let out, Bao had driven to Pao Fa temple. The temple's ugly square building sat on the edge of town in an industrial park. The city wouldn't grant them permits for the temple; that's why they were out here, on county land, stuck between an awning manufacturer and a welding shop. Danh's public rebuke had burned in his head as he lit the incense in the courtyard outside the temple, the stench of soldered metal puncturing the incense smoke. Bao thought he was being pragmatic, which was the opposite of naïve. They were unwanted guests here. And no host would tolerate accusations thrown at him in his own home. Until the Americans saw them as Americans, they were sleeping in a guest room with the bathroom down the hall and they would have to take what was fed to them at dinner, no matter how terrible the dish.

And when he got home an hour later, he had found Ai in their bed, the television flashing a rerun of *Love Boat.*

"Mình ơi," he said, climbing into bed and placing his hand on her back. "You frightened?"

"Vâng," she said. "A little, yes." She was cocooned in the blankets as though it was freezing in the house. "Are you?"

"No," he said, rubbing her left shoulder where the muscle cramped when she was anxious. He was often frightened, but it was his duty to never show it. "No."

Now he was in the living room, halfway into his glass of scotch. The headlights of Linh's Honda suddenly brightened the street. Her front tire hit the curb when she tried to park, and she rushed across the grass as though escaping something.

"What's wrong?" he said, when she burst into the foyer.

She startled. "Dad, you scared me."

"Something's wrong."

"Yes," she said, smiling now. "You scared me."

She dropped her book bag and noticed the glass of scotch. "Did you leave any for me?"

He laughed. "Tất nhiên. I always leave you a drop or two."

"Well, get me a drop or two then."

They sometimes drank together, in the backyard alone, in the kitchen or living room if it was raining or cold out. She told him things when they shared a drink—things about young men, about her fears, about the American literature she was reading. When she'd quit pre-med, he was angry at first—and Ai was still bitter—but he'd come to appreciate her love for the words. He'd learned a lot about American history, too, from her retelling of the books. This country, for all the beautiful stories it told about itself—which he loved and sometimes believed—could also be a dark place, at least in some of its books.

He handed her the glass and they sat together, in the low light of the table lamp, sipping their scotch.

"How was the group?"

"Fine," she said. "Slavery, racism, metaphor, simile, et cetera—you know."

He marveled at her, always, the scar on her forehead throwing him back to the day he'd almost lost her. He remembered how she kept her eyes open when the army surgeon pulled the shard from her forehead and sewed up the wound. He didn't know what that meant, a ten-year-old child who kept her eyes open during such a thing. But it seemed to epitomize her, the way she took things straight-on.

"I'm sorry you had to find that this morning."

"It's okay," he said.

"No," she said. "It's not. Don't try to make it so because you don't want to frighten me."

"I'm okay, is what I meant."

She looked at him a moment, a sad smile on her face, and then she took his hand and held it.

"You work so hard," she said. "You always have. You and Mom both."

He could hear the thank-you in her voice.

"And for that," he said, "I get to sit here and drink expensive scotch and talk with you."

She let out a sigh, as though she had breathed her first full breath of the day.

"I almost feel American," she said. She slipped into Vietnamese then, and Bao's shoulders eased a bit. He often spoke English with her, but he preferred their time alone in the house, speaking their words almost as natural as breathing. "But then I'm reminded."

"This morning reminded you."

She nodded and took a sip.

He never felt American—at least as most Americans seemed to think of it: white and Christian. Bao knew some refugees who proudly raised the American flag above their store or ran it up the flagpole in front of their house, but something about that felt like an abasement to him. He was still here on a green card, would live his life as though on one long work trip. But Linh was a citizen. As soon as it was allowed, they got her citizenship, planted her roots into solid dirt. No longer the refugee, no longer on the run, a citizen, a home.

"You know why I changed my major?" she said. "I'm sorry, I know it hurt you, but do you know why?"

He hadn't asked her. He had just accepted it. He had been afraid, at the time, that his questions would sound like an interrogation.

"With medicine," she said, "I was doing it for you, for the community. I felt I owed you and Mom that. Felt I owed that to all these people who lost so much when they came here." She paused. "But I thought I owed myself, too. I thought I owed you my honesty about who I wanted to be."

He nodded. Bao knew she wanted to be a teacher someday, a professor. In the hierarchy of things, a professor wasn't as respectable as a doctor, but it would still make people take notice.

"When I read these stories from all over the world," she said, smiling now, "I realize our story, our history is not so unusual. It feels like it is, living here, the daily reminders that we're different—both the reminders we tell ourselves, and the ones thrown at us." She waved her hand at the street outside, which Bao took to mean the reminder that was dropped in the alley behind their grocery this morning. "But it's not. Our history is common—war, migration, starting over somewhere else. There's nothing unusual about it. To say anything different would be ignorance."

She paused and took a sip. "You know, I kind of feel sorry for a lot of people here. Most of them don't know their story, don't know, really, where they came from." She smiled at him. "Sorry. I've just been thinking."

"No," he said. "It's good. I'm glad the stories help."

She squeezed his hand and let go, took a sip of her drink, and looked out the window to the street. He felt a distance grow between them then, as though her mind was floating away into one of her stories.

"I want you to know that I never mean to hurt you with the decisions I make about my life."

She was still looking out the front window, and Bao had the feeling she was both being honest with him and keeping something hidden.

"In my Contemporary American Lit class," she said, "we're

reading this book called *Beloved* by Toni Morrison." She looked at him and smiled knowingly. "It's sad, so you wouldn't like it."

He raised an eyebrow, and she smiled.

"I underlined something that hit me the other day: *Definitions belong to the definers, not the defined.*" She nodded and looked out the front window again. "I like that."

She finished her drink, kissed him on the cheek, and went to bed. But Bao sat up, replaying the moment in his mind when he first saw the dead dog, the way he'd been sure it was a child at first, the coyotes gnawing on it like something out of the war. He poured another scotch and found his pad of paper and charcoal pencils and started sketching a Townsend's warbler. He'd seen one yesterday on his walk home, a winter visitor from the North, sitting in a pine tree, devouring a grasshopper. He heard the toilet flush and listened to the water running in Linh's bathroom. He sketched the shape of the body, then started in on the face, filling in the beak, shading the dark area around the eye, like a thief's mask. *Definitions belong to the definers, not the defined.* He drew until the light was off in Linh's room and the house held the silence of sleep. Then he set aside the half-finished bird, reached across the couch, and zipped open his daughter's schoolbag. He wanted to read the line in the book, to see the context in which it was written. A notebook of college-lined paper, a *Norton Anthology of American Literature*, a water bottle, but no Toni Morrison. Morrison, that's what she had said. He was sure of it. He zipped closed the bag and sketched until the whiskey heavied his eyes, wondering what secrets she kept.

Chapter Six

"You've got an admirer, it seems," Mendenhall said to Natasha the next morning as he hovered over the body of the state senator's kid, the one who had OD'd on heroin. "Detective Vanek wants you on Pajama Man. The guy in the pool. Says it's a priority. You should have told me it was Vanek you were working with."

"It was written on the paperwork."

"Real pain in the ass, that guy," he said. "You can have that case."

She almost said *thank you* and then caught herself.

"You're welcome," he said.

At her desk, she found Detective Vanek's card in the file and called him.

"What are you doing?" she said when he answered. "What's with this requesting me?"

"I need you on this case," he said. *No, I need the juvenile files,* he said to someone away from the phone. *Yes, '83 to '86.* To Natasha: "I need your expertise. Mendenhall's sloppy, lazy. You know that."

"All right," she said. "But I'll handle my business and you handle yours."

"Fair enough," he said. "This is what I need." And then he laid it out: any methamphetamine present, dead before or after hitting the water, approximate time of death, instrument of killing. "Looks to me like his skull was beaten in, but no blood present, no contusion. Strange, don't you think?"

Not necessarily.

When she was off the phone, she wheeled the man's body onto a floor scale and recorded his weight, 172 pounds. In the examination room, she pulled back the sheet. Walter Brennan was fifty-six years old, graying at the temples but otherwise a youthful brown head of hair. She clipped a lock and slipped it into an evidence bag, then she stripped him of the pajamas, his bloated body a grayish white in the examination lights. Despite the bloat, he was muscled, the kind of carefully cultivated muscles carved in a gym—the pectoralis major, the deltoids, the trapezius—as though each muscle was attended to.

She clipped nails from his manicured right hand and placed them in an evidence bag, too, and examined the broken pinkie finger. The knuckles were flaked with dried blood. If he'd landed a punch or two, it would have hurt his attacker; he was muscled enough to leave a mark. In the margins of the examination form, she wrote: *Suspect may have facial contusions from a punch.*

She started at the calcaneus and the metatarsals, then moved up the anterior and posterior muscles of the legs—each muscle carved as though he'd purchased bionic limbs. She worked up his torso, past a curved scar marring the lower third of the abdominal oblique—a tummy tuck scar. Could never look too good on the beach. His pectorals were square slabs, but even this body could be broken—the rib contusion, a purple nebula, marring the skin atop the 8, 9, and 10 false ribs. She pressed the skin there, felt a jagged snag where the bone had been snapped. One hell of a punch, if that was the cause. Kicked, maybe? After he'd fallen? Baseball bat?

She ran her gloved hands over the clavicle and jugular notch, pressed her fingers against his jaw. Intact, it seemed. She could tell the skull was fractured by the slight displacement of his right eye lobe. There was blood, too, in the corners of both eyes. True, there was no blood at point of impact, just an ugly concaved contusion—a depressed fracture, she guessed, compound, too, by the broken-eggshell feel of it. But she wouldn't know for sure until she got under the skin. Considering the violence of it, it *was* strange that the skin wasn't broken, that there was no abrasion.

His prettily perfect nose wasn't broken, the plastic surgeon's work left intact. A small gash of dried blood specked each oral commissure, as though the upper and lower vermilions had been stretched to breaking. She opened the mouth then, the beautiful teeth like two rows of Chiclets, and saw something stuffed down into the pharynx. She found the forceps on the steel table and slid the instrument past the tongue and soft palate, down past the tonsils, and pinched the object—paper, she could tell by the way it crumpled in the esophagus—and drew it out into the light.

She laid the crumpled paper on the examination table now and unfolded it slowly, careful not to rip it. The letters reassembled themselves as she spread her hands across the sheet. *TRAITOR!*, it read, in bold black ink. *Posse Comitatus*.

———

Jacob ditched classes after lunch and hoofed it over to La Bonita shopping center. He stood outside the store, leaning against the wall, watching the Chinese man work the register. His old man gets a mysterious phone call last night, he's suddenly got an emergency claim over at La Bonita shopping center, and Jacob finds his dad with his arms wrapped around a girl in the park. He wasn't that stupid, he could put two and two together. The girl worked at this store. He was sure of it.

The place was busy, five or six people inside, a couple streaming out and a few more waddling in. An older woman was stocking bins with strange fruit, weird-looking things like something out of a sci-fi movie or something. Then he saw her, the woman who kissed his dad last night. She came through the back door, backpack slung over her shoulder. She dropped the bag and sat down on a stool, leaning over the counter, talking with the man. The old woman stocking shelves rushed into the back room and returned carrying a bowl of something—soup, it looked like—and the woman who had kissed his dad dug into the bowl with chopsticks. Soup with chopsticks! Fucking stupid.

Jacob's chest burned this morning, like his muscles had been shredded. He'd spent two hours last night in Michael Rowan's garage, terrified to go home, cracking pool balls with Ian, sucking down a Colt 45. Usually Michael hung around, too, but when Ian got back from helping with Jacob's dad, Michael had gone inside the house. Jacob didn't know what was up, but he figured Michael and Ian had had a fight. They were brothers, after all. About an hour in, four other dudes showed up—two of them he knew, Fisker and Clocker, both dressed in dark jeans, black work boots, and bomber-style flight jackets. Pinned to the chest of Fisker's jacket was a small British flag pin. Clocker slipped a cassette tape into the boom box, and thrashing punk music rattled the walls.

Jacob had hung out in the garage before, for the last couple of years, playing pool, watching the older boys lift weights on the driveway bench press like it was their own clubhouse or something—most of them already graduated from high school. Jacob occasionally tuned in to Ian's theories about the greatness of Nordic culture, about how his name, Ian—originally spelled Iain—came from Viking raiders of Ireland. Ian's work boot look was a pretty new thing. Jacob, who had always kept an eye on the older boys, had noticed that Ian'd started dressing like this a few months before. Then Fisker and Clocker followed, the twins, too, like they were a small army. They looked slick, kind of like the mods who wore trench coats and cruised around on Vespas. But these guys were tougher looking, clean-cut tough. Ian stretched out on the bench press, wore black boots ladder-laced all the way up to mid-calf, black jeans, a white tank top, his muscles tributaried with veins, like some mercenary soldier in training.

Jacob wouldn't be able to explain what he felt last night hanging with them, couldn't articulate to himself the gravitational pull tugging at him in that garage; it was sort of like the way he felt when he saw Gina down the street, like he'd let her eat him alive if she asked. He'd thought Ian was pretty cool for a long time now, but last night, when Jacob sat there, watching Ian pump an incredible amount of weight above his chest, he felt such jealousy toward him that his throat caught on the edge of crying.

"Let's put some meat on you, Tough Shit," Ian had said to Jacob when he finished his reps. He nodded to Fisker, and the two of them stripped off the largest donuts of weight.

On the bench, Ian dropped the bar on Jacob's chest. Five times and his biceps were burning, the bar shaking above his head.

"Do one more, Tough Shit," Ian said. Fisker was down on his haunches, practically licking his ear, snarling, *Push it, push it.* "One more," Ian said again. *Push it, push.* "Shove your old man off you." He'd remembered then his dad swinging the rake at him—"Get him off you"—and the brutal and lost look in his father's eyes. And the bar started to lift, slowly; he raised it above his head, his arms ropes of fire.

"You got it, Tough Shit. You got it."

Tough Shit. He liked that.

Then his mom showed up at Michael's, her eyes hollowed

out, asking him to come home, holding out her hand as though he were some fucking baby, like he'd even think of taking her hand in front of these dudes. "Mi casa es su casa," Ian said as Jacob followed his mother down the driveway home, where he was forced to sit at the kitchen table with his parents, his fucking father in tears. *I swear,* he'd said. *I swear I'll never hit you again.* Yeah, right.

Now the grocery store looked empty of customers; just the old man, the woman, and the girl were there, hunched over bowls of soup at the counter. He stepped inside, the old man saying "Hello" with a stupid accent, and then Jacob was a fumbling idiot with no idea what to do next. He walked the aisles, looking at the strange fruits—one had spikes like some medieval battle weapon—and the vegetables, the shitty-smelling dried fish, the aquarium stuffed to the gills. Circular mirrors in the corners of the shop reflected distorted Chinese people looking back at him.

"Can I help you find something?"

He turned to find the woman who had kissed his father standing in front of him. She didn't recognize him. He'd been a ninja last night, after all. She didn't have an accent, sounded like an American, but there were those eyes and the skin that looked like coffee with milk poured in. She had this scar, like her skin had been melted away above her left eye, and for a weird moment he'd wanted to touch it.

"Candy," he said. Stupid thing to say! "You got any candy?"

"Up front."

And he followed her like a fool to the front of the store where the old man stood behind the counter. It was all stupid foreign candy, with funny-looking faces on the wrappers and crazy letters.

"You got any American candy? Like SweetTarts or something? This is all Chinese stuff."

"Vietnamese," the woman who had kissed his dad said, her eyes narrowing. "They're Vietnamese candies."

The old woman came up behind them. She was hunched over a bit, tiny, wearing Air Jordans—fucking AJ IIs that cost a hundred bucks! That was funny, a Chinese woman wearing Jordans, as though she was about to go out and play a pickup game.

"This one's tasty," the old woman said, pinching one off the shelf. "Like papaya."

He took the candy, paid for it, and then turned to the woman who had kissed his father and said, "My dad's married."

She blushed and then flashed a guilty glance at the old man. "I don't know what you're talking about," she said, throwing her backpack over her shoulder. The old dude rattled off some Chinese and then she was stumbling toward the front door now, panic flushing her face.

"He's married," Jacob said again, following after her. "Leave my dad alone."

He stalked her into the parking lot. It felt good to scare her. Made him feel big, like Dietwaller or something, like one of the football fuckers, or like Ian Rowan. She squeezed between two passing cars, glancing over her shoulder, and rushed into the sea of metal in the parking lot.

When he turned around, the old man was blocking his way.

"What do you want?"

Jacob tried to push past him, but the old man grabbed his wrist and clamped it so tightly he thought he'd stop the blood in his veins.

"Let go," Jacob said.

"What do you want?" the man said, glaring at him. Jacob felt like a schoolboy being scolded by a teacher, but then he remembered the man was Chinese—Vietnamese—whatever.

"Let go, chink," Jacob spat, ripping his hand away.

When he strode away, he saw the old woman, the one who had handed him the candy, hunched in the doorway, her arms wrapped around her waist, her eyes drilling into him as though he were the most dangerous animal in the world.

Natasha called Vanek immediately and told him about the note stuffed in Brennan's throat.

"Posse comitatus?"

"Yes."

"Power of the county," Vanek said. "Any word on the methamphetamine, or the weapon?"

"Not yet," she said. "I figured you'd want to know about this pronto."

"You figured correctly," he said. "I need answers to those other questions. Why don't you finish up and meet me at Mr. Brennan's place."

And then he hung up, as though her yes was a foregone conclusion. Somehow, though, it didn't seem rude or condescending. More like he was too deep in thought to bother with politeness.

She bagged the paper note and asked Jerry to open up Brennan's body. A Britannica encyclopedia sat on a shelf near her desk, and she thumbed through it. She got the posse part, but the whole phrase had to have more resonance. Page 576: Posse Comitatus Act—*a law*. "A federal statute prohibiting use of the military in civilian law enforcement."

"I need blood samples," she called out to Jerry. "Femoral vein, vitreous, liver, and spleen."

"Right, boss."

Jerry did the dirty work and didn't complain.

So separation of powers, keeping the federal government out of local concerns. And she understood the colloquial use of *posse*—which she'd always thought of as vigilantism. That didn't explain why someone would stuff the words down a local real estate magnate's gullet.

She sat there thinking and said the words over and over in her head until she just repeated *posse, posse, posse*. She remembered the note stapled to the dog's ear. No, it didn't make any sense. Twenty miles separated the two crimes. Yet she marched down the hall to the coolers anyway, pulled the dog out of number 28, opened up his snout, and examined the throat. Nothing. A hunch that was nothing. Still, something itched in her. She swore, sometimes she thought they spoke to her—the bodies in the morgue. That was irrational, she knew, and certainly a dog wasn't communicating with her, but that's how it felt. She'd come to understand it as her mind trying to tell her something—some shadow of memory swimming up to the surface, like the eyes had caught something the brain wasn't able to process the first time around. You couldn't always get everything from a single autopsy; sometimes you had to sit with the dead.

She ran her finger along the ridges of the dog's soft palate, then started working the gums, no idea what she was looking for. Then she saw it: tiny, lodged in a back molar, a thin red thread. She flashed on the red thread Detective Vanek had snatched out of the pool the other morning at the Huntington Beach scene. The itch scratched.

At first sight, Ian looked like a dead body, his legs sticking out from beneath the truck like he'd been run over.

"Playing hooky today, huh?" Ian said from under the chassis.

Jacob just looked at the ground, like an idiot. He hated when he did that.

"Don't worry," Ian said, his head peeking out from beneath the car. "I'm no snitch. They teach you all the wrong things over at that school anyway." He turned back to the car chassis. "Get down here."

Jacob scooted himself under the carriage, the guts of the car twisted above him. Between them sat a metal bowl.

"So, you just unscrew this," Ian said, a wrench working a bolt loose, "and . . . bleed the oil out of the fucker."

A line of warm oil streamed into the bowl between them, a strange earthy metal smell wafting into the air.

"You gotta learn to do things on your own," Ian said. "When the war comes, you gotta be self-sufficient."

"What war?" Jacob said. The oil slowed to a trickle.

"There's always a war coming." The oil stopped, just an occasional drop plopping in the bowl. Ian handed him the bolt and the wrench. "Screw that back in."

Ian scooted himself out and Jacob wrenched the bolt into the oil pan. His dad had an old Firebird in their garage, but when his dad was working on the car, you were supposed to leave him alone.

"Now get up here," Ian said. He showed Jacob how to O-clamp off the oil filter and replace it with a fresh one from Pep Boys. He poured the oil in, four and a half quarts, because you didn't want to overfill the reservoir.

"Take it for a ride," Ian said, tossing him the keys.

Jacob laughed. "No license, man."

"So."

So. That's all you had to say in the face of laws? At that moment it sounded like the most powerful word in the English language.

"All right," Jacob said. Ian slipped into a flight jacket he'd left draped over the driver's side door and climbed into the passenger seat and told Jacob what to do—foot on the brake, yank the steering column shifter into reverse, slowly press the gas pedal, the growling V8 radiating up Jacob's leg—and he backed the truck down the driveway, hitting the gas a little too hard once. *Take it real easy,* Ian said. Then they were cruising, all the stupid little houses rolling by them.

"My big brother died in the last war, in 'Nam," Ian said. "In '74. I was eleven. It was tough, real tough. Turn right here."

He turned onto Jupiter Street, where the backyards pushed up against the train tracks. They passed an unmarked cop car, parked on the street next to the footpath that joined the streets. You could tell it was the fuzz by the spotlight near the side-view mirror.

"Just stay cool," Ian said. "He's not looking for us."

Jacob held his breath as they passed the cruiser and he felt like some big-deal dude, breaking the law right in front of a cop. After they passed, Ian watched the cruiser for a few seconds out the back window, like he was memorizing the car or something.

"He was barely eighteen," Ian said, back to his dead brother, "been there two months and some fuckin' gook shoots him through the neck." Ian hit the dashboard with the palm of his hand. "We had to drive over to El Toro marine base on a Sunday to pick his body up. Just rolled his coffin out the back of a C-130, like it was shitting him out. My mom . . . Man, my mom . . ." He rubbed his palm then with his thumb, kept making a fist around the finger. "Worst day of my life. Turn left."

Jacob did and then Ian told him to park halfway down the street.

"Less than two years later, *they* were flying into El Toro," Ian said, nodding toward a house a few doors down. There was a Chinese woman outside—or, he guessed, Vietnamese—picking something out of a garden. "On Pan Am flights. Fucking first-class ticket to America—that *our* tax dollars paid for. When we heard they were coming in, I'd ride my bike over to the base and stand at the fence and watch the planes land and I remember I wanted a machine gun, a rocket launcher, anything to blow them out of the sky. I was thirteen and I couldn't believe they were walking on the same tarmac my brother's dead body was rolled across." He was quiet a moment. "Still can't believe it."

Jacob watched the woman stand and shuffle into the house. The house looked like the other houses, though it needed a paint job.

"I think my dad's . . ." Jacob was embarrassed to say it. "I think he's dating one of them."

Ian looked at him, anger flashing across his pupils like a gun had gone off inside his head.

"Your dad's . . . messed up," Ian said. "It's not his fault. The war screwed him up, okay? That war shouldn't have happened, those assholes in DC sending us to fight in places we don't belong." Ian dropped his hand on Jacob's shoulder and held it there. "Your dad was having a flashback last night."

"My mom calls them rememberings."

"They're kind of like that," Ian said.

He turned his attention to the house again. The woman they were watching came back out with a kid, a toddler maybe two years old.

"These people," Ian said. "Jesus Christ, sometimes I just wanna blow them all up."

The kid was naked, his little wiener pointing out for everyone to see. Man, put a diaper on the kid at least.

"You ever feel that way, Tough Shit?" Ian smiled then, flashed his green eyes at him. "Yeah, you feel that way." Ian stared hard at the woman now, anger radiating off him like heat off the truck's hood. "These people are here because of a mistake. They don't belong here. We're living a mistake."

When they got back to the house, Ian told him to wait. "I got a present for you." He pulled a ratty paperback from the cinderblock shelves in the corner of the garage and slapped the book onto Jacob's chest. "I know, Tough Shit, things feel confusing." He pressed the book to Jacob's heart. "There's some clarity in this book." He smiled. "Classes start tomorrow."

"You have anything on those other matters?" Detective Vanek asked Natasha.

They were sitting in his unmarked cruiser at the end of

18th Street in Huntington Beach where the pavement met beach sand, the engine on, the heater blowing warm air against her neck. She handed him the file. Vanek was wearing a three-piece suit, buttoned-up vest and all, with a little tie bar that pushed up his Windsor knot. She noticed a red-white-and-blue pin affixed to his lapel.

"The Czechoslovakian flag," Vanek said, not looking up from the file.

Before he touched the case folder, he produced a handkerchief—she had always liked a man who carried a handkerchief—from his coat to wipe off his already seemingly clean hands. His whole getup—the clothes, the demeanor—was so old-school, she glanced to see if he had a chain watch dropped into his vest pocket. Nope, a Casio digital calculator watch was strapped to his left wrist.

"There was no meth present in the blood or hair," she said.

"So not a user?"

He held the edge of the papers delicately, as though afraid to injure them.

"At least not in the last couple of months."

"You have very neat handwriting," he said.

"As far as a weapon goes," she said, not sure what to do with that statement, "head trauma's a compound, radiating fracture. Intracerebral hematoma."

He was looking at an autopsy picture now, Brennan's waxy face filling up the frame.

"Bleeding on the brain."

She nodded. "The radiating fracture caused some diastic fracturing along the coronal suture and the sphenoid."

"So pretty brute force? Not likely a punch?"

"Not unless the killer's George Foreman. The depressed fracture, the center of the radiating fracture"—she pointed to the circular indentation in the picture—"is between fifty and sixty millimeters wide."

"No abrasions," he said.

"So something round."

"And heavy," Vanek added.

"He was dead when he hit the water," she said. "They wouldn't have pulled him out to stuff that note down his throat."

Vanek folded closed the file and handed it back to her. "A very well-put-together report. Thank you."

"It's my job." She went on: "There's something else. Ben Wade down in Santa Elena is working a dead dog case." She laid out the details—the dog left behind the Phans' grocery, the sawed throat wound, the poisoned meat, the note stapled to the ear. "Remember that sliver of red thread you got out of the pool?"

She pictured him a moment, soaking wet, his hair matted against his forehead.

"I do."

"The two notes, on the dog and on Brennan, got me thinking," she said. He was watching her, his brown eyes unblinking. "I went back in on the dog and found a red thread lodged in one of the molars. Checked it against the one we found in the pool, and they match. Herringbone. An oxblood red."

He was nodding now. "Let's take a walk, shall we?"

It was still foggy along the coast, a thick gauze of white slicking everything with salt water. Natasha could taste it on her lips, the brine of kelp and barnacles, the scent of wood rot. They were walking the footpath to the public beach, just three blocks down from the modernist house where Brennan's body was found. Vanek kept to the edge of the path where sparse tufts of Bermuda grass held the earth together, and she followed so they didn't upset any footprints in the sand.

"City only let us block this off for a day," Vanek said, down on his haunches now, a ballpoint pen pinched between his fingers, like some accoutrement of gentried title.

"See there?" He was pointing to a footprint—or half print, some of it obliterated by the outline of a bare foot. He circled it in the sand with the writing end of the ballpoint. A horseshoe of straight-edge tread surrounding a half dozen little crosses.

"Not exactly beach shoes," she said. "Some kind of boot."

Vanek walked them fifty yards down the beach where the yellow tape surrounding the firepit fluttered in the breeze. A pod of surfers were out, riding long rights toward the beach. It didn't seem to matter that the beach was a crime scene; if there was a swell, surfers were going to carve it up. The firepit was surrounded by boot prints, too, little crosses dotting the sand.

"Doc Martens," Vanek said. "Steel-toed, I believe. Seem to be a new kind of fashion among some of our younger folks."

"The contusions to Brennan's ribs were more diffuse," Natasha said. Could be kicks from steel-toed boots. "More crushing. The hematoma oblong-shaped."

"Let's keep going," Vanek said.

The house was fifty yards down the beach. She could see it through the fog—steel gray, rectangles of black windows, crime scene tape, and three uniforms standing outside. Natasha and Vanek followed the line of boot prints.

"Five or six of them," Natasha said.

"That was my guess, too."

The boot prints were muddled together, collapsed where the sand was too soft. But you could make out the strides, if you looked closely. And then they were gone. The sand had been swept clean and flat, a few flakes of seagrass dotting the sand.

"I'm guessing it's like this all the way to the house?"

"As clean as a Club Med beach at sunrise."

She glanced around the beach, her eyes landing on a clump of seaweed.

"Kelp," she said. She walked ten yards over and picked up a frond of the beached seaweed. "They swept it with kelp." She got down on her haunches and swept the seaweed over one of the boot prints; they both watched the print disappear. "You can see the indentations from the gas bladders." Furrows were dug into the swept sand from the balloon-like structures that clung to the fronds.

Vanek got down on his haunches, too. "They're almost smart," he said, nodding to where the sweeping stopped. "There was sand in the house, all the way to Brennan's office where it looks like a bunch of files were taken."

She glanced around again, taking in a larger swath of the beach. The 15th Street entrance was directly to their right. "So they wipe it down to here on the way out and then make a break for it down Fifteenth." Sure enough, the line of boot marks pocketed the sand—though they were more torn up, less clear. Running, for sure.

"Funny," Vanek said, "that Brennan doesn't seem to be a user. After the snow melted the other morning, we found three meth pills on his patio tile."

"A bad drug deal?"

Vanek shook his head. "I don't think so. Looks to me like Mr. Brennan was a bit of a health nut—all organic in his refrigerator, no hard spirits, just a couple bottles of red wine." He was quiet a moment. "It'd take a lot of energy to beat someone up like that."

"So the killers are the users? Jacked up on speed?"

"It's a theory," Vanek said. He glanced at his Casio. "C'mon, chili cheese fries on me."

—————

By late morning, Ben was back in the Connollys' neighborhood, canvassing residents about Duke the dog. Five houses bordered the Connollys' backyard, three on Aries Street, the next block over, and the two on either side. So at least five immediate persons of interest, Ben thought, though surely these weren't single-occupancy residences. A paved footpath with six-foot cement walls on either side ran along the right side of the Connollys' house, separating their place from the neighbor on that side. This footpath hooked into other footpaths, joining streets through the whole development. So, yeah, he could count the whole damn neighborhood as suspects.

This morning, he'd checked in on Dr. Lofland in the crime lab at the station. The labs on the green sludge he'd scooped out of the snow the other morning had come back: superwarfarin, confirmation of Mendenhall's and Natasha's tests. Whoever dropped the dog in the alleyway behind the Phans' grocery started their grisly work here.

He walked the footpath first. It was the most obvious spot from which to throw a poisoned rib-eye into the backyard. The walls offered cover from witnesses and an easy sprint away onto the next street over. A Bartles & Jaymes bottle lay broken against the fence, a Big League Chew wrapper fluttered in the breeze. Some crude graffiti graced the walls—CYNTHIA GIVES GOOD HEAD, an anarchy sign, the number 88 scrawled in red spray paint, the cryptic IØIBIGDADI, a Santa Cruz skateboard sticker. He wrote it all down on his yellow legal pad, though he doubted poor Cynthia had anything to do with this. But that 88 interested him. He underlined it twice.

The old lady to the right of the Connollys', Mrs. Partridge, was so hunched over, she could hardly lift her eyes to see him. *The Price Is Right* was blasting from the television in her living room, and each time he asked about the dog she said, "I don't understand what you're saying." Doubtful that she would notice much of what happened on the footpath, and he was certain she wasn't pitching any steak over the wall. No one answered at the house to the left. He slid a business card between the gap in the two front doors, a *Please call me at your earliest convenience* written neatly on the back.

Back in the cruiser, he circled around to Aries Street. "Dog's a pain in the ass," a Mr. O'Brien said. "They let it run around. Shits on everyone's yard." The man pointed to his grass, little brown circles where, Ben assumed, Duke had dropped a couple of loads. "Not losing any tears over it," he said. "But poisoned?"

He seemed genuinely surprised. No one was home at the other two houses, so he walked the backyards. A six-foot privacy fence separated the properties from the Connollys', but it'd be easy to toss something over. He glanced through the closed-up sliding glass doors, family pictures on the mantels at both houses, a pile of stuffed animals spilling off a couch at the last home. A shih tzu with a bow tied on top of its head yapping at him from behind the glass door. You own a dog, you're not killing a dog.

He cruised Venus Street, then turned back onto Jupiter Street, trying to figure the territory of a free-range dog. He made a right onto Comet and slowly cruised the neighborhood, his window down, the cold desert air dry as parchment. About three-quarters of the way down the street, he ran into a muscled kid bench-pressing on the driveway. Another kid was standing behind him, all shaggy hair and acned awkwardness, spotting the big kid.

"How you guys doing?" Ben said when he was out of the cruiser. The acned kid looked spooked. "You got a nice country club going here."

They did, a pool table, a mini fridge where most people parked cars. Some ugly thrash-punk-type shit playing on a boom box. A Dodge Power Wagon pickup truck was parked on the right side of the driveway.

"Officer," the kid at the bench press said. He had just dropped what looked like a couple hundred pounds on the bar stands. He rested his elbows on his knees, the veins of his arms engorged with blood. Ben unfolded the MISSING poster he'd slipped into his breast pocket.

"I'm just checking the neighborhood—any chance you can turn that down?" The acned kid adjusted the volume a couple notches. "Checking to see if anyone knows anything about this dog."

"Is that the one that turned up dead behind that Vietnam grocery?"

Not Vietnamese, *that Vietnam*. A small thing, but it hit Ben's ears wrong.

"That's right," Ben said. "What's your name?"

"Do I really need to give it to you?"

"You trying to hide something?"

"Ian." Not really a kid, early twenties maybe. "Ian Rowan."

The kid wore a white T-shirt and black suspenders, dark jeans with thick-soled shoes. It was the suspenders that threw it off; they didn't make any sense. Suspenders with a suit, sure, but with Levi's? Made him think of the cholos in the gangs up in North Hollywood, the long shorts, the knee-high socks; places to hide weapons, sure, but really just an identifier, a signal to one another.

"You hear any rumors about it?"

"Nah," he said. "They let it loose, let it shit—excuse me, *crap* on people's yards. A lot of people hated that dog."

"So a whole lot of people would've had reason to saw open its neck?"

The kid stood up now, slipped on a black polo shirt, and suddenly he looked like any other clean-cut kid.

"I don't know. People're messed up."

Preaching to the choir.

"You hated it, too?"

"It's just a dog."

He asked the acned kid, too, and he just shrugged, like he wasn't working with a full deck. Kid should be in school, but he wasn't going to play truant officer right now.

"You hear anything," Ben said, handing the buff kid a business card, "call the station."

"Sure thing, Officer Wade." Then he cocked his head, his eyes narrowing. "Hey, you're that cop, aren't you?"

"Yeah," Ben said. "I shot the Night Prowler."

"No," Ian said. "That other case. You're the one with the swim coach, right?"

Ben imagined planting a fist in this Ian Rowan's face, but the kid had rights, even asshole kids did.

"Keep that music down." He turned to walk back to the cruiser. "This is a family neighborhood."

"Sure thing, Officer Wade."

———

No chili cheese fries for Detective Vanek, apparently. He'd raved about the fries on the walk back to their cars, Tommy's, the best in Orange County, he'd said. She followed him over here, completely across town and past at least fifteen other burger joints. He brought her a cardboard bowl of the layered mess, and a cod sandwich for himself.

She nodded at the fish. "You were waxing poetic about these fries."

"I love them." Vanek had removed his coat, rolled up his sleeves, and was now picking the onions from his fish sandwich and stacking them in the corner of the paper plate. "But my wife got me off red meat a few years back. Had a bit of a health scare." He patted his chest. "Now I enjoy them vicariously."

Vanek closed his eyes and seemed to say a quick prayer. She dug in. The fries *were* tasty, thick with meat, gooey with melted cheddar.

They were sitting outside at a stone table, in the shadow of a red-and-white-striped metal umbrella. Whitney Houston's "I Wanna Dance with Somebody" jingled through an outdoor speaker. Vanek scraped the mayonnaise off the bun. "Always tell them no mayo, but they never listen." Now he placed the bun back on the fish, took a bite, and watched a few teenagers leaning up against a VW Bug, music blasting from the car speakers.

"Nice to have someone care about you like that," Natasha said.

"It was."

She glanced at the ring on his finger and her heart sank. "I'm sorry to hear that."

He nodded and took a small bite of the sandwich. "Cervical cancer."

"How long ago?"

"Two years next Tuesday."

"Any kids?"

He shook his head. "Didn't get the chance."

"I'm very sorry," she said.

"Turns out the real health scare was hers." He nodded at the fries. "Good, right?"

"Best in Orange County."

He smiled at her and then nodded across the parking lot to the teens. "We seem to be developing a gang problem here in Surf City."

Natasha watched the boys—their dark jeans cuffed short to the tops of their shin-high dark boots, their white shirts strapped to their chest by red suspenders.

"Doc Martens?" she said.

He nodded. "This has become a little hangout for them."

Now that she was paying attention, she registered the ugliness of the music—thrashing guitars, the singer's guttural scream. One of the boys, the one leaning against the Volkswagen, had an 18 tattooed across his neck, the curve of the 8 crawling up the edge of his jaw.

"I'm guessing eighteen's not his age."

"First and eighth letters of the alphabet."

"*A* and *H*," Natasha said.

"Yes."

She thought about it a moment, eyeing the young men—the Volkswagen, the brutal ugly music, the militant edge to the clothes.

"Adolf Hitler?"

"Right." Vanek smiled as though very pleased. "Dr. Betencourt, you do live up to your reputation."

She wasn't aware that she had a reputation.

"That's what we're dealing with here?" she said. "Nazi kids?"

"Neo-Nazis. Skinheads. White supremacists. A lot of names for them, but boils down to the same thing: hate."

"This Brennan guy," Natasha said. "Was he Jewish?"

"Not if the crucifix on his bedroom wall is any indication," Vanek said. "I've been running my own sort of task force the last couple of years. My chief of police doesn't think it's all that important yet, so sort of my side gig. My wife, actually, was the one to get me onto them."

"Was she a cop?"

He shook his head. "She had the instinct for it, but she was a public defender. Was finding herself assigned to represent some of these 'gentlemen'—you know, beating up Mexicans on the street, defacing public property with graffiti. Finally had to defend a perp who curbed a black man."

"Curbed?"

"Get a man's jaw biting a street curb and then kick the back of his head."

"My lord."

"The perp found out she was Jewish," Vanek said. "And refused to let her represent him. Deborah was relieved. Was a real moral conundrum for her. If she was assigned to defend him, ethically, she really had to do it. But she didn't think she could." He laughed. "The fool defended himself and got five to seven on attempted. She probably could have gotten him off on criminal assault and six months in the pen. So it worked out. Anyway, she got me looking around on this, and here we are."

She watched the teens. Three of the kids had white shoelaces, laced strangely up the face of the boot. Not crisscrossing, but laced like ladder rungs. But one boy, the one with the 18 tattoo, wore red laces.

"The red laces," Natasha said. "Everyone else has white, except that one kid."

Vanek looked at her. "Means he spilled blood for the movement."

"Not his own, I imagine," Natasha said.

"It's not that kind of movement."

"Shoelaces," Natasha said, pieces clicking into place. The red thread in the pool, the red thread caught in the dog's molar. "The thread's from bootlaces."

He smiled, pleased, it seemed, and for some reason she liked pleasing him.

"Maybe got ripped off when they were kicking Brennan, got caught on the pajama button?" Felt thin, but stranger things have happened.

"Question is," Vanek said, "to which fool's boot do they belong?"

"I'm thinking it's a Santa Elena fool," she said. "Brennan's a target killing, the dog is more opportunistic, a not-in-my-neighborhood type of thing."

Vanek nodded and smiled, again that pleased look on his face.

"Neighborhoods," Vanek said, mostly to himself. "That's the thing, isn't it? Who gets which neighborhood? Sometimes a life-and-death decision."

"What about this posse thing?"

"Posse comitatus," he said. "I'm still trying to piece some things together on that. It's a reference to a law from 1878 that got federal troops out of the South following Reconstruction. More generally, it restricts the US military from policing American citizens."

"States' rights," she said.

"Something like that," he said. "Eisenhower suspended it in '54 when he sent troops down to Little Rock following *Brown versus Board of Education*. Not sure, yet, what it means to have the words stuffed down the throat of a murdered real estate investor in 1987."

Vanek pulled his business card out of a silver holder and slid it across the table. "Please pass it along to Detective Wade. I believe we'll be working together on this."

The teens finished their chili fries and drove away, blasting their rage music down Katella Boulevard. She and Vanek watched them go before they walked out to their cars. She opened the door and was about to climb in when Vanek called over to her.

"Dr. Betencourt."

She turned around to look at him. His unmarked cruiser was between them, his arm leaning on his half-open door. He started to say something and then stopped, his chin pressed to his chest like he was embarrassed to have even thought of it.

"You all right, Detective?" she asked.

"You know, you could be a detective, Doctor."

She was pretty damn sure that was not what he had wanted to say.

"Believe I already am."

―――――

"Two threads?" Ben said.

She'd paged him when she left Huntington Beach, a sudden desire to see him. She was only a few miles from an old haunt of theirs up in Long Beach and it was as good a place as any to mix business with pleasure. *122*, she had typed into the pager. *7366. 615*. He was at the Reno Room by 6:14. By 6:20 they had drinks in hand and he was throwing her a hundred pounds of doubt.

"Yes, two threads," she said with all the declarative power she could muster to counter him.

Then Natasha explained—the red thread in the dog's molar, the red thread from Brennan's pool in Huntington Beach, the match under the microscope. She didn't mention Vanek yet, not entirely sure why.

"C'mon, Ben," she said. "How often do I throw you a line of bullshit?"

"Huntington's twenty miles away from the Connollys' house."

"Hello, twentieth century," she said. "There are these things called cars. You drove one to get to me."

He flashed her an ironic smile and took a sip of his Coors. His hair was saltwater-bleached and mussed, his skin blotched with sun damage. His coat, a tweed blend, had a small stain on the lapel, like something he should have dabbed with stain remover before washing. He was a beach bum at heart.

"I thought you were off this case," Ben said. "Thought Mendenhall was taking it."

"I was requested," she said. Even she could hear the pride in her voice.

"Requested?"

"By the detective on the case," she said. "His name's Joseph Vanek."

"Vanek?" Ben said.

"You know him?"

"Worked with him a couple of times in South Central LA, before I transferred to North Hollywood. Worked the real-deal crack cocaine wars. He's a good cop. A little fussy, but good."

He finished his beer and pointed at the empty, and the bartender fished him out another.

"Well," she said. "He's running with the thread theory."

"You didn't mention him before."

"It wasn't my case before."

He was watching her now. "Thread?" he said, biting a little on the theory.

"Yes," she said, a bit ticked that it was the mention of Vanek that made him take her theory seriously. She should have been enough for him to bite on it. "I think it's from shoelaces."

"Shoelaces?"

She told him about Vanek walking her through the Huntington scene—the boot prints, the meth pills, the neo-Nazi gangs, the Adolf Hitler tattoo.

"I saw it myself," she said. "These kids with knee-high steel-toes. Red shoelaces ladder-laced."

"In the field with him?" Ben said.

She pulled out Vanek's card and set it on the bar top.

"He asked for a hand," she said. "I'm assigned to the case. Besides, it's nice to get out of the office."

"Get out of the office?"

She laughed at him. "Is this what we're going to do, Ben? I messaged *you* the one two two."

He smiled sheepishly, like a boy still embarrassed by the mention of sex. It endeared him to her, it always did. His skepticism wasn't wrong, though, exactly. It *was* unusual for a medical examiner to work the field with a detective, at least after the body was at the morgue. Her investigative arrangement with Ben was born, of course, out of their personal relationship.

"One two two," she said, in a lilting voice now, leaning into him. "I. Want. You."

He smiled a crooked smile and stared into her eyes for a few moments. He touched her hand then, turned it over in his, and ran his thumb along the heel of her palm and down across the veins of her wrist. A charge shot up her side with the touch. Didn't matter if they were talking a case, they could spark a fire as fast as the Santa Ana winds.

"Want another?" he said, nodding to her empty glass.

"If you got the money, honey."

He laughed, the bartender dropped her drink in the wet circle from the last, and it was back to business.

"The number eighteen, huh?"

She nodded.

"There's some graffiti on one of the walls of a footpath next to the Connollys' place. Eighty-eight."

"*HH*," Natasha said. "Heil Hitler, maybe."

"Nazis?" he said. "In Orange County?"

He let go of her hand then and they were fully back into professional mode, though the charge still pulsed in her body, a fringe benefit of crime fighting with Ben.

"White supremacists," she said. "Is it so hard to believe?"

He raised an eyebrow at her. "Describe these kids' threads."

She explained it to him again—the boots, the rolled-up jeans, the suspenders, the tats.

"Throw that back," he said, nodding to her Dewar's. "And let's take a ride."

She followed him back to his house, dropped off her car, and jumped into his cruiser. And forty-five minutes after leaving the Reno Room, they were casing a neat little ranch-style home, a single light on in the window, pansies in the flower boxes. Ben had told her about the buff kid on the way down, his buddies, and the way they dressed. No tattoos, though, as far as he could tell; nothing obvious to give them away. It was a nice street, like most streets in Santa Elena, every house painted a shade of beige, little squares of mowed green grass, sprinklers draining the Colorado to keep that green. If there was a picture of "California suburb" in an encyclopedia, this is what it would look like. They sat there in the night shade of a huge jacaranda tree, the garage door closed, a bench press sitting unused on the driveway, nothing doing at the house. A couple walked their golden retriever around the block, a man stepped outside to smoke a pipe on his porch, a woman retrieved a box from the trunk of her car. The street was so sleepy, it was, in fact, difficult to imagine this could be the epicenter of some murderous neo-Nazi gang.

Rain pelted the windshield of the cruiser. Natasha jumped it was so sudden, and it took her a moment to realize it was sprinkler water, shooting from a mis-aimed sprinkler head.

"C'mon," Ben said, firing up the car. "We're wasting our time. I one two two you, too."

Chapter Seven

When Linh left for class on Friday morning, Bao hopped into his Ford Taurus and followed her. He made excuses to Ai, said he needed to go up to Little Saigon for a case of fish sauce—which meant he really would have to drive up to Westminster and pick up a case of Three Crabs—and left the grocery to her and the police keeping an eye on it from the fire lane.

He was three cars behind his daughter now, following her down Universidad Road. He would watch her park the Honda, he hoped, watch her walk through the gates to her class—safe, learning things he'd never learn—and then drive back to the grocery, reassured he was overreacting. Something was off with Linh: her silence at dinner last night, the way she locked herself in her room, her rejection of his invitation for a late-evening drink. *He's my father and he's married.* He swore that's what the boy had said yesterday, but sometimes Americans spoke too fast and the syllables bled together in his ears. But he heard the words *married* and *my father.* He had understood the other word for certain, the one the boy had spit at him when Bao had grabbed his hand. *Chink.* Yes, he knew that word.

When she reached the entrance to the university, she drove right past it, despite her 9:00 A.M. class. He followed her car up the switchbacks into the hills, where they were terracing the land for new houses. When she changed lanes, he changed lanes, keeping at least two cars between them. He was ashamed of himself for doing this. She was a grown woman and she had a right to her personal secrets, just like anybody else. But the dog in the alley and the angry boy yesterday had upset the architecture of their lives, and Bao suddenly felt like it all could collapse—and he was afraid for his daughter, afraid the dog and the boy and her secrets were all connected.

She turned her Honda in to an apartment complex. Bao drove beyond the entrance and made a U-turn at the next intersection, to make sure she wouldn't see him. He made a left into the parking lot, one of the older ones in the city—just two weathered wooden buildings with rows of white doors, like the one they lived in when they first arrived in the States—a broken-down apartment he had vowed they would move out of within two years, and they had; he and Ai had worked sixteen-hour days, sometimes more, starting the first grocery, and they had gotten out into a small house near Little Saigon in just eighteen months. For a moment, Bao felt like he was following his daughter into the past, a fragile time when they seemed to live on a razor's edge between opportunity and destitution.

He drove past her parked car, which was empty now, and pulled into a spot down the row, near the end of the lot where weeds separated the cement from green rolling hills. He hadn't seen which apartment she'd gone into, and his heart jumped each time a door opened—a white man carrying a briefcase, a woman hauling a bike down the stairs, a mother walking her son to her car. He sat there for an anxious thirty-three minutes, watching the clock, watching each door, trying to peer through the sun glare of apartment windows. Then there she was, coming out of Apartment 16. She turned to talk to someone—from his angle he only saw a shadow cast across the doorframe. The door closed, then, and she climbed down the stairs, stopping at the bottom to tuck her blouse into her jeans, before getting into her car.

He watched her drive off, waited to make sure she was gone, and then he crossed the parking lot, climbed the stairs, and knocked on the door.

He was overreacting. It was probably just one of Linh's college friends—Lucy, the redhead with the loud laugh, or Andrea, the woman who always blasted pop music from her VW Rabbit convertible. The door handle turned, and when he saw who was standing in front of him, smiling as though expecting Linh to be standing on the threshold again, rage jolted his body, and he knew then that he was capable of anything.

Jacob sat in the passenger seat of Ian's truck, blurring past orange groves on the Santa Ana Freeway, windows rolled down, punk music playing on the stereo—freedom, it felt like fuckin' freedom, like his stupid little goddamned house and his goddamned parents were on the other side of the planet.

"You're not going to that ZOG school, are you?" Ian had said this morning, pulling up alongside him and Michael while they walked to school together.

"Shit," Michael had said under his breath when he saw his brother.

Ian glanced at Michael. "What did you say?"

Jacob hadn't noticed it the other night, but this morning there was a clear bruise under Michael's right eye. Yeah, him and Ian had had a fight.

"Nothing, all right," Michael said. "I've just got a test, that's all."

"Can you believe that?" Ian said, looking at Jacob now. "ZOG school test? Get in the truck. I'll give you a real education."

Jacob threw up his palms to Michael and got in the cab of the truck, leaving Michael to walk alone to school. Jacob wasn't learning a goddamned thing in school anyway, except to hate himself.

Now they were driving north, out of Santa Elena, into the low-slung flats of northern Orange County, where the houses looked like poorly assembled moving boxes.

"What's ZOG?" Jacob asked.

"Zionist Occupied Government," Ian said. "The Jews control it all—the banks, the lobbying groups in Washington, the businesses. The schools." He tapped the heel of his hand against the steering wheel, frustrated it seemed. "My brother, man . . ."

He was quiet a moment, apparently at the thought of Michael.

"So what'd you think of *The Diaries*?" Ian said after a few quiet seconds. *The Turner Diaries*, the book he'd given Jacob after they changed the truck's oil.

"It was cool," Jacob said, finally.

"Cool?" Ian said, smiling. "That's it? Like you just got done reading a fucking surfing magazine?"

Shit. *The Diaries* was more than cool, but he didn't know how to talk about it without sounding lame. Chapter 6 was fuckin' amazing. In that chapter, when they drove the stolen delivery truck with the dead body and the bomb loaded in the back into the basement of the FBI building, Jacob's heart had jumped into his throat. It wasn't a bad feeling. It was like seeing a hot girl, the way he could imagine getting inside her pants. He loved the way they fought the corrupt System, the repressive government that kept the Organization down. When they ran the cable from the detonator to the bomb, the feeling was almost unbearably awesome. He walked away with them in his imagination, the two blocks down Pennsylvania Avenue, until the blast shuddered the pavement and sheared away the façade of the FBI building.

But chapter 5 was even better, when Earl Turner puts the blasting gelatin in the applesauce cans. Actually, chapter 5 was the reason chapter 6 was so fucking rad. Turner pouring the gelatin. Turner priming it. Turner setting the timing mechanism. All that careful preparation and then *Kaboom!*, a device serving its perfect destructive purpose, to destroy the government in DC, to destroy the System.

"The System that gets destroyed in the book is supposed to be the Zionist Occupied Government, right?" Jacob said, putting one and one together. "ZOG?"

"Right," Ian said, smiling at Jacob like he was real happy. "You got it."

The System was the real-life ZOG, the government that sent Jacob's dad to Vietnam to get his head scrambled. The world, for Jacob, had felt like a black hole, something you got sucked into and thrown around in. Spinning around in the darkness of his parents, the teachers and their fucking tests, the fucking girls who wouldn't even look at him, the whole goddamned world on spin cycle. But the book made order of things. Why the hell were they in Vietnam anyway? His history teacher had tried to explain the war, went into all the complicated reasons going all the way back to World War II or something, but it didn't make sense to him—none of it. The System—ZOG, he meant (it was hard to tell fact from fiction)—sent whites off to die in foreign countries. Just like in the book, ZOG wanted races to mix because it made white Europeans weaker, while they controlled the banks, the lobbyists in DC, the entertainment industry, the whole damn thing. He got it, all the pieces fell into place.

Ian swerved the truck into the slow lane and sped down the off-ramp into the city of Anaheim. Jacob could see Angel Stadium and the Big A with the stupid halo on top pointing up to the blue sky.

"You know Andrew Macdonald's not really the author's name, right?" They were sitting at a stoplight, a Mexican man hawking bags of oranges from the sidewalk. "That name's a pseudonym. His real name's William Pierce. The leader of the

National Alliance. Real smart dude. He used to be a physics professor up at Oregon State."

Ian leaned across Jacob's lap then and opened the glove compartment. Inside was a pistol. The gun had a bluish tint, like it was made of plastic, and for a moment Jacob thought it was a kid's toy.

"Can't be too careful in these neighborhoods."

He set the gun on the bench seat between them, its barrel pointed at Jacob's thigh.

They drove down the first street, Ian rolling the truck slow, the little houses cement squares with bars on the windows. Ian's eyes flicked around, from mirror to mirror, from house to house. He smiled once, about what Jacob didn't know. At one house, a Mexican man in a cowboy hat sat smoking a cigarette on the front steps. When they passed, he flicked the butt into the dead grass and watched them roll down the street, Ian staring right back at him. On the next street over, Ian parked the truck in the driveway of a little house and they sat there for a few seconds, Ian watching the rearview. Jacob glanced over his shoulder and saw a car make a right onto the next street. It looked like a police cruiser, but he couldn't see if there was a light hanging from the side.

"Sit tight," Ian said. He shoved the gun into the right pocket of his flight jacket, grabbed a bag of something from behind his seat, and then walked three houses over, strolled up the driveway past a tricked-out Impala, and disappeared down the side of the house. Blood thrummed in Jacob's ears and he sat there, looking at the bars on the windows of the little house in front of him, waiting for—well, he didn't know what. Something moved in the periphery of his vision—an old man, standing outside on his lawn, watering a rosebush. The old man stared at him hard; if his eyes were pistols, Jacob would be bleeding in the cab of the truck. Then Ian was walking back down the driveway, strolling down the sidewalk, all swagger and calm.

He threw an "Hola" at the old man, but the old man didn't catch it. Just stared him down.

Inside the truck, Ian set the pistol back on the bench seat between them. Unused, as far as Jacob could tell. Then he pulled out of the driveway and cruised down the street, not a word about what happened in that house.

"I'm going to tell you a theory," Ian said, his head swiveling back and forth from house to house like he was hunting. "It's by this other smart guy, Wesley Swift. He's a Methodist minister, so, you know, a man of God who knows his Bible."

They passed a house surrounded by chain-link fence. A dog in a spiked collar barked.

"Now, Swift says Adam and Eve weren't the first people. They were the first made in God's image. These other people, the ones before Adam and Eve, were *not* made in God's image."

Two girls threw a red ball to each other in a weedy yard. When they drove past, a young woman gathered the girls up and hurried them through the barred front door of the house, glancing over her shoulder. Jacob realized then that she was afraid of the truck, of them. He glanced at the gun on the bench seat between them, his own fear gone now.

"These people might have been related to Neanderthals, I don't know," Ian went on. "But they weren't endowed with what he calls the divine likeness." Jacob thought sometimes Ian sounded like a professor. "These are the ancestors of the non-white people on earth, the mud people."

These houses were more like mud huts than homes. Mud huts for mud people. He couldn't imagine living here, in this ugly neighborhood. It pissed him off, how ugly it was. This was America. How could it be this ugly? What he knew of America was Rancho Santa Elena—brand-new homes, freshly cut grass, greenbelts, parks to play baseball in.

"Since the muds weren't made in the image of God, they've got no souls. At least not a soul as we know it. When God made Adam and Eve, he made them in God's image and they're the ancestors to all white people on the planet. We're all related, a tribe, you know? Now, these people here," he said, nodding toward the houses, "they're mostly Mexican, maybe a few Hondurans or Nicaraguans. Sure, some of them go to church, though not Protestant churches, papist churches. The Catholics are happy to have anyone get down on their knees for the pope." He rubbed imaginary greenbacks between his fingers with his free hand. There was a tattoo on the suicide part of his wrist, Jacob noticed, just a number: 1488. "Now, if you went down to Mexico, you'd find white Mexicans. Those are the Spanish, the Europeans who conquered the Americas. But you don't see them here much. Since they're endowed with the divine spirit of God, they've got education, good jobs, the sweet houses down there in Mexico. You see this all over the world—or at least you used to—the divine white folks in charge, keeping order. But these people here are mestizo, mostly. You know what that is?"

Jacob shook his head.

"Mixed," Ian said. "Means whites slept with the Indians, the muds in Mexico. Thinned out the white bloodline, dimmed the divine in them a little. And now these people come here, sleep with each other, have kids, and do it over and over again and thin the divine even more until they become mostly muds again."

"Who says God didn't give Indians this divine thing?" Jacob was kind of sympathetic to the Indians. They got screwed, as far as he could tell. And they seemed cool—their headdresses, their bows and arrows.

"The Bible," Ian said. "Adam and Eve were in the Garden of Eden and the Garden of Eden was somewhere in the Middle East, probably near Babylonia or somewhere like that."

What did that make the Arabs then? he thought to ask. But Ian was preaching and he let it go.

"So then, you see, we have all these half muds and mostly muds here, in this country, and they start asking for equal rights, good jobs, then they want to get into government—like that Mexican police chief of ours. Soon you and me—your old man—start sleeping with them, making kids, and in a few generations there's no Anglo-Saxon anymore—no more divine. It's a slow genocide."

That girl, the one at the Chinese store, was pretty. He'd never seen pretty like hers before. Was it wrong to think she was pretty? He didn't ask Ian. He figured he knew the answer.

A group of men were standing on a corner up ahead, leaning against a lowered El Camino. Two police cars were parked on the next street—one across the street from the men on the corner, the other pulled against the curb in front of the El Camino.

"What about Jews?" Jacob asked.

"Think back to Eden," Ian said. "You know, Eve being tricked by Satan to eat the apple—the fruit of knowledge?"

"Yeah," Jacob said.

"Well, that's a metaphor," Ian said. "A symbol of seduction, of the power of Satan. But there were two seeds in Eve. Satan, as the snake, actually seduced Eve, physically impregnated her. And Adam, not knowing the evil growing inside Eve, got her pregnant, too."

Was that even possible? You could have twins, but for a girl to get pregnant twice? He thought he remembered something about that in sex ed. But he guessed if a snake could get a girl pregnant, anything could happen.

"Cain was the progeny of Satan, Abel was the son of Adam. Cain, who killed Abel out of jealousy, is the father of the Jews. We—you and I and all whites—are descended from Adam and Eve through Abel's brother Seth. So we're really the chosen people."

Ian pulled the truck to the curb, about twenty yards from the men standing on the street.

"We didn't choose this role," Ian said, shifting the truck into park. "It's actually a burden. We've got to be better, stronger, morally clear-minded. It's our heritage."

"How do you know all this stuff?" Jacob asked.

Ian looked at him, like he was sizing him up. "We've got our own school now," he said, smiling, "a place where people tell the truth, not the ZOG lies. I'll show you when you're ready."

Jacob noticed the yellow police tape then, the dude in the street taking pictures of something circled in chalk. Another standing over a puddle of something.

"Muds are killing each other," Ian said, "shooting people in the street. Saw it on the news last night." Ian pointed at the men across the street. "See how those muds are dressed?"

Long shirts buttoned at the neck, the button-downs opened to tank tops. Baggy chino shorts, long white socks. A few of them wore blue bandannas wrapped around their heads. Another had one hanging from his back pocket.

"Cholos," Ian said. "Gang members."

Ian set his hand on the gun. He didn't lift it, just laid his hand on it like it was something holy.

"Right now, these muds're killing each other. Up in South Central, too. Watch the news tonight. You'll see. Those blacks up there're blowing each other away. One day, though, they're going to figure out that killing each other is stupid. One day soon, sometime around the millennium, they're going to come for us. The Jews—the government in DC, the ZOG-run UN— will come for our guns. And then the muds will overrun our neighborhood, slit our throats, steal our women." Ian rested his forearms along the top of the steering wheel and leaned his chin against them. "But we'll be ready."

He put the truck into gear and eased it around the corner. Cops or no cops, Ian didn't put the gun away, just left it sitting between them on the seat. Ian, it seemed to Jacob, was a fucking demigod. The dude feared no one!

"Hey, homies," Ian said, leaning out the driver's side window.

"We're not your homies," one of the homies said. "What, you looking for a Del Taco?"

"Good one," Ian said, laughing. "A fucking comedian."

The cholo glanced back at one of the officers sitting in the squad car. Then he stepped into the dead grass separating the sidewalk from the curb. The cop opened the door to his patrol car and stepped out, too.

Ian laughed, made a gun with his hand, and pointed it at the man's head. "Boom," he said, before easing into the gas and rolling off.

———

Rachel had a before-school conference this morning, so Ben drove Emma to school. After dropping her off, he was cruising south on El Rancho Road, intending to have a look in on Comet Street, when he saw the Power Wagon pulled over to the curb on the northbound side. He passed the pickup truck and watched out the side-view mirror. The buff kid from yesterday, Ian Rowan, was leaning out the driver's side window, jawing it up with a couple of boys. From here—thirty yards away doing thirty-five—he couldn't get an ID on the kids, just that they were sloppily dressed like teenagers. A shrub-filled island ran down the center of the road, and by the time Ben could pull a U-turn at the light, one of the kids had hopped in the truck and they had driven off.

Ben slowed the cruiser and eyed the kid left behind as he passed—fifteen, he guessed, huge backpack bouncing against his ass, cropped dark hair, tall and skinny like puberty had recently assaulted him. Ben thought about pulling over, but the Power Wagon was stopped at the next light up so he tried to remember the kid's face—a trick he'd gotten pretty good at over the years. Not the kid from yesterday—that kid was stockier, hair longer with a bit of a mullet.

Five minutes later, Ben was three cars behind the Power Wagon, riding the ramp to the 5 freeway. Traffic was moving, but the lanes were packed and it was easy to follow him—too many cars to arouse suspicion, no need for dramatic maneuvering for position, just a slow cruise north. It was like that all the way up to South Harbor Boulevard in Anaheim, but once they hit West South and turned in to the neighborhood all he had was distance and the kid's oblivion—hopefully.

The Power Wagon crawled down the street, the driver's elbow resting on the frame of the driver's side door—like he wanted everyone to see him, or like he was looking for someone. Made it damn hard to be inconspicuous following him since any normal driver would swerve around the ten-mile-an-hour cruise, but Ben decided it didn't much matter if the kid knew he was being followed. If this Ian Rowan was clean, he'd stay clean. If he was dirty, it might shake him up. This was Vatos Locos territory—the VT FAMILIA tags on the cement walls gave it away. There'd been a shooting near here last night; he'd heard it on the OC Sheriff's scanner on the way home from the bar. So the obvious question: What's a white kid from Rancho Santa Elena doing cruising the barrio? Nothing good, that was the answer.

The Power Wagon suddenly pulled into a driveway and all Ben could do was roll on by, play it cool like he was attending to other business. He watched the truck out his rearview, but nothing happened. They just sat there. He rounded the corner, rolled the next street until the block ended, and by the time he'd U'd it around back to the first street, the Power Wagon was gone.

He parked the cruiser across the street from the house where Ian had pulled in, watched it a minute, and decided it was abandoned—the overgrown grass, the empty driveway, the boarded-up side window. He got out and pushed through the rusted aluminum gate and started up the walkway to the front door.

"It's three doors down," a middle-aged Hispanic man said. He was wearing a T-shirt screen-printed with the image of Cesar Chavez. SI SE PUEDE was written beneath the picture.

"What's the word on the place?" Ben asked.

"Shit pinche five-oh," the man said. "You all know the *word*, but you don't do jack shit."

———

"Bạn không thể nhìn thấy anh ấy nữa," Bao said to his daughter. "You can't see him again."

They were in the grocery, the door locked, the sign turned to read CLOSED. He'd waited for her to come back following her late-afternoon classes, which she did, as though everything were normal, as though she'd come from studying American literature instead of from Lucas Clay's apartment.

"You followed me?" She turned to him, her face shocked with anger.

"I was worried," he said. "The dog, this boy yesterday. I was afraid you were in danger."

"We've been meaning to tell you," she said, the edge coming off her anger a bit. "We were just waiting for the right time."

The *we* was a punch to his gut. How long had he been lied to? How long had this gone on behind his back? "No," he said. "Bạn không thể nhìn thấy anh ấy nữa."

"We should have told you," she said, "but I *will* see him if I want to see him."

His body thrummed with adrenaline. He didn't know what angered him more, that she was seeing a married American more than a decade her senior or that she replied to him in English. They spoke English together, yes, but the important things, the matters of the heart, were discussed in Vietnamese. Using English now was a show of disobedience, a knife to cut the familial connective tissue.

"The man's married," Bao said, moving toward her now.

Her face flushed and she looked lost for a second. "He doesn't love her."

Bao knew enough about the tricks men play to get what they want. How could she be so naïve?

"Việc đó không quan trọng."

"It *does* matter," she said.

His head roared. *Speak Vietnamese,* he wanted to say. *Please, please stop speaking English.*

"He's going to leave her."

Bao huffed a bitter laugh at that. "The fantasy of every mistress," Bao said in English now, an attempt to blunt her defiance.

Someone was banging on the front door. She was being erased from him, his little girl who had been cut open with shrapnel, his little girl who had clung to him on a shuddering helicopter above the Pacific. This place that took and then lost his country was now taking her.

Ai, who had been in the office paying bills, stepped onto the grocery store floor now and asked what was going on. Both of them ignored her.

"You think if you marry a white man," Bao said, "they'll see you as American?"

"Dừng lại," Ai said, her hand on his forearm now, trying to calm him.

Linh threw her shoulders back and raised her chin. Someone was knocking on the door again. The astonished anger on his daughter's face frightened him.

"That's what you think this is?" She was shaking her head now. "That's what you think of me?" Then she took a step toward him and looked him in the eyes when she said it: "I love him."

His hand clapped her cheek. It happened so fast, it took his mind a moment to catch up to what his palm had done. Ai ran to Linh, her arms around their daughter's shoulders. His wife screamed at him, but his head was spinning and he was suddenly afraid of himself. He turned and shoved open the front door, the metal frame slapping a customer across the chest before Bao nearly ran him over.

———

Ian raced the back roads into Santa Elena, riding the edge of the Santa Ana Mountains, tunneling through rows of orange groves. A crop duster buzzed their heads, malathion misting the windshield. Edging a strawberry field, hazed by pesticide spray, Jacob saw dozens of people bent over, picking berries from the plants. They looked like hunchbacks in the early-evening chemical light, something grotesque out of a storybook. And when they passed the camp, plywood shacks on the edge of the drainage ditch, Jacob realized Ian was right: Here they were, on the edge of town, mud people just two miles from his house.

The houses back in Santa Elena looked like mansions to him now. The clean rows of red-tiled roofs, the tidy lawns, the newly paved street, black like ink had been spilled. This was a whole different world from the mud world he'd just come from, and suddenly he felt how fragile it was. Like this perfectly organized street was the last stand of order. Whatever happened inside his house, people weren't getting shot on the street here—at least not yet. He'd never felt important before, never felt like this place was one he deserved—and he sure as shit hadn't thought about God, the Garden of Eden, or the divine.

Ian pulled into Heritage Park and parked near the library.

"We're going on a mission tonight," Ian said. "Midnight. Can you get out?"

He could. He could climb out his window, step onto the bump-out kitchen's roof tiles. From there he could jump to the grass.

"Yeah," he said. "I'll get out."

"Meet here," Ian said. "Don't go to my house."

Jacob walked home from the park. Ian said he wasn't going home right now, said they were going to keep it quiet at his house for a while. Told him, too, to use the pass-through walkways if he was going out, to stay off the street as much as possible. That was cool, felt like he was a secret agent or something. Jacob got home a half hour before his parents, and he made a big show of spreading his binders across the kitchen counter, pretending at homework.

"How was school?" his father asked when he reached the kitchen, something weird in the tone of his voice.

"Cool," Jacob said. "Miss Barrow was back."

"No more cancer?" his father said, looking hard at him.

Shit, he didn't think his father was listening the other night. "She seemed all right."

"Well, that's good news," his mother said, hanging her coat in the hallway closet.

His dad shot bullets at him, looked like he had a thousand things to say. His Chinese girlfriend had told him Jacob had visited the grocery, Jacob was sure of it. But what the hell was his dad going to do? Accuse him, right in front of his mother?

"I need to meet a potential client," his father finally said.

He went into the den and made a show of pulling contracts out of his desk and stuffing them into his briefcase before heading out the door, saying he'd be back in an hour, but dinnertime rolled around and he was a no-show. His mother fried up three pork chops, set the table for three, even poured three glasses of Pepsi and they sat there alone together, staring at *Facts of Life* on the television. His mother downed a glass of wine while cooking, another when they sat down to eat, and now she was topping off another at the refrigerator, the laugh track on the television echoing in the house.

"The school called." She lit a cigarette, blew smoke, and

watched him from the kitchen. When she was drunk, her eyes became someone else's, as though some darker soul possessed her body. "You're spending time with that Rowan boy, aren't you?"

He just stared at his plate, the soggy Shake 'N Bake pork chop, the blood-smear of ketchup. On television, Blair said, *I just had another one of my brilliant ideas.*

"I like Ian Rowan." She blew smoke and nodded. "Takes care of his mother, the poor woman."

Jacob didn't know what the deal was with Michael and Ian's mom. He'd seen her a couple of times, once when she brought chocolate chip cookies out to the garage. She seemed nice, but quiet, a sad fake smile painted across her face. Anyway, he didn't get how his mother could feel pity for her, as though her own situation was that much better.

"Dad's seeing a Chinese girl," Jacob said. He didn't know if he was trying to hurt or help her. It just jumped out of him and plopped onto the table between them.

She didn't say anything for a few long seconds, just sat there stretching out time with her cigarette between her fingers, rolling the ash to a point in the ashtray.

"She's Vietnamese," she said finally. Then huffed a bitter laugh. "You think I didn't know?"

If there was love for him in her, he didn't see it in her eyes. Her legs were crossed at the knee and she shook her dangling foot back and forth.

"You're just like your father," she said. "You think I'm too stupid to see what's right in front of me." She turned away from him, staring at the crack in the sliding glass door. "He cried at our wedding. That's how happy he was. Did you know that? As soon as he saw me coming down the aisle, he turned to water."

"Mom," he said. "I'm sure he lo—"

"Go to your room." She took a drag of the cigarette. "This is my house. I want to be alone in it."

Ben was back on Comet Street by early evening, parked four doors down from the Rowan place, putting down a cold chicken quesadilla he'd picked up at El Rancho Market. He'd forgotten to eat lunch after the trip up to Anaheim, remembered only after his head began to pound on the drive over here.

The house Ian had stopped at was a meth lab, he was almost certain of it. When he knocked on the door, he saw the light on the peephole blotted out for a moment and then he watched through the small lens as a man escaped into the back room. But he smelled it, that ammonia chemical stink radiating beneath the door. He figured the dude inside was cowering somewhere, praying he'd drive away, so he checked the side yard, keeping away from the windows in case he figured wrong. Yep, burned patches of grass where they'd dumped chemicals. He opened one of the lids to the trash cans—paint thinner cans, Drano bottles, empty plastic cold tablet tabs. He didn't have jurisdiction, so there wasn't much he could do right then but alert the Anaheim cops.

When he called it in on the Motorola, a Detective Hollis told him, "I'll put it on the list," so Ben didn't have much faith a whole lot would get done on that end. Ben had then checked the white pages in a phone booth outside a liquor store around the corner from the place, looking for a name to give him a lead. The address was unlisted. Back at the Santa Elena station a lawyer was waiting for him. Ben was fifteen minutes late for a deposition on a home invasion case he'd completely forgotten about, so three afternoon hours were wasted on lesser concerns before he could get back to Comet and stake the place.

Nothing doing at the Rowan house—the garage door closed, no Power Wagon. He sat there for two hours, watching neighbors drive home from work, a dad and kid playing a game of catch, lights going on in dining rooms, the obnoxiously perfect little suburban idyll, when he got a ring on the Motorola from Detective Hollis.

"That place you called in about today," Hollis said, chuckling.

"What about it?"

"Looks like you were right," the detective said. "I'm watching it burn right now."

———

Hollis wasn't kidding: The whole damn place went up. The flames were out, the fire department spraying hot spots, but the structure was mostly gone; just the fireplace, one charred south-side wall, and the cement foundation remained.

"Must have burned real hot," Detective Hollis said. "Fucking meth fires."

Sure, meth labs go up in flames all the time, but this one felt awfully coincidental.

"Body?"

"We don't know yet."

Ben doubted it. After he'd checked the trash cans of the place earlier today, he'd talked to the Mexican man down the street again. *No one really lives there,* he'd said. *White people just come and go, usually late at night or early in the morning.*

Ben saw the Mexican man now, standing in his front yard behind his fence. Ben wandered over to check in.

"They already asked me," he said, nodding toward the Anaheim officers. "I didn't see anything."

"No snitching," Ben said, nodding, irritated. "I get it."

"No," he said. "I'm not one of those scared coños. I really didn't see anything."

"You hear an explosion?"

"No," he said. "Smelled smoke and came outside to see."

They set it themselves, Ben guessed. If it was accidental, if they were baking, it most likely would have blown up.

"What about that truck today? You see it around before?"

He nodded. "Drive in, drive out. Like a goddamned In-N-Out Burger."

Ben asked some of the other neighbors, standing around in the flashing lights, watching the fire department clean it up. But no one else would say anything, some of the coños, he guessed, the man was talking about. Ben got it, though, the fear was real because the threat was real. No way the Vatos Locos tolerated snitching, Ben was sure of that. People terrorized in their own neighborhoods.

"Mind if I take a look around?" Ben asked Hollis after the fire truck had gone.

"Knock yourself out," Hollis said. "Seems pretty cut and dried to me."

Ben remembered the Mexican man's *You don't do jack shit* from earlier today. If this neighborhood was near Disneyland, Ben figured, the Anaheim PD would have already sent in a SWAT team. This neighborhood earned one fire truck, two uniforms, and a single incompetent detective. And all of them would be gone within the hour.

It was completely dark now, the nearest streetlight out and the next one, too, like the world didn't care enough about this place to offer it light. He stepped around hot spots, flashed his Maglite across melted aluminum cans, the spring-coiled remains of a couch. No signs of a body, no burned corpse, no smell of burned flesh. He ran his flashlight across the remaining wall. A half-burned flag hung from a couple of nails. It was pretty badly charred, but he could make out what looked like a baby-blue shield set against a red background. The bottom half of the flag was burned away, but at the top a yellow crown sat on top of a white cross. Crowns and crosses, a bad combination if you asked him.

He went out to the cruiser, grabbed a Polaroid camera out of the trunk, tiptoed back in, and took a few shots.

Jacob was stretched out in the bed of Ian's truck, tanked on Colt 45, back pushed up against the open cab window; the guitars thundering the stereo speakers tremored his lower back. Between his legs lay a homey sock, a billiard ball lodged in the toe of a white knee-high. Ian swerved around a corner and Jacob's sloshed brain pulled three g's, the billiard ball rolling against his calf.

They were cruising out toward the hills, past the El Toro air base and the flaring afterburners of the F-4 fighter jet night maneuvers. He was ramped up, electricity pulsing his limbs. Ian had given him a white pill before heading out. "It'll make you strong, Tough Shit." And he had thrown it down his throat. Then they'd sat in the park, slipping their hands into latex gloves, drinking forty-ounce cans of malt liquor, while they made Jacob slip the balls into the socks. Probate, that's what they called him. *Hey, probe. Now wrap the sock in that duct tape so it doesn't split open.*

In the bed of the truck, he spun between euphoric drunkenness and desolate anger. Earlier, Jacob had punched a hole in his bedroom door. Hurt like hell, maybe broke a pinkie finger, but it was a good pain, the kind that got your blood pumping. Someone had made this door and his parents had paid for it and he, with one swing, had unmade it. Then he'd grabbed *The Turner Diaries*, hid in his bed, and immersed himself in the war against the System. He imagined himself a soldier in the book, a freedom fighter to save his people. He heard his father's car rumble up the drive. A door slammed. His mother yelled. But who the fuck cared about his stupid parents? He let himself be transported into the novel until all was quiet and dark, and then he climbed out his window and jogged down to the park.

Thank God he was alone, not in the cab with Ian and Clocker, not in the VW Bug with Fisker and the twins, because he could barely hold his shit together. His mother fucking *knew*. Lies. All lies. The face of the girl in the grocery flashed across the screen of his memory—her brown eyes, her milk-coffee skin, that scar like something you wanted to smudge away with your thumb. She'd jumped into his head the night after he yelled at her at the grocery. Just came out of nowhere while he was lying on his stomach in bed, an erection pushing into the mattress. But his dad was doing her. Jesus.

Ian careened another right and they were on a dirt road now, white robes of dust rising in the city glow. Campfires flickered out across the strawberry field to his left, three undulating orange dots a couple hundred yards away. Spotlighted by the flames, he could see the walls of the migrant camp, a shitty stack of plywood and cardboard. It was the same camp they'd passed today, he realized, on the detour back from Orange.

Ian swung the truck beneath a row of eucalyptus and parked next to a cement water tank. Clocker was already out of the Dodge, lighting a cigarette, hopped up on adrenaline.

"Whoo-hoo," he said, swinging his homey sock between his legs like a ball sack. "Let's get some mud blood."

"Shut up," Fisker said, slapping him on the back of the head. "This is a stealth operation."

"Didn't some fucker blow his brains out here last year?" one of the twins said.

"Yeah," Fisker said. "I watched them carry the body bag into the ambulance. Some illegal scum. Fucker was even going to the high school. I mean, our goddamned taxes were paying for it."

"Shut up, Fisk," Ian said, laughing. "You don't even have a job. It's your parents' taxes."

Jacob vaulted out of the truck bed, his head spinning but nothing he couldn't control with a little concentration. Ian crushed a can beneath his right foot and then pulled Jacob aside.

"Look, Tough Shit," Ian said, grabbing the homey sock out of Jacob's fist. "You swing it up." He tossed the ball end into the air, like he was clocking someone in the chin. "You swing it down." This time he whipped it overhand, like he was tossing a football. "Or you swing it backhand." And he took a swing like he was in the ATP or something. "Don't swing it across your body. You miss and the cue ball's pummeling your ribs."

Ian gave the sock back to Jacob, and Jacob threw a couple of practice swings.

"And hold your arm out here," Ian said, grabbing his wrist and pulling it away from his body. "So it swings past your waist."

"Yeah," Clocker said, laughing. "Or else you crack yourself in the huevos."

The others leapt across the drainage ditch and marched the service road running the edge of the strawberry field. "Probe gonna lose his cherry tonight," Jacob heard one of the twins say.

"Listen," Ian said, his hand on Jacob's shoulder. "These guys aren't going to trust you unless you get a shot in, all right?"

The fires across the field spun blurry for a moment. His stomach roiled, but he swallowed it down.

"Yeah," Jacob said. "All right."

"Just bring up the rear. You can get a second shot on one of mine. Make it real easy, all right?"

Then they were across the drainage ditch, into the dust and gravel of the service road, the homey sock swaying from his fist. The air was like steel against the exposed skin of his neck. Up ahead, he could see puffs of freezing breath from Fisker and the crew. In the distance, Saddleback Mountain glowed milk white in the crescent moon. Between the mountains and them were the fires. He could see the pickers now, crowded around each firepit—some of them standing with hands in pockets, a few sitting on what looked like upturned crates. Voices murmured across the night air—no language, no way to tell if it was Spanish or Chinese or Swahili—just the hum of people talking.

As they turned the corner at the edge of the field, he and Ian gained ground on the gang. The four in front of them were silhouetted by the fires—Fisker and his limp, Clocker a head taller than everyone—and beyond them two kids chased each other around the pits. A couple of men in cowboy hats hunched near a fire, and a woman drew water from an orange cooler. Someone was strumming a guitar, a man crooning some sad stupid song, his face turned toward the moon as his voice trembled a note. Spanish, it was definitely Spanish. He recognized some of the words—Sí, No, También, Gracias.

"You good?" Ian said.

"I'm good."

But his body felt like an electric transformer about to fuzz out. It was so fucking cold. This was SoCal, how did it get so goddamned cold?

The muds were twenty yards away now and his head started to spin. He remembered the girl, the one sleeping with his dad, the one he got an erection over, and his mind wigged out like the television between channels. How could he find her pretty? She was a mud, these people were muds. They didn't have souls, not like us. They lived right on the edge of town, and the muds were coming for them.

And then he heard a scream and Fisker yelled, "Don't let him get into the grove." A dull thud and the heave of someone throwing up. Something whipped by his ear, Ian's homey sock and ball, he realized, and he got his vision back.

The ball end cracked a mud in the cheek, dropping the fucker right next to the fire. He heard the guitar hit the dirt, a tonal thud that resonated in the cold air. Then a body flashed in front of him, bent over like a linebacker coming in for the tackle, and Jacob swung, the sock blurring before his eyes until he felt the crack. The man screamed like a kid, a grown fucking man shrieking like that!

He swung again, the ball thudding the man's torso. Something broke open in Jacob then, the fear winging out into the darkness, and for a beautiful moment he saw the muds scattering like rabbits, and he didn't care anymore, didn't give a goddamn about his father or his mother or the fucking Vietnamese girl or her mother with the stupid candy or the father who had grabbed his wrist and made him feel small. He swung again, blindly, swung like he was pummeling the shit out of his old self, killing the boy who cared about a stupid woman handing him candy. He was a soldier, a soldier for the Organization and he was fighting his own goddamned war and all wars had casualties, all wars had atrocities; that was the nature of war, you were a victim and a killer, and they called you Soldier. And he swung and swung into the darkness.

PART TWO

PART TWO

Chapter Eight

Ben got the call at 12:23 A.M, Saturday morning.

"Detective Wade," the voice said, a Spanish accent, someone he recognized. "Detective, nos atacaron. Nos atacaron."

"Santiago?" He'd given Santiago his personal number, last year after Lucero's funeral. "Who attacked you?"

"Please," the man said. "Please, I'm at the Texaco station near the camp."

He and Natasha got dressed and tore off for the migrant camp, speeding the cruiser down the emergency lane of El Rancho Road. They pulled into the Texaco station in five minutes, across the street from where the boy's body, Lucero's body, had been found last year after he'd killed himself. Santiago lay clumped on the curb next to the pay phone. A woman stood at one of the pumps, filling her Cadillac, staring at the man.

"Jesus," Ben said. Blood was running down Santiago's cheek, pooling in the crescent of his ear.

"They came after us," Santiago said. "We were around the fires and they just came out of the dark."

"Can you get up?"

"Don't move him," Natasha said. She started examining him, checking the wound on his head, pressing her fingers against his ribs. *Does this hurt? No. How about this? Sí, yes.* "We have to stop this bleeding."

Ben stumbled with Santiago over to the bathroom door. Locked. Dammit. Natasha let Santiago lean against her while Ben sprinted to the station office for the key. The office was closed, no one inside. CREDIT ONLY AFTER 10 P.M., a hand-written sign read. The woman was still at the pump, not even gassing up anymore, just watching the scene. Back at the door, he kicked it in and the two of them hauled Santiago into the foul restroom, sitting him down on the toilet.

"They chased Javier into the arboledas."

Natasha grabbed a handful of towels and pressed them to the gash above the man's hairline. In the fluorescent light, the blood was so deeply red it was nearly black. Santiago was speaking a quick Spanglish Ben had a difficult time interpreting. Nosotros weren't doing nada. They comenzo a golpearnos.

"He needs stitches," Natasha said. "I think his skull might be fractured."

"Who's they?" Ben asked. He could see that Santiago's right eye was dilated.

"He's concussed," Natasha said to Ben.

"Gringos. White kids."

Natasha wiped blood from Santiago's cheek. The man's pan-icked breath, as he streamed broken English, puffed against Ben's face. Santiago's heart pulsed a vein near his temple.

"They hit Javier, he's an old man. They broke Sylvia's— I shot at them."

Shit. "You hit anybody?"

"I shot in the air," Santiago said. "We didn't do nothing. We didn't do nada."

As soon as they saw Ben's cruiser lights the migrants scattered—ghosts dashing away from his headlights. By the time he threw the cruiser into park, the only people left were the injured, their bodies strewn on the ground in front of the campfires—a young man with a shard of his mandible knocked left of his upper jaw. A mother with a broken wrist, her teenage son, crying dios mío, trying to splint the bone with sticks and duct tape. A man, still sitting in a plastic chair next to the fire, pulling shards of guitar out of his left arm, the body of the instrument exploded on his lap.

Five minutes earlier, Ben had left Natasha with Santiago at the Texaco station, called in EMTs, and sped the berm of the drainage ditch, not knowing what the hell he was going to find. White kids, Santiago had said. Unprovoked. Jesus, by the look of things they'd attacked the camp with steel bars or baseball bats.

A young girl grabbed his wrist and started pulling him toward the orange groves. "Mi abuelo," the girl called. "Mi abuelo, la policía, esta aqui."

Her grandfather was laid out beneath a ripening orange tree. The man, his torso twisted to the right, gurgled a breath. Ben shined his Maglite on the man. He was bleeding from the mouth, and his right eye was swollen over. The man must have been in his seventies, these assholes going after grandfathers, too. Jesus. Ben could hear the ambulance sirens now and he stayed with the man and his granddaughter, Ben holding the old man's hand, until the EMTs arrived and triaged the scene.

Once the EMTs were working on the grandfather, Ben called over one of the uniforms.

"I need you to do a drive-by of 19473 Comet Street, over in California Homes. Just roll by, tell me if there's a Dodge Power Wagon parked outside and come on back."

"Sir."

Then Ben tried interviewing witnesses.

"No se" was all he got, from six different witnesses. *I don't know*, like they were under some contractual obligation to be silent, like they were more frightened of him than the assholes that had just attacked them. No se, No se, No se.

He saw the little girl again, the granddaughter. She was hugging an older woman, her grandmother, Ben guessed, who was sitting on a red plastic chair, her eyes wide with shock.

"Abuela," Ben said. "Please help me. Who did this?"

"No se," she said, her brown eyes catching the firelight.

To them, he could be immigration or working with immigration. If some other detective was on this case, he might put a call into the feds after it was cleaned up, have the migrants arrested at the hospital once they were healthy enough to be trucked down over the border. That shit *did* happen, but that wasn't Ben, that wasn't his deal.

"Look, we need to know if she saw anyone," Ben said to the girl. "That's how we do it up here."

The abuela's face changed then, a sharpness in her eyes that cut him.

"No. Se."

"Jesus, please work with me," Ben said. "I'm trying to help."

"Señora," someone said, coming up behind Ben. He turned and found Lieutenant Hernandez, his boss, striding up next to him, dressed in a double-breasted suit as though he slept in the thing. "Por favor toma tu tiempo," he said to the woman, taking her hand in his and holding it. "Sé que esto es aterrador. Take your time. I know this is frightening."

The grandmother nodded and took a deep breath and after a few moments she started speaking. Ben understood some cursory Spanish, could order tacos in a taquería, converse the basics, but the lieutenant and the abuela were talking so fast he lost much of it. He stood there stupidly, on the edge of their conversation, the EMTs working the scene around him.

"Excuse us, Detective," Hernandez said.

Then Hernandez, the abuela, and the girl stepped into one of the cardboard homes, shutting the flimsy door behind them.

The ambulance, with Santiago strapped inside, burned off toward Hoag Hospital. After, Natasha stood there a moment, looking at the splotches of blood darkening the cement, thinking. From where she stood at the Texaco station, she could see the cruisers' light bars raking the orange trees. *Posse comitatus. Posse comitatus. Power of the county.* "It's not that kind of movement," she remembered Vanek saying. If the government wasn't going to kick immigrants out, she thought, trying to imagine herself into a neo-Nazi's mind, then they would do it themselves. They would be the "posse."

She found the white pages dangling inside the phone booth and tried to look up the Phans' home number. She didn't care that it was nearly 1:00 A.M., she was frightened now. If these were the same people who left the dog at the Phans' grocery, the dead dog was just a prelude to more violence.

No number. They must have been unlisted.

She thumbed to the *S*'s in the yellow pages and found the number for their market, Sunrise Food Mart. The phone rang just once before someone picked up.

"Linh?" An urgency in Bao's voice.

"No, it's Natasha."

"Oh, xin chao," Bao said, a false lightness coming into his voice. "Hello."

"Xin chao," Natasha said.

"You remembered your words," Bao said. "Very good, Miss Natasha."

"A little." He'd taught her phrases years ago, just as she had taught him some English. It embarrassed her that hello was all she could remember. "Is Linh okay?"

Why was Bao at the store, seemingly waiting by the phone for a call from his daughter?

"Yes, yes," he said. "She's fine. She's just had problems

sleeping since the dog. She's at home in bed. I'm paying some bills."

He was lying. But why? He hadn't even asked her why she was calling so late.

"Please, lock your doors," she said. "We don't know who they are yet, but the people who left the dog at your grocery are dangerous."

"Of course," he said. "Since the Night Prowler we always do."

"Bao, have things like this happened before? Things like the dog? Is this how it's been for you here?"

It was quiet a moment, just the static of late-night silence. "No. This is a good country. I have a house, a grocery." He sounded like a used car salesman trying to pawn off a lemon. "Linh's going to college. She can be anything she wants to be."

"I asked how it's been for *you*."

Static again. She had the feeling he was writing a script for himself before he spoke. "A lot of work, Miss Natasha. What is it they say? Pull yourself up by the bootstraps?"

"Yes."

"I like that," he said, sounding very tired. "I don't wear boots, but I like that."

———

"Calcetines," Hernandez said, when he climbed out of the makeshift house.

"Socks?"

"Filled with rocks, bricks, maybe."

Rocks? Bricks? Jesus, like they were hit with steel beams from the look of it.

"She couldn't say that in front of me?" Ben said. "Had to have a little private powwow?"

Hernandez looked closely at him, like he didn't like what he was seeing. "Some things you shouldn't take personally, Detective."

It had been like this in LA, too. The North Hollywood families, terrorized by the gangs, shutting their doors against the police. Pissed some of the guys off—well, pissed most of the good cops off, anyway, and some of the guys cultivated a resentment of the families, of the whole Latino neighborhoods. It frustrated Ben, too—even though he knew some asshole cops used their badge to exercise their own terror on the community. Still, it made you feel like the enemy, and no one wanted to feel like the enemy when they were trying to help.

"That all she give you?"

The bonfires were still smoldering, casting the camp in a deep ocher burn. Lieutenant Hernandez had been in there for fifteen minutes, maybe twenty. The EMTs were gone, the injured ferried away, the ground littered with detritus—but the migrants hadn't returned. They were huddled out there somewhere—in the groves, in the hills, who the hell knew where. Out there in the dark unseen. And why shouldn't they be? Ben conceded to himself. Who the hell could you trust when you were illegal, when you could be assaulted without provocation?

"She said they called them barro," Hernandez said. "Mud people."

A black-and-white came rolling down the access road and parked next to Ben. "Anything?"

"Yeah," the officer said. "A Power Wagon parked on the curb. Right in front of the house."

———

Some mud had pulled a shotgun on their asses and popped off a shot as they blazed through the field, crushing strawberries under their feet. They had raced the cars back through town, pulled up behind a Lucky's, ripped the duct tape from the homeys, and tossed the bloody socks in a dumpster. Jacob got back to Comet Street sometime after 1:15—his dick dad's car still not parked out front. He climbed the tree to the kitchen roof and then pulled himself up by the windowpane into his darkened bedroom.

And now he stood in front of the mirror in his bathroom, the fluorescent light cutting angles out of his face. He'd had to piss when he climbed into his room, and when he was washing his hands he glanced in the mirror and noticed something in his hair. He dried his hands and untangled it: a piece of bloodied skin with black hair curling from the follicles.

A slice of scalp, he realized. A mud's scalp.

It was pressed into his palm like a beach shell. He stood there watching himself, his hooded sweatshirt speckled with blood, and tried to think what it meant to hold a piece of someone's scalp in your hand. The moment felt important, like he'd crossed into some new territory from which he couldn't return, but he couldn't put words to the feeling.

He pulled a Kleenex from a box sitting on top of the toilet, wrapped the scalp inside, placed it in a shoebox with his baseball cards, and slid it beneath the head of his twin bed. No Polaroids for him: skin and bone, viscera and spilled blood.

Chapter Nine

He'd struck his daughter.

Bao was alone in the grocery this morning, an un-ashed cigarette burning between his fingers. A delivery of star anise and ginger sat on the floor, unopened, unshelved.

After he had slapped Linh and she had run off yesterday, Ai had stormed off, too, telling him that she was going to her sister's. *Anh phải làm cho mọi việc tốt hơn!* she'd said, a fury he'd never seen from her. *You have to make things better.* But he didn't know how.

He'd slept on the couch in the office last night, nodding off well after 3:00 A.M. He'd tried to stay at home, but the empti-ness of the house was like an accusation. He hadn't given Linh a moment to explain, hadn't listened to her. But it had felt to him that she was seeing this American to punish him for some parental crime he didn't know he'd committed. It didn't help that Natasha had called, clearly frightened, telling him to lock his doors. Yes, he could lock his doors, but to protect what? His daughter was in another man's house, his wife at her sister's. Let them come for him. He had his anger, had his Smith & Wesson.

He watched the hand that held the cigarette, the hand that had flown away from him and slapped his daughter's cheek. When they had arrived in America, Bao had sworn to Ai that they wouldn't be like some Vietnamese families, that he wouldn't punish Linh with his hands. Ai was grateful for it; she'd been hit by her father, spanked by her mother. Bao, too, had been struck as a child. It wasn't for a lack of love—he and Ai did not doubt their parents' love—but he'd wanted his fatherhood to be a soft one that guided Linh into the world. But this loose use of her body, this—this betrayal. The Americans had lost his country and now they were taking his daughter, and she, it seemed, was willing to be stolen. Did he not have the right, after all his work, to say, *No, some things cannot happen, some things are too much to ask,* and have his feelings, his decision— his life—respected?

Now the door jingled and Lucas Clay walked in. Bao's mind flashed to the gun in the safe. 18-28-9, and he'd have it in the palm of this hand.

"Leave," Bao said.

Yesterday, when Bao had climbed the stairs to that apartment and knocked on the front door, Lucas Clay had turned the tables on him. He had invited Bao inside, said he'd been wanting to talk with him about Linh, said they had been waiting for the right time. Bao had stood there paralyzed by the realization that his daughter was sleeping with this man, confused, too, by the sudden deference Lucas showed him, before Bao stumbled down the stairs and drove blindly back to the grocery, burning with rage until that rage found expression in his hand striking his daughter's cheek.

"Linh's upset," Lucas said. "We should talk."

"Get out," Bao said.

"Please, Bao." Lucas had something in his hand, a bottle of Chivas Regal that he set on the register counter in front of him. "I know it's a shock, but let's talk like adults."

A bottle of whiskey for a daughter? He thought Bao was that easy? Worse, Linh had told him it was his favorite; his daughter thought he might be bribed into giving her away, too. 18-28-9. The combination to the lock on the safe flashed in his head. 18-28-9. Bao had pulled the trigger on the gun before, at a target practice range in Westminster, and again, once in the air, when hoodlums tried to rob his first grocery up in Little Saigon.

"You've made her a mistress," Bao said.

Lucas dropped his head and nodded, as though ashamed of the fact. Bao wanted to believe he felt ashamed, but did he really? Americans spoke a lot about sin, but he didn't see much evidence of their shame.

"I'm leaving my wife," he said.

Not, *I'm sorry*. Not, *I know it's wrong*. Just, *I can discard one woman and have another*.

"I'm just trying to make it easier on my son right now."

The son. Yes, Bao remembered the boy's face. He remembered the ugly slur that shot from that boy's mouth. Maybe it was the son who had left the dead dog in the alley.

"I know he came here yesterday," Lucas said. "I'm sorry you found out that way. He's . . ." He trailed off, shaking his head. "He's having a difficult time."

"You're stealing her," Bao said.

"Stealing?" Lucas said, an edge coming into his voice. "You don't think she can make her own decisions? Who do you think you raised, Bao?"

Bao slammed his hand against the counter. "Leave."

"I'm not going to take her away," Lucas said, sounding desperate now. "You can have a traditional wedding, I'll receive her at your house, she can wear an áo dài. I will keep her here in Santa Elena, near to you and Ai."

Bao counted the *I*'s in his head. I, I, I, always *I* followed by *want*. In Lucas's mind, she was already his possession. Bao had imagined his daughter in a Western wedding dress, not the traditional áo dài. Ever since he'd arrived here, he'd wanted a big wedding for her. Like the ones in the movies, the ones that looked expensive. Though he'd wanted Linh to marry a Vietnamese man. He wanted it both ways, both ways always. He was a split man.

"How did it happen?" Bao said.

"After the Palm Springs earthquake. When your driveway cracked."

In his own house, under his own roof. Bao remembered the night. They had just poured the concrete, and Bao invited Clay to stay for Ai's sour curry shrimp. Linh had been unusually quiet, and they'd joked about Lucas's third bowl of the dish. Most Americans, Bao had found, didn't like the fish sauce, didn't take to sour, but Lucas had devoured the meal like he'd been starving.

"I want her home," Bao said. "Today."

Lucas glanced out the front window of the store, staring at the cars shining in the morning light, before looking back at Bao.

"Don't make her choose between us," Lucas said. "You don't want that."

"She's not yours. I want her home."

———

Ben and Lieutenant Hernandez were at the station, filling out paperwork, processing photos from the crime scene in the strawberry field—Hernandez typing up the forms on one of the Macs as if he were still a street cop. The lieutenant had called in the detectives to a special Saturday morning meeting, and Ben was talking it all out before heading into the briefing room—the murder at the beach house in Huntington Beach, Detective Vanek's neo-Nazi idea. The poisoned little boy, and Duke, his slashed dog. This posse comitatus thing, whatever that meant, the red thread that matched. Hernandez had been silent since leaving the migrant camp, and his silence was starting to get on Ben's nerves.

They'd come straight from working the scene, a night of generator hum and spotlights. They'd combed the place for evidence, followed a line of footprints, all identical in tread—a half circle of what looked like a horseshoe of missiles surrounding a constellation of crosses. Boot prints. Probably the same prints Natasha and Vanek had seen up on the beach at HB. "I want casts of the shoe prints and the tires," Hernandez had said. "Pictures, too. With a tripod. Want them clear, no blurring." They'd followed the prints down a dirt access road edging the strawberry field until they found the tire marks near a water tank. Measuring the axle width against the other tire tread marks, a truck for sure, four-by-four most likely. A few crushed Colt 45 cans littered the ground. A ripped shirt, an empty negro frijoles can, broken sunglasses. Santiago had said socks, with something hard in them. But no socks, not at the crime scene at least.

"What was that business about a Power Wagon parked outside of a house?" Hernandez said now.

"I've got an eye on this place over in California Homes," Ben said, "near the street where the dog disappeared and the kid was poisoned. This guy, Ian Rowan, smells like trouble. Buffed out. Listens to this shitty music. Got a real edge to him."

Hernandez stopped typing, leaned his elbows on the desk.

"Rowan?"

"Yeah."

"Paul Rowan," Hernandez said, mostly to himself.

"The city councilman?" Ben said. "His son?"

"California Homes? Comet Street?"

"That's the one."

Hernandez just nodded.

"Right," Ben said. "Paul Rowan led that resistance to district-to-district voting."

Hernandez nodded again. Danh Phan, an airline industry executive and a councilman hopeful, had led a campaign for district-to-district voting. Seemed to get a few councilmen on board with it, but ultimately the council voted to stick with at-large voting, effectively diluting the minority vote. No way minorities in the La Bonita section of town, where some of the Asians lived, were going to get their man elected if he was running against all the other white candidates in the city with all the other white residents in town voting regardless of district. Snowball's chance in hell with district-to-district even, but would be *a* chance at least if only La Bonita residents voted for La Bonita candidates. If you bothered to think about it for two minutes, it wasn't hard to see the legal injustice in that decision, but either people didn't think much or they were happy about it. Danh Phan had threatened a lawsuit, and his pitch to the Asian community to elect him centered on the promise to change the election process.

"Rowan was the vote against you becoming chief, right?" Ben said.

"He was."

Ben remembered it now. Paul Rowan had been interviewed by the *Rancho Santa Elena World News* after the vote making Hernandez chief, angrily calling it affirmative action bull crap, or something along those lines. Ben remembered the "bull crap," thought it was funny at the time. The biggest assholes, Ben had often noticed, had a sensitivity to four-letter words. There wasn't necessarily a correlation between politeness and kindness.

"I ran a check on Ian Rowan yesterday," Ben said. "Came up clean. But get this, I followed him up to East Anaheim yesterday. He stopped at a meth house in Vatos Locos territory and then disappeared. That house burned down last night."

Hernandez looked at him, his glasses on the edge of his nose like a schoolmarm. "Ian's *not* clean. I arrested him. When he was sixteen."

"On what?"

"Animal cruelty," Hernandez said. "He doused a cat with gasoline and lit it on fire."

Ben thought about Natasha's fear the other night. Animal cruelty, the gateway crime to murder.

"He pled, spent a little time in juvie, then probation and mandatory therapy. Dad sent him off to some kind of Outward Bound program when probation was up. Then he was back in school middle of his junior year."

"Well, he's an angel as far as the state's concerned."

"Meth house?"

"Yeah, and look at this." Ben found the case file, pulled out the picture of the flag from the meth house last night.

The lieutenant studied the picture, handed it back to Ben, and went quiet again, like he was going deep into something, until sunlight streamed through the dirty windows and the day-shift uniforms were putting creamer in their coffees for the long day ahead. When it was time for morning meeting, all the detectives already sitting around the table in the conference room, shooting the shit, Hernandez pulled Ben aside.

"I'm making this a priority," he said to Ben. "But keep the councilman out of it in the meeting. This is between us for now, all right?"

"All right," Ben said. "But I'm going to want an explanation."

It wasn't like Hernandez to withhold information, especially from his own cops.

Hernandez nodded. "I figured you would."

Then the lieutenant burst into the conference room, all business, calling out the case numbers of the strawberry picker attack and the slaughtered dog, letting everyone know what was what.

———

Vince Sessions started bitching immediately about his cocaine-trafficking case losing top billing: "Sir, we're close on the Jenkins case. Got a line on a shipment coming through San Ysidro. We've been working this for months."

Theirs was the big case, the hot one the department had gone full-court press on. A broken cocaine syndicate was a good news story. *Miami Vice* had made coke dealing sexy, a bust made the department look tough—and all of it gave Santa Elena a certain swagger: Where there was coke, there was money. A win–win on the PR front.

"I want *all* resources on this," Hernandez said, "until we have an arrest."

All of them—Carolina, Marco, Vince—were sitting around the table, leafing through the files Ben and Hernandez had been up all night assembling. Vince glanced at Marco, full disdain flashing across his face. All resources were admittedly not much. Santa Elena was still a small-town police department, just starting to deal with big-town problems.

"With all due respect, this is stupid shit," Sessions said, a you-called-me-in-on-a-Saturday-for-this look on his face. "A dog? Red threads? A couple of beaten-up illegals? Are we serious?"

"Detective," Hernandez said, his voice uncharacteristically raised. "I don't give a damn if half of Santa Elena is snorting coke off their glass coffee tables tonight. Everyone in this room is on this case until we get an arrest. You take exception to that, I'll be happy to meet you in my office to discuss your future with this department."

Vince—well, everyone in the room—stared at the lieutenant, and the lieutenant gave it right back, his glasses on the tip of his nose, his eyes hardened to a fighter's stare.

"Detective Wade," Hernandez said, his voice finding its keel again. "Please walk them through the evidence."

And Ben did—the Huntington Beach murder of Walter Brennan, the real estate dude, the dead dog, the two notes on the bodies, on Brennan's and on the dog's, the boots, the red shoelaces, socks made into weapons. He left the meth house out for

now, wasn't sure how to deal with that without mentioning the
Rowan kid. All the while the lieutenant had his chin pressed
against his chest, his eyes cast down at the floor as though the
tile had something illuminating to share with him.

"The HB DB had broken ribs, fractured skull. Two of the victims last night had broken ribs. Boot prints in the dirt—both at
the site of the attack last night, and all the way back across the
field where they parked their cars."

"Rocks?" Marco said. "Bricks in the socks."

"Possible," Ben said. "Mostly contusions, though. Not a lot
of cuts."

"Something round then," Carolina said. "A baseball?"

Sessions rolled his eyes and tapped his pen against the table.
"I'll start interviewing Little Leaguers then."

Hernandez pressed his chin against his chest, as though trying to maintain his composure.

"I don't get how the dog fits," Marco said.

"They say they eat 'em," Vince said. "The Vietnamese."

Mrs. Connolly's face floated up into Ben's memory, the look
in her eyes like she'd believe a Vietnamese killed JFK if someone had said so. Truth is, he'd heard this before, last year when
a shih tzu disappeared from a couple's backyard. *Maybe it's the
Orientals,* the older woman had said to him. He showed her the
coyote tracks in the dirt near a hole in her fence, but she looked
doubtful. Why was it easier to believe that people eat dogs
rather than the simple fact of a hungry coyote?

"Jesus," Carolina said. "Vince, you're a—"

"It's terrorism," Hernandez said. "The dog and last night."

Everyone glanced up at him.

"Terrorism," Hernandez said, looking at Vince, "perpetrated
by people who believe that the Vietnamese eat dogs."

"Or by people who want you to believe that," Ben said.

"Who want you to believe that," Hernandez said, nodding at
Ben. "Right."

After morning meeting, Hernandez called Ben into his office. Inside, the lieutenant closed the blinds to his floor-to-ceiling windows, cutting off the view from the detectives' floor. The lieutenant leaned back in his chair and looked out the window at the brand-new city hall, modernist-lite architecture, curved glass façade across a courtyard where a soybean grove used to be.

"Rudy Boysen," Hernandez said. "You heard of him?"

Ben shook his head.

"First parks superintendent for the city of Anaheim. The man who created the hybrid boysenberry."

"Knott's Berry Farm." It was an amusement park now, a place that put on fake high-noon shoot-outs.

Hernandez nodded. "When I was a kid, my father drove us over to Pearson Park. Wanted to have a picnic outside with his family. It's got this nice lake."

"Yeah. I know it."

"Well, back then," he said, "if you were Mexican you couldn't get near that lake. Mr. Boysen had a patch of grass cordoned off for the Mexicans clear on the other side of the park. Ticked my father off—and mi padre had a temper. He was born here. He wasn't some 'wetback' carrying everything he owned on his back out of Tijuana. So he dragged us over—my mom protesting the whole way, first time I ever heard them argue—and set our blanket down right there on the edge of the water. I remember there were big orange fish in the water, koi, like huge goldfish. I was six or seven, probably, and I got down on my knees and watched them swim around the lily pads. I was about to stick my hand in the water, thought I could catch one of them, when two police officers showed up. One of the officers said something, my dad raised his voice, and then I heard a thud. When I turned around my dad was crumpled on the ground, a cop standing over him with a billy club, my mom on her knees next to him, crying. They cuffed and hauled my father away. Didn't let him out until the next morning. A cut above the left eye, a fat lip, probably a bruised rib or two."

"I'll never eat a boysenberry again," Ben said.

"They're good on ice cream," Hernandez said. He was quiet a moment. "The worst thing about those cops beating my dad," the lieutenant went on, "is that back then, when I was that seven-year-old, I blamed my father. I remember thinking he should have kept his mouth shut."

Ben thought about that a moment. "It must have scared the shit out of you, having your dad hauled away like that." A little girl's face flashed in Ben's mind, a girl up in North Hollywood, her face behind the bars of her home's front door when he hauled her dad away. She was probably frightened, but what he remembered seeing was hatred in her eyes.

"Later," Hernandez said, "when I was older, it pissed me off I ever felt that way, that I had ever blamed my father."

"That why you became a cop?"

"Maybe," Hernandez said, looking at him like he had more things to say about that. "You know there're still streets and parks up there in Anaheim, in Orange named after KKK members? Starbuck, Byerrum, Powell. Tidy streets with nice little houses. You'd never know, if you didn't know."

Ben hadn't known. He knew the KKK had had a presence in Orange County, sure. But those streets were just names to him, names of old men long dead.

"That's why the abuela didn't want to speak in front of you," Hernandez said.

Ben nodded. He got it, but he still felt that impulse to defend himself, to say *Not all white people are KKK*. Since the deal with the dog, though, Ben's eyes had been opened a little bit wider. He'd started noticing things—the SOUTH VIET GOOKS! penned on the Blow Hole Café's bathroom wall, BEANERS SUCK spray-painted in a drainage ditch running next to El Rancho Road. These little everyday things suddenly becoming a part of his world and making him think.

"You were in there talking to her for a long time," Ben said.

Hernandez frowned in acknowledgment. "She was telling me things, things that have been happening lately." He paused and looked out the window. "She said they thought things would get better, when I became chief."

"They have to report things, Lieutenant. Otherwise, what're we supposed to do?"

Hernandez glanced at him. "I was here last night. That's how I knew about the call. Was looking through old reports. When the dog report came through, I thought I'd poke around. I found at least fifteen incidents in the last six months—dog shit burned on a doorstep, Korean woman screamed at in Ralph's, swastika spray-painted on a car . . ." He twirled his hand in the air, a frustrated *et cetera*. "Not one of them was followed up on, except for the car."

"Because the insurance company needed the report."

Hernandez nodded. "The councilman, Mr. Rowan, chairs the fair housing commission."

"He's also into real estate, right?"

"He is," the lieutenant said. "Orion Brokerage."

"He doesn't strike me as a real fair kind of guy."

Hernandez wrote something down on a notepad. "He's got the mayor's ear, too."

Right. Keep Councilman Rowan out of it for now.

"You say this Mr. Brennan, the DB up in Huntington Beach, was a real estate broker?"

"According to the detective working the case."

They were both quiet a moment, adding things up in their heads.

"Don't step on any toes, but you might stick your nose into real estate," Hernandez said. "I'll have Carolina do surveillance on the Rowan house." Hernandez wrote something down on a pad of paper and circled it. "A whole lot of dots—"

"And no lines," Ben said, nodding. "Yet."

———

After his closed-door meeting with Hernandez, Ben cruised over to Comet Street. He trusted Carolina, but he wanted to check something out on his own first. When Ben got there, Ian Rowan was standing in the bed of the Power Wagon, tossing crushed Colt 45 cans into a trash bag. Ben parked the cruiser a couple of doors down and watched him. Ian was wearing khaki pants, a long-sleeved shirt buttoned all the way to the top, the thick-soled, black steel-toed boots, white laces but not crossed over like normal, laced like ladder rungs. Outside of the boots, Ian Rowan looked like a clean-cut middle-class kid. The garage door was open, though, and Ben wanted a look.

"Good party last night, huh?" Ben said, when he got to the sidewalk.

Ian glanced up at him, a flash of something—anger, fear, both maybe—lighting his face briefly. He recovered quickly, though, tied off the bag, hopped out of the bed of the truck, and started walking toward the trash cans on the side of the house. "You wanna see my ID?"

It was a cold morning. An Oldsmobile Cutlass was idling in the driveway. The Power Wagon was idling, too. The V8 engine rumbling, the huge tires caked in mud, the jacked-up suspension, the flood lamps welded to a roll bar above the bed—a big-dick truck if there ever was one. When Ian set the trash bag down, Ben noticed the tattoo on his wrist, where the shirt had pulled up: the number 1488.

"Nah, I know your birthday already," Ben said. "November 7, 1963."

"You know the hour, too?" Ian crossed in front of him on the driveway and closed the garage door.

Ben smiled. "I can find out."

Councilman Paul Rowan and a teenage boy came out of the house then. Ben watched the councilman, dressed in a double-breasted suit and tie, the kind David Letterman might wear on his show. The kid, Ian's brother, Ben guessed, was wearing an Angels baseball cap and carrying a first baseman's glove. He glanced at Ben, a bruise blooming on his right cheek, then dropped his head and slipped into the passenger seat of the Olds. Ben remembered Natasha's report on Brennan: *Suspect may have facial contusions from a punch*. It was the kid from yesterday morning, the one that didn't get in Ian's truck. The councilman made a beeline for Ben and Ian.

"Detective Wade," the man said, holding out his hand for a shake.

"Councilman," Ben said, taking his hand. "Never really met, as far as I remember." Ben didn't like being known by people he didn't know.

"I keep an eye on things," the councilman said. "It's my job. And you've been in the news."

Ben nodded. The Coach Lewis Wakeland abuse case. Some over at city hall were pissed about the way Ben exposed Wakeland, about the bad press for the city, the way it blew up the big-time high school swim program. Ben's blood burned for a minute with the reference, but he kept it cool; he was getting used to his troubled past being common knowledge now.

"What can I do for you?" the councilman asked.

"Had a little incident with one of your neighbors' dogs the other day."

The kid in the car didn't turn around, never glanced back at them. In Ben's experience, a cop on-site usually got a kid's attention.

"Just canvassing the neighborhood again. See if anyone knows anything."

"No," the councilman said. "Don't know anything about it."

"Yeah, the dog was poisoned, someone slit its throat. Amazing what people'll do, huh?"

"Imagine you know as well as anyone," the councilman said. "Excuse us. I need to get my son to baseball practice, and I have a ten-thirty appointment."

"Of course," Ben said. "Councilman? One more thing, if you don't mind."

The man paused while opening the door to the Oldsmobile.

"There was an attack on a camp of migrant workers last night. Out by the air base."

"I'm sorry to hear it," the councilman said.

Most people would ask *What happened?* or *Is everyone okay?* Natural human curiosity—and concern.

"Looks like the perps four-wheeled over there." Ben spun around and looked at the truck. "You know, maybe in something like this. I mean, I imagine that thing can go anywhere, right?"

"It does all right," Ian said, climbing into the cab of the truck now.

"Can haul a lot in the bed there, too, huh?"

"Detective," the councilman said, "I trust your colleagues in the police department will do all they can to catch the people who did it."

"I have no doubt," Ben said. "Protect and serve."

"If I can be of any help," the councilman said, slipping into his car, "please just let me know."

Ben got in his cruiser and waited for them to pull out. Then he followed the councilman's car and Ian's out of California Homes a mile down El Rancho Road, just to let them sweat it out a bit. The councilman turned in to the high school and Ben followed Ian another half mile, the Power Wagon's tires shedding clumps of dried mud until the kid pulled into the line at Checkered Flag car wash. At the next light, Ben spun a U-turn, circling back around to Comet Street. He parked a couple of doors down, walked up to the garbage cans, untied the trash bag, and grabbed two of the crushed forty-ouncers. Back in the cruiser, he slipped them into an evidence bag. On the way back to the station, Ben saw the Power Wagon cruising southbound on El Rancho, sparkling as though just driven off the showroom lot.

Chapter Ten

The Orange County Recorder's Office was in the hall of records in downtown Orange, just off the 22 freeway. Ben wanted to take a look at some real estate records. Councilman Rowan had a real estate company, and so had Walter Brennan, the man murdered in Huntington Beach. Two dots. Maybe the real estate records could offer Ben a line to connect them.

He drove out of the south county master-planned neatness of Santa Elena into the jumble of cement and warehouses, early-century bungalows, and industrial rust of north county. Santa Elena didn't allow billboards, phone lines were below-ground, nothing but the uninterrupted Southern California sky down there. Here in Orange the basin felt more like LA, cemeteries of dead industry rusting on the banks of cement drainage ditches, midcentury shopping centers with miles of cracked cement parking lots, the sky spiked with telephone poles and peeling billboards. And people on the street—not joggers or bicyclists in their neon getups, but men selling oranges, elderly sitting in wheelchairs on corners watching the traffic burn by, young men in their gang-banging chinos and white tanks guarding the front of liquor stores.

Ben's mother had grown up here, back in the 1930s and early 1940s, when the town had been populated by Dust Bowl Okies and middle-class whites working at the Goodyear factory and Trulite Glass and Aluminum—companies long since dead or moved. He remembered his grandparents' house, a Craftsman bungalow his grandfather had ordered through Sears and Roebuck for twenty-one hundred dollars and built himself. Ben had loved the house—the small backyard with the hammock, the doves that cooed in the fronds of the palm tree swaying above the roof—but mostly he had loved the neighborhood, kids outside riding bikes, kids playing tag. Growing up out on the ranch had been a lonely life, despite his love for the horses, for the land. Then, suddenly, his grandparents sold the house and moved to Ashland, Oregon—"to God's country," as his grandfather put it, whatever that meant.

Seven years ago, early 1980, when Ben and Rachel were looking to move back to Orange County, they'd driven by the old house, Ben moved by a nostalgia for the place. The house still stood, but the south side of the porch had sunk, and the windows were welded with metal bars. The neighborhood, a childhood idyll as he remembered it, was a world of cracked cement, pocked with rusting cars and forty-ouncers in the gutters. No way they were going to raise Emma where people cared so little they left beer bottles in the street.

But there was life on the street here. Idling at a stoplight, Ben watched families picnicking in El Modena Park. A man carrying a guitarrón crossed the street, the instrument slung over his shoulder. A kid walked up and down the line of cars, selling Mexican candies.

"Una De la Rosa, veinticinco centavos," the kid said.

Ben fished a couple of quarters out of his pocket. "Two, por favor," he said, handing the kid the change.

Ben popped the marzipan in his mouth. Damn good candy.

Hernandez had made a couple of calls, and got a clerk to meet Ben at the recorder's office to let him in.

"What's so important you need sales records on a Saturday?" the clerk asked, keying open the front door. Inside, the room smelled like a moldy cardboard box.

"Official business," Ben said.

The clerk sighed and led Ben back into a darkened warehouse with at least ten thirty-foot-long rows of deed books filed on metal shelves. The clerk switched on the fluorescent lights. Check that, at least ten more shelves appeared out of the darkness.

"Organized by name?" Ben said.

"More or less chronological. Eighteen eighty-nine is down at the south end, row number one. Nineteen eighty-seven is north end, last row."

"So you gotta know the date?"

The clerk sighed again, as though this interaction were killing him.

"There are also grantor/grantee indexes," he said, pointing to a couple of tables with built-in drawers. "Alphabetical, as I'm sure you've guessed."

"One more thing," Ben said. "Can you find me ownership for 1576 Valencia Street, Anaheim?"

The clerk sighed and walked away.

Ben found the grantee index for A–C, hauled it out of its drawer, and dropped its dusty binder onto the table. He ran his finger down the list until he found Brennan, Walter. There were at least three dozen Brennan, Walters. Brennan, Walter A., Brennan, Walter F., Brennan, Walter H., Brennan, Walter J.— *Description of Land: Single Family Dwelling. Location: Huntington Beach. Volume: AF 324, pg. 597.*

Took him five minutes to find it and he stood there in the aisle, flipping the pages to 597: *30C Pacific Ave.* That was it, that was the house on the beach. The grantor a Mr. Charles Lind, sold in '83. But so what? That didn't tell him shit, really. Ben remembered Natasha saying to him that Vanek said Brennan was involved in the redevelopment of downtown Huntington Beach.

He went back to the grantee book, ran his fingers down the list of Brennan, Walters, looking for another Huntington Beach listing. Nothing. He thumbed back two pages and found the beginning of the Brennan section, looking for Huntington Beach again. He found two entries, both listed as commercial. The grantee was listed as Brennan Holdings. He ran his eyes down the *Grantee* column and I'll-be-damned, a whole page of Brennan Holdings. Most properties were listed in Westminster, a smattering in Garden Grove, and then, on the next page, he found six properties in Rancho Santa Elena, Brennan Holdings the grantee.

"Winston Heimel," the clerk yelled from across the room. "The owner of the Anaheim address."

Ben wrote it down, "*Ei* and an *e*?"

"You can spell."

After checking the Brennan properties, Ben searched for Orion, Paul Rowan's real estate firm. More than two dozen properties were listed under Orion Brokerage, almost all of them in Rancho Santa Elena. *Pays to be a councilman running Unfair Housing,* Ben thought.

"I'm going to need to make some copies," Ben yelled down to the office.

The clerk was a good twenty yards away, but Ben swore he heard a sigh.

———

Two dudes with shaved heads stood outside Iron Eagle Army/Navy Surplus, smoking cigs. One had a lightning-bolt ss tatted on his neck. The other, H A T E inked into the knuckles on his right hand. Now that he knew what the tats were, Jacob was amazed that they didn't try to hide them. It was like tattooing a big Fuck You to the world. Ian nodded to the dudes and they lifted their chins in response.

Inside the store there were dummies dressed in army clothes, one of them rocking a gas mask. There were rows of camouflage jackets and camo hats and a shelf of dummy heads wearing camo earmuff hats.

"Be right back," Ian said. "Check the place out."

Ian had picked him up at the high school, opened the side door to the truck, and said, "Let's go shopping." A half-hour drive later, they were here, near the surf breaks in Huntington Beach.

Jacob cruised the row of officer hats, their gold-and-black insignias, the eagles and the stars, the arrows and crossed rifles. Inside a locked display case lay rows of Rambo knives and butterfly switchblades and a kick-ass inlaid sword. A rack of dog-tag chains dangling used M16 shells sat on top of the case, and behind the case, stapled to the wall, hung a DON'T TREAD ON ME flag, the coiled snake reared to strike. He loved the place immediately, the bucket of defused hand grenades, the MREs, the old walkie-talkies and World War II radios, the hard hats and the canteens. It smelled like his father's war box—of machine and weapon, of gunpowder and gasoline.

"Mom's all right," he heard Ian say, "if we can keep her on her meds."

Ian cocked his head and looked at the ground. Jacob had never seen that look on Ian's face before, like something had needled him in the kidneys.

"Hear you, mate. That's tough." The man, his head shaved and shined like a bowling ball, was standing behind the display case, in the corner near the cash register and a sign with the barrel of a six-shooter pointed at the viewer. GO AHEAD, it read, MAKE MY DAY.

"My man here," Ian said, turning toward Jacob, "needs some braces, some boots."

The big dude retreated to the back room, where Jacob could see him sorting through a box.

"Take that sweatshirt off," Ian said.

He did and laid it on a bench next to the boot rack. The man behind the counter came out with black suspenders. Ian took off his flight jacket and showed Jacob how to put them on. Crossover in the back, tight along the shoulders, clipped right next to the belt loops.

"Now roll up those jeans."

He did, his stupid white legs with only wisps of hair.

Ian threw knee-high socks at his chest, like the ones they'd slipped billiard balls into last night. And then the man behind the counter came out with a pair of black boots, mid-calf-high, shining like they'd just been blackened. They were radical looking, leather and thick soles, stitched with thread that looked like yellow staples.

"Put them on."

And he did, the leather like armor around his calves and feet. He could feel something hard at the toe and he pressed his finger against it.

"Steel," the bald dude said, smiling.

"No one'll step on your toes again."

"And if they do," the bald dude said, "you can kick their balls into their stomach."

Jacob stood up, felt the inches the shoes gave him, felt his shoulders and rib cage expanding, his whole body growing rigid as though the steel had seeped into his veins and hardened his muscles.

"Gonna show you something," Ian said, the bald guy handing Ian a roll of red laces. "These because you spilled blood last night." Ian dropped to his knees then and started untying the black laces from Jacob's boots. Jacob could feel Ian's hand on his ankle, the other hand pulling the laces through the eyes. It felt weird, being treated like this. Then Ian started threading the new laces, from the bottom up. "You don't cross them over.

You straight-lace them. Like a ladder." And he ran his hands up Jacob's ankle and calf, did the same for the next boot, and then tied the laces so tight that Jacob's feet felt strangled.

"Because you spilled blood," Ian said, standing now, "but also for blood and soil—your blood, spilled to defend the white race and the soil on which it lives, if necessary."

"Banger Jones," the bald dude introduced himself, throwing his hand out for a shake. "Blood and soil." Banger squeezing Jacob's hand. "Blood and honor."

Jacob kept thinking, *Remember this. This is important.*

"Step outside," Ian said, "and let me settle up."

Jacob did. He walked out into the California sun, the desert light flecked with Pacific salt. The dudes were still outside, standing like sentinels of the surplus castle. The taller one blew smoke and took him in.

"Brother," he said, holding out his hand and nodding.

And Jacob clasped it, skin against skin.

———

Three of the seven victims in the strawberry pickers attack had fractured skulls.

Dr. Sinan Akpinar, the Hoag Hospital emergency radiologist, was pointing the tip of a ballpoint pen at the three X-ray shadow graphs clipped to the backlight. "Two of the fractures were internal"—he ran the pen along the round shadow on one skull and then the other—"with only topical contusions."

Yes, Natasha could tell from the X-ray, a round gray area where the radiating fractures split the skull like an eggshell.

"But this one," the doctor said, again pointing the pen at the third image, "was a compound fracture." The same eggshell fracturing, but a bright white snag of bone breaking open the skin. It was Santiago's skull.

Natasha had been up much of the night, sitting at her desk in the county morgue, the evidence from Brennan's murder laid out in front of her—the thread, the autopsy report, the button pulled from the pajamas, a few pieces of an unfinished puzzle. This morning, she had called down to Hoag Hospital, requested a visit with the emergency radiologist, and now here she was, staring at the inside of skulls.

"You think different weapons?"

"Not necessarily," the doctor said. "The internal damage is similar." He used the pen to circle each fracture again.

"What's the radius on the fractures?" she said.

"Hmm . . ." he said. "This is scaled at a hundred twenty percent." He pulled up an X-ray marker and measured each. "Five and a half, six centimeters."

"So fifty to sixty millimeters," she said, recalling her measurements from Brennan's autopsy.

"Approximately."

"So same weapon then," she said. The contusions looked like a match to Brennan's shattered skull. The crushed bone, but no abrasions, no cuts. Except for Santiago's wound. "Why the compound fracture here and not on the others?"

"Force," the doctor said.

"And repetition," she said, nodding. She pointed to Santiago's skull. The image was darker than the others, the contusion deeper.

"Yes, likely," the doctor said. "Bone perforated the scalp. Surgeons had to graft the skin."

"Graft?"

"Part of the scalp was missing," the doctor said. "I'm shocked he came in here conscious. He took one hell of a beating."

When she left radiology, she asked at the info desk for Santiago's room number, bought a bouquet of flowers in the gift shop, and rode the elevator to the third floor. He was asleep when she got there, his head bandaged, the heart monitor beeping. She tiptoed into the room and left the vase of flowers on the nightstand, blooming sunflowers and yellow lilies set against the drab white wall.

"Dr. Betencourt speaks highly of you," Vanek said on the line. "And I respect her opinion."

Ben had called Vanek as soon as he found out about the Brennan real estate properties in Rancho Santa Elena. He expected to leave a message, but Vanek had picked up before the second ring; the detective was putting in the hours, too.

"Yeah," Ben said, "I think she's pretty all right herself." Most likely Vanek's interest in Natasha was purely professional. She was good at her job, after all. But Ben had decided he might as well establish some parameters immediately.

"Some of those addresses are in Little Saigon," Vanek said now, shifting down to business. "Let's go take a look."

Ben knew a lot of refugees had settled in the area, but he was surprised at how big Little Saigon was. Ben met Vanek on Bolsa Avenue in the parking lot of a huge grocery store, the name of the store spelled out in bright red letters. Across Bolsa was a large pagoda, the curved green-tiled rooftop, the carved wood symbols, like a Vietnamese Arc de Triomphe.

"I remember you now," Vanek said when they got out of their cars and shook hands. "We worked the Crenshaw Four killings in Inglewood before you got transferred north."

Vanek was in his early forties, but he dressed like a man twenty years older. A sort of dapper, verging on dandy, look—navy-blue suit, art deco tie with tie bar, his shoes shined, his hair pomaded.

"That was nearly fifteen years ago," Ben said. "I got the soft detail up in the Northeast after that." And no shit he believed it, too. The South Central crack wars were medieval in their violence. Made North Hollywood look like kindergarten.

"None of it was soft," Vanek said.

"What brought you down to paradise?" Ben said.

Vanek glanced at Ben, as if to size him up. "Daryl Gates," he said. "Among other things. The Pacoima raid kind of finished me off. I wasn't real comfortable with cops in tanks, you know?"

Ben had already left the LAPD by 1985, but he'd watched Gates, the chief of police, swagger his way through a television press conference announcing the new weapon to fight "The War on Drugs," the V-100 tank with its fourteen-foot-long battering ram on display behind him. The Pacoima raid, one of the first in which LAPD SWAT battered its way through the front wall of a house, yielded two women, three children, and less than a tenth of a gram of cocaine. So little, the DA wouldn't prosecute. Still, there was anecdotal evidence that the battering ram had helped clean up some hardcore rock streets, but, yeah, Ben had to admit, it was a bit disconcerting to see a municipality wield a weapon of war against its own citizens, dealers or not.

"Shall we?" Vanek said, changing the subject. He held out his hand and they walked across the parking lot.

Westminster was the city directly east of Huntington Beach and it felt like a completely different world. The green-tiled rooftops of the strip mall shopping centers, the flower markets lighting up the street, the bolts of colorful fabrics hanging in open storefronts, people picking through boxes of fruit that spilled onto the sidewalk. The shrines to Buddha with burning incense. As in the Mexican neighborhoods of Orange and Anaheim, things in this part of Westminster tumbled out into the street, as though life couldn't be contained inside the four walls of a strip mall box. Santa Elena had zoning laws against that kind of disorder. Tantamount to treason if the sidewalks were blocked down there.

They stepped into a sort of deli—hot foods steaming in stainless-steel bins, rows of plastic-wrapped foods on refrigerated shelves, colorful small cake-like things. In the corner of the front window was a small sign, BRENNAN HOLDINGS, taped to the glass.

Vanek greeted the woman behind the counter in Vietnamese. He picked up a pair of cheap sandals that were piled in a bin, bought them, and then flashed his badge, smiling. She bowed and smiled back and they spoke for a moment, basic pleasantries, as far as Ben could tell. Ben guessed Vanek was a vet, had learned a little of the language when he was over there.

"You lease the space?" Vanek said now, in English. "Sorry, that's all the phrases I know."

They both laughed. "It's very good," the woman said in English. "You know many words."

Vanek pointed to the little sign in the window. "Brennan Holdings. Is Walter Brennan the owner of the building?"

She nodded.

"Is he a good landlord?" Ben asked.

She glanced down at the linoleum floor. "I don't want to speak ill of the dead."

So the word had spread.

She looked at Vanek. "I've dropped five bowls of soup in the last two days."

Vanek nodded. "Thank you." Then he said something in Vietnamese, bowed his head, and they were out the door.

"I did a couple of tours," Vanek said when they were out on the sidewalk, as though he had read Ben's mind. "Down in Truong Lam."

Ben nodded. "My respect to you."

"You didn't serve?" Vanek said.

"No." Ben felt that pang of guilt. "What was that about? The dropping-the-bowls thing?"

"The Vietnamese believe in ghosts," he said. "Literally. Especially if it's a violent death."

"She thinks the ghost of Brennan is knocking the bowls out of her hands?"

Vanek nodded. "Something like that. Murders sort of haunt us all, don't they?"

Couldn't argue with that.

"House shoes?" Ben said, nodding at the slippers dangling from Vanek's hand.

"Brennan was wearing this type of slipper when he was killed."

The next five addresses checked out, little BRENNAN HOLD-INGS signs in the window. At the sixth, a fish market, the owner didn't seem to be too concerned with ghosts.

"He charges too much," the man said, scaling what looked like a catfish, the little translucent circles piling up on the cutting board. "Raises rent whenever he wants to. Doesn't fix things when broken." He pointed with the scaling knife at a window-unit air conditioner that apparently didn't work. "We're unlucky. There are no spaces, so we rent from him."

He threw the scaled fish aside, with some anger, it seemed to Ben, and started on the next one.

"Let Mr. Brennan go down south," the man said. "He can take the rich people with him, the ones who don't want to be up here with us."

Vanek shot Ben a quick glance. Yeah, he caught that, too.

"We have Mr. Jao." The man's voice filled with pride now. "He's going to open the Asian Garden." He pointed the knife in the general direction of west. "He'll buy up Brennan's properties. He'll be fair."

"Sir," Vanek said. "You said Mr. Brennan is taking people with him down south, in Santa Elena?"

"He buys properties down there," the man said. "All over south county. Then he tries to get the richest shop owners to lease from him. Overcharges, of course, but some people don't care." He whacked the tail off the fish. "Not Mr. Jao, though. He stays here."

Vanek and Ben stepped into a sandwich shop, bought a couple of banh mi, and settled outside on a bench. Ben didn't know if it was just that he was starving, but it was a damn good sandwich—the baguette, the sweet pork, and the pickled vegetables.

"Brennan's got six properties in Santa Elena," Ben said. "Pretty new ones, just in the last three or so years."

"Whoever murdered Brennan stole some files from his home office," Vanek said.

"Paperwork on his south county properties?"

"A lot of money to make down there in Santa Elena, all that new development."

They were quiet a moment.

"Natasha mentioned something about this posse something or other," Ben said.

"Posse comitatus. Grab your sandwich and follow me."

They settled into Vanek's unmarked. He fired up the engine, slipped a cassette tape into the player, and started rewinding it. Ben tore back into his sandwich.

"I've been doing a little research on this," Vanek said. "Bernhardt Klassen. You heard of him?"

"No," Ben said.

"Mr. Klassen is the founder of this pseudo-religious movement called The World Church of the Creator. He believes Christianity is something the Jews created to make whites weak." He lifted an eyebrow at that. "I won't insult your intelligence to lay it all out for you, but he believes there needs to be a race war, whites against people of color, to reclaim the planet."

Vanek went on about ZOG, the Zionist Occupied Government. Ben couldn't believe what he was hearing. A crazy theory about the federal government run by a cabal of Jews bent on taking over the world and killing off white people in the process. Vanek told him about William Pierce and the National Alliance, about Pierce's "novel" (Vanek doing air quotes with his fingers), *The Turner Diaries*, written under the pseudonym Andrew Macdonald. Told him about Richard Girnt Butler and the Christian Identity, another supremacist movement up in Eastern Washington.

"These guys Christian or not?" Ben said.

"Not the type that actually read the Bible. But they got a lot of theories to justify their prejudice. The problem with these guys is that they look like stand-up people," Vanek said. "Butler started a Presbyterian church, Pierce was a physics professor, and Ben . . . Bernhardt was a Florida state representative, invented the wall-mounted electric can opener."

The tape stopped rewinding.

"And then there's this gentleman," Vanek said. He pressed the button and a staccato voice, full of self-righteous anger, started spitting what sounded like crazy shit.

"There's a bunch of empty skulls in Washington, DC. We're going to get them filled up or cracked open—one or the other real soon. These government officials are going to get back to the Constitution of the United States or they're gonna hang by the neck until they're dead— make examples of them who won't. These judges, these government officials who are tearing the Constitution apart, will be brought down, judgment upon them, by the law of posse comitatus. The law is that you citizens—a posse of good American men—will hang an official who violates the law and the Constitution. Take him to the town square at noon and hang him by the neck. Let the body dangle until sundown as an example to those other government officials who are supposed to be servants to you that they will abide by the Constitution or suffer the death of traitors."

Vanek pressed STOP on the cassette.

"This is from 1982, broadcast on local radio out of Nebraska and spread around much of the Midwest. A fellow by the name of Richard Potter Wales. *Reverend*, as he likes to be called."

"Nineteen eighty-two?"

"Right," Vanek said. "Not '62."

"So this guy threatens congressmen with lynching," Ben said, "if they violate the Constitution?"

"It's worse. This Mr. Wales believes—or trades in the snake

oil—that whites are the descendants of Abel and the Jews are the descendants of Cain. You know, so whites are close to God and Jews come from the seed of evil, idiocy like that. He holds with the ZOG theory, the conspiracy of Jews running the government, trying to destroy Anglo blood. You can probably guess how this 'movement' feels about blacks, Hispanics—"

"Asians."

Vanek nodded. "When he gave this speech, he was speaking to midwestern whites who had their farms foreclosed on, blamed the Federal Reserve."

Ben was jotting down notes on his legal pad, filling it up as fast as he could.

"A few months later a farmer, this guy named Ross Morrison, who was about to be arrested for tax evasion, killed the federal agents trying to arrest him. He escaped, holed up with a Wales sympathizer down in Kansas. Killed an Osage County sheriff down there when the law caught up with them. Agents went all-in then, shot the place up. Killed Ross and his hosts, including a teenage girl who just happened to be in the house."

"Jesus," Ben said.

"Wales ran with that, screamed all over the radio that Morrison was killed because he was invoking posse comitatus, his right to fight oppressive tax laws that were funding the ZOG in DC. Says Morrison was killed fighting against an unjust banking system. A freedom fighter and all that."

"A lot of sympathetic farmers heard that, I guess?"

Vanek nodded. "And the movement got their first martyr." The detective ejected the cassette, slipped it into a case, and placed it in the center console.

"So Wales starts his own little group: Posse Comitatus," Vanek said. "Declares the federal government illegitimate. Thinks there's no higher authority than the county sheriff. Believes, too, if the sheriff doesn't carry out the will of the people, the Posse has the right to hang him as an example."

"Where'd you get this stuff?" Ben asked.

"Went to school with a federal agent in Alcohol, Tobacco, and Firearms," Vanek said. "They've been keeping an eye on them. Apparently, these gentlemen have some sort of message board system on the internets where they all can talk to each other—sort of like a members-only computer party. Guys from Idaho and Pennsylvania can have direct contact with guys in California."

Ben knew vaguely about the internets, thought they were mostly a government thing, but he had no clue how message boards could be set up for guys from all over the country to talk to one another.

"So this guy is based out of Nebraska?"

"No. He's a Californian. Been sort of syndicating his radio program to sympathetic outlets. Years ago, he was a mechanical engineer out of Long Beach," Vanek said. "Left, complaining about the 'mongrelization' of Southern California, and got a place up in Mariposa, in the foothills of the Sierra Nevada. That's still his listed address, but apparently it's sitting vacant. No one's seen him there for a couple years, not since after the Ross incident."

"Someone's sheltering him then."

"My guess, too," Vanek said.

They were quiet a moment, their minds whirring separately.

"The Vietnamese are building something here," Vanek said, nodding out toward the shopping center, "and a lot of white folks don't like it."

"Didn't seem to bother Brennan," Ben said.

"Predatory opportunism doesn't equal tolerance, now, does it?"

Good point.

"What would a fourteen eighty-eight tattoo stand for?"

"Not sure about that fourteen," Vanek said. "But eighty-eight is Heil Hitler." Vanek explained about the numbers and the alphabet, a secret code so the supremacists could signal one another without announcing it to the public. "Twenty-eight, for instance, means blood and honor. Means they're willing to die or spill blood to keep the country 'pure.'"

"This kid with the fourteen eighty-eight tat, name's Ian Rowan," Ben said. "He's the son of a Santa Elena councilman, Paul Rowan. The councilman chairs fair housing. Owns a real estate company. I followed Ian up to Anaheim to a meth house yesterday. Last night that house burned down." Ben pulled the picture of the flag he saw at the house out of his case file and handed it to Vanek. "This was hanging on the wall."

"Wolfsangel," Vanek said, pointing to the black slash through the cross. "Symbol of the Second Panzer Division Das Reich. They committed a number of massacres in the war. The worst was in 1944." He handed back the picture. "They slaughtered something like six hundred and fifty civilians in the French town Oradour-sur-Glane."

"Jesus."

"Any idea if Brennan was leasing to Asians in Santa Elena?" Vanek asked.

Ben said he wasn't sure. He would have to get back down to Santa Elena to check out the addresses.

"These folks have this idea about race traitors," Vanek said. "If you're a traitor to the race, you're a target, too, lily white or not. If Brennan was buying up property to lease to Vietnamese, that's how they'd think of him."

"Hence the piece of paper stuffed down Brennan's throat."

Enforcers, Ben thought. Ian and his gang were enforcers to keep non-whites out of Santa Elena. He thought Vanek had landed at the same hypothesis, but it was just a theory and it needed to be proved.

"Let me get down there and check these addresses out," Ben said.

As he was driving down Bolsa Avenue on the way out, a car pulled in front of Ben. A sticker pasted to the silver bumper read, WILL THE LAST AMERICAN TO LEAVE WESTMINSTER BRING THE FLAG?

Ian and Jacob were cruising PCH, lines of waves barreling over his right shoulder. Jacob glanced at his new boots—black like bat skin, red laces stitching skin together.

"I can't pay you back for these," Jacob said.

"Did I ask you to?"

Jacob shook his head once.

"We're a sort-of family," Ian said, his hand dangling over the wheel. "We're the kind of family you choose." He glanced at Jacob. "Not the one you're born into."

Jacob looked out the window, all that water, the endless blue of the Pacific. It was the end of the Western world, the last-stand coastline. They drove for a few minutes in silence, PCH pulling away from the beach and easing into the three-story beach homes of Newport and the bayside restaurants and the Ferrari and Porsche dealerships.

"Last night," Jacob said, "there was . . . there was a piece of someone's scalp in my hair."

Ian looked at him a moment, his eyes narrowed like he was trying to be real careful. Jacob kept hearing the Mexican guitarist's scream in his head. He'd never heard a grown man sound like that.

"It's tough the first time," Ian said. "A skull feels like a skull, a rib feels like a rib. But these muds don't belong here. They're trespassing. I mean, what would you do if a stranger jumped the fence into your backyard and refused to leave? *And* the cops wouldn't do anything about it? We don't do something, they'll outnumber us. In just ten years."

Ian tapped the steering wheel with the side of his fist, thinking, it seemed. A Ferrari and a Lamborghini swerved into their lane, weaving between traffic, their engines whining like something about to explode.

"You gotta get rid of this hippie hair," Ian said, yanking on the curls behind Jacob's ear. "People around here see long hair, they think you're smoking grass, trying to overthrow the government. Keep it clean-cut—no knuckle tats like those dumb shits at Eagle, no cue-ball skinhead, no rolling up your jeans to show off your boots, no obvious symbols. You gotta keep it subtle, be a sort of ghost skinhead, you know what I mean? Clean-cut is camouflage. To white folks you're just a nice young man, like their sweet little grandkid or something. Got it?"

"Yeah."

A half hour later, Jacob was in a barbershop near the university, his brown hair curled at his feet, looking at his new face in the mirror—fresh cut into new flesh.

———

When Ben got off the San Diego Freeway and crossed over into Santa Elena, he took in the brand-new pseudo-Mediterranean houses, the tidy shopping centers, the clean ordered streets, and it struck him, suddenly, that South Orange County looked like the kind of place Nazis might have built if they had occupied California. The cultivated perfection, the homogeneity of it felt, well, fascist, though a seductive fascism, a type of authoritarianism that made you feel like you wanted to be controlled. Behind the "orange curtain" for sure.

The first three addresses Brennan had leased checked out— a Korean grocery; Taiko, a sushi joint; and a little pho place, all of them with the BRENNAN HOLDINGS sticker in the corner of the front windows. The next three, too, all buildings listed as owned by Brennan Holdings, were leased by Asians. Looked like he and Vanek had their fingers on something. If Paul Rowan used his real estate company and his position on fair housing to keep out minorities, it must have frustrated the hell out of him to have this Walter Brennan guy break through the wall to lease to them.

The last address was the newest of Brennan's purchases, from summer of 1985, according to the information Ben got up at the county hall of records. It was a construction site on the far east of town, where the new city was gnawing away at orange groves. The ground was graded for building, the foundation laid, a line of I-beams forming one side of the L-shaped complex. Ben parked the cruiser on La Mirada Street and walked around the wire fence closing the site off from the street. LOS OLIVOS MARKETPLACE, COMING SOON! PACCOAST REAL ESTATE, INC., read a faded sign hanging from the padlocked front gate. As far as Ben could tell, nothing was coming soon and no one was working to make it so. There were no construction workers, no trucks or tractors on-site. Rainwater puddled in dredged holes, rusted rebar poked out of cement foundations. Looked abandoned, if you asked him. Construction was happening all over town, new places going up at a shocking rate, cheap land turned into real estate gold, the economy a runaway train, so it seemed pretty damn strange to have construction suddenly halted.

At the Phans' place, Sunrise Food Mart, there was no sticker in the corner of the window, just a clean plate of glass. When Ben stepped inside, Mr. Phan was behind the fish counter, matchsticking a cucumber. The bell on the front door jingled, but the man didn't look up from his work. Ben said hello, but Mr. Phan seemed to be having a conversation with himself, his lips moving silently, his hands working furiously at the cucumber.

"Excuse me, Mr. Phan."

The man startled and nicked the edge of his thumb.

"Sorry." Ben quickly grabbed a napkin on the counter, handed it to him, and Mr. Phan stanched the blood. "Didn't mean to sneak up on you. I guess you had something on your mind."

"Paying bills," Mr. Phan said, pointing to his skull. "You found the people who killed the dog?"

"Not yet," Ben said. "But we will." Man did a pretty good job on his finger, the blood blooming on the napkin. Ben handed him another one. "Mr. Phan, do you know a Walter Brennan?"

"I leased my first grocery from him. In Westminster."

"But not anymore, I guess," the detective said. "Who do you lease from now?"

Mr. Phan threw the bloodied napkin in the trash with the peels of chopped-up vegetables. He looked furious, like something Ben said had pissed him off.

"This is my store," Bao said, hitting his chest twice for emphasis. "I own it."

His parents were arguing when Jacob got home. He ran upstairs, listened to a cassette tape Ian had given him. Skrewdriver was the band's name—the thrash of guitars, the growl of the singer, like sonic power fuel for his body. A door slammed, his mother yelled, and he turned the music up to drown it out, the ripping guitars burning him clean of his fucking parents and their fucking problems. Then someone was banging on his door. He stopped the cassette and his dad was there, filling up the doorway.

"You hungry?" he said.

Jacob was fifteen. He was always hungry.

And then he was in his dad's Buick, rolling down El Rancho Road, out past the new construction where an orange grove was being bulldozed. Five minutes of silence, just Kenny Loggins on the radio followed by some stupid song about wang chunging tonight, whatever that meant, until his father parked in front of a strip mall restaurant. Faded Chinese letters on a sign above the door mixed with English read PHO YOU, with a picture of a Chinese girl wearing a triangular hat. Inside, his father bowed his head and spoke to the waiter in a language that sounded like baby talk. Jacob didn't even know his dad could speak another language. The waiter glanced at Jacob, taking in his boots, before standing at the next table, cleaning the rims of a water glass with a white napkin.

"You join the army?" his father said now, sitting across from Jacob, gesturing at Jacob's new haircut. The table was near the kitchen, the heat of the stoves radiating around them.

"Mom was crying," Jacob said. "You hit her or something? Have one of your fits?"

The waiter was suddenly at the table and his dad spoke to him in Chinese. His dad was a fucking communist or something. Then they were alone again.

"I didn't hit her," he said quietly when the waiter was gone, wiping his hand across the table, as though sweeping crumbs. Someone whacked a cutting board, like they'd just cut off a limb. Then the waiter dropped bowls of soup in front of them and a plate full of weird-looking stuff—donut-shaped peppers, curly seaweed-looking things, green leaves with the stems still on.

His father said something to the waiter in Chinese.

Jacob stared at the soup—noodles, shavings of beef, some kind of meatballs. A sweet smell, too, like sweet dead fish.

"I don't like those boys," his father said.

"I do."

His father narrowed his eyes then, hearing the accusation in Jacob's voice. *You chased me with a metal rake,* he was really saying, *and Ian saved me from you.*

"Something happens," his father said, pointing an index finger at his temple, "and then I'm suddenly over there again. I can't explain it."

Jacob's pussy-self softened toward his father, like always. One moment he hated the man and the next he'd get all teary over him.

"Ian says it's not your fault," Jacob said.

"That's what Ian says, huh?" his father said, using the chopsticks to pinch a shaving of meat. "What *else* does Ian say?"

Jacob shut his mouth. His father nodded, as though he could guess the things Ian said, and chopsticked some bean sprouts.

"This is what you do," his dad said, piling more stuff into the bowl—the peppers, the sprouts, the green leaves. He poured a little red sauce in, too, and stirred it. But Jacob just sat there, staring at his father, the steam rising between them.

"You said you were hungry."

"Changed my mind," Jacob said, but it smelled good, with it all mixed together. He almost dug in, his stomach rumbling with hunger ache. But how the hell could he be a soldier in a war if he couldn't discipline his stomach? His father set the chopsticks on the table, leaned back in his chair, lit a cigarette, and leveled his concrete eyes at him.

"When my draft notice came in," his father said, "I almost made a run for Canada. But your mother . . . she begged me not to, said they'd call me a traitor." He nodded at this, an ironic smile splitting his face. "Traitor.

"So I stayed, let them send me over there." He paused again, took another drag, the smoke fogging the fluorescent light above the table. "Your mother got pregnant just before I left. We tried for you. She said she wanted something of me if I didn't come back. I wanted you, too. Wanted to know I had left something in this world if I got killed over there. I almost convinced myself I was defending you from commies, from the Russians, the Chinese, all that bullshit." He laughed and shook his head. "Domino effect."

Jacob didn't know what the hell the domino effect was and he didn't give a damn.

"And when I got back you were already walking." He smiled at Jacob then. "You wouldn't let me hold you at first. I was a stranger, as far as you were concerned, and I didn't blame you. It was almost like you were someone else's kid. In a way you were."

He took a drag and looked out the window as he blew a line of smoke to the ceiling. Jacob stared at the soup; the meatballs had the ridges of a brain, the shavings of meat like curled skin.

"What did it feel like?" Jacob said. His father's 'Nam pictures flashed through Jacob's mind—the severed leg, the melon-head, the charred flesh on the dirt road. "To kill some-one?"

His father's eyes were as hard and as clear as Jacob had ever seen them.

"Like nothing," he said. "Just shooting shells into the jungle." Drag, blow of smoke. "It's what you feel afterward, when it's quiet again, when you know."

He leaned across the table now, his hands between their bowls of soup as though he wished Jacob would take them in his.

"Nothing I've done to you is your fault," his father said. "I know you're angry with me . . . and you've got a right to be so."

Jacob got that feeling on the back of his throat, the tickling that preceded tears. *Don't do it. Don't fucking do it*. He thought about hitting the muds with the homey sock, the way it unfastened him from his softer feelings.

His father fell back in his chair now, disappointed, it seemed, that Jacob hadn't leaned across the table and called him Daddy or something.

"Me and your mom are getting a divorce."

The floor fell away, Jacob's chair spinning in empty space, but then he remembered the piece of scalp he'd held in his hands the other night and the room reassembled itself.

"It's that Vietnamese girl," Jacob said.

"It doesn't happen to me with her," he said quietly, nodding. "I don't know why, but it hasn't happened with her."

"You're leaving me and Mom for one of them?"

"I'm not leaving you," his father said. "I don't want to hurt you anymore, I can't live wit . . ."

He watched his father's lips move, but his voice sounded far away, like it was down a deep well. Something thrummed Jacob's head, a white noise blotting out sound. *You're a mud lover,* he said to himself. His father's lips moving, stupid tears in his eyes now. *Mud lover.*

Chapter Eleven

"**H**ow's your sister, Banger?" Vanek said to the guy behind the counter as soon as he and Ben walked into the surplus.

"Shit," Banger said. He was a refrigerator of a man, bald head, real tough-looking dude who was sewing something. "How long you gonna keep me on the hook?"

Banger was Vanek's confidential informer, and like any good street cop Vanek would keep him on the hook until his probation ended, maybe longer if he could find an angle to keep him hanging.

Vanek sat down on a stool pushed up against a display case showing off army-issue survival knives and smiled. Ben stayed standing. "How long's your tail again?" Vanek asked.

"Don't mess with me," Banger said, setting down the army epaulet he was mending a hole in. "You know how long I have left on my parole."

Carolina had followed Ian and another kid to Iron Eagle Surplus on Saturday. She'd tailed Ian from the house over to the high school where he picked up a kid, and then she followed the Power Wagon up to Huntington. Kid went in looking like a stoner teenager, she'd said, and came out looking like a clean-cut soldier. Not only that, came out wearing spiffy boots with—get this—red shoelaces. She'd followed them halfway back to Santa Elena, too, before losing them at a light. Ben had put in a call to Vanek Saturday night, confirming what they'd heard up in Little Saigon, that Brennan was leasing to Asians in Santa Elena, and told Vanek about the empty construction site also. Filled the detective in on what Natasha had discovered at Hoag Hospital, that the blunt-force fractures on Brennan and at least three of the migrants were caused by the same type of weapon.

It was Ben's day with Emma on Sunday, the surplus closed for the day anyway, but Carolina had given them a direct lead, and he and Vanek met up at Iron Eagle at 9:00 A.M. Monday morning, walking through the front door as soon as the neon OPEN sign was switched on.

Vanek turned to Ben, an easygoing smile on his face. "Banger here thought it'd be a good idea to walk into the Silver Fox up in Long Beach with some of his Aryan buddies and beat the shit out of a couple of fags."

Vanek's demeanor had changed, *shit* and *fags* sounding strange coming from his mouth.

"I was drunk."

"He even introduced himself to the victims before breaking their jaws. *Hi, I'm Banger Jones,* and then, bam!"

"Not very polite, Banger," Ben said.

Vanek placed his elbows on the glass case and got real serious. "Here's the deal, Banger. We just need some info on an Ian Rowan. That's the name, right?"

"Real buff dude," Ben said. "Has a fourteen eighty-eight tattooed on his wrist."

"Don't know him."

Bullshit.

"See," Vanek said, turning to Ben again, a wry smile on his face, "Banger's sister here likes to tweak. Got this supplier over on Tenth Street. I mean she practically lives over there. You should see her teeth. How long inside for a Schedule Two offense?"

"Up to four," Ben said.

Banger ran his hands over his bald head, like he was looking for some hair to pull on up there. Vanek was working Banger two ways—probation and his druggie sister. Vanek just smiled at Banger, his elbows still perched on the glass case, in no position to defend himself if this bull went off. For Ben's part, his right hand had crept up to the small of his back, where he could snatch his revolver in a pinch.

"I know the guy," Banger said. He let out a sigh, the perp's universal sign of letting go. "He was in here Saturday, with this kid, getting outfitted."

"New recruit?"

"I didn't ask questions."

"Braces, boots?" Vanek said. "Red laces?"

Banger just nodded.

"How old?"

"I don't know, fifteen, sixteen."

"Shit," Vanek said, serious frustration in his voice. "He's in then."

"Kid's name?" Ben said.

"Don't know. They didn't say."

All Vanek had to do was stare at the man.

"I swear, man. Was just a kid. Real quiet, sort of wide-eyed and stupid-looking."

"You assholes ever think twice about brainwashing kids?" Vanek said, standing now. "That ever prick your conscience?"

"I don't recruit. And I wouldn't call it brainwashing."

"Don't recruit, BS," Vanek said. "With the uniform in your back office."

"There's a demand, I supply it," Banger said. "Capitalism, you know?"

Vanek grabbed Banger's hand and twisted it, the big boy tugged into a wrist lock in a flash. It was a shock to see Dapper Dan enforce such violence, but it looked like he did it well.

"You're in no position to sass me," Vanek said.

Ben looked at Vanek, the first time he'd seen the man lose his composure. They needed cooperation, not coercion. Vanek caught Ben's eye but kept Banger's wrist twisted behind his back.

"Yeah, yeah," Banger said, standing on his tiptoes to keep the edge off the pain. "I get you."

Vanek let the wrist go, and Banger, flat-footed again, leaned on the glass case, breathing hard.

"Here's the thing," Ben said. "A guy by the name of Walter Brennan turned up dead the other night over on Fifteenth."

Banger grabbed at his bald head again. "I heard, but I don't know nothing about that."

"What'd you hear?" Ben said.

"Just that the dude turned up dead," Banger said. "Some rich prick in some fancy house. People were talking about it. Doesn't happen very often around here, you know?"

"And a couple nights ago, some dudes wearing real fancy boots beat the shit out of some Mexicans down in Santa Elena."

Banger couldn't help a small smile, an involuntary expression of joy.

"You think that's funny, huh," Vanek said.

"No, man," Banger said, getting himself under control. "I mean, Mexicans should stay down in their shithole country. So I'm not all torn up about it, you know. But I don't know anything about that shit. I'm playing it straight, man. My girlfriend's pregnant."

"Well, congratulations," Vanek said, his voice all sarcastic lightness. "A little Hitler youth."

"Where were you three nights ago, around midnight?" Ben said.

"At home, in bed with Tabitha."

"You know, Banger," Vanek said, "we've had a long-term relationship now, and I think I believe you. But I'm having lunch tomorrow with your PO, guessing he'd be real interested that you're hanging with a suspected murderer."

He wasn't really a suspect yet, just a person of interest. But, you know, technicalities.

"You can check with my PO, man," Banger said. "I called him by ten, from my home phone."

Vanek glanced at Ben. Sounded like the truth, but Ben trusted Vanek would do due diligence on that later. Banger was sweating now. Literally.

"Let me ask you again," Ben said, "in light of the situation. What do you know about Ian Rowan?"

He looked pained, like some sudden cramp had seized his gut.

"Look, man. I don't want to fuck with Ian."

"You don't want to fuck with us," Vanek said.

"You'll just arrest me. Who knows what he'll do? Like I said, I got a kid coming."

Vanek pulled his handcuffs from his belt. "Then let's get this party started."

"All right, all right," Banger said. "There's something about Ian, man. I don't know. He's scary, like he could go off any second. He's got this whole crew, but I don't run with these guys. I just see them around the community, you know?"

"The *community*," Vanek said. "Like some little church group."

Banger glanced at Vanek.

"People say he's got connections to a crew up in Big Bear. Some Christian Identity thing. Got some compound up there near the lake. Say they're planning something big."

"You know anything about Posse Comitatus?" Vanek said.

"Nothing, man."

"What about fourteen eighty-eight?" Ben asked. "Eighty-eight, Heil Hitler, we know."

Banger smiled, almost as if hearing those two words together turned him on.

"But what about the fourteen?"

"I don't know. *A* and *D*. Haven't seen that one before. There's a whole bunch of groups out there now, all over. New numbers, new sayings. Some of these guys, some of these new crews talk about a race war. I'm not down with that, man. I just don't want to live with them, you know?"

"Very progressive of you," Vanek said.

"We hear there's some kind of computer bulletin board thing," Ben said, "where all of you people all over the country can talk to each other. You know anything about that?"

Banger was quiet a second. "Yeah, I've heard something about that," he said. "Liberty Net or something. But I've never been on it."

"There's some special little club," Vanek said, "where assholes like you can get together and talk your bullshit, and you expect me to believe that?"

"I run a surplus store," Banger said. "You think I can afford a computer? Besides, it sounds like some stupid *Star Trek* shit to me."

Vanek laid down a stare on Banger, trying to decide if the man was telling the truth.

"Look, Ian . . ." Banger said, "something's off in his head, man. I don't know if it's because of his mother or what. I guess she had some kind of mental breakdown, after Ian's brother was killed in 'Nam. Whatever, I don't really like the dude, to be honest."

"Thought you all were brothers in the cause?" Vanek said.

"Mexicans should stay down in Mexico. Let the Asians have Asia. But I'm not going around curbing people."

"Unless they're fags," Vanek said.

Banger twisted his head. "I was drunk, man. I was stupid drunk."

"Stupid's right."

The tuition bill from the university had arrived at the grocery mailbox this morning. Bao was hung over, glasses of whiskey to stone himself into two hours of sleep last night. He opened it, had the amount memorized, but this morning the sum had sat on his chest like a boulder, this $3,235. It was the reason he worked fourteen hours a day, it was his pride, his ability to do this for Linh.

He had tried to work, tried to be pleasant with the customers, tried to cut just the right fillet of meat for their soups, tried to offer them the freshest basa fish. It had been a quiet morning, only a few regulars came in—Hao to buy sea urchin for his restaurant, An for two packages of rice noodles. Maybe he was imagining it, but they were quieter than usual—no gossip about whose son was marrying whose daughter, no whispered drama about who was going broke—just business-like, polite but reserved. And he soured with a feeling of shame and scandal about his daughter that he was suddenly sure was public. Ai was at her sister's, surely people knew about that, surely word had spread.

Now he turned the lock on the front door and sat at the counter, smoking cigarettes, adding up in his head all the money he'd spent to send Linh to college, all the hours he'd worked in this store, the weight of it burning his stomach. Linh had a 3:00 P.M. class, he knew. Modernist Literature. It was 12:45. He grabbed his car keys. It would take him fifteen minutes to get to Ai's sister's house. Linh would come home, she would leave this man. Three thousand two hundred thirty-five dollars. She couldn't pay that on her own. Only he could cover that cost. He was her father and she would listen to him. He had held her hand as they pulled shrapnel out of her skull. He had helped her with her math homework each night. He had signed her up for AYSO soccer and cheered for her on the sidelines. He'd brought her to this safe place where no planes would strafe jungles with napalm. He loved her more than any-thing, loved her so hard his heart was bruised with it. She *would* listen to him. She *would* come home.

—————

Judge Sullivan rejected Ben's affidavit for search and seizure of the Rowan place and admonished him in the process. *As the detective surely knows, there must be a nexus between items to be seized and criminal behavior. The discontinuity of the evidence presented does not warrant a seizure or search under Amendment Four of the Constitu-tion.*

Vanek had gone off to check out PACCOAST, the commercial real estate company that just happened to have offices in Hun-tington Beach, and Ben had rushed back to the station, written up an affidavit for a search of the Rowan house—all their evi-dence was circumstantial, not enough, he knew, to hang an arrest warrant on yet. He laid all the evidence out—the shoe-lace threads, the boot prints at the migrant camp similar to those up at the crime scene at Brennan's, the four-wheel-drive Power Wagon covered in mud the morning after the migrant attack, Brennan leasing to Vietnamese in Rancho Santa Elena, the tats, Banger at the surplus saying they were "planning something big." If Ian and his gang were connected to the Bren-nan murder, that *KILL 'EM ALL!* stapled to the dog was more than a scare tactic. He ran the affidavit by Hernandez, who was skeptical but didn't shut him down, and now here he was with a big fat official roadblock.

"Let's get a beer," Hernandez said when Ben got back to the station from the courthouse. "Better we talk away from here."

And then Ben was riding shotgun in Hernandez's personal Chevy instead of his cruiser, first sign that something was up. It was 1:33, not beer time for Hernandez, as far as Ben knew.

The lieutenant parked in front of Turk's Saloon in the Alta Vista shopping center. Inside, a half dozen people huddled over the bar, a man alone in the corner, a red candle illuminating his face. The unhappy hour. Hernandez chose a table in the back, not far from the restrooms. They both sat and angled their chairs so they could scope the room. No backs to the doors, ever—off duty at a bar, out to dinner with the family, ever.

The bartender, unbeckoned, dropped a couple of cold Coors on the table.

"Got this place on retainer?" Ben asked.

Hernandez smiled. "We all have our places."

They both took a sip, a woman clinked quarters into the jukebox and the Shirelles' "Will You Still Love Me Tomorrow?" floated through the speaker.

"I got a call from the mayor this afternoon," Hernandez said. "Seems Councilman Rowan feels he's being harassed."

Shit. "I had one conversation with him, followed him and Ian a little way down the road."

"And the affidavit."

"I know this Rowan kid's dirty," Ben said. "He's our guy—for both the dog and the attack on the pickers. And according to Natasha the blunt-force trauma to Brennan's body could have been caused by the same weapon used on the pickers. This is all connected. We get a weapon on the migrant attack, we might be able to connect it to the Brennan murder."

Hernandez took a sip.

"We only get two bites at the apple," Hernandez said. "We bring him in now with a case built on circumstantial and the DA chooses not to prosecute, we've got one more chance, and that's it. Besides, what are we arresting him for? Animal cruelty? Assault? We barely have anything to make those charges stick, much less to get him on murder. Everything we've got right now is either circumstantial or hearsay."

That's why he needed the search warrant, to get the goddamned evidence—prints, a weapon, something concrete. What he needed was in that garage on Comet Street, he was sure of it.

The lieutenant finished his beer and another promptly arrived. The man didn't even have to lift a finger. If he didn't know better, Ben would say he had something on the owner. Hell, maybe he did. *We all have our places.*

"I would have rejected that affidavit, too," Hernandez said.

"Why'd you approve it then?"

"Sometimes it's good to poke the nest," Hernandez said. "Judge Sullivan's usually a rubber-stamp man, right? Usually doesn't give cops too much grief before handing out warrants?"

Ben nodded and finished his beer and, sure enough, the bartender dropped a fresh one on the wet ring left by the last one. Magic.

"Generally, yeah. Never had any issues with him. Real police-friendly."

"I *do* have issues with him," Hernandez said. "Seems to me he signs off too quickly, gives cops like Vince a whole lot of latitude. And now he's suddenly Mr. Fourth Amendment?"

"Judge gets it right," Ben said, "and you're pissed off about it?"

"I'm wondering about the judge's motivation to get it right." He took another sip. "You know what redlining is?"

"Yeah, a little," Ben said. "Can't say I'm an expert."

"All these folks—black, Mexican, et cetera—come out to LA in the 1930s and 1940s to get in on the growing aerospace industry, move into neighborhoods like Watts, which was mixed—working-class white, black, Mexican. Government starts this program, Home Owners' Loan Corporation, part of the New Deal, to get more people to own homes post-Depression. This program relies on local real estate agents to make a map, grading neighborhoods based on the perceived safety of the bank's investment. Most of these agents were white men, because—well, you know why. Which neighborhoods do you think got the lowest grade? Not a trick question."

"Black."

"And Latino. Marked in red on the map. You pretty much couldn't get a loan in these neighborhoods—to buy your own home, to fix it up, to start a business. If you could get a loan, the rates were so high you'd get choked by the payment."

The lieutenant gulped the beer. In Ben's experience, Hernandez wasn't much of a drinker.

"Whites, though, in the nice neighborhoods could get loans. Or whites who didn't want to live among blacks and Latinos applied for loans in green or blue neighborhoods and moved out of the red towns. You can guess what happened when blacks and Mexicans applied. I mean, this whole county is less than two percent black. Shit, it's white all the way down the coast to Mexico." He swept his hand toward Tijuana. "Are we to believe that blacks don't like clean streets, beautiful beaches?"

Hernandez paused a moment.

"These are the histories we remember"—his voice hardening—"and you people forget."

Ben threw him a look.

"Why'd you move back here?" Hernandez said, leaning across the table as though Ben's irritation was a challenge. "I mean, you were shot, I know. But that possibility comes with the territory."

"I wanted my dad's house," Ben said. "Wanted a piece of the old California, before the developers destroyed it."

"Why else? You knew what the developers were planning down here. You knew they were going to carve up the hills and kill that old California. You had a nice place in Marina del Rey. You weren't living in the hood."

"I was sick of North Hollywood, tired of LA. I was sick of seeing what those people did to each other. Sick of bringing it home with me."

"Those people."

"Look, Lieutenant," Ben said, angry at the man for throwing his words back at him. "I didn't make them poor. I didn't create the gangs. I didn't make the shitty schools."

Hernandez leaned back. "You just policed them. You just

kept them in their place. And then drove back to the nice streets of Marina del Rey every day."

"I sure as hell wasn't going to live in North Hollywood," Ben said. "Wasn't going to send Emma to LA Public."

"Santa Elena," Hernandez said, "has excellent schools."

Ben leaned back in his chair, his chest buzzing with blame. "It does." He heard his voice again—*those people*—and he burned with shame.

"So you left," Hernandez said. "Moved forty miles away to escape it—to a place made for whites to escape to."

He did, it was true. "I didn't really think of it that way," Ben said. "Just wanted to come home."

Hernandez stared at him a moment. "My family got redlined in Boyle Heights," he said. "Somehow my father managed to get a loan for a tiny house in a blue neighborhood in Anaheim at an interest rate three times a white man's, and then crosses started burning on our lawn."

He paused, seeming to remember the burning crosses.

"My father moved us down here to Santa Elena because back then, when this place was a working ranch, if you were willing to castrate cattle, get your body beat to shit riding horses all day through these canyons, they didn't give a damn if you were black, Mexican, Chinese, or Martian. Labor is labor.

"But whites kept moving south," Hernandez continued. "And now there's nowhere else to go to get away from minorities—at least in Southern California. This is it. Santa Elena and the south counties."

"I thought redlining was outlawed twenty years ago."

"It was."

"Councilman Rowan and the fair housing commission," Ben said, nodding now. Assholes could always find ways around the law. "The last line of defense."

"And the prodigal son and his gang," Hernandez said.

God's country. He got it now. Somewhere white and Christian. If you asked white folks, they'd say that's not what they meant, just someplace clean and beautiful, but that *is* what they meant. That's what Santa Elena had been for him when he moved back, someplace safe and clean, a place that could ignore the rest of the world.

"Why'd you stay here?" Ben said. It wasn't an accusation. He was genuinely curious. Why stay where you weren't wanted? Why put yourself through that?

"It's my home, too," Hernandez said. "And I figured it was going to change. I wanted to be here when it did. And it *is* changing. I figured, too, there was going to be a fight over that change, and so here we are." He smiled. "Also, I like the irony of me being here, chief of police, in a place I was never meant to be."

Ben smiled. Lieutenant Roberto Hernandez, a Trojan horse.

"Detective, there's a chain of power here—from the councilman, to the mayor, perhaps to the judges—that works to protect itself. I would like to break that chain."

"You think the mayor's in on this?" Ben said. "The Brennan murder? The DA, the whole shebang?" Ben wasn't a fan of most politicians, and the mayor wasn't the kind of guy he'd want to sit and have a beer with, but that level of conspiracy felt a little too much to him.

Hernandez stared at his beer a few moments, thinking. "I think," the lieutenant finally said, "that a lot of white folks are happy to turn a blind eye to the ugly things some others do to keep this town as Leave-It-to-Beaver as possible. Let's put it that way."

"All right."

"We need a weapon, eyewitnesses—blood, if we can get it. Circumstantial won't get this done, no matter how many lines we draw between dots. We need it so tight, no arrest affidavits can be rejected, no trial dismissed for insufficient. So airtight a jury can't pretend they don't see the truth."

"There's something else," Ben said. "Vanek mentioned something about a computer bulletin board thing, Liberty Net or something, that some of these assholes might be using to connect with each other. Might be nothing as it relates to this, but—"

"If they're planning something big," Hernandez said, nodding, "that might be a good place to do the planning."

"Exactly."

"Check in with our tech guy."

"The department has a tech guy?"

Hernandez nodded. "Nick Talbot. Been with us for six months. Someone has to maintain those new Mac computers we got a year ago."

Ben imagined a dude wearing glasses, sitting at a desk in a closet somewhere, surrounded by computer chips. He swigged the last of his beer, stood to go, but hesitated.

"Lieutenant, I've known you since I was a kid," Ben said. "Saturday's the first time I've heard about the lake and your old man. Today's the first time I've heard about the crosses on your lawn."

Hernandez glanced up at him. "People don't want to hear those stories. Makes the good folks feel guilty, and no one likes to feel guilty."

―――――

After his father told Jacob that his parents were getting divorced, Jacob's stomach burned. All day yesterday it burned, an inferno in his gut. It burned today, too, through fucking algebra, burned through bullshit ZOG history. He sat alone at lunch in the quad, burning, watching the football dicks and their girlfriends act like kings and queens of the world. If he had a bomb, they'd be dead already, their fat-ass limbs strewn in front of the cafeteria doors. Thank God it was an early-release day, something so the teachers could learn more ZOG lessons to teach to the stupid-ass students.

When school let out, Jacob followed Dietwaller off campus,

through the park, all the way back to his front door—the dumbass never looking over his shoulder, never even thinking someone might be coming for him—and snuck up and punched him in the back of the head. Diet fell and smacked his face against the door, and then Jacob steel-toed him in the kidneys.

"Give me my fucking bike," he yelled. Steel drilling the soft tissue of his torso.

"All right, all right," Dietwaller said, tears in his voice. "It's in the backyard."

He kicked the asshole again to punctuate the beating and then found the bike leaning against an aluminum trash can in the side yard. He pedaled the mile and a half down El Rancho Road—swearing he'd never let anyone steal anything from him again—to the apartment complex and sat beneath a row of eucalyptus on the edge of the parking lot, watching the front door. Number Sixteen. His father had told him the address. *When you're ready*, he'd said at the restaurant. *You can visit*. He stood there in the shadows for an hour, maybe more, and then there she was, coming out the door and down the steps and into her car.

It was surprisingly easy to follow her on his bike. She'd punch the engine, joining the rush of the other cars, but every hundred yards was another stoplight and he'd catch up to her while she idled at the intersection. It was kind of funny, actually. Made you wonder about cars—all that horsepower and a kid on a bike could get across town just as fast.

He almost lost her at the university but pedaled a couple of rows of the parking lot and found her stepping out of her Honda, backpack dangling from her shoulder. He followed her up the pathway into the campus, walking his bike behind her, like he was a fucking student, and watched her glide into the liberal arts building.

His father chose her. He couldn't get that out of his mind.

Later, he followed her to Lucky's grocery. Walked the aisles she walked—watched her buy a bottle of white wine, a bunch of asparagus, a hunk of steak. Then he followed her to the gas station, watched her fill up the car. She was oblivious to him, just a kid on a bike. The town was full of them.

She was the one who made him feel like shit. Fucking mud. No mud should make him feel like this. No Chinese, no Vietnamese. This was *his* country, *his* town. *His* family.

He pedaled behind her back to the apartment and watched her carry the groceries up to #16 and go inside. Around the back of the apartments, he found an empty lot where he could see into the window. Then his dad was there, helping her unload the groceries. The stupid normalcy of it burned a hole in his stomach. They sat at a little dining room table, eating cheese and crackers, her hand touching the back of his dad's neck, her head thrown back in laughter. Jacob had almost forgotten that laughing was something people could do together. Then she stood at the sink, steam rising to slick the window, her face melting in the gathering condensation. He watched his father dry the dishes she handed him. He watched his father kiss her on the neck as she dried her hands, watched her head fall back in a swoon he'd only imagined a girl might do with him one day. He watched them, through the windows, as his father pulled her by her hand from the kitchen, into the dining room, and finally into the bedroom. And Jacob stood there, his imagination running wild about what was happening behind the curtains.

When he got back to Comet Street, his heart hammering his ribs, he found Ian on the driveway, benching a stack of weight so heavy it bent the bar. Jacob told him about what he'd just seen, spit it out like recounting a terrible crime.

———

Bao drove over to his sister-in-law's house and apologized to Ai, begged her to listen to him. They sat down on the patio of the backyard of the house, and he told her about Linh's affair. When he tried to explain himself the other day, when she berated him for striking their daughter, he simply told her that Linh was dating an American man. He couldn't bear then to tell her that it was an affair, that the man was married. But today he told her everything, said it out loud like an indictment.

Ai was immediately—and secretly—furious. If you hadn't lived with Ai for twenty-four years, you wouldn't have noticed the tightness of her lips, the chill in her eyes as though some wall had been constructed around her heart. She packed her bag, thanked her sister without betraying anything, and then sat next to him in the car burning silent rage.

At home, they sat together at the dining room table, crafting a plan to separate Linh from Lucas Clay. They would no longer pay tuition, if she stayed with him. They'd no longer make the payments on her car or cover the insurance cost; no more gas money. They had spoiled her, Ai said, given her too much, turned her into a rich girl who thought she could have everything. If that didn't work, they'd tell her—this was almost too much to imagine—that they wouldn't speak to her until she ended the affair.

Then they drove over to the university, stood outside her three o'clock class, and told her, right there in the courtyard in front of the student union. They were saving her from a greater pain, at least that's what Bao told himself. A man never married his mistress, never settled down to have kids with her. A thing that starts out bad, ends bad.

He would never forget the look on Linh's face, never. Water swelled in her eyes—shades of her childhood face colored her complexion—but then something dried up in her and her pupils hardened. It was like watching your child's soul vacate the body to be occupied by a stranger's—the new soul locked against you.

"You lied to me," she said, cutting her eyes into him. "All the things you said I could be. It was all lies."

And then she simply turned and walked away, joining the crowd of students shuffling to class, their threats made impotent.

Chapter Twelve

Natasha noticed the small discoloration on Linh's cheek. She looked like she'd been crying for hours, her eyes red and puffy, her nostrils raw.

"I don't know who to talk to," Linh had said on the phone a half hour earlier. She sounded desperate, angry, so Natasha cleaned up and left County immediately, leaving a couple of death certificates unfinished on her desk.

Now they were sitting outside in the late-afternoon sun, underneath a heat lamp at the Blow Hole Café in Santa Elena, Natasha holding Linh's hands while she tried to calm down. She had already told Natasha about the affair with the older married man, a vet no less, and Natasha tried to hide her surprise—and her disappointment. What a mess Linh had gotten herself into, was all Natasha could think. But then she chided herself. Who was she kidding? Love was love—if this was love. Things had started with Ben before he was officially divorced. The heart isn't rational; it follows its own Darwinian laws.

"This man hit you?" Natasha said, nodding to the bruise.

"No," she said, her eyes so furiously clear Natasha had no doubt she was telling the truth.

Linh looked at her coffee, of which she hadn't taken a sip. Simply warmed her hands against the mug.

"It still feels unreal," Linh said. "Like it didn't really happen, but then I look in the mirror."

It wasn't hard to put one and one together, but she couldn't believe it.

"Your father?" she said. "He's the one who hit you?"

Linh just looked at her and started crying again, angry tears—a cry of injustice.

"Oh, sweetheart," Natasha said. *Sweetheart*, the term of endearment she used at the camp at Pendleton all those years before, when she played checkers with the little-girl-Linh in the army tent. The term of endearment she used when she helped them find a sponsor and move to Westminster, the term she used when she took Linh shopping for clothes. She had felt something maternal for the girl, a feeling she hadn't experienced before. She had been a girl herself, really, and the feeling—the intensity of it, the need in it, the feeling of possession—frightened her. Linh wasn't hers, Linh would never be hers. And later, when Natasha was in medical school, caught in a loop of late-night study and daytime residency, newly cutting open dead bodies, digging deep into the flesh and finding all the easy ways it could be destroyed, she had let Linh go. There hadn't been any dramatic severing, but Natasha called less, gapped weeks and then months between dinners with the family, until the Phans simply faded away. They never called her, never asked her why she was disengaging, and Natasha interpreted that silence to mean that they had moved on, too. But now here she was, playing the mother—or the dutiful aunt—to this young woman she didn't really know anymore.

"I thought he loved me too much to do that," Linh said.

"He loves you more than you can imagine."

She wanted to say, *That's why he hit you.* But that was a message she'd never utter. No way Natasha would act as an apologist for Bao, but she understood the possessiveness of love. She understood the fear of loss. And she could imagine how the sacrifice, how the toll of Bao's life could be endured through the hope in his daughter. Love, she thought, could birth monsters in all of us.

"But he shouldn't have hit you."

"Slap," she said. "He slapped me. I was being a bitch, too. He kept asking me to speak Vietnamese and I wouldn't. I knew what I was doing."

"Look at me," Natasha said.

She did.

"He shouldn't have hit you,"

Linh nodded. She was silent a few moments and Natasha waited. Sometimes the most important things needed to be waited for.

"They're making me choose," Linh said. "They say they won't speak to me again until I end it with him."

Oh, a true mess.

"My friend Andrea said that was bullshit," Linh said. "She told me to go it alone. But she doesn't understand. I love Lucas, I do, but I love my parents, too. I can't weigh one against the other, as if they're mutually exclusive—as though only my happiness matters, like Lucas alone would make me happy."

"But your happiness does matter."

She nodded. "Maybe," she said. "But my happiness can't look like Andrea's. It can't be that selfish." She rapped two fingers against the coffee mug. "My father said something terrible to me."

"What did he say?"

She shook her head. "I don't want to repeat it," she said. "I hope he's ashamed of it—or will be. If he is, I don't want it to be a public shame for him, too." She glanced at Natasha. "That's part of the reason why I'm talking to you, and not someone in the community. When he said what he said, though, it infuriated me. Now I think he said it because he was frightened."

"They're frightened now, and they've made a mistake."

"I know," she said. "But fear can last a long time."

It was quiet a moment, as though Linh was working up to something.

"Will you talk to him, Natasha?"

Natasha glanced away, out over the parking lot.

"He always respected you," she said. "For a while after we stopped seeing you, he talked about you."

"I'm sorry I stopped calling, stopped coming around," Natasha said. "I think I thought I was an imposition to you all after a while."

"I don't think so," Linh said, shaking her head. "But people lose touch sometimes." She offered Natasha a smile. "So will you talk to him?"

What was she going to say to Bao? What was she going to ask him to do? She tried to see what Bao would see, herself as an American woman, basically a stranger so many years after Pendleton, telling him how to live his life, how to raise a daughter, how to change to fit this place. He might need to change, if he wanted to keep his daughter—but she wasn't the right messenger, she was almost certain of it.

"I want to help," Natasha said, "but I don't think my talking to your father right now would be helpful."

Linh's shoulders dropped and she sat up, her chin struck in a defiant gesture as though she felt betrayed.

"I think my talking to your father might make things worse," Natasha tried to explain, but she could see that something had turned in Linh. "I think he might feel judged, condescended to."

Linh took her first sip of the coffee and set the mug and a couple of one-dollar bills on the table.

"It's on me," Natasha said.

"My father always says," Linh said, standing up now, "pay your own way here. Never any gifts."

———

Nick Talbot's office smelled like plastic and burning metal. Ben found him standing at a table strewn with parts, bent over one of the Macintosh computers the department had bought last year. The machine's cover was stripped off and Nick, wearing a Kraftwerk T-shirt, OP shorts, and checkered slip-on Vans, was bent over the guts of the machine, soldering metal circuitry.

"Did you check all the cords?" Nick said, impatience in his voice. "If so, then try shutting it down and starting it up again."

"It's not a computer problem," Ben said. "It's an investigative issue."

Nick looked up from the computer and set down the soldering iron.

"I need to get into a so-called bulletin board system," Ben said.

"Well, let's do it," Nick said. He looked pleased. Ben followed Nick to a computer desk strewn, again, with spare parts, floppy disks, a phone, a nearly finished Rubik's Cube. The man couldn't have been older than twenty-five, and he bounced into his desk chair and swiveled it around like it was an amusement park ride. "I've been telling the chief computers are the future of policing."

Ben was skeptical, but the future liked to surprise. Most cops stayed away from the computers, used them only to type up reports, as mandated by Lieutenant Hernandez after the city invested in the machines.

Nick pushed a button on the Mac, flipped a switch on a box sitting next to the keyboard, and picked up the phone receiver.

"What's the phone number?" he said, his fingers hovering over the buttons.

"You need a phone number?"

"Of course," Nick said. "How d'you think you reach the board?"

"I don't know," Ben said. "Thought maybe you typed in 'Liberty Net' and the thing came up."

Nick set down the phone, clear disappointment on his face. "This isn't magic, Detective. This is technology."

"In the white pages?"

"It doesn't work that way. Usually, the sysop, the guy who set up the board, invites his friends and then they invite friends and so on and so forth."

And then Nick launched into a long explanation of phone lines and processors and RAM and Ben thought Nick would have talked all day about it if he hadn't told Nick he had a meeting and escaped out the door.

Back at his desk, Ben looked over his case notes for anything that might reveal a phone number. Then he sifted through the report Lofland and the PhDs in the crime lab had left on his desk. The prints on the cans picked up at the Mexican crime scene didn't match the ones Ben had nabbed at the Rowan house. That didn't mean anything, when you were dealing with a gang. But it would have made things a whole lot easier had they matched. Tire prints matched, though, from the alley with the dog and the strawberry field attack. Goodyear Wrangler 215s. Ian's Power Wagon had Wranglers on them, but how many trucks out there rolled on Goodyears? He'd counted at least sixteen on his drive through the Connollys' neighborhood. He needed soil samples from the strawberry field. Should have scraped them off the truck when he had the chance.

His desk phone rang.

"Wade."

"Dad, please come and get me," Emma said into the receiver, clearly hysterical with tears. "Mom's teaching. I need you to come get me."

He grabbed his blazer, jumped in his cruiser, and burned it down El Rancho Road, flipped on the dashboard emergency

light to slip past a red light—an emergency is an emergency—
and was there in five minutes.

When he got to counseling, a Miss Saldana lobbed him a
sympathetic look. "She's in my office."

Inside, Emma jumped out of the chair and clung to him, wet
tears slicking his shirt.

"It's all right," he said, stroking her hair. "What the hell happened?" he said to the counselor.

"I don't know. She didn't want to tell me."

"Take me home," Emma said.

In the cruiser, his daughter curled up against the passenger
door as though someone had gut-punched her, Ben said,
"Emma, what's going on?"

"Nothing."

They drove across town, her wet cheek pressed against the
closed window, an occasional sob as though her heart were
being torn out. When they got to the house, she walked straight
into her room over "nothing" and slammed the door about
"nothing" and then he was left alone in the house, her door
closed, imagining all manner of disasters: from a failed math
test (a ride in the hills and A-okay) to a pregnancy (heart pal-
pitation) to some kind of assault (8.3 on the heart Richter)
until his imagination got away from him and everything went
apocalyptic in his mind and he paged Natasha. She called him
back in five minutes, enough time to imagine all manner of
catastrophes, and listened to him as he relayed the state of his
daughter.

"I'm already in town," Natasha said. "I'll be there in five."

———

"Emma," Ben said, knocking on the door. "Emma, please."

Natasha was in the kitchen, percolating a pot of coffee,
watching him standing outside Emma's locked bedroom door.
My lord, she'd just gotten over the shock of watching Linh walk
out the door of the café when Ben paged her in the kind of

panic he reserved only for his daughter. The man could chase serial killers, hunt down murderous gang members, but when it came to Emma he had the emotional wisdom of a fifteen-year-old boy. Must have driven Rachel crazy, always having to be the adult in the room.

"Emma, honey," Natasha said, grabbing Ben's hand and pulling him away. "You take all the time you need," she said to the door. "You come out when you're ready."

Natasha dragged Ben into the front room.

"Sit down and be quiet," she said. "Don't make this about you." She pulled out a chair for him at the dining room table. He sat. "She asked for you, now you need to wait."

She poured him a cup of coffee, sugared up the way he liked it, and they sat there for eleven minutes (Ben keeping tabs on the digital clock on the stove), watching the evening marine layer ooze through the canyons, until suddenly he got up, grabbed a Phillips-head screwdriver out of a drawer, and started unscrewing the wall-mounted can opener from the kitchen wall.

"What're you doing?"

"Not a fan of these things anymore."

When Emma's door swung open, Natasha raised her eyebrows at him and smiled. Emma, looking like someone had painted her cheeks with black watercolors, zombied into the room.

"Let's get you some tissues," Natasha said, finding a box on the kitchen counter. When Natasha held them out to her, Emma fell into Natasha's arms and re-commenced sobbing.

Natasha glanced at Ben. She'd been working hard to win Emma's confidence. Worked through the She's-weird phase and the You're-not-my-mother phase and had just recently graduated to the She's-okay-I-guess phase, so she was a little surprised that Emma chose to snot all over her chest.

"We broke up," Emma said, finally.

By the look on Ben's face, Lance was about to be executed. She gave him a calm-down face.

"Men stink, don't they?"

Emma laughed, sniffed away her tears, and then pulled free. "No offense. But I kinda want to go home—to Mom."

Her mothering duties abruptly canceled.

———

Home—to Mom. Emma had paused, as though she realized what she had said. Home was not here, in the house where she'd spent most of her childhood; the house that was his father's and his childhood home; the house with the horses out in the barn that she loved. Home was a post-divorce condo down in the center of town—a cheaply made, overpriced cookie-cutter square.

"Yeah, sure," Ben said. "You got it, sweetheart."

Emma stepped into the bathroom.

"Jesus," he said to Natasha when Emma shut the door. "I thought it was serious."

"It is."

He put in a call to Rachel, who was still at school grading papers, and then he and Emma were rolling down the gravel road in his truck, kicking up dust until they hit the pavement and slid into the river of BMWs and Mercedes. Two minutes into traffic purgatory, he asked, "Was he nice about it, at least?"

She let out a frustrated sigh. "Dad, he cried when I told him."

It took him a moment to recalculate. He eased the cruiser down the street and had to work to suppress a smile. Lance wasn't a bad kid, really, but he didn't see much of a future for the boy. The only direction Lance was heading was to the beach at 32nd Street to *Shoot a barrel, dude.*

When they got to Rachel's condo, his ex was standing in the doorway with a mug of hot cocoa. Cocoa. Why didn't he think of such things? Emma hugged her mother and then squeezed inside to flop down on the couch.

"I knew this was going to happen," Rachel said, shaking her head. Her hair was pulled into a ponytail, her down-to-business look. He could smell lasagna, the meal of crisis, baking in the oven. Home indeed.

"It's not what you think," Ben said.

"You mean, he broke up with her?"

He chuckled. "No, it's exactly what you thought."

"He's not smart enough for her," Rachel said. "It was just a matter of time before she figured that out."

"Yeah," Ben said. "He's not going to Cal Poly."

"I've got to triage, Ben."

And he was out, the important parenting being done on the other side of the door.

He pulled his truck back onto El Rancho Road. *She* broke up with him. For the year or so they'd been together, he had prepared himself for the Armageddon of him breaking up with her. But he was raising a heartbreaker, apparently. He drove the ten blocks over to Lance's house. He'd grown to like the kid, actually. He was a surfer, and a pretty damn good one, to be honest. Hell, they'd even spent a couple of days down at the beach together—him, Natasha, Lance, and Emma—and he'd watched the kid try to teach Emma how to catch waves. She kept tumbling off the board and Lance was patient with her. He'd decided then he would stop making fun of him. But in the future, when things got serious with a man, he wanted to add smart to kind. The brain needed sustenance as much as the heart.

What was he expecting to find? Lance curled up on the porch, sobbing away the thought of his daughter? Yeah, he guessed that was what he thought he'd find, maybe would feel some pride over it, thought he'd say, *Sorry, kid. Some things just don't work out.* Instead, as Ben rounded the corner, there Lance was with his buddies, pirouetting the skateboard ramp as though nothing had happened, and Ben just cruised on by, leaving the kid to the rest of his life.

———

Ian had let him cry, his hand cupping the back of Jacob's head. When he was done, Ian cracked a forty-ouncer for him and sat down on the couch in the closed-up garage. They'd been lying low since the Mexican camp, keeping it real cool.

"This can't stand," Ian said, pacing in front of Jacob, something feral and electric about him. "Your old man and this mud girl." Ian's pupils were pinpointed, like two drill holes. "You know that, right?"

Ian sat back down and handed Jacob a white pill, like the one he'd taken the night they clobbered the Mexicans.

"One pill makes you larger," he said, a wild smile on his face.

Jacob washed the pill down with malt liquor. And an hour later, they were in the Power Wagon, heading down Universidad. Ian had called Clocker and Fisker, told them the plan. They'd slipped on the gloves, they'd weaponized the homey socks, Jacob dropping the cue ball into the deep bottom of the fabric, duct-taping the sock around the ball like bandaging a broken knee. Ian clipped a magazine into the pistol, and now Jacob's homey sock rested between his thighs, the gun planted on the bench seat between them. Electricity zipped Jacob's veins, like silver running the synapses of his body. His teeth tasted metallic, his muscles felt like lubed steel, like he was the Terminator or something. He imagined he had that red eye, that searching killing machine eye. Ian punched the V8, rumbling a small earthquake through the floorboard, the lights of the university coming into view now. Jacob knew he had set something in motion, something bigger than him, like Earl Turner had in the book, something heroic and brutal. And he swore he'd never cry again.

———

Later, when Ben got home from dropping Emma off, he and Natasha sat out on the porch and talked it all out, Natasha offering dubious parental advice about Emma—how in the world was she to know what to do in these situations?—until Ben got loose enough to focus his attention on her.

She told him, then, about Linh, about the slap and the affair. Ben played out possible connections between the affair and the dead dog, but it was just speculation and a couple of drinks in she knew his mind was set on other things. When they got back to the bedroom, her body was with him but her mind was crowded with Linh, with Emma and Rachel, who was at home with her daughter, trying to sort out heartbreak. It seemed to Natasha that was one of the essential duties of motherhood—to teach the heartbroken to feel it and then let it go. She imagined herself in Rachel's condo—she didn't want to, it just happened, a very unfortunate imposition at the moment—sitting on the couch, handing tissue after tissue to Emma, knowing that there was no more important job in the world. A heaviness crowded in on her and she tried to wrench her mind back into the bedroom, back with Ben.

Who was doing a whole lot of gymnastics, trying to take care of her, but her mind wasn't up to the task.

"It's all you tonight," she said, putting her hands where he liked them.

Soon enough she was alone with her thoughts, remembering that feeling she had toward Linh all those years ago. Natasha was now thirty-five years old. She wanted to nurture something into this world, wanted to leave something behind other than autopsy reports. The minute on the digital clock flipped: 12:47 A.M. Ben snored quiet breaths against her shoulder blades, the whole empty night open for her deliberations.

1987

The Hate Network

THE RULES:

- You never visit or speak about The Reverend's church, America's Divine Promise Ministries. You never donate to His church.
- You do not call yourself a white supremacist, a neo-Nazi, or a skinhead.
- You dress and comport yourself as a white-collar business-man.
- You vote for politicians vetted by The Reverend and his Council on Politics.
- You do whatever The Reverend asks, when He asks you to do it, or His money will be withheld and you will be Ex-communicated.
- If you are arrested, you will not speak The Reverend's name or reference America's Divine Promise Ministries. If you do, you will be silenced.
- You will dedicate yourself to creating the Edenic Adamic Israelite Colony, wherever you may be in the country.
- You will work to prevent the mixing of races in order to preserve untainted white DNA.
- When the time comes, you will be armed and ready to fight, for *We must protect the existence of Adamic peoples and a future for our children.*
- If The Reverend calls, you go to Him.

None of this is written down. The rules are memorized.

Richard Potter Wales got the call at 7:30 A.M.: "The Reverend asks that you meet him at Hacienda del Sol in Newport Beach at 2:30 P.M. today. Come alone."

Wales left the mountain compound early, at 11:40; you weren't late to a meeting with The Reverend, especially when he had been as generous with you as he had been with Wales. The cash The Reverend had gifted him in the briefcase eighteen months ago, on the day he was ordained, had simply been a down payment. It had helped Wales resettle into the compound in the eastern ridges of the San Bernardino Mountains near Big Bear Lake, far down a dirt road where police rarely ventured. It had helped fund the erecting of prefabricated trailers used to house the young men, and some of their families, who followed him from his old compound. That compound, some three hundred miles up the mountainous spine of California, sat empty following the killings in Nebraska, the FBI monitoring an empty shell. The money purchased assault rifles and ATVs, it paid for the tie-down for the Comanche at the Big Bear Airport. And when the money ran out, more arrived, wired through Western Union from Promise14Ministries, LLC, to a rotating cast of young men who resided at the compound—never to Wales himself. Everything was purchased with cash—no checks, no credit cards, no trail.

Wales's pilot—another gift from The Reverend—met him at the municipal airport at noon, the Comanche was in the air by 12:30, and by 1:45 Wales was staring at a restroom mirror in the Revolution Air executive terminal at John Wayne Airport. He splashed water on his face, ran a comb through his hair, straightened his tie twice, making sure there was a dimple in it, just like The Reverend's, and then he sat nervously on a bench outside until a car arrived for him.

Hacienda del Sol sat on a cliff overlooking the Pacific Ocean, a sprawling white adobe single-story home surrounded by a fortress of wrought-iron fence. At the gate, two men in suits frisked him, and then he was led past a fountain into an enclosed courtyard and left alone for fifteen minutes to ponder the wonder of the gardens. It was both an honor and a concern to be called by The Reverend, and Wales concentrated on the trickling fountain water to help keep calm.

A young man in a slick suit, the one with the glasses Wales had met eighteen months before at Elias Klein's church in Idaho, led him down a stone path shaded by palm trees and giant ferns until the ocean opened up before them. They followed the path across a large backyard toward a pool where a woman was swimming laps, her white swimsuit shining against the deep-blue tiles. On the far side of the pool, The Reverend sat at a white wrought-iron table in the shade of a retractable awning. He was dressed in his signature blue suit, his legs crossed at the knee, watching the woman spin a flip turn and race down the pool. When they got closer, Wales could see that The Reverend was stemming a strawberry with a coring knife.

"Brother Wales," The Reverend said, flashing his electric smile, which, at that moment, reminded Wales of a young Ronald Reagan. The Reverend gestured with the coring knife to the seat next to him. "Please sit."

Wales sat and the young man disappeared. Behind him Wales heard the sucking of air and a splash.

"She loves it when we come to California." Wales had never met The Reverend's wife, but he had seen her on television, in pictures in celebrity magazines at the grocery store. Like The Reverend, she seemed both gracious and remote, as though she would do anything for you and nothing at all.

"I didn't know you had a home in California," Wales said.

"I don't," The Reverend said, slicing the strawberry into quarters and dropping them on a china plate. "California doesn't suit me. But it's an important state and"—here he swept his hand toward the house—"we have important friends here."

Celebrity? Politician? Both? Wales knew not to ask.

The Reverend spooned powdered sugar from a small bowl

and sprinkled it on the quartered strawberry. "Have a strawberry," he said. "That's something California does well."

Wales spooned a strawberry out of the wooden bowl and dropped it on the plate set in front of him. He wasn't hungry.

"Please," The Reverend said, his fork held in the air as though he'd been interrupted, "eat your strawberry."

It sounded like a command. Wales ate. The Reverend watched him. His wife spun a flip turn in the pool.

"Your idea of creating the bulletin board," The Reverend said, "has been very helpful."

"Good," Wales said.

"Much better than your old radio broadcasts," The Reverend said, smiling.

Yes, he had reached some people with the radio broadcasts, but the actions taken by his followers had been limited and isolated—Ross Morrison martyred for killing two federal agents in Nebraska, and David Schneel's "farm revolution," in which he and an accomplice tried to dynamite a natural gas pipeline in Missouri, resulted only in a dented pipe. And Wales had spent months traveling out to the fallow fields of the Midwest, or the isolated valleys in the mountainous Northwest, living in motels in ruined American small towns, only to sit in tiny studios anchoring steel transmission towers that rose into the empty sky, knowing that his voice would reach only as far as the horizon, where the curve of the earth silenced him.

"Seems you're a bit of a visionary," The Reverend said.

Wales relaxed a little with the praise. "We now have connections in at least twenty-eight states."

"I want all fifty," The Reverend said. "And Canada."

"Europe as well," Wales said, "eventually."

"Good," The Reverend said. "Ambition is the passion of character."

It was amazing, actually, that the single encrypted Commodore 64 computer he bought at a Kmart in San Bernardino for $595 could reach so many people. It was just a plastic box filled with integrated circuitry and computer chips attached to a television screen, a floppy disk drive, and, most important, an eight-line 300 bps modem that was plugged into the telephone landline. The computer itself was a simple enough instrument to understand. Wales had worked as a mechanical engineer before starting his ministry, designing hydraulic cylinders for construction equipment. But the software for the BBS, Color64, took some time to negotiate. With help from a book, *How to Build Your Own Computer Bulletin Board System*, which he bought at a Radio Shack, and the prompts in the software itself, he had learned the language of the computer. After a few months, the BBS was ready to debut with Richard Potter Wales the sysop, the systems operator.

On the day the bulletin board went live, almost a year ago now, Wales sat in front of the machine and gazed out the windows of his office. Miles of desert spread before him, the rest of the nation out there beyond the horizon. Elias Klein, the reverend in Idaho, had advertised the BBS in his inter-movement *Liberty Front* magazine, using coded language people in the movement would understand for the access code, but there was no way to tell how many patriots it had reached. Wales pressed the POWER button and the machine whirred to life, the screen sending its green glow into the room. He had already handwritten his first message, and he typed it into the bulletin board, his chest swelling with the quiet momentousness of it all.

MSG LEFT BY: SYSOP
AT LAST, WE ARE ALL GOING TO BE UNIFIED AT
ONE POINT IN TIME. IMAGINE, ALL THE GREAT
MINDS OF THE MOVEMENT JOINED TOGETHER BY
ONE COMPUTER! ALL THE YEARS OF COMBINED EX-
PERIENCE AND WISDOM AVAILABLE TO ANYONE IN
THE MOVEMENT. NOW IMAGINE ANY ARYAN CHRIS-
TIAN PATRIOT IN THE COUNTRY, IN NORTH AMER-

ICA, IN THE WORLD, EVEN, BEING ABLE TO CALL UP
AND ACCESS THOSE MINDS, TO SHARE IN THE
GREAT STRUGGLE TO FREE THIS NATION FROM
TYRANNY. YOU NOW ARE ON-LINE WITH THE IDEN-
TITY MOVEMENT'S BRAIN TRUST. IT IS HERE TO
SERVE THE PATRIOTIC SOULS OF THIS COUNTRY!
POSSE COMITATUS.

He sat there and waited, computer engine fan humming, green cursor flashing, his words staring back at him. Then, text flashed across the page:

MSG LEFT BY: CHRISTIAN DEFENDER
I AM A WHITE SOLDIER OF MY CHRISTIAN FAITH
AND MY RACE! I AM A DESCENDENT OF A GLORI-
OUS LINEAGE THAT HAS SHED BLOOD AND TREA-
SURE ON THE BATTLEGROUNDS OF EARTH. I AM
PREPARED TO DO THE SAME TO SAVE OUR RACE
FROM ANNILHATION. FOURTEEN WORDS!

Then a flash and another message filled the screen.

MSG LEFT BY: ARYAN SOLDIER
HAIL TO YOU! THIS IS A GREAT DAY. WE ARE ALL
A PART OF THE GREAT WHITE RACE WHOSE SPIRI-
TUAL ESSENCE WAS CREATED BY YAWEH IN THE
CELESTIAL PLANES OF HEAVEN.

The screen flashed again.

MSG LEFT BY: LIBERTY OR DEATH

And again . . .

"I can tell you're proud of your work," The Reverend said now, watching him closely. "You should be."

"It's just the beginning," Wales said.

The Reverend's wife made another turn. Wales noted that she had not stopped swimming since he arrived.

The Reverend folded his cloth napkin into perfect thirds and set it on the table. "I don't like what I'm hearing out of Rancho Santa Elena." The Reverend's voice changed then, an edge to it. "A Vietnamese running for city council, a police officer looking into some of our affairs. That's why I've called you here today. Perhaps the bulletin board has distracted you from your other duties?"

"I know about these things," Wales said, unable to keep the irritation out of his voice. The Reverend flashed his eyes at him. Wales adjusted his suit coat. "Yes, it's true. I've been busy with the bulletin board." You never knew if you were in or out of favor with The Reverend.

"Councilman Rowan's son is a bit reckless," The Reverend said.

"We're covering our tracks," Wales said.

"Yes," The Reverend said, "you burned that house down."

"Detective Wade has no jurisdiction over the meth house," Wales said, feeling accused, "and we have people inside at the Anaheim PD."

The Reverend said, "Please, brother. I'm not blaming you. If I blamed you, we wouldn't be having this conversation in this garden." He smiled. It was amazing how he could threaten and comfort at the same time. It was a powerful tool Wales would have to learn to emulate. "Drugs are a dirty business anyway, and it exposes us. Our other sources of income are sufficient." The Reverend sighed. "I've been touring some of our other towns, too. These problems are everywhere—Mexicans trying to move into our town in Ohio, Muslims in our town in Pennsylvania. The Mexicans have already infested Utah, Idaho."

"It's difficult when we have to deal with ZOG laws," Wales said, feeling suddenly like he had failed.

Flip turn, a splash of water against Wales's loafers.

"True," The Reverend said, "some of these things are out of our control, for now." He was quiet a moment. "We may be closer to the moment, to The Tribulation, than I thought." The Reverend leaned forward now, his elbows on the table next to the bowl of strawberries. "Tell me," he said, "how secure is the BBS?"

Wales explained. The bulletin board contained five different security levels, all of them password-restricted. The lowest levels, Levels 1 and 2, could be accessed with simple electronic codes, available to Identity Movement members and other chosen white supremacy groups. On Level 1, there was a board for leaving messages, posting names of enemies, and links to access Wales's archived sermons. Level 2 was a board for recruitment. Level 3, a board for sharing documents—by invitation only. Level 4 was a place to meet with sympathetic politicians—again, by invitation only. The fifth level was available only to those with the highest security clearance—codes shared only among individuals who were planning or executing missions.

"This level," Wales said, "has new access codes for each meeting, no two ever the same."

"In theory," The Reverend said, "if law enforcement cracked the codes, they could access the first two levels, yes?"

"Yes."

"Of course, that's a risk *you* have to take—access versus security," The Reverend said. "However, I cannot take such risks."

"Everyone with access to the fifth level," Wales said, "will be people already vetted by you."

"If it's compromised, you—"

"It *won't* be compromised."

The Reverend stared at Wales a moment, a flush of anger on his face at the interruption, but thinking, too, it seemed. "This may not be *the* war, but I believe some action needs to be taken. I've visited with some of the other reverends, too."

Wales nodded. He'd been waiting for this moment, been

praying for it. Yet, The Tribulation had always been out there, somewhere over the horizon, like some unattainable dream.

"Ian Rowan is reckless," The Reverend said, "but he could be useful. He and his group of young men."

Then The Reverend leaned in close to Wales, his voice growing quieter, and Wales listened.

PART THREE

PART THREE

Chapter Thirteen

Boneyard was hitting hard. A swell out of New Zealand was pushing across the Pacific, stacking a line of waves that raked the reef at Abalone Point. Ben sat low in the water, egg-beatering his legs to keep his chin above the rising swells. It was 7:15, a cloudless desert-dry morning, the water only in the high fifties. His full-length wet suit made it bearable, but his fingers and toes tingled with numbness. Two kids were out with him, surfers; they straddled their fiberglass boards, eyeing the stacked-up swells.

Ben kept his distance; he didn't want to be impaled by a board tip, strafed by a fin. But he kept an ear to their conversation—the "dickweed" admin at school would call home, one of them said, he'd be in deep shit with his parents tonight, but he wasn't going to end up like his prick father, no way, driving to LA at 4:30 every morning to avoid rush-hour traffic, dressed like a clown in a three-piece suit, selling latex gloves to hospitals. He wasn't going that route, man; he was going pro in a few years, picking up a few sponsors, out the front door of his little suburban prison when he was eighteen, waving to his parents in the rearview as he flew off to Hawaii to ride Pipeline or even Teahupo'o in Tahiti.

Ben quietly laughed at the kid, that teenage idealism expressed in disdain. They were Emma's age—their bodies hormone-flooded, their minds rattled by molecules they couldn't understand. He thought about Emma last night, hysterical about killing her relationship with Lance. It had rattled him a little, the violence of her emotion and his helplessness at dealing with it. *Teenagedom is a form of insanity,* Natasha had said. *As a parent you manage a loving (hopefully) asylum.* She was right. She usually was.

And for a few moments last night, he thought they might want to have a child together. They'd played around with the idea before, postcoital and mostly joking. *She should have your nose and your eyes. He should have your height*—a smile before she said it—*and my brain.* They weren't too old yet, but getting close, both in their later thirties. He'd almost said it out loud last night as they walked back to the bedroom, something about the way she talked about Linh, the way she'd patiently won over Emma, pushing the idea to the edge of spoken reality. And he imagined it while they were tussling in bed, an extra spark in the action thinking about the intention in it. But once he uttered those words, there was no going back on it, he knew it, half drunk or not. So he climbed out of bed this morning, leaving her tangled in the sheets, and drove out here to clear his head before heading to the station.

He hadn't been out body surfing for a couple weeks at least, and his body felt heavy in the surf. He'd ridden three nice lefts that dropped him into a forest of seaweed. He could see the ropes of bladder kelp beneath him now, a submerged forest swaying with the tide. The blades and bladder pods tangled around his ankles. It used to freak him out when he was a kid, about the surfers' age; the kelp fronds felt like limbs rubbing up against his body, or fingers trying to pull him down into the darkness below. But he loved it now, a whole world beneath the surface of the water, a world that sheltered rockfish and gari-baldi, top snails and abalone. To get your feet offland was to forget for a while all the shit people do to one another, to exist on a separate plane.

A set of three came in. Ben started kicking, but one of the surfers dropped in first, cut left, and got thrown over the falls, his board coughed into the air by the churn.

"You all right, kid?" Ben said, when the boy surfaced from the spin cycle, a bloody cut above his left eye.

"Yeah, man, I'm fine."

They both dove beneath the breaking third wave.

"Might want to swim in," Ben said when they were breathing air again. "Make sure that head of yours isn't rattled."

The left leg of the kid's wet suit was gashed open, too, and a trickle of blood swirled like oil among the kelp fronds and salt bubbles.

"Dude, that looks pretty gnarly," his friend said, paddling over to check on him.

"Ah, man. Just a flesh wound," the kid said, sounding like the Black Knight from Monty Python.

"Let me see your eyes," the friend said.

"Dude, Logan, I'm fine," the kid said.

"They dilated?" Ben yelled to Logan.

Last year Ben saw this surfer from Dana Point go down hard. Next thing, he slid off his board and had to be dragged to shore by his buddies, Newport EMS hauling him off to emergency.

"No, man," Logan said. "They look good."

Ben spun to see the next stack of waves rolling in, real big ones, morning sunlight glancing off the windblown peaks.

"Whoa," the bloodied kid said. "What was that? Dude, something rubbed against my leg."

"It's just seaweed," Logan said.

"No, man. It was big."

A shark, maybe, the kid's blood chumming the water for leopards. Ben tried to peer down into the darkness of the kelp, but the morning sunlight sparkled the surface, the water as opaque as aluminum. A burst of air, like a small pipe punctured, and there, fifty feet away, bobbed the bullet head of a sea lion, its black, intelligent eyes staring at them.

"Fucking seal," the friend said, laughing.

"Sea lion," Logan said.

"Shut up, Mr. Marine Biologist. That freaked me out."

It had been two, maybe three seconds between the nudge against the kid's thigh and the surfacing sea lion. They were fast underwater, for sure, but not that fast. Ben watched the sea lion, maybe seventy feet away. It wasn't the sea lion the kid had felt, no way.

"Set," Logan yelled out.

The boys slipped belly-first onto their boards and kicked toward the break. Ben spun around, too, and started kicking, the Viper Fins lifting his chest in the water with the speed, the adrenaline rush of chasing down a wall of water. The swell rose green and translucent, a peak of Pacific obliterating the horizon. The surface of the water shifted like a table being lifted, and Ben, for a moment, thought he'd be flipped backward until the energy threw him forward toward shore. The kid took off on the wave, too, but Ben wasn't giving it up to him. He'd carved it first, the kid dropping in at the last moment. Ben cut left, so did the kid, his board rocketing him below Ben, who was laid out to stay high on the wave. Then Ben slammed into something, and he was rag-dolled onto the lip of the wave before it bludgeoned him headfirst into the spin cycle.

Ben turned, expecting to see the kid's torso floating above the line of his wave, but something else tumbled through the backwash, something white and limblike—a piece of driftwood, a hunk of rotting porpoise? The wave thundered the shore and the white thing spun, two arms Ferris-wheeling into the white-wash.

For a moment, Ben was terrified it was the kid, concussed and drowned, but Ben found him, arm grasping his board, his eyes wide and startled, looking toward the shore, too, as the next wave lifted the dead body into the sky.

———

When Natasha arrived on the scene, her official white Ford perched on the cliff above the beach, Ben watched her hike the trail down to the sand, trying to figure out how to break this to her, feeling terrible that he hadn't told her over the phone, hadn't prepared her. He'd ordered a uniform to hold her at the perimeter until he could talk to her, and now her kit was at her feet, her badge shoved into the officer's face. He left the body and trudged through the sand. He was still dressed to the waist in his wet suit, the neoprene shoulders and arms dangling from his hips, his T-shirt wet where it met the damp suit, and he shuddered from the morning cold,

An hour earlier, he and the surfers had pulled the body from the water. Logan uttering *Holy shit, holy shit, holy shit* with such breathlessness it almost sounded profound. Ben had stayed with the body—her seaweed-tangled hair, sand clinging to her legs—and sent the kid on a mission to the Texaco on PCH to put in the 911 call. He stood alone with her for nearly twenty minutes—shooing away an occasional gull, stomping at crabs—until the sirens screeched on PCH and the first black-and-whites arrived on scene. He'd tried to reach Mendenhall at the ME's office from one of the Motorolas in a patrol car, but the chief medical examiner wouldn't be in until 9:00. Ben didn't like working with Mendenhall; he did careless work as far as Ben was concerned. Mostly, though, he didn't want Natasha on this scene. But she was the ME on call this morning, and he had no choice but to call her in.

"On Detective Wade's orders?" he heard Natasha say to the uniform.

"Yes, ma'am."

Ben ducked under the crime scene tape, took her by the elbow, and walked her up the path some distance from the cops and the television crews, the joggers and their leashed golden retrievers.

"What's going on?"

He faced her now, her chin raised to him, her green eyes narrowed.

"It's Linh."

Her eyes shot back and forth, searching his face, and he made sure he looked right back at her. She glanced toward the beach where Linh's body lay in the sand, looking like tide detritus—tangled rope kelp, a washed-up log. Then she took off down the hill. Twenty yards down the beach, she ran, her heels kicking up sand, and he followed slowly behind her, giving her space. At the body, she stabbed her foot into the sand to keep her balance. She spun away then, and stood on the edge of the waterline, gazing out at the empty Pacific, waves washing over her shoes.

They stood like that for a couple of minutes, Natasha staring at the horizon, Southeast Asia out there somewhere, thousands of miles away. He didn't dare move, just planted his feet in the sand ten feet away from her, the body between them.

"Get my kit," she said, finally.

"Tash, let's get Mendenhall in here to do this. Or call someone down from LA."

"No. I want my kit."

He trudged the fifty yards back to the perimeter, trying to get his head straight, trying to turn off Benjamin Wade and make the detective inside him take charge.

———

Hernandez arrived on scene ten minutes later, dressed in a tan suit and alligator-skin boots. The lieutenant walked out across the sand, hands behind his back, eyeing Natasha and the body, while Ben and Carolina gridded the beach.

"Word has it she knows the deceased?" Hernandez said, nodding toward Natasha.

"Word's true."

They both watched her work the body. She was on her knees, snapping pictures, and from here, some twenty yards away, she looked all professional, like this deceased was any other victim washed up onshore.

"It shouldn't be her."

"She and I already had that discussion."

Hernandez glanced back at the perimeter where the surfer kids were being interviewed by an Eyewitness News reporter.

"Deceased has a contusion around the left eye socket," Ben said. "Looks like her skull was fractured."

"Dumped or post-drowning?"

Ben glanced out at the water, waves breaking against the rock reef and tide pools. Years ago, he'd ridden a long right into those rocks, tearing open his back.

"Hard to say," Ben said. "Could've been beaten first then dumped in the water. Could've drowned and then slammed up against the rocks. Will need to see if there's water in the lungs."

"That fire fresh?"

"Looks that way." Ben glanced back at the pit, a wisp of smoke spinning into the coastal breeze.

He remembered the firepit up at Huntington Beach.

"She related to the grocer with the dog incident?"

"Daughter," Ben said. "The victim was sleeping with an older man. The insurance agent for the family grocery. Guy named Lucas Clay."

Hernandez glanced at the smoke curling from the fire. "Looks like a party to me," he finally said. "But we should question the agent anyway." He glanced at Ben again. "You have any clothes or is this your choice of off-duty attire?"

"In the truck," Ben said. "I didn't—you know—I didn't want to leave her alone with the body."

"Go get dressed, Detective. It's too damn cold to be out here wet."

Ben trudged again across the sand and climbed the footpath

up the cliff to his truck. There he wrapped himself in a towel and changed, and watched Hernandez kneel down next to Natasha. From here, he couldn't tell what he was saying to her, but she never stopped working, never stopped snapping pictures; hell, didn't even look like she acknowledged the lieutenant. And when Ben was hiking back down the cliff, Hernandez finally stood and strode away from the body.

"She's one tough pain in the ass," Hernandez said.

"Yep. We could arrest her, I guess."

"And put the chief medical examiner on it?"

Ben just nodded once, turning his lips down in acknowledgment.

"You keep her clean on this."

"She'll be clean." *Don't know what she'll be afterward,* he thought, but kept that to himself.

"It'll be Mendenhall's business when the body gets up to County."

Then they let her work as they combed the sand, Ben keeping an eye on her as they tagged anything unusual—a silver fork, a couple of beer cans, a discarded O'Neill sweatshirt, a shriveled-up condom behind a rock. Jesus, you looked too closely at a beach and you'd never want to set foot on one again. At first glance, there was little to go on around the fire. The bastards had raked the sand clean, just like up at Huntington— no footprints, no tire marks, nothing. But this time with an actual rake. A fucking Zen garden.

———

Ben and Natasha were on the 5 freeway, heading back into Santa Elena, passing the strawberry fields where the pickers had been attacked the other night, past the new United Artists mega-plex movie theaters advertising "stadium seating."

An hour earlier, he had followed Natasha up to the county coroner's office to drop off Linh's body. He helped her move a body out of the first bin—senator's kid OD. Then together they wheeled Linh across the examination room, silent, just the rattling of the steel gurney, the click, click, click of a bum wheel. For a minute, Natasha braced herself against the gurney, her face inches from Linh's covered face. Beneath the sheet, you could see the contours of Linh's face, the point of her nose, the conjoining lines of her lips.

"Okay," she finally said, and Ben helped her push Linh inside bin 1.

Now he pulled the truck into Hacienda Estates, wondering briefly if any of these developers actually knew Spanish, and flashed his badge at the guard at the gate. As soon as he pushed the truck up against the curb, the front door opened and both Mr. and Mrs. Phan were there—Mr. Phan stepping outside in his socks and Mrs. Phan crowding the door in a robe.

"I can do this," Ben said to Natasha, his hand on the driver's side door.

"No, you can't," she said and shoved open the passenger door.

He fell back in his seat and watched her make her way up the pathway to the house. She took Mr. Phan's hand and Mrs. Phan stumbled against the doorframe, her mouth yawned open in a silent wail. They went inside the house together, the door left open to the early-afternoon light, the darkened doorframe revealing nothing of what was happening inside.

Natasha stepped out into the light ten minutes later, closing the front door behind her. He watched her stumble down the walkway, her eyes cast down at the cracks in the pavement. She opened the door and climbed into the passenger seat and then stared through the windshield to the green winter hills.

"That's the worst thing I've ever had to do," she said.

Chapter Fourteen

They were driving back to his place—he was going to boil her some soup, feed her drinks, anything she needed—when Hernandez dialed him on the Motorola.

"Lucas Clay's in the house," Hernandez said. "Walked in to file a missing person report. Got Carolina taking his statement, but haven't broken the news yet."

When he hung up with the lieutenant, he told Natasha. "I have to get over there, but let me take you to my place, get you comfortable."

She shook her head and said, "I'm coming with you. Let's go."

When they got to the station, Carolina was finishing up with Lucas Clay in an interview room. Hernandez tried to get Natasha to rest in his office, but she wasn't having it, so the three of them huddled in the viewing room, watching Lucas Clay scour his fingers over the knuckles of his left hand. Ben noted the man's shoes, Nike sneakers.

"If he's lying," Hernandez said, "give him an Oscar."

"Wouldn't be the first," Natasha said.

Truth. In LA, Ben had assisted on a case of a missing waitress/actress. Her high-profile cosmetic surgeon boyfriend called her in missing, sobbed them a detailed account, fed them an alibi. Woman turned up in a ravine in Griffith Park a week later, neck sliced with what the coroner determined was a medical scalpel. The alibi confessed to taking a bribe. Surgeon arrested a day later at his office, photos of the stars he'd cut hanging in the waiting room.

Carolina stepped out, handed Ben the evidence file. "I'd say the man's in love," she said.

"It's not a crime of passion," Ben said. "Unless the man keeps a rake in the trunk of his car."

"Let's tell him," Hernandez said.

Inside the interview room, Ben sat down opposite Lucas at the bolted-down table. "Get you anything? Water? Coffee?"

The man looked trashed, his eyes rimmed with black circles, the whites bloodshot.

"There's something you all aren't telling me."

"You were having an affair?"

"A vulgar word for it."

"Her father found out?"

"He came to my apartment the other day. I tried to invite him in, to talk with him about it."

"But he wasn't having it?"

"No," he said. The knuckles of his left hand were raw from his scratching. "Linh was staying with me for a few days until Bao calmed down."

"Your wife know about the affair?"

"What the hell is going on?" he said. "Where's Linh?"

Ben put his elbows on the table. "Mr. Clay," he said. "Linh is dead."

When Jacob shifted in his desk chair, a sharp pain zapped his side. This morning when he tried to get out of bed, his head spun with pain and he nearly threw up in the toilet. *You gotta act normal, Tough Shit,* Ian had said last night. *No matter what. You got it?* Yeah, he got it, so he managed to drag himself downstairs and pop a couple of aspirin, and he managed to walk himself to school. It wasn't so bad when he was standing, but sitting here, in English class now, Miss Russell blah, blah, blahing about *The Great Gatsby,* it ached, and whenever he tried to stand or sit that lightning strike of pain lit him up.

"Shit, man," he remembered Ian saying last night. Ian's flight jacket splattered with blood, the front of his white T-shirt, too. "You might have broke your rib or something."

Jacob had been leaning against the passenger door of the truck, holding his side.

"You flipped, man," Ian said. "I mean, you went nuts. Even nailed Fisker once. Must've tagged yourself, too."

"Is she dead?"

He remembered parts of what happened, drunken blurs of moments—Clocker laughing, the girl's hand touching his, her voice saying, *You don't have to do this, Jacob,* before he swung the sock.

"You don't remember?"

"Only some of it."

His memory flashed with fragments of the night—a streak of firelight, his arm swinging the homey sock, screaming, her body splayed out in the sand. He'd been loaded, on beer, on the white pill, his memory blurred. Clocker had grabbed him around the waist and yanked him away from the fire, and then he was up on the cliffs where the trucks were, watching the waves roll in.

"Mr. Clay," Miss Russell said now, shaking him out of his memory. "How about joining this world, huh?" A few kids chuckled; Sarah Greenblatt smirked. "What do you think Dr. T. J. Eckleburg's spectacles symbolize?" Miss Russell was standing at the chalkboard; her hand, pinching a piece of chalk, rested on the board where she'd apparently just drawn a huge pair of glasses.

"I don't know," he said, his head swimming with pain. "God or something."

As far as he could tell about American lit, it always came back to God.

"Would you like to elaborate?"

"Not really."

Laughter. *Fuckers.* "God or something," David Feller said, mimicking Jacob's voice.

"Mr. Feller," Miss Russell said. "How about you enlighten us?"

And then all eyes were on the sputtering David Feller.

Last night, Ian had driven them into the new Bonita Vista housing complex and circled up the ridge of the hill, past the newly framed homes and then off the pavement onto a dirt trail that rolled high into the darkened wilderness the serial killer had hidden out in last year. Ian had pulled out the pistol when they crossed the cattle grate onto the dirt road, and it sat there between them, small and gunmetal gray, but loaded and locked. Ian drove for a long time, the city lights fading until nailhead stars punctured the black sky. They passed an old cabin, half of it knocked down and the other half sagging toward the dirt, until they got to the reservoir, still and black as used oil.

"Take your shirt off." Ian stepped out of the truck, stripped off his jacket and his shirt. "Now. Take it off." He found a rock, tied his shirt and flight jacket around it, and flung it into the water. "Find a rock. Tie your shirt just like I did."

Jacob found a hunk of limestone, tied his shirt off, and then Ian snatched it away and hurled it into the water.

Five minutes later they were sitting in the cab of the truck, a couple of blankets wrapped around their shoulders, the city lights sprinkled in the valley below. The pistol was still on the bench seat between them. The radio was turned low, but it wasn't picking up any music, just the hushed static of radio wave emptiness. Something moved out in the open field below.

Deer, Jacob realized, their heads bowed to the long winter grass.

"Look," Ian said. He picked up the pistol, held it in his hand draped over the steering wheel. "From here on out, forever, until you fucking die, you say nothing." He pointed the gun at Jacob's face now. Jacob couldn't tell if Ian meant to be threatening him or if the gun had just become an extension of his hand, but one pull of the trigger and his head would be oatmeal. "Never say anything about this to anyone, you got it?"

"Yeah."

"No one, man. Not even to me. Full radio silence."

Ian drove them to a twenty-four-hour pharmacy, put on a ratty sweatshirt that was stuffed behind the driver's seat, left him in the car to his pain, and returned with a bag full of shit.

"Sit up." Ian pulled the blanket from Jacob's shoulders and tightly wrapped his torso with a bandage. "Look. You can't go to the hospital. They can't do anything for you anyway. It just has to heal on its own, got it?"

"Yeah," Jacob said, but it hurt like hell.

"Fuck, Tough Shit," Ian said, shaking his head and smiling as he put the truck in gear. "We gotta work on your technique."

Miss Russell was talking again, stalking the rows of the class like she was hunting something. He tried to go back in his memory, before the ride into the hills, before tossing the bloodied shirts. It was like with the Mexicans, his head exploding with light, the sock swinging, the crack of bone, and then the thump of his own side. But he didn't really feel anything then, not until later, when they were in the truck and he was coming down off the buzz of the pill.

"Mr. Clay."

He was back in the classroom—the scent of sharpened pencils, a tinge of hairspray and body odor spicing the air, a poster of David Bowie reading a book. Students were scratching chairs across the floor, class apparently over. Miss Russell was sitting down in the desk next to him now, her chin resting on her hand, her eyes full of concern. T. J. Eckle-something's glasses hovering behind her.

"Jacob," she said now, her tone softening. "Are you okay?"

He wanted to say, I think I killed someone. *Never say anything about this to anyone, you got it?* He wanted to say, My side hurts like hell and I'm scared. *Forever, until you fucking die.*

"Yeah, Miss R," he said. "I'm just tired."

———

After they told Lucas Clay about Linh, the man flipped out. It had taken all three of them—Ben, Hernandez, Carolina—to get Clay down on the interview room floor, an indescribable wail wrenched from his throat. He thrashed around until Natasha pressed a thumb behind the man's ear and he finally let them have his arms.

"What did you do?" Hernandez asked, huffing air.

"Pressure point," Natasha said. "Thumb to the mandibular nerve."

"How'd you know to do that?"

"I study the body, Lieutenant."

Then they sat there on the linoleum for five minutes, the man crying, Natasha talking to him, soothing him, before they locked him in a holding cell. They'd have to let him go in the morning, though. His alibis had checked out—the next-door neighbor whose door he banged on, asking her if she'd seen Linh. Linh's abandoned car at the university with his panicked note folded beneath the windshield wiper. *Cục cưng*, it said in slashing letters. *Call me, please! I'm worried, cục cưng.* Darling. Cục cưng meant "darling," according to Danh Phan, whom Carolina had called once the evidence had made it back to the station.

Now Ben and Natasha were back at his place, sitting at the kitchen counter. Ben's back muscles had spasmed a half hour earlier, but he'd taken three Tylenol and their grip on his torso had loosened. He'd turned on some Teddy Pendergrass to take the edge off, but Natasha asked him to switch it off. *I want to sit with this,* she'd said. *I don't want to try and pretend it hasn't happened.* And now they sat in silence, just beginning what he imagined would be a long night, and watched the cutout black hills, framed by the basin lights, out beyond the window.

"You know how the Phans got out of Saigon?"

Ben just shook his head.

She told him about how Bao's brother had stolen a helicopter during the fall of Saigon. How he had piled his family inside and flew out into the Pacific in search of the American ships.

She was quiet a minute. "Can you imagine doing that? Leaving everything, flying your family out into oblivion, not knowing if you were going to find those ships?"

Ben admitted he couldn't imagine it, though he could imagine being desperate enough to act. Bravery usually wasn't bravery, but desperate action. Or desperate action in the face of terror *was* bravery.

"You know how Linh got that scar?" she said, touching her own forehead.

"No."

"They had to land on an American destroyer, which really only had room for one helicopter. When they hit the deck, the tail rotor clipped another helicopter. Shards of metal went flying. She nearly lost that eye."

Ben stared out the window, catching a glimpse of the lights of Balboa Island and Newport Bay, and then the dark expanse beyond, pushing toward Asia. Coyotes yipped at one another. Beyond them the freeway hummed.

"The first time I saw her, down in Pendleton," she said, "I felt this incredible anger. Anger at the war, at our country. At myself. It scared the bejesus out of me, that feeling. First time I felt like we were the enemy."

"You were a kid when the war started."

"I voted for Nixon," she said. "I knew what that war was,

and I still voted for him. My first time voting, just doing what my parents did." She paused and looked out at the dark ridges of the hills, the bruised blue of the sky above. "That anger woke me up. But not for long."

"You're a good person, Tash."

"That's not why I'm telling you this."

"All right."

"It was my fourth year at UCLA," she said. "I showed up at Camp Pendleton for months—even after my parents' church mostly stopped volunteering there—combing out Linh's hair, teaching her English, playing soccer in the street. I mean, I started skipping classes to be down there, almost dropped out the spring semester." She paused, thinking about it. "I helped find them a sponsor, a job packing tiles in a warehouse for Bao, a stupid job for a man who was a teacher. I helped them move to Westminster. I stayed in touch, visited for dinners, translated for Linh's parents at school conferences, even helped them move into their first grocery. Then I started med school and I just let them go."

"Med school's a bitch," Ben said.

"That's not it, Ben. After the grocery opened, after Linh started school—she had friends, she had soccer, dance lessons, like any other kid. They didn't need me anymore. I realize now," she said, "that all of that—the volunteering, the searching for a sponsor, the way I threw myself completely into their lives—was really just a way to deal with my own stuff. I used them—used Linh—and I thought I was being some goddamned saint."

Ben thought she was being hard on herself, but he suspected he had done the same thing up in North Hollywood, the white cop riding in on the Ford Mustang cruiser, ready to vanquish all manner of evil.

"When I realized," Natasha went on, "they didn't need me—the grocery was successful, they had family and friends—I was hurt. It felt like real loss at the time, but I think it was resentment. I resented them for not needing me and I severed them from my life. How selfish is that?"

"We all lose touch with people."

"Please stop trying to make me feel better about this," she said, reprimanding him with her eyes.

He wasn't going to be able to ease this for her. Why did he think he could? Like she said, she wanted to sit with this, to feel it. Why couldn't he just sit and feel it with her? Well, he could and he would.

"Linh wanted me to speak to Bao," Natasha said after a couple minutes. "I said I wouldn't. She asked me for help, Ben, and I said no. I didn't think he'd listen to me, thought it would make him angrier, thought it'd make him feel like I, an outsider, was closer to his daughter than he was. And now this."

He covered her hand with both of his, and the two of them stared out at the black hills in silence, watching the lights of the city curl around the edge of the wilderness down toward the ocean, until she said, "Okay," and he walked her into the bedroom. He thought he was just going to hold her, but she started kissing him, devouring kisses, and before he knew it they were both naked and he was inside her, something overwhelming about it, something frightening in the rawness of it.

After, she lay next to him, her back turned, his arm draped over her hip.

"What are we doing, Ben?" she said, quietly. "I mean, what is this?"

"I love you," he said to the back of her neck. "That's what this is."

She was quiet a moment, like she had other things to say. "I know."

———

It was all lies. Linh had been right; Bao could hear her voice declaring it. The last words she would ever say to him.

Bao sat in his chair in the living room, a carving knife in his lap, imagining his dead daughter's face. He had lied to her—that all his work was for her, that he wanted her to be an independent woman, that she could be anything she wanted. They'd proven their lies with their dumb, mean plan, he could see that now.

After Miss Natasha told them about Linh, Ai had thrown herself on their bed and unraveled. He stayed with her until the early morning, holding her, but he knew she blamed him—or at least he blamed himself—and when Ai had calmed, he moved into the living room, sitting in this chair in the dark, unable to share his shame and grief with her. *You think if you marry a white man*, Bao remembered saying the other day, *they'll see you as American?* It was a mean thing to say, a terrible thing, to suggest Linh was trying to make herself more white through marriage; it demeaned her and it shamed him, a shame he'd never get forgiveness for now.

Sometime in the night, he'd pulled the knife from the butcher block and set it in front of him on the counter. He imagined stabbing it into his heart so fully he was surprised to find his hands pinned to the countertop. He almost called Danh then—he wanted to confess his selfishness—but he couldn't make himself move. So he sat with it then, the knife on his lap in his chair in the living room, and sometime in the early morning, he didn't know when, in that timeless space of grief, something vibrated in him. That's the only way he could explain it—something vibrating with life moved through him. If Linh had an energy, this was it. If he was asked to describe the feeling, he wouldn't have been able to. It wasn't warm or cold, it wasn't physical, wasn't molecular. He could only say that it felt like Linh, as though something like air had entered his bloodstream, had blown into his synapses and DNA. She stayed with him—for how long, he didn't know—something warm vibrating in his solar plexus, and then she was gone.

The sun shone through the backyard door now, that pure

unfiltered desert light. He was astonished that light could ever
shine again. It was the beginning of the world forgetting Linh
Phan had ever existed. The birds chirped, someone started a
car, and he swore he could feel the earth cruelly spinning.
Gripped by a sudden impulse to stand, he set the knife on the
coffee table and pushed himself up. He had to prop himself up
by the armrests until his feet tingled back to life, and then he
stumbled down the hallway to Linh's room.

For a moment, he thought he'd find her in her bed, the night
a terrible dream from which he was just now waking. Her perfume wafted into his nose, the citrus tang of the soap she used
to wash her face. She was in the house. Her physical presence
was so powerful, he even knocked on her door, "Con yêu," before pushing it open to her empty bed. Then his hands were
sliding under her covers, his palms searching the indentations
of the mattress, the dip where her hips once weighted the foam,
the canyon where her shoulders once lay. He threw off the covers and swiped his palms across the bare mattress, his hands
with minds of their own, until he found the strands of hair.
They tangled around the fingers of his right hand and when he
realized what they were, he pressed the strands to his nose, the
scent of his daughter's shampoo filling his head.

———

After Natasha fell asleep, Ben snuck out to the barn and cleaned
the horses' stalls, thinking about the cases, trying to link all the
pieces into a cohesive narrative. He could think out here,
the quiet, the clean-grassy scent of hay. After taking care of the
horses, he sat at his desk inside the barn and listened to his
home answering machine. Vanek had left him a message, told
him he had some intel on PACCOAST. Told Ben to call him,
anytime. Ben took him at his word. It was 12:47 A.M. Vanek
picked up after the first ring.

"I had a conversation with the construction superintendent

at PACCOAST," Vanek said, getting straight to business. "The man said the Los Olivos site was blocked because of a zoning dispute. City maintained they didn't have enough parking spots for the shopping center. Apparently when they started the complex, the city only required them to have seventy-five spots. After they laid the foundations, suddenly they needed a hundred."

"So the whole thing got shut down over twenty-five parking spots?"

Ben was scribbling notes on his legal pad.

"Officially anyway," Vanek said. "Brennan was an early investor in the project. The superintendent said they tried arbitration, but now it's tied up in litigation. The company's leaning toward cutting their losses and moving on. Says there's too much money to be made elsewhere—down in Mission Viejo, Laguna Niguel, et cetera."

On his pad, Ben wrote: *Brennan killed for leasing to Vietnamese. Phans targeted for owning their property. Too much of a foothold, owning property. But what about Linh?* He underlined that. Something didn't fit easy with that.

"Brennan bought one space in the complex on September third and was apparently considering a second when the zoning issue came up on September fifteenth, according to the supervisor."

"Well, that's one way to keep them out." The councilman, the mayor maybe, who knew who else, getting in the zoning board members' ears.

Ben told Vanek about Linh then, about the affair, told him about how she was being asked to choose between her family and Lucas Clay, about how her head was bashed in, about the raking down of the beach sand, just as the perps had done up in Huntington Beach.

"Any chance this young woman jumped?" Vanek said. "She must have been upset."

"Possible," Ben said. "But the tide would have been too far out for her to hit water from the cliffs. If she jumped, I think we would have found her in the sand."

"And the raking down of the beach," Vanek said. "Just like the Brennan scene."

"Right," Ben said. "But there's a missing link here."

"Something personal," Vanek said.

"Exactly."

"Her father? He was making her choose, I would guess, because they were ashamed."

"Don't think it's him," Ben said. "Natasha knows the family."

"She knew the young woman, too?"

"Yeah," Ben said. "She did."

He told Vanek about the Phans' escape from Saigon, about Natasha's time volunteering at Pendleton. Vanek was quiet for a minute. Ben heard him clear his throat through the receiver.

"How is she?"

"Torn up."

Quiet another moment. "What about the lover? Maybe she told him she was breaking it off, told him she was choosing family."

"No," Ben said. "He showed up at the station in the morning to report her missing, just about tore the place apart when we told him. Besides, his alibis check out."

"His wife then," Vanek said.

"Maybe," Ben said, "but—"

"How'd she get the young woman down to the beach?" Ben could practically hear him nodding. "How'd she beat her and get the body into the water?"

"Right," Ben said. "It'd have to be a strong dude, if it's a lone killer."

"Or a group."

They were silent a minute together. Ben heard an owl hooting from the oak tree on the edge of the property.

"The re—"

"Recruit," Ben said, finishing Vanek's thought. "The kid Ian Rowan got outfitted."

Ben hung up and drove down to the station, got there at 1:18, the midnight show buzzing around him—the drunken howlers in the overnight cells, the low-on-the-totem-pole cops questioning high-class prostitutes, writing up reports on late-night bar fights. He found the report file from the wrestling match with Lucas Clay this morning. They didn't arrest him, but Ben had slipped a copy of the incident report in the murder book for Linh's case. The address Clay gave was in Corona del Mar. Ben found the white pages in the left-side drawer. The address wasn't listed among the residential listings in Corona. He checked the yellow pages. There it was: the office address of Clay Insurance. But where in the hell did this guy live? He went back to the white pages, found the Clay listings, and ran his finger down the line. There were thirteen Clay listings in the county, but no Lucas Clay, no Katherine Clay.

In fifteen minutes, he was in Corona del Mar, parked behind the Clays' insurance building. Inside, all the lights were off, except for a desk lamp. He tried the back door, but of course it was locked. Ben kept a bump key on his key ring for just these occasions. He slipped it into the door lock, found a brick discarded near the trash bin, and tapped the bump key. The lock clicked open.

What he was doing was strictly illegal and anything he found here would be inadmissible in court, but sometimes you needed to bend the law a bit to enforce it. It didn't take long. A quick look through desk drawer files, a fingering of desktop paperwork, and then, stuck inside a stack of mail, he found it: a letter addressed to Lucas A. Clay, 19476 Comet Street. Holy shit, on the same street the Rowans lived on.

Ben put the mail back, locked the back door again, and sped over to Comet Street immediately, most of the street dark, the slumber of a bedroom community, and sat a half block down thinking. Clay's wife would have motive, if she knew about the affair. But, nah, that didn't work out, for all the reasons he and Vanek ticked off earlier. No coincidence this Lucas Clay lived right across the street from the Rowans, and in the same damn neighborhood as the Connollys' poisoned pooch. Ben got out of the car and strolled the sidewalk. A light was on in one of the upstairs bedrooms of the Clay house. Two twenty-two in the morning, shadows windmilling up there, like someone swinging figure-eights in the air. But he couldn't see anyone, just the shadows moving like some kind of frenetic ghost. He crossed the street and was trying to get a different angle when the movement stopped and suddenly he could see the face, a kid's face, just before he reached over and flipped a light switch and the room went dark. The recruit. The recruit was Lucas Clay's son. He was almost sure of it, that feeling like everything clicking into place.

From Comet Street, he drove down to Crystal Cove. He swung the cruiser around onto Los Trancos and took the dirt road underneath the freeway until he reached the parking area where the old bungalows, abandoned and dilapidated now, glowed like a bombed-out memory of paradise. The headlights of the cruiser lit the surf, and using that harsh light he combed the beach where they found Linh. It was low tide now, the water sucked away from the sand and rocks, exposing the tide pools. You could smell it, the stink of piled seaweed, the rot of stagnant salt water. A weapon. They needed a weapon. He walked the beach for a half hour, flashlit up the trail threading the cliffs, thinking about the shadow swinging figure-eights. Nothing.

It was 3:18 when he got back to the house, slipped back in with Natasha, and lay in bed thinking. Natasha was up by 4:15, quietly sliding out of bed, silently slipping on her clothes.

He lay there, pretending to sleep as she hovered on the balls of her feet, avoiding the creaky floorboards, and floated into the living room. He knew what she was doing. He heard her keys jingle in her hand. Knew where she was going. Her Z fired up outside in the early-morning darkness, and he swung his feet over the edge of the bed and watched her headlights fade down the driveway. He also knew there was no point in his trying to stop her.

When her taillights receded past the eucalyptus trees, he picked up the receiver on the bedside phone and dialed the number.

———

Of all the horror yesterday, the worst was telling the Phans they'd have to perform an autopsy on Linh. Ai had kept slapping her hand against the Formica counter—*No,* she said, *no*—smacking her palm so hard it had frightened Natasha.

"Please," Natasha had said, "you'll hurt yourself." Then she gently flattened Ai's hands against the countertop. "On my life, I swear to you, we'll catch who did this. *I* will catch who did this."

Now she was in the examination room, 5:17 A.M., more than three hours before Mendenhall would arrive. Linh's body lay before her on the stainless-steel table, the sheet pulled tight over her. Natasha sat across the room on a metal stool, looking at her. She'd been sitting here for at least twenty minutes, the scalpels laid out on the tray next to the body, but she'd been unable to move. Linh was not Linh anymore, whatever made up her soul had bled away into the Pacific, but her body, the container of what had been Linh, still seemed intact enough to hold that ephemeral ghost. More than ever, Natasha felt the brutality of her job. When she opened up Linh, peered inside her body, she'd look like any other person—deconstructed to parts, as though she were a machine. What she knew for sure, though some genetics professors theorized the opposite, was that there was no race beneath the surface of the skin. In here, inside the bone and viscera, within the fluid and gall, there were no markers that the skin contained. In here, you couldn't say, *Oh, that's a black heart*. The lungs didn't have a Mexican look to them. All things were equal here, in death, in dissection, unless you wanted to get beneath the surface with your own prejudice. What a terrible irony that was, death the great equalizer. She wasn't ready to do this yet, though, wasn't ready to deconstruct what was the beauty of Linh, the singleness of her.

But that promise she'd made. To catch whoever did this.

She had to make herself nothing—nothing but a trained physician, nothing but an investigator. A medical examiner: the job and not the person doing it.

She gathered up her instruments and pulled the sheet from Linh's body. She understood the myriad ways a body could be destroyed, could identify almost every one. Because of this, she understood how the body worked, perhaps better than some physicians, but she didn't understand, not really, how the body came to be made, how the smallest of things—an egg, a sperm—could create something so profoundly complex. Yes, science made rational arguments for most of it, but there was—and by God she hated this word—a miracle in it. That human beings could so easily destroy that miracle was and had always been terribly disturbing to her. Why would God—if there was one—make something so miraculous so fragile? Why would he give us such power to destroy his creation?

She picked up the scalpel and held it above Linh's body, trying to find her trained self, her disciplined physician-self.

"Dr. Betencourt," Mendenhall said from the far side of the examination room, his shoes squeaking across the floor. "There's no way you can perform this autopsy with any objectivity."

He was right, but she couldn't stand the thought of someone else touching Linh.

"I'm going to do this. If you need to fire me afterward, you can."

"Doctor," he said, his voice softening. "I don't want to fire you."

Then he was next to her, covering Linh's body again with the sheet. At the moment, that gesture felt astonishingly gentle to her.

"Ben called you, didn't he? He let you know I was here."

"Natasha," Mendenhall said, in a quiet voice she'd never heard from him before. "You know I can't let you do this one. You don't want to do this one."

She almost handed the scalpel to him. She wanted to be relieved of this duty, she did.

"I promise you I'll take my time, I'll be careful," he said. "And you can check all my work afterward."

She looked at Linh's body, intact, veiled under the sheet. *Remember her like this,* she thought. *Remember her as she was two days ago, alive, sitting across a table.* Then she set the scalpel on the stainless-steel tray and walked out of the examination room.

———

"It's time to take a bite on this," Hernandez said a minute after Ben arrived at the station. "Get Ian Rowan in here."

"And Lucas Clay's son," Ben said. He told Hernandez about Lucas Clay and the recruit theory.

"Juvenile," Hernandez said. "Can't question him without a guardian present."

They'd already released Lucas Clay. Ben thought about bringing him in, but Ben wasn't about to put him in the same room with his son if the kid was in on this. From what Ben saw yesterday with Clay, they might have another murder on their hands.

"Let's get Clay's wife in," Ben said. "I'm thinking she knows about the affair, if her husband's keeping an apartment. Let's see what happens when they're in the same room together."

"Two in one," Hernandez said.

———

Vince Sessions was supposed to pick up Ian, bring him in on suspicion of animal cruelty on the Connollys' dog. That way they wouldn't have to spend one of their two shots on murder charges until they had concrete evidence that would make it impossible for the DA not to charge. Only get two bites at the apple. The plan was for Vince to talk him up on the way over to the station, make it sound like Vince was one of those cops sympathetic to racist views. See if he could soften Ian up, make him feel comfortable. Vince would be putting on an act, sure, but Ben suspected—and he imagined Hernandez did, too— that it wouldn't be all that difficult for Vince to play this particular part.

Ben got Jacob Clay. He drove over to the high school, checked in with Helen Galloway at the attendance office. When he got there, she scooted around the little desk to hug him.

"Howdy, sweetheart," she said when she saw him. Helen had been the attendance lady at the high school for twenty-seven years, and it seems she never forgot any of the kids who passed through the school's halls. On occasion, Ben worked with her on cases that involved students. "You're not here just to say hello, are you?"

He nodded. "You know a Jacob Clay?"

"Mr. Clay's been missing some classes," she said, immediately going back to her desk to thumb through her files. "Something's going on with him. Absences are one thing, but he's changed his whole style, too. They look one way one day and another the next, something's up." She studied his file. "Usually something at home."

"You know anything about gangs on campus? Neo-Nazi gangs?"

She shook her head. "The closest we got to a gang is the football team. Or maybe the rockabillies, but they're too worried about their pompadours to throw a punch." She looked at Jacob's picture in the file. "He's got angry eyes. Nothing more dangerous than an angry teenage boy. No offense, but testosterone's a lethal weapon."

"Should register every one of them once they turn fourteen."

She smiled, but it was a sad one.

"He should be in history class, unless he's continuing his vacation."

Outside the classroom, Ben leaned up against the lockers and waited for the bell to ring. When Jacob came out of the classroom, Ben held out his hand and introduced himself. The kid looked spooked, sweat beading his forehead, but he shook Ben's hand and then kept on walking, not even asking him what it was about. Ben noticed the shoelaces immediately, red, ladder-laced like the dicks in Huntington. Ben kept pace with him.

"I'd like to sit down with you and have a talk," Ben said.

"I got math next."

"I'll write a note," he said. "Besides, I'm thinking school isn't your thing—or hasn't been lately."

"What if I say no?"

A kid bumped into Ben's shoulder.

"You could do that," Ben said. "But it wouldn't start us off on the right footing."

"So."

Ben stopped, planted both his feet on the ground. He'd heard So's before, uttered by teenagers in LA. ¿Y que?—as though the word had actual power. He threw his hands in his pockets and looked the boy over. The newly sheared head, the jeans and suspenders, the flight jacket. The boy kept walking until some internal social mechanism clicked in and Jacob stopped to see what the hell Ben was doing. Ben strolled over to him real slow, chin cut low to look the kid straight in the eyes.

"So," Ben said. "I'm going to be real straight with you. You have a few options, some are better for you than others." He was a few inches from the boy now, staring down at him. "You can say no to me, I arrest you and take you to the station anyway."

The kid looked away, into the courtyard where his peers were strolling to class with backpacks strapped to their shoulders.

"Look at me," Ben said. "I want to be real sure we're on the same page about this."

The kid did, brown angry eyes, just as Helen had said.

"You can say *So* to me again, walk away, I arrest you and take you to the station anyway. You can run, I chase you down—in front of all these kids—arrest you and take you to the station anyway. Or you can take a quiet stroll with me out to the parking lot, go on a leisurely ride to the station, where you'll sit down with your mother and have a chat with me and a couple of friends. You decide."

————

Ian was in one interview room, the kid, Jacob, in the other. They'd called the boy's mother to let her know they'd brought Jacob in for questioning, but she hadn't arrived at the station yet, and she didn't seem to be in a hurry to do so. *Usually something at home*, indeed. They were letting Jacob sweat it out, door closed, air conditioner off, in the chair facing the wall—*feel what it is to be locked up, kid*—and decided to start in on Ian.

Ben was watching him through the window now, Ian calmly smiling at the wall, his foot handcuffed to the bolted-down table. Ben grabbed his legal pad and a pencil, stepped into the interview room. The air warm, stale. He sat down on the chair opposite Ian, crossed his legs, leaned back and propped the pad on his knee so that Ian couldn't see his notes.

"I'd appreciate knowing why I'm here," Ian said.

"Detective Sessions should have made it clear to you."

"I know what you're charging me with," Ian said, smiling like he had everything under control. "But I don't know why *I'm* here."

"What does it feel like to burn a cat?" Ben said.

Ian just looked at him, that placid smile on his face.

"You were arrested on that in 1980, right?"

The smile, the boot dangling from his crossed leg shook once.

"You're arresting me for something that didn't happen when I was sixteen?"

"It happened," Ben said. "I mean, I know there's no record of it. It's nice to be able to erase history, isn't it?" Ben leaned his elbows on the table. "Here's the thing, people have memories. People know things."

His boot shook three times and then stopped.

"You like the beach?" Ben said.

Nothing in Ian's face changed when Ben said it. His eyes never left Ben's, that smug smile.

"I don't like the sand," Ian said, shaking his head once, "the way it gets into everything, you know?"

"Like boots, right?"

Smile.

"I love the beach," Ben said. "I'm a body surfer. I especially like Crystal Cove. You know down there at Abalone Point? Some good waves over there. Huntington Beach's okay, too. Some nice peaks right around Fifteenth Street. You been up there?"

"Like I said, I'm not real high on the beach."

"Right there in front of this three-story modernist house. You know it? That real big one—all glass, a nice pool in the front yard. It's nice because you can surf all day, and then have a bonfire at night in one of those firepits they got there."

"Guess I prefer the mountains."

Ben wrote it down.

"Is that where you went after burning the cat?" Ben said. "Heard you went to some Outward Bound thing, or something like that. Some place for troubled kids."

"You mean after that thing that didn't happen when I was sixteen?"

Ben smiled and underlined *mountains*. Remembered Vanek saying Richard Wales had a place up in Mariposa, in the foothills of the Sierras. He wrote down *posse comitatus*. Said it out loud to himself a couple of times, just loud enough for it to be heard by Ian.

"How's your mother?" Ben said after a few moments.

Ian's face shifted then; the smile was still there, but his eyes darkened. "She's fine. Thanks for your concern, Officer."

"I can't imagine losing a child," Ben said. "I think I'd go a little crazy, too."

"She hasn't gone crazy."

Good, got under the skin. Quicker than he thought. Even assholes care about their mothers. He wrote *Has to take care of his mother—a burden* on the pad. *Would protect his mother at all costs.*

"That must have been real hard on you, too," Ben said. "Losing your brother over there."

Still angry over brother's death.

"Are you a therapist or a cop?" Ian was sweating now, a smell coming off his skin—like metal and cat piss. Meth sweat.

Tweaker. Pills on the scene at Huntington Beach.

"I remember when I lost my dad," Ben said. "It felt like the world spun out of control. Didn't know up from down. He was hit by a speeding car. Hit-and-run—the guy just clipped him and took off. Never found the guy. Still, to this day, I think about finding that guy and killing him."

Wrangler 215s, blood sourced from strawberry fields on tires. Traces of methyl bromide on tread. The last two about the blood and pesticide were bullshit. He'd never gotten the samples off the truck after the attack on the strawberry pickers, and hadn't run any soil samples, but sometimes bullshit worked.

"Maybe you need a therapist," Ian said. "That shit with the coach, Wakeland, that break up your marriage?"

He slammed the asshole's head against the side of the table, in his imagination. Deep breath and wrote, *Steel-toed boots used as weapon.*

"You hate Vietnamese people because your brother was killed over there?"

Wrote down, *Red shoelaces. 1488.*

"Did you find out you liked men?" Ian said.

Ben eyed him like he was pulling the trigger. Shoot at center mass. Ian's smile was back, pleasure in his eyes.

"No, found out I pretty much hate them," Ben said.

Ben wrote on his pad: *First-degree murder, death row, electric chair. I'm going to nail you.* Underlined three times.

"He must still have a hold on you then," Ian said, elbows on the table now. "You must think about him a lot."

"What I think a lot about, Mr. Rowan, is what causes people to murder." He set the legal pad faceup on the table, leaned forward and placed his arms across it, closing the space between himself and the asshole. "What I tend to obsess about is what causes people to murder innocent young women. I mean, what goes on in the mind of such a sicko?"

"I've always wondered the same thing about faggots."

"I've got your boy next door," Ben said. "He looks a little freaked, you know that deer-in-headlights look before they get plowed by a car? You see, his dad was sleeping with the very woman who turns up dead—but you know all this, because you were there. You're not stupid—I mean you're a fool and there's something wrong in your DNA, or your brain got scrambled or something. I don't know, maybe there was something wrong with your mom and you were warped the moment you came out—some genetic defect that runs in your family. Maybe you're just a frightened little pussy who thinks it makes him a big man to attack vulnerable people. I don't know what the fuck it is, and with you I don't much care. No, you're not stupid, but that kid over there . . . well, I'm not so sure about him. I mean, anyone who looks up to you can't be that smart, you know what I mean?"

Ian just stared at him, betrayed nothing—his breathing as calm as though he were sunning on the beach. Ben leaned back and smiled, the pad of paper in full view between them. Ian's eyes scanned Ben's notes, but nothing about his face changed.

"You know anything about the Liberty Net bulletin board?" Ben said.

Ian's eyes flashed back at Ben. Yeah, he knew something about it.

"Your daddy makes enough money for a computer, right?" Ben said. "He's got you all set up—the computer, the modem, the floppy disk. Sit in your room and chat away with other assholes?"

Ian smiled then, but Ben knew he'd gotten him. "First Amendment, Detective."

"I hear they're planning something big."

Silence.

There was a knock on the door.

"I know what you are," Ben said. "I know where you've been, and I know where you're going."

Knocking again. Ben got up from the table and walked to the door. Fuck. Hernandez was outside, a red-faced Councilman Rowan at his elbow.

———

Bao opened the combo lock to the safe in the grocery office and pulled out the revolver.

He'd dropped Ai off at her sister's, said something about needing to see his brother, and then drove over to the grocery, kicking flowers out of the way that had been left at the doorstep.

He checked the bullets, closed and spun the chamber, and then he was burning down the road, the revolver hanging heavy in the pocket of his windbreaker. Once a war started, it never ended—not really. You kept fighting it in your head, or you were forced to fight its aftermath—the displacement, the anger and shame, the forever bitterness of violence. This was his

American war, fought against people who felt they could just keep taking.

It took him five minutes to get across town, lights green the whole way, his mind lasered on the one thing he needed to do. He parked in the handicapped spot nearest the apartment and climbed the stairs, his fist clamped around the revolver in his jacket pocket. This man had taken his daughter. He would take the man. It was simple math. Halfway up the stairs, a woman rushed out of an apartment and squeezed by him. The air filled with her perfume and something about the delicate scent burned a hole of doubt in his stomach. He remembered his daughter's hair wrapped around his finger, remembered her child-self ripped open by shrapnel, remembered the anger in her eyes when he slapped her in the grocery. He remembered the dead in My Tho, once flesh now bones in graves in Vietnam. And he found himself shaking at the top of the stairs, his finger on the trigger, the door to the man's apartment just three footsteps away.

Ian was already un-handcuffed, but Ben wasn't ready to let up yet. When Ben had seen the councilman outside the interrogation room, he'd asked Ian where he was the night of Linh's murder, wanted something on record before Ian slipped out of the station.

"Watching the Lakers game," he said. "Ordered a pizza, had a couple of beers."

Hernandez, whose cuffs had been on the asshole and who had just unclicked them, stood in the doorway, clear frustration on his face.

"Who were they playing?" Ben said to Ian.

"The Seventy-Sixers."

"What was the score?"

"You want to question my son anymore," the councilman said, "you'll do so in the presence of my lawyer."

"One sixteen to one eleven, Sixers," Ian said, standing now. "Barkley had a double-double."

"Where were you the rest of the night?" Ben said.

"Reading, then I went to bed." Ian was standing next to his father now. Ben hadn't noticed the resemblance before—the green eyes, the high forehead, the doltish look of privilege certain white men affected. "*The Camp of the Saints* by Jean Raspail."

"What pizza place did you order from?" Hernandez said.

"Lamppost," the councilman said.

"I'd like to see a receipt."

"I believe I threw it away," the councilman said. Father and son were standing in front of Hernandez now, but Hernandez didn't look too interested in moving.

"I suggest you find it," Hernandez said. "Sir."

———

"Blunt-force trauma to the head," Mendenhall said. "Depressed skull fracture with subdural hematoma."

Mendenhall had found Natasha in her office. She'd been reading *The OC Register*'s front-page story on Linh's murder. ASIAN WOMAN FOUND DEAD ON CRYSTAL COVE BEACH. Mendenhall had changed out of his scrubs, which was thoughtful of him, she thought.

"Radius of the fracture?"

"Fifty-five, sixty centimeters," he said. "Same weapon as the Brennan case, right?"

"I think so," she said. "Water in the lungs?"

"Only a little," he said.

"So she was dead before she hit the water."

Mendenhall nodded.

"And there's one more thing," he said, some hesitation in his voice as though he was nervous to tell her. He laid a ziplock bag on her desk. Inside was an unraveled strip of paper. In red ink, someone had written: *We must protect the existence of Adamic peoples and a future for our children.*

"You found it in her esophagus, right?" she asked.

He nodded. "What do you think *Adamic* means?"

She read over the lines again. "White," she said. "It means white."

Her desk phone jumped off the hook. She answered on the first ring.

"Please, Miss Natasha," Bao said, when Natasha picked up, "I need someone to stop me."

"Slow down, what's going on?"

"I have a gun," Bao said. "Please, send someone to stop me."

———

Ben was ready to blow a hole in someone when Jacob's mother, Katherine Clay, arrived at the station. She was painted up like a bird—blue mascara, black eyeliner, her lips a glossy pink—sporting an off-white dress with Stevie Nicks–like lace knitting down the arms. In fact, she sort of looked like Stevie Nicks, the feathered hair, the pouty lips. He almost expected her to twirl.

"Where's my son?" she said, with an urgency she apparently did not have an hour ago.

Hernandez escorted her to the interview room while Ben grabbed a file folder and stuffed it with random papers stacked in the corner of his desk. He wrote CLAY, JACOB—MURDER on the front cover and then stood with Hernandez in the viewing room and watched the two a few moments. Mrs. Clay didn't hug her son, no dramatic displays of love and fear, but simply lifted the boy's chin and looked into his eyes, as though to make sure he was okay. Ben entered the cubicle then, quietly laying the folder on the desk before sitting down. He let Jacob and his mother give the file a look-over before clasping his hands over the label.

"Two nights ago a Vietnamese woman was murdered and dumped in Crystal Cove."

He should have niced it up with them, built a rapport first, let them get their guard down, but he wanted this kid shaken up. You could tell, just looking at his face, he was holding on tight—his skin pale, sweat running down his temple.

"The woman was having an affair with your husband," Ben said, leveling his eyes at Mrs. Clay. She looked confused at first, but then an unmistakable gleam of pleasure colored her face before she tried to tuck it away.

"That gives you both motive. We have boot imprints from the beach." It was bullshit. They had nearly nothing from the beach, but the kid didn't need to know that. "That match the ones on your boots." Ben took a glance under the table. "Doc Martens, right, from England? Size eleven?"

The look on Mrs. Clay's face shifted again, her maternal instinct kicking in, it seemed.

"He was home in bed," she said. "I check every night before I settle in."

Jacob glanced at his mother, something unreadable in his face. Ben leaned back in his chair, picked up the file, opened it, and pretended to read through it—a report on a robbery at a Security Pacific Bank, a memo about a new policy for submission of ballistics work, Bob's Big Boy take-out menu.

"I never said your son's a suspect," Ben said, closing the file. "Just that both of you have motive." He leaned his elbows on the table, closing the gap. "I mean, I know what it feels like to be cheated on. Angriest I ever felt in my life. I could have killed someone."

She glanced at him, not sure if he was being sympathetic or setting her up.

"And I can't imagine what you felt, Jacob. When you found out. If it was me, I'd want to defend my mother. I might even think about hurting my dad, maybe try to take the woman away from him."

Nothing. The kid was a vacant room.

"How old are you?" Ben asked. Ben knew, but wanted him talking. "Sixteen, seventeen?"

"Fifteen," he said.

"I did a lot of stupid stuff when I was fifteen," Ben said, nodding. "Wanted to look tough, wanted the girls to like me. But, you know, they didn't really. I was kind of a geek."

The kid just watched him, a stupid look on his face that could have been the absence of a brain—or savvy silence. He was sweating, though. Hernandez had dialed up the heat in the room, starting to feel like the inside of a tin can.

"See, we're looking into a couple of other things here," Ben said. "Another murder, an assault on a group of Mexicans. The Mexicans said it was a bunch of kids who attacked them—in jeans, boots, flight jackets."

"It's just the style with the kids these days," Mrs. Clay said.

"A friend and I visited a store up in Huntington Beach the other day," Ben said. "Iron Eagle Surplus? You know it?"

The kid looked away briefly and scratched his arm. Yeah, he knew it. He was the recruit.

"This guy up there says Ian Rowan showed up with a kid and bought him some threads—some red shoelaces, too. This guy said Ian told him the kid had 'spilled blood' the night before. Said he beat the shit out of some Mexicans. And it just so happens some Mexicans got beat up the night before down here."

Mrs. Clay glanced down at her son's shoes, the red shoelaces new and unfrayed.

"Here's the thing," Ben said. "We've got red shoelace fragments at a murder scene up in Huntington Beach. We've got them at a scene here, with a dead dog—the grocery that just happens to be owned by the father of the deceased woman."

Mrs. Clay looked frightened now, but the kid was stone-faced—a black hole, it seemed.

"From what I understand, your husband told you he wanted a divorce a few nights ago," Ben said. "A lot of things adding up, you know what I mean?"

"We're separating," Mrs. Clay said.

"And he hit you."

"He's not well," she said. "And the VA up in Long Beach is useless."

"You still love him, don't you? And after all you've been through with him, he runs off with a Vietnamese girl a decade younger than you."

"I wouldn't kill anyone."

"Just said you had motive," Ben said. "You and your son."

The door opened then and Lieutenant Hernandez stepped inside. "Detective," he said. "Can I see you a moment?"

Outside, they watched the two through the one-way glass. Mrs. Clay lit a cigarette and blew smoke to the ceiling. The kid stretched and winced. Bad stomach? Cramp?

"Let's bring Mr. Rowan into it," Hernandez said.

They watched them for a couple more minutes, wanting them to sweat it out. Mrs. Clay leaned over, her left hand on her son's thigh, and whispered in his ear. They couldn't hear what she said, but the boy nodded. When Ben got back inside, Mrs. Clay glanced at him guiltily and then stubbed out her cigarette in the tin tray.

"Ian's sitting in the next box over." Bullshit, of course. "Says you put him up to the job, going after Linh. Says you were pissed at your dad."

Jacob's eyes widened. "Bullshit."

"Says he hadn't intended to kill her, just scare her. But things got out of hand."

The kid looked frightened now. He cringed, shifted his weight around in the seat.

"Says you wanted her dead," Ben said.

"No way Ian said that."

Ben raised his eyebrows and nodded. "My lieutenant did the interview. I can bring him in and he can share with you what he was told."

"Don't say a word to him," Mrs. Clay said.

"But I think he's bullshitting me. I think he's setting you up to take the fall. I mean, he'd just get charged as an accessory, be out in two to three years." This was bullshit, too; he'd be charged with aiding and abetting and face murder charges, but what chance the kid or his mother knew that? "But you would get first degree. Might even get a judge to try you as an adult. Could be in Quentin for the rest of your life, maybe on death row with that crazy killer, the Night Prowler."

The kid's eyes were narrowed now, as though something stabbed his stomach.

"We might be able to help you," Ben said, "if you tell us about Liberty Net."

"Liberty Net?" the kid said. "What's Liberty Net?"

"Don't talk to him," Mrs. Clay said. "They trick you. That's what they do."

"I think you just got into Ian's gang. Think you weren't in when the Huntington murder happened. I'm thinking Ian Rowan pulled you in, pressured you to attack the Mexicans. I'm thinking Ian killed the girl and he's selling you out. Maybe even threatened you to keep you quiet."

The kid's face was white now.

"My lieutenant's in there right now," Ben said. "Who knows what Ian's dropping on you."

Then the kid threw up, green bile all over his boots and the linoleum floor. A splattering on Ben's slacks.

His mother let out a little yelp and then put her hand on her son's back.

"Is my son under arrest?"

The kid was holding his stomach, bent over at the waist.

"Not yet."

"See," she said, pointing a finger at him. "That means you've got nothing. I know a little about the law." She was helping her son up from the chair, guiding him by the arm out of the inter-view room and down the hall. "Harassment, that's what this is. Police harassment of a minor."

"Well," Hernandez said. "You scared the shit out of the kid at least."

Ben flashed the lieutenant an annoyed look as he pulled a paper towel from the wall dispenser near the bathroom and started dabbing at his pant leg.

Then Carolina was coming down the hall, passing Jacob and his mother, calling his name. "Betencourt just called," she said quietly, when she got to the observation area. "We got a possible 217. Says the perp is Bao Phan."

Ben knew the gas station; it was across the street from Lucas Clay's apartment. Shit. He gunned the cruiser down El Rancho Road, slipping by traffic in the bike lane. Dispatch sent out the Code 3 over the radio. "Suspect is armed."

Ben swerved to miss a Coke delivery truck trudging through the intersection, then he clicked into the radio. "Suspect is trying to turn himself in," Ben said. "Repeat, suspect is trying to turn himself in."

"Listen, Ben," Natasha had said on the phone at the station. "He's got a gun, but he's begging for someone to stop him."

Three patrols called themselves in on pursuit. Ben weaved through commuters, rode the emergency lane down Junipero, and then cut across town on the bike lane paralleling the drainage ditch. Who knew what would happen if one of these young uniforms, used to writing up traffic tickets and nabbing shoplifting teenagers, got there first?

He swerved into the parking lot, spinning the drive-through of a Wendy's. One black-and-white was already on scene. Both officers were crouched behind their thrown-open doors, revolvers aimed at Bao, who stood slope-shouldered at the pay phone, pistol dangling from his right hand. Ben slammed on the brakes and threw open his door, fingers on the butt of his .38.

"Don't shoot," Ben yelled to the uniforms.

"He won't drop the gun," one of the officers yelled back.

"Mr. Phan," Ben said. "Put the gun down and we can talk."

But Bao didn't say anything. He just stood there, the gun clutched in hand. He looked lost, as though he'd found another level of grief. Did he want them to shoot him?

"His daughter was just murdered," Ben said to the uniforms. "He's not thinking straight."

"Don't fucking care," the officer said. "He needs to drop the gun."

"You pull that trigger, Officer, I'll personally have you brought up on murder charges."

The officer glanced at Ben, venom in his eyes. He was bluffing, though, and the officer knew it. They'd be justified in shooting Bao. Man with a gun equals clear and present danger—to the public and to cops.

"Mr. Phan," Ben said, coming around his open door now, walking slowly toward the man. "I'd want to kill him, too."

Bao glanced at him.

"But it's not bringing Linh back," Ben said, slowly gaining ground, putting himself between the barrels of the officers' revolvers and Bao's body. Sirens screamed down the street. Another minute, and there'd be a half dozen loaded and cocked police issues bull's-eyeing this man. "Think about your wife. Think about Ai. What happens to her if you're in jail—or dead?"

"I'm not strong enough," Bao said. Ben was close enough to see his eyes now, an anguish in them that would cut a hole through any feeling person. "I was so close. I could have done it."

Bao still had not dropped the gun. Ben's revolver was still in his dirty harry, his right hand gripping the handle, a fucking risk for sure, but if Bao couldn't kill Lucas Clay, he wasn't going to kill a cop. This kind of rage and grief, Ben knew, turned inward now. At this point, he was trying to keep Bao from blowing his own head off.

"You're not weak, Mr. Phan," Ben said, his hand raised to Bao. "Please, give me the gun."

"Why do you take so much?" Bao said, his cheeks streaked now.

"I don't know." He was five feet from Bao now, his hand outstretched, and Bao hadn't moved, his feet planted on the cement walkway next to the restrooms, the phone receiver dangling from the cord. Then Ben leaned forward, took the man's hand in his, and gently pried the revolver out of his grip. And when he did, Bao's legs gave out, Ben catching him just before he hit the pavement.

———

When Jacob's mother saw his father's car pull up to the curb, she locked the door and latched the dead bolt. She ran to the sliding glass back door and locked it, too, yanking the curtains shut. Two days after his father moved out, she'd hired a locksmith to change the locks. Now Jacob's father was coming up the pathway that led to the front door; Jacob could see him through the little stained-glass window, his eyes sunken into his skull, his face misshapen by the warped glass.

Jacob had just gotten himself cleaned up, changed his clothes, took off the boots. His mouth still tasted like shit, though, and his side was throbbing with pain. His mother had been silent on the way home, three cigarettes one after another, the car buzzing with unsaid things. She didn't ask him a goddamned thing, as though getting drilled by the cops was an everyday deal, like going to the grocery or something.

Now his father was two steps from the door, his hands cramped into fists, and Jacob was sure he was going to knock the damn thing down. But his dad just stood there on the other side, slump-shouldered, his ear pressed up against the glass. "Let me in, Jacob," he said. The door handle turned back and forth, his father trying it from the other side.

"Go away, Lucas," his mother said, running into the front room after closing all the windows in the bedrooms.

"I just want to talk."

"Get away from the door." Then his mother stumbled out of the room again.

"Did you do it?" his father said through the door, his voice slipping toward chaos.

The ungrounded electrical current of his father's pain passed through particleboard and glass.

"Were you there, Jacob?"

His mom was back in the room, a small pistol in her shaking hands, the one his father kept in the safe, the blunt nose of the gun aimed at the stained glass.

"Jacob, I love you," his father said. "Open the door. If you were there, I know you didn't mean to do it."

"I have the gun, Lucas," his mother said, her voice trembling. Her finger was on the trigger, a little red button showing on the body of the gun. "It's loaded, like you showed me."

The door shuddered then, a warping bash that splintered the frame along the edge. His mother jumped backward, but the lock held and his father didn't hit it again. Instead, he stalked down the pathway and crossed the street, his shoulders sloped, his hands at his sides balled into fists. Jacob knew where he was going, but the Power Wagon wasn't parked on the street, the garage door was closed. His father strode up the driveway, ripped a weight off the barbell, and heaved it against the closed garage door. He grabbed the next weight and splintered the wood with it. And by the time he was hurling the bar itself through the air, Jacob's mother was on the phone, dialing 911.

───────

They stood outside on the driveway and watched the cops arrest his father. One of the officers asked them a few questions while the other cops led his father to the car. Jacob answered the questions, but it was hard to concentrate with his dad drilling his eyes into him from the back seat of the cruiser. Jacob didn't know what the look meant—was it hate, was it love, was it hate and love? All Jacob knew, if a look was a weapon, he was dead.

When they were gone, his mother sat at the kitchen counter—the gun sitting on the edge of the sink, a glass of wine shining in the pendant light above their heads. She traced the edge of his hairline with the side of her hand, as though gently pushing away a strand of hair that would have been there a week before.

"Jacob, honey," she said, pausing a moment, as though for strength. "Did you kill her?"

He couldn't read her face, but if he had to swear to it, he'd say there was an excitement in her, like maybe she'd be proud of him if he said yes. You protected family, you took care of your own. He heard Ian in his head, *From here on out, forever, until you fucking die, you say nothing.*

"No," he said.

She leaned back in the bar chair, disappointed or relieved, he couldn't tell—maybe both.

"Did Ian?"

I like Ian Rowan, he remembered her saying.

"I don't know," he said. "I was up in my room, sleeping."

1987

Aryan Army

"The Reverend is not happy," Wales said.

The councilman shifted in his seat and glanced at the two young men standing guard at the office door, the same young men who had driven down the mountain to pick up Councilman Rowan and bring him here. Each had a Ruger P85 holstered to his waist. Each had killed before, and each would do it now if Wales gave the word. Councilman Rowan knew this, and Wales wanted him to know it. Wales could have flown the councilman up here, but he wanted the man to live with that fear on the two-hour drive up and down from the mountain.

"It was an inopportune time to kill that young woman," Wales said.

The councilman unbuttoned his sport coat and then buttoned it again. "I know," he said.

"With that detective already investigating the dog incident, and the Mr. Brennan murder investigation," Wales said, his hands folded together on the desk before him, his voice quiet, unemotional, just as The Reverend would be, "your son is making himself a liability."

"It wasn't Ian," Rowan said. "It was another boy."

"Your son is in charge of this group, yes?"

Rowan just twisted his neck with the truth thrown at him.

"He recruited the boy, didn't he?"

"Yes." The councilman was looking at his hands now, which were resting on his thighs. "She was sleeping with the new recruit's father—race mixing."

"The motivation for the killing is not the problem, it's the timing," Wales said. "The Reverend is questioning you and your son's intelligence. I am, too."

It was difficult to find the right level of intelligence for the people you were using. The councilman had been useful—to this point, at least. The councilman's real estate company, Orion Brokerage, had a near monopoly on construction in Rancho Santa Elena. His vote and influence on the city council often gave them favorable local laws—from restrictive zoning codes to at-large elections that diluted the minority vote, keeping whites in charge of local government. Rancho Santa Elena had been Wales's personal project, and suddenly that seemed under threat. If that should fail, it reflected badly upon him—something The Reverend had reminded him about. And failure was not an option, something The Reverend also had reminded him about.

"I'll get him in line," Rowan said.

Wales just looked at the councilman, let the silence settle in for a few moments.

The councilman looked up at Wales now. "I will. He'll do what I say."

"I understand the police interrogated him."

"Yes," the councilman said.

"Did he mention the bulletin board?"

"He was asked about it," the councilman said. "But he didn't say anything."

Wales waited, let the councilman think about the men with the Rugers.

"With the bulletin board system up and running," Wales said, "The Reverend thinks now might be an opportunity for us and our other allies around the country."

The councilman nodded. A look of relief had washed over his face when he heard Wales say *an opportunity for us*. Still in the club, not going to be dragged outside and shot in the back of the head.

"Missions are being planned," Wales said, leaning forward now on his desk. "I can't tell you, now, what they are, but they may be dangerous. We will need your son—"

"Not Ian," the councilman said, shaking his head. "No, not him."

Wales leaned back in his chair, folded his hands again on the desk in front of him.

"Is he a soldier or not?"

"You know I lost my older son," the councilman said.

"Yes," Wales said, nodding apologetically. "I know." Wales glanced at the young men guarding the door. They stood at attention, like soldiers. Their heads shaved, their dark jeans and flight jackets, the shined steel-toed boots, and, of course, the pistols. The councilman did not follow Wales's gaze. "The Reverend will be disappointed," Wales said.

"The new recruit," the councilman said, a panic in his voice now. "He has special skills that might be useful to you—and The Reverend."

The man was willing to give up another man's child to save his own—and to save himself. Wales supposed that was love, but it was ugly. Wales didn't believe in love; he was motivated by another, stronger emotion.

"Skills that might be useful to a mission," the councilman said.

Wales leaned his elbows on the desk, closing the distance between them.

"Tell me," he said.

PART FOUR

Chapter Fifteen

Danh Phan, Bao's brother, had organized the rally on Thursday, two days after Linh's body was discovered and after word had gotten out that they were holding Bao in jail for attempted murder of Lucas Clay. Danh had recently announced his intention to run for city council next year (the flyers he'd left rubber-banded to people's front doors spelled his name *Dan*), and the rally was a combination vigil/protest/political rally. He'd already been on the local and LA news, swearing the vigil would last until Bao was released and they "won" justice for Linh. "The community is tired," he'd said, on Eyewitness News, "of the daily abuse and the racial attacks."

Now a group of a dozen or so from the Asian community stood in front of the police station, signs in hand. JUSTICE FOR LINH! BAO PHAN IS NOT A CRIMINAL. STOP ATTACK-ING US! Ben could see them through the front window of the station, a mix of men and women and a couple of kids, plod-ding a stoic circle in front of the entrance. Local news had al-ready shown up, the mayor, too, with a bullhorn, asking them to break it up. When that didn't work, the mayor visited Her-nandez, complaining that the gathering was illegal, but the lieutenant wasn't having it—they had a constitutional right to protest, he told the mayor to his face in front of all the cops on the floor. Then the mayor shut the door to Hernandez's office, drew the shades, which meant real business, and it had been a tomb like that for nearly fifteen minutes now.

Earlier this morning, Ben had stopped over at the impound lot and found Linh's car pushed up against the back fence next to a Mercedes 450SL. He searched the inside—McDonald's wrappers, a couple of hard candies, Depeche Mode and Smiths cassette tapes, a dog-eared book, *Beloved* by Toni Morrison. An air freshener tree hanging from the rearview. He sat there in the passenger seat, thinking. Whatever happened the other night had started at the university. When they got to the car three nights ago, Lucas Clay's note was still there, pinned under the driver's side windshield wiper. The doors were unlocked, the passenger door only half closed. Sitting on the passenger seat was her book bag, which he had taken in for evidence. She'd walked back from class, opened the door, set down the book bag, and then someone kept her from closing the door. They'd fingerprinted the door handles, the metal frame edges of the windows—but only her prints and Bao's came back. Not even Lucas Clay's. When he got back to the cruiser, he'd called in to Carolina asking her to get someone out to fingerprint the right rear panels of the deceased's car.

Then he'd returned to the station, to the growing commotion outside. In a meeting room now, Ben had pinned a piece of butcher paper to the wall. He'd mapped out each crime scene, listed all the evidence gathered at each, pinned the photos of the flag from the burned-down meth house, photos of the 1488 graffiti in the alleyway, and written down the three messages found on the dog, Brennan, and now Linh. *KILL 'EM ALL! TRAITOR! Posse Comitatus. We must protect the existence of Adamic peoples and a future for our children.* He glanced outside to where the protestors had gathered and there was Natasha, holding a JUSTICE FOR LINH sign.

She'd been furious last night when he told her Bao was in jail.

"He never confronted Lucas," she said. "He called and asked someone to stop him."

They had been at his place, an untouched pizza going cold in front of them on the kitchen counter.

"It was a full Code Three," Ben said. "I had to keep two uniforms from popping him. He wouldn't put the gun down. He admitted his intention, too. I'm sympathetic to the man, but that doesn't leave us a lot of wiggle room."

"Bao in jail," she spit. "And those assholes are out there."

Ben knew their hands were tied. If they let him go, uncharged, and he did discover he had guts enough to shoot Lucas Clay, they'd be in a shitstorm. But yeah, sometimes there wasn't a whole lot of justice in the law.

"Natasha," Ben said. "I swear he was about to blow his own head off. Better he's in custody until we nail these bastards."

Natasha stepped outside then and smoked two cigarettes. He watched her light the first with the second, the light from the dining room window cast across her face. When she came back in, she pulled Linh's file from her bag and set it on the table.

"You sure you want to do this now?" Ben said.

"I want those bastards in jail—or dead, if you have the opportunity."

Her voice was full of real-deal fury.

"You're scaring me a little," he said.

"Good," she said. "Be good for all of you to be frightened, to live in the world the way women have to."

She looked at him hard, but then took a deep breath and opened the autopsy report.

"No sexual assault, no cuts, no broken bones. Except her skull, which fractured where the frontal and the parietal bones met."

There had been no abrasions on the scalp, Natasha explained, which suggested she hadn't bashed it against the rocks. Jagged rocks would break the skin. He was amazed by Natasha; she had switched from murderously angry to all business; didn't betray any emotion while she walked him through the report. You'd have thought it was just another body. Only a small amount of water in her lungs, too, which suggested death—or near death—before her body was in the water.

"He did good work," she said.

"Who?"

"Mendenhall," she said, looking over the file a moment. "Whatever fractured her skull didn't have any sharp edges—something smooth, and heavy."

"It's the same weapon used at the migrant camp," Ben said. "The same fracturing on Brennan."

"And Santiago at the strawberry field attack," she said. "And of course"—she slipped the ziplock bag in front of him with the paper inside declaring the need to protect Adamic peoples—"their calling card."

Now he was in the conference room at the station. He'd written it all out on butcher paper, drew lines between the dots, playing it all out in his head. Ian and this kid Jacob were in on this, but it wasn't provable yet. No eyewitnesses, no blood, no prints, no weapon. *We must protect the existence of Adamic peoples and a future for our children.* That phrase wasn't something stupid racist kids came up with on their own. It was corporate sounding, an organizational doctrine. Ben thought of Banger up at the surplus store the other day, *Some Christian Identity thing,* he'd said. *Say they're planning something big.* These kids were small-time players in something much bigger. He flipped through his notes, looking for something to click. IØIBIGDADI. That cryptic bit of graffiti in the alleyway from the other day. He hadn't paid much attention to it, but something caught him this time. Ten letters. If they used numbers as codes for letters, they could do the reverse. He started writing it out. *I* the ninth letter of the alphabet. Ø is 0. 92974149. He rewrote it, his heart starting to pump: 909-297-4149. A phone number.

Fifteen seconds later, he burst into the tech guy's office.

"Try this number."

Nick fired up the modem, dialed it in, the machine making a screeching sound. Then the screen flashed. WELCOME TRUE PATRIOTS TO LIBERTY STORM NET!

"We're in," Ben said.

"Wait," Nick said, pointing at the screen. "You need a password."

"Shit."

Then Hernandez darkened the door, a grim look on his face. "Detective, I need to see you in my office."

———

"You're kidding me, right?" Ben said.

He was across the desk from Hernandez, the shades still drawn, the door firmly shut.

"I am not."

Ben was off the case—worse, he was being placed on temporary leave. Mayor swinging his dick around—Councilman Rowan going Machiavellian. ZOG pulling the levers of government? Yeah, sure.

"Jesus, Lieutenant," Ben said. "Have a little backbone, huh?" Ben was standing now, spinning one frustrated circle on the industrial carpet in front of the desk.

"Detective, sit down."

Ben stopped and looked at him, considered going full insubordination and storming out the door—but he respected the man. He sat.

"Listen to me carefully," Hernandez said. "One of the things men like the mayor—and the councilman—believe is that a man like me, a Mexican, will follow their directions. That's what they're used to—telling the Mexican mowing the lawn how high to cut, underpaying an illegal building their backyard patio. There're some good men on the city council—DiPatri, Rosenberg—who want change and voted for me. Others voted for me because they figured I'd be so grateful for the position I'd kiss their asses. For a certain kind of man, that's the best thing possible—to be able to daily show someone their place."

"You trying to prove their point, about the ass kissing?"

Hernandez leaned his elbows on the table. "When you suggest I need a backbone on this, it seems to me you might not understand the rage—" He put his chin to his chest and composed himself. "How I feel about this one. It seems to me you might think about me the same way some other men in this town do."

"Jesus, Lieutenant. I just didn't want to be called off."

"If I didn't agree to this, I'm fired and you're on leave regardless. Maybe on unemployment yourself. And where would that leave us? Putting Vince and Marco on this case? You have to care about this one because you'll be cutting some viscera from the social body—and maybe committing professional suicide. I can put Carolina on it, yes, but she's only one cop."

"Not a lot I can do except get a suntan."

"How much do you care about this case?" Hernandez said. "I mean, I've got skin in the game."

It was a strange question and he wasn't sure how to answer it. He cared about every murder case. Being a homicide detective was a sort of calling, a missionary of crime fighting. Was he supposed to conjure up more feeling about a young woman he didn't know than any other murder victim? It hurt Natasha, and that hurt him, but a cop who gave his heart away to every murder victim was a cop who eventually put a bullet in his own head.

"Last year," Hernandez said, "when I realized what had happened to you as a kid, with Coach Wakeland, I couldn't sleep until we took down that bastard. What happened to you never happened to me, but it was like someone had hurt my family."

Ben looked away, his gut burning with the mention of it.

"And all the silence in this town," Hernandez said. "All the people who knew or suspected what he was and didn't do a goddamned thing about it."

Ben looked back at Hernandez—burning with shame about all the years he'd been silent. But the lieutenant was right, a lot of people in this town had let the cancer that was Coach Wakeland live among them, something ugly they didn't want to look at because they hadn't been one of his victims. But Ben could hear the real questions now: Can you sleep at night while those racists are out there attacking people? Do you care enough about it that it keeps you up at night?

"I've known you most of your life," Hernandez said. "How much do you know about living with this kind of hate? How often have you asked me about what it's like?"

Ben couldn't remember a time when he'd asked Hernandez about anything like this. He knew it had ruffled some people's feathers when Hernandez won the lieutenant's position. But Hernandez was a tough son of a bitch when he needed to be, and the lieutenant had always been an authority figure to Ben, someone he cared about, sure, but someone he looked up to, someone in charge.

"What's it been like?" Ben asked.

Hernandez looked away, thinking, and then right back at him. "Como estar infinitamente enojado."

Like being endlessly angry. Yeah, Ben knew that feeling.

"Look," Hernandez said. "The mayor's not as smart as he thinks—and Rowan's overplayed his hand. I intend to make it bite them in the ass."

Ben nodded, the clouds opening up a bit. If they nailed Ian, pulling Ben's badge would make it look like the mayor and Rowan conspired to get the police off the case. Yeah, Ben could see where Hernandez was going with this.

"Also, by evening," Hernandez said, "Ian Rowan is going to know that Daddy threw his muscle around and got you off the case."

"That's going to make him feel pretty damn powerful," Ben said. When the whole system works for you, is even corrupt for you. "Make him feel like he can get away with anything."

"Yes, Detective." Hernandez leaned forward on his desk. "If you really care about this, you have a duty as a citizen to do whatever's in your power—within the limits of the law—to stop it. And concerned citizens"—he slid a REVOCATION OF POLICE POWERS AND NOTIFICATION OF DUTY STATUS form across the desk to Ben—"*always* have the ears of this chief of police."

Ben glanced at the form, still didn't like signing it despite their tacit agreement. Then he set his badge on the form, pulled his revolver from his dirty harry, emptying the chamber of bullets, and set them on top of the badge. When he got outside, he joined Natasha in the circle of protestors, chanted along with them. *Justice for Linh! Let Bao go!*

"Taking a lunch break?" Natasha said.

He pulled his coat pocket back, revealing his empty dirty harry, the belt without his badge.

"No," she said.

Stop attacking us.

He just raised an eyebrow in confirmation.

"Means you're close," she said.

"Doesn't matter how close we are," he said. "Only matters if we can touch 'em."

Ben handed her a strip of paper with the phone number on it.

"Get this to Vanek," Ben said. "It's the number that gets you into the BBS."

"You got in," she said.

"Almost."

———

After Ben left, a VW Bug pulled into the parking lot. Natasha noticed it because they were blasting music, the ugly music she'd first heard up in Huntington Beach when she met up with Detective Vanek. They parked the car in the lot at the top of the hill facing the protest and then they got out. There were four of them, two leaning against the hood of the lowered-down Bug, the other two standing to the right of the car watching the protestors—their stupid boots, their flight jackets, their shaved heads.

The sight of them charged her with anger—the brazenness of their display of power, standing on the hill, in direct sunlight, staring down at the protestors. *Here we are,* it said, *and you can't do a damn thing about it.*

She set down her sign then and charged up the hill to the parking lot. It was a stupid move, reckless even, but she was driven by a boiling-over she had no desire to control. She wanted to be rage, wanted to be judgment. Two of the boys started laughing, the kind of laughter only young men can produce, laughter lathered in the authority of testosterone and spoiled privilege. The Clay kid wasn't among them, she noticed. Closer now, she could hear the lyrics to the song, *A cleansing battle throughout the land / the final solution, our triumphant stand.* Then the singer started screaming, something guttural and ugly.

"Hey, Doc," Ian Rowan said, turning down the music when she got to the top of the hill.

That caught her off guard.

"Yeah," Ian said, sitting in the passenger seat, his arm—elbow to fingertips—resting along the top of the door. "We know who you are."

Maybe it was because he'd frightened her, the alchemy of anguish and fear, but she walked right up to the passenger door and clapped him across the cheek and nose.

The kid in the driver's seat started laughing immediately. "Holy shit," he said.

Ian snatched her hand and started to twist her wrist. "That's all you have?" he said. "That's what you came all the way up here to do?"

She leaned down, got in his face. "I just wanted to see, face-to-face, what evil looks like. And you know what? It looks like fear. It looks like a frightened little boy in dress-up clothes."

One of the boys behind her laughed, but there was an edge of doubt in it now. She had her back to them, letting them know she wasn't frightened. What did all their dress-up mean, their posing on the hill, if a five-foot-three-inch woman gave them her back?

"There *is* a hell," she said, looking straight into those green eyes, "and it's just up the freeway, twenty short minutes from here. If there's a heart in there"—she pointed at his chest—"I'll be the one dropping it in the incinerator, and all that hate will just be ash and char. It'll take about three minutes while I pour myself a cup of coffee."

———

She tried to return to the protest, but it felt like something you do when you are powerless. Her threats meant nothing to the boys. They just sat there, leaning against their car looking down on the protestors, smug smiles on their faces, laughing occasionally as though telling jokes. That's how she felt, utterly powerless, carrying the signs—JUSTICE FOR LINH! Walking around in circles, howling out chants, like screaming into a strong wind. How much could cardboard, Sharpies, and a few dozen voices do? How soon before the mayor could quietly shut it all down?

She found the nearest pay phone and called Vanek.

"You drink?" she said when he answered.

"Occasionally."

"Well, how about you make this an occasion?"

He drove to her, pretty damn quickly, she noted, and they met at The Hook and Barb on Jamboree. They sat in the back, keeping an eye on the front door.

"They've taken Ben's badge," she said, laying the ziplock

with the paper inside on the table in front of him. "So it's up to you to nail these bastards."

She'd ordered a Dewar's, but she was too angry to drink it. Vanek took a sip of his red wine and looked at the numbers. She couldn't remember the last time she saw a cop drink wine in a bar. Pinot noir, for God's sake.

"The bulletin board number," he said.

"Yeah," she said. "But we need a password."

"I'll get on it." He folded up the paper, slid it inside his coat pocket, and looked at her.

"I'm very sorry about your friend," he said. "Linh."

Natasha almost lost it, but she had a rule about that with detectives. Only with Ben. She only allowed herself to cry with Ben.

"She was . . ." She didn't really know how to say this. "For a while, she was sort of like a daughter for me. Back before I realized I wanted kids."

Vanek just watched her, a softness in his eyes that drew her in. She remembered his *Didn't get the chance* the other day. He took a sip of his wine, then folded his hands on the table.

"You know, South Central was brutal," he said. "But there was logic to it. It was a war over drugs, over territory, over money. It was mafia in the hood. But this . . . this is just hate. Nothing rational about it."

"Hate and power," she said.

He was quiet a moment.

"There was this rumor in South Central," he said, "that the CIA was supplying the drugs in the inner city, to keep the black man down. I didn't believe it. It seemed too sinister to me."

"But if they can take a cop's badge," she said, nodding.

"It doesn't matter," he said, "that conspiracy theory. It's just a way to express other truths about the way we treat people in those neighborhoods."

They were quiet together for a few moments.

"I slapped Ian Rowan today." She told him about the kids, looking down on the protestors, gloating in their power. "I could've killed him. If they want a race war, I could have started one today. White-on-white murder."

He smiled, a sad one, though.

"Be careful with them."

She didn't like the sudden paternal tone. "I can take care of myself."

"I know," he said. "But not with these people."

He pushed aside his wine and leaned toward her.

"At home, I have a box full of anonymous notes," he said. "Sometimes they're left on my windshield, sometimes they're in my mailbox, a few have been sent to the station."

"The station?"

"Yes," he said. "Two days ago one was left underneath my windshield wiper at the grocery store."

He let that sink in for a moment.

"Dr. Betencourt, these people have concocted this notion that they're living through a white genocide. That these are the end-times for the Anglo race. They believe they're soldiers in a war to stop it. They think we're enemies, and they don't think it's murder when they kill. They think it's a successful operation."

He almost touched her wrist, almost. Instead he laid his hand on the table, less than an inch from hers.

"So please," he said. "Be careful with them."

He seemed to suddenly realize he was too close to her and he leaned back against the wall.

"You wanted to say something to me the other day, but you stopped," she said. "What was it?"

She knew she should leave it alone, but she had kept thinking about it. He looked down at the table, a sad smile on his face.

"Dr. Betencourt," he said, looking at her now. "We shouldn't always say what we want to say."

Chapter Sixteen

Three days in a row, Ben did daily drive-bys of the Rowan house in his Chevy. Apparently, Ian felt invincible following his daddy's power play to strip Ben of his badge, because he had a small crew with him now, four college-aged young men with shaved heads and the same stupid boots. But no Jacob Clay; his mother was keeping him under lock and key, it seemed.

Ben had looked up the BBS phone number the afternoon Hernandez told him he was removed from duty. It was unlisted, but 909 was Big Bear, up in the mountains like Banger had said. He did daily check-ins with Vanek, too, but no luck yet on accessing the board.

So Ben decided to do surveillance, to let them know he was keeping an eye on them. He would park a couple of houses down from them, pulling a U-turn in the middle of the street so they could see him, and watch them lift weights on the driveway. He followed them when they cruised across town in the Power Wagon, leaned against his truck in the parking lot and watched them kick a soccer ball in the park. Sometimes Carolina was there on Comet Street in her unmarked, but she just ignored him, let him keep them on their toes. He trailed behind them in Lucky's while they picked up a twelver of Budweiser, stood in the next checkout line while they waited to pay, stared at them. *Fucking mud lover,* Ian whispered. Ben just ignored him, kept his mouth shut. He sat in the row behind them at El Rancho Cinemas when they all chain-ganged it to see Schwarzenegger in *Predator.* "Let's beat the shit out of this fucker," one of the kids said to Ian, staring Ben down during a preview. "Watch the movie" was all Ian said, and Ben didn't say anything, didn't even really look at them at all. He was just their shadow, hovering behind them, while the Alien picked off the special-ops guys one by one.

Monday evening, Ben showed up at the city council meeting and sat in the front row, directly in front of Paul Rowan, while they discussed leash rules for dogs in public, a special zoning ordinance for a new shopping center, detailed general disbursements. Ben kept his eyes trained on Rowan, the councilman glancing his way a few times. Ben stuck around, too, while the councilman glad-handed citizens who turned out for the meeting. He followed the councilman out of the building, had his back up the steps to the parking lot, until Rowan finally turned around and got in Ben's nose.

"Detective," he said. "I'll bring you up on charges."

"Just walking to my car," Ben said, stepping around the councilman and climbing into his truck, which just happened to be parked next to the councilman's Oldsmobile.

Then at 3:00 A.M. that night, something crashed through the living room window. Ben and Natasha jumped from the bed, blasted from sleep. Ben knew who it was immediately, ran out in his boxer shorts, his personal .45, which he'd been keeping under the bed, gripped in his palm. Three shadowy figures sprinted down the gravel driveway. He blew through the front door and chased after them barefoot, the gravel ripping open his feet. When he got to the end of the driveway, he caught the last figure diving into the bed of a Ford truck—not the Power Wagon, not the VW—and raised the .45 to pop off a shot, but they were fifty yards away, swerving onto the road, too far away to hit and too far away for a plate number.

When he trudged back up to the house, mostly naked, his left foot bleeding, he found Natasha holding a three-pound shot put of a boulder—nothing attached to it, no note, but message received. He got dressed and checked the perimeter of the house, stuck his nose into the barn to make sure the horses were safe. On the way back to the house, he noticed his Chevy, all four tires slashed, the rims resting on deflated rubber. Luckily, Natasha had parked her car behind the barn, an old hold-over from when they were still a secret item, or else they might have slashed hers, too.

Back inside, Natasha was sitting at the dining room table, boulder in hand, studying it.

"You said awhile back these skinheads had a pool table in the garage, right?"

"Yeah," he said. Of course, he thought. No abrasions, just crushed bone.

"That's the weapon."

"A pool ball," Ben said, nodding. "Stuffed down in a knee-high sock."

The next morning, he drove Natasha up to County for her shift and borrowed her 280Z. The tires on the Chevy could wait.

Her car was tiny, his knees knocking the dashboard, even with the seat all the way back. But the sports car was sure as hell fun to drive, tight around corners, quick jump off the line. No wonder she liked these wheels. He came into California Homes through the back entrance and parked three doors down from the Clays' and Rowans', pushed up behind a lowered Toyota with some stupid Richter scale design taped on the rear window. Nothing doing for a half hour—closed garage door, the wood still splintered from Lucas Clay's meltdown, the shades drawn on both houses.

Nearing 10:00, Ben took a little walk down the sidewalk to the Rowan house. He came up the side, pushed through the open backyard gate; he wanted to make sure no one was home, thought he might be making a little bit of noise inside the garage. Something flashed through a window, and he turned to see the television screen, Bob Barker standing in front of a spinning wheel. Ten feet in front of the television a woman sat slumped in an armchair, her blank face shining blue in the light. He couldn't have been more than fifteen feet from her, the shades pulled up, the midmorning light shining down on him, but she didn't move; her face, expressionless as a statue, just watched *The Price Is Right* wheel spin round and round. He'd have to keep it quiet, but he doubted she was leaving that chair unless someone forced her to.

Back at the garage, he pulled one of the wooden slats aside and squeezed inside. Technically, the garage wasn't locked. The wood was splintered, three large holes opening up to the little clubhouse inside. So technically, he wouldn't be breaking in.

He took the place in—the couches, the fridge, the trash can full of beer cans, the pool table. No computer. If they had one, it was inside the house. Three balls sat on the pool table felt— the 8 ball, the 1, and the 6. He searched the pockets, counting them as he went: four, seven, nine, twelve, fifteen. Fifteen. No cue ball. He searched the pockets again. He checked around the garage. Nothing. The cue ball was gone.

A truck rumbled in front of the house. Shit. The Power Wagon. He crouched beneath the pool table and watched through the broken slats as it parked in front of the Clays'. A few moments later, Jacob was out the door, climbing into the truck with Ian. When they rolled past, Ben slipped out of the garage, jogged to the Z, and caught up to them on El Rancho Road.

Ten minutes later, he kept two cars between them, on the 405, and followed them up to the MacArthur exit, where Ian pulled a left and headed toward the airport. Ben followed them down the departure lane, past the bronze statue of John Wayne, all decked out in his *Searchers* getup, the fake cowboy stuck in permanent stride toward some unseen horizon, until Ian pulled the Power Wagon through the opened chain-link gate of Revolution Air. Ben cruised on past and turned in to the parking lot of Martin Aviation, rolled the Z around the back of the hangar, and nosed it up against the fence, where he got a clear view of the Revolution lot.

Ian and Jacob were inside the office for a few minutes, and then came out with a pilot dangling Bell headphones in his right hand and a topo map rolled up under his arm. They walked out to the tarmac, climbed into a single-engine Piper Comanche, and three minutes later the wheels were up and the little plane banked into the desert sky.

Ben drove back around to Revolution Aviation's parking lot and stepped into the office, remembering at the last moment that he didn't have a badge to flash, no authority whatsoever to get information out of the man behind the counter. Ben greeted the guy and then walked around the office, reading the signs. FAA CHECK RIDES AVAILABLE HERE. SIGN UP TODAY. GET ABOVE IT ALL! INQUIRE ABOUT OUR HOURLY RATES. 24/7 AOG SUPPORT, 714-876-3491. Photos of Learjets, a signed photo of the Blue Angels, a sepia print of the original airfield.

"How much does it cost to rent out one of your planes?" Ben said. "Like that one that just took off? What's the rate for an hour or two?"

"The Comanche? That one's private. Some rich guy up in Big Bear."

"Must be nice," Ben said. "I mean, what's the cruising speed on one of those?"

He thought for minute. "That's a 250, so"—he turned down his lips—"maybe one hundred and eighty."

"Whoa," Ben said. "That *is* cruising."

"It's a damn nice plane," the guy said. Then he started rattling off specs and Ben nodded along like some true aficionado.

"That where the plane's headed?" Ben said. "Big Bear?"

The guy glanced at the paperwork. "According to the flight plan."

"Imagine that," Ben said. "A half hour and you're up in the mountains, in God's country."

———

It scared the shit out of Jacob, flying in that four-seater hunk of metal as it banked over the empty Pacific. Worse, he kept thinking about what the detective said the other day, that Ian had sold him out, that Ian had said that it was his idea to attack the Vietnamese girl. He watched Ian now, up in the front seat next to the pilot, wearing the same fancy headset the pilot was wearing, like he was in charge or something. It was Ian's idea to go after the girl, not his. But it did get out of hand, that was true. Way the fuck out of hand.

The compound was up in the mountains. A place he'd never been. He'd seen the mountains on clear days, snowcapped in winter, dry rocks thrust into the sky in summer. He'd watched *Grizzly Adams* as a kid and thought it'd be cool to live in a cabin, have a bear as a pet, but as the plane shot back over land, all the houses packed together below, the winter-green hills rising above them looking small at this height, he just felt sad. It felt like his life had been taken out of his control, like the plane was whisking him toward some unknown moment that was coming soon. It felt inevitable, preordained. Like God himself had taken him into the sky toward that destiny. So he sat there, leaning away from the window, the nails of his left hand digging into his jeans, and yelled, "It's fuckin' radical," over the hum of the engine when Ian pulled aside one of the headphones and asked him what he thought of flying. What Jacob knew, for sure, was that if you were scared you kept that shit to yourself, especially around Ian. A scared kid was a liability, even Jacob knew that, especially now, after what happened at the beach.

"There's a little get-together tomorrow," Ian had said yesterday, calling him on the home phone when Jacob's mom was out grocery shopping. Since the police station, his mother hadn't let Jake out of the house, the whole place locked up like they were hiding from the serial killer again. He was supposed to be back at school today, though, the district threatening his mom over his truancy. When Jacob mentioned that fact, Ian just said, "This is the kind of get-together you don't miss, Tough Shit," and Jacob couldn't tell if that was a threat or an invitation or both.

It took them a half hour, and soon the land was shoved up under the fuselage of the plane, huge hunks of rock smothered in gleaming snow as the plane descended between peaks. From here, to the west, he could still make out the line of the beach, and to the east, on the other side of the mountains, the great empty desert—dry and ugly and stretching into infinity, it seemed. Beneath the plane now lay a deep-blue lake, the water rising toward the wingtips. The plane circled around and seemed to slide down an invisible cable to a landing at a cement strip near the water's edge.

Then they were in a jacked-up jeep, camo-colored, doors off, despite it being winter. The dude driving it wore mirrored aviator glasses, didn't say a word to Jacob except "Hop in," and before he knew it they were barreling through banks of snow, an empty road snaking through mountain ridges. At first there were huge pine trees, like something out of *Bonanza*, massive trunks layered with broad green branches reaching to points in the sky. But soon the land started to shift, the trees getting shorter until there was mostly brush and snowy ground, and beyond that, down the winding road, the bare, desolate desert. It was so empty out there, layered with treeless ridges and canyons, that he realized they could leave his body in the desert and it would never be found. His mother would never get an answer to his disappearance. Off to school one day and, poof, gone forever.

In twenty minutes, they were there: a peaked-roof building that looked like a barn, a large aluminum-sided hangar, a clump of four mobile homes, and a large wooden cabin with boxes of dead flowers under each window. It was a relief to see the house, to know, at least for now, they weren't driving him into the desert emptiness. Parked in front of the house was another jacked-up jeep, a couple of beat-up Chevys—Jacob counted seven cars in all squeezed into the driveway, a couple of bikes, too. The driver parked the jeep next to a Dodge Charger and slammed the gear shift into park. Above the house a remote-controlled toy plane zoomed a loop in the desert blue sky. Jacob watched it and smiled. They were flying fucking toy planes and he thought they might kill him. Man, he was a wimp.

"This is more than a social call," Ian said to Jacob as Aviator Glasses turned the engine off. "We're on the edge of something here, something that might be big, all right? These guys are heavy hitters—got connections in Idaho, Washington, Pennsylvania, see? We're tapping into something that's been beaten down by the ZOG-loving liberals. But not anymore. You need to know these guys, and they *want* to know you, so be cool, Tough Shit."

They *want* to know him. That *want* bloomed in his chest and he swore to himself he'd be cool, he'd be the coolest goddamned dude ever.

It was late January, but the sun was high and warm and little rivulets of melting snow ran down the driveway. A bonfire was burning in the dead grass of the backyard, a tepee of crackling tree trunks throwing black swirls of smoke into the blue sky. About a dozen people were hanging out around the warmth of the fire—three women chilling at a wrought-iron table, a cluster of dudes on the patio, Buds in fists. There were kids there, too; not teenagers, like himself, but kid kids. Kids sliding down an aluminum slide, kids stumbling around giggling like the world was made of rainbows. He kind of expected machine guns, backyard targets, knives—something more like Rambo carving spikes out of tree branches, not an elementary school playground.

There were more people inside the house, figures he could just make out on the other side of the window glare. A short, wiry guy was turning some meat on the grill near the back door. Two guys standing out on the dead grass, one with a remote control in hand, looking up at the zooming toy plane. It was chill, normal—some rock music coming from inside the house—not Pantera, not Skrewdriver, just classic rock crap, little bowls of Ruffles potato chips, a bag of Cheetos. The only things that gave this away were the boots, the tats, and a red flag with a blue shield and a white cross. Other than that, it was some Norman Rockwell lameness.

"Rowan, my brother," some dude said, breaking away from the Bud crowd to slap Ian's hand. Ian nodded Jacob over and introduced him to the dude, Heimel was his name, whose smile flipped to a scowl reeking of violence.

"Blood and honor," Jacob said, holding out his hand, feeling the test in the dude's eyes.

He looked Jacob up and down, took in the boots and the laces, then slapped Jacob's hand so hard he thought his fingers flew off. He pulled Jacob in close, then, their clasped hands fisted between their stomachs. "You're welcome here, but this place is off the fuckin' map, got it?"

"Yeah. Got it."

"Hammer," Heimel called across the yard. "Get Jake here a cold one."

Hammer reached into a bucket of ice and pitched the can, Jacob snatching it out of the air like he was playing first base.

He and Ian made the rounds, Whitman Kavanaugh, "Bam Bam" Flaherty, Mick Pruitt, Gunnar Kelly, until Jacob couldn't remember the names anymore, just faces and fragments of tats—the fringe of an eagle's wing, the intersection of a Celtic cross, a couple of 88s, most of them partly hidden by T-shirt sleeves or crew necks. Then Ian and Heimel, "Bam Bam," and Brian Pence all slipped into the house and the sliding glass door, which had been open to the breeze, slid closed behind them. Jacob could see the four of them sitting at a dining room table, the sunlight against the window streaking their shapes. Jacob cracked a second beer and some guy named Garrett Bolton started chatting him up about his allergy to cats, which was a big fucking problem since his girlfriend had three cats and every time he stayed over at her place he broke out in hives. But it was worth it, man, because he loved her and she was really good in bed. Jacob listened to him and read his handwritten T-shirt—QUEERS, JEWS, FAGOTS, JUNKIES, ADMINISTER OUR BELOVED COUNTRY—but he was really keeping an eye on the four men in the house, Ian's elbows on the table, listening and nodding. After ten minutes, the four disappeared—who the hell knew where—and Jacob snatched a third beer out of the cooler, his head starting to roll, the edge coming off his ribs.

Four beers in, Jacob found himself playing horseshoes with a chick, Aryanna was her name, who liked to hip-bump him out of her way. She'd come out of nowhere while he was flying the toy plane. It was a World War II Luftwaffe model, the dude told him, complete with painted German crosses on the wings. He'd just managed to make the thing do a loop, and then all of a sudden she was there, her hand on his forearm. "Hey flyboy," she said. "How 'bout throwing a few ringers with me?"

"Where you from?" she said, sending a horseshoe flying into the sandbox.

"Santa Elena."

"Oh," she said, her voice going all superior sounding. "The Rancho."

She popped her hip into his and giggled. Not a stupid chick giggle, but an I-got-you-on-the-hook-and-I-know-it giggle.

He'd never been on the hook before, and he'd tried—with Amy Beerman, with Sandy Neederbacher.

She rung it, the metal swinging around the iron stake.

"What about you?" he said. His shoe landed behind the stake, in the weeds beyond the box.

"Ooh," she said, giggling again. "Strong, but you need some finesse." She stepped up to throw. "Norwalk. It used to be nice, a lot of middle-class families." Ring. She was killing him now. "But they're all moving out, to the valley, the desert, you know? Going to be all Mexicans soon."

He picked up the horseshoe and got into his stance, the pain in his side only a dull throb.

She laughed. "Here," she said. She put her hands on his left calf and spread his legs. Then behind him, her breasts softly against his back, she slipped her hand under his wrist. "Like this," she said, swinging his hand. "Finesse."

He swung the shoe. It hit the stake, spun around, and then rattled off into the sand.

"Close. You're almost there."

She rung another. "They're in there talking about you," she said. "Ian likes you. And Ian doesn't like a lot of people, not even his little brother."

He looked at her. She had hazel eyes. She was wearing a red polo shirt buttoned to the neck, a short black skirt with knit stockings lacing her legs. "What're they saying?"

"Not sure," she said, bumping him out of the way. When she lifted the horseshoe, he saw part of a tattoo running up the inside of her arm, WE MUST PROTECT THE EXIS— "But I heard your name."

Ringer.

"Come on," she said. "Show me what you got."

He stepped up, remembered her body against him, her hand on his wrist. The shoe flipped three times, hit the spike, spun around, and came to a rest on top of hers.

"Oh," she said. "I like quick learners."

A half hour for the Comanche was two hours for the Z, if traffic was light. But he knew where all the speed traps were—the Corona corridor, on the 215 in Riverside, after the 60 junction—so he punched the sports car, burning eighty in the fast lane, weaving in and out of traffic and braking it down to fifty-seven for the traps, playing the model citizen. The Z zipped the mountain curves on Highway 18, speeding past the ski resorts and the spandexed rich people carving snow, riding the edge of the lake blue with reflected sky, until he reached the Big Bear Airport on the east side of the lake and nearly seven thousand feet in the air. It took him an hour and twenty-five.

He found the Comanche in two minutes, tied down in front of the Mountain High Air hangar. What he realized pretty quickly was that plane people really like to talk about planes, and the dude behind the counter, an older man with a mountain-man beard and a WAYLON WILLIE TOGETHER AGAIN shirt, was no exception.

"Damn nice Comanche out there," Ben said. "Those 250s are hard to find."

"Sure are." And then he waxed poetic about the retractable wheels, the cruise speed, max altitude, the lift and pitch, Lycoming engine, vectors and victors and blah blah blah and Ben just stood there smiling, occasionally offering an "Oh, yeah" or some other expression of awe about this little four-seater can with wings.

"I'm in the market," Ben said. "Think the owner'd be willing to sell?"

"Reverend Wales?"

Bingo. Richard Potter Wales. Ben remembered the "sermons" Vanek played for him in the parking lot of Little Saigon. Wales had fallen off the radar after his sermons inspired a farmer to kill two federal agents in Nebraska; he'd left his place in Mariposa and disappeared. So he'd been hiding out up here.

"You'd have to ask him."

"Well, I'm real interested," Ben said. "Would pay over market value if I had to. How would I find him?"

"Got a place out off Rim of the World Drive," the man said. "But I wouldn't go knocking on his door."

"Why's that?"

"Let's just say they like their privacy. Got a whole compound out there," the man said. "Ask me, looks like some kind of barracks. Got guys coming in from all around, a lot of 'em coming out of jail, people say. Like it's kind of a sort of rehab facility or something."

"Rehab?"

The man lit a cigarette and blew smoke. "All's I'm saying is that I wouldn't go knocking on their door. You don't buy a place up there 'cause you're looking to shoot the shit with strangers."

———

"C'mon inside, son," the man said to Jacob. His voice was soft.

Ian had found him out at the horseshoe pit with Aryanna, told him the reverend wanted to greet him personally. Reverend? Nothing about Ian had seemed religious, so what was this reverend thing? The man stood behind a wooden desk, backlit from the sun streaming through the windows, and Jacob couldn't make out his face, just his voice.

"Please, sit down." His arm gestured to two chairs turned toward each other in front of the desk. Ian closed the door behind him, and now Jacob was alone with the man. He came around from behind the desk and Jacob could see his face. He looked like a grandfather—tall, gray hair, black suit with a sweater vest, red tie, and red hankie in his coat pocket. Jacob sat and the man sat down in the chair opposite him. At school, whenever he was called to the principal's office, the man sat behind his broad desk, but the reverend was practically knocking knees with him.

"Jacob," the reverend said. "That's a strong name. One with a lot of history." The reverend leaned back and crossed his legs at the knee, smiling the whole time. Jacob noticed the ring, same as the flag outside, red background, blue shield, white cross and crown. "Please, tell me about yourself."

Jacob had never been asked to talk about himself, didn't know what the hell to say.

He shrugged. "I'm Jacob Clay, I live in Rancho Santa Elena, go to the high school. That's about it, I guess."

The reverend smiled. "You don't like yourself very much, do you?" It didn't sound mean, didn't sound like an accusation. It sounded kind, thoughtful. It sounded true. "Why don't you like yourself?"

"I don't know," Jacob said. "I'm not really good at anything."

"That's not what I hear," the reverend said. His smile faded. "It's not your fault. Your father doesn't like himself, either, doesn't respect himself."

Jacob must have given something away with his face.

"I'm sorry," the reverend said. "Ian told me about your parents' separation. I'm very sorry to hear it. And I don't mean to speak ill of your father. But his problems are instructional for you."

The reverend folded his hands on his knee. Something about the man made him seem like a shrink, or at least what Jacob thought a shrink would be like.

"I hear the policemen gave you a hard time."

The reverend just looked at him a moment, as though he was determining something important about him. It was the first time his face didn't seem kind.

"I didn't talk to them," Jacob said.

"I know," he said. "Most of the boys here, the young men, have been in jail. You know why?"

"They broke the law?" Jacob shrugged.

The reverend smiled. "They were depressed. They lost themselves. Forgot who they are. When we lose ourselves, we do petty things, stupid things—alcohol, drugs, steal things, beat our women. Young men, when they lose themselves, self-destruct."

He paused. "You know how I came to know Ian?"

Jacob just shook his head.

"He burned a cat," the reverend said. "Who burns an innocent cat if they're not in pain?"

Jacob could tell he wasn't supposed to answer.

"Lucky for Ian his father's a friend of mine. When Ian came up here, he found himself, and now he's found you. Hating yourself is the most dangerous thing. And you, Jacob, are in a very dangerous place."

He went on, "It's not your fault, though. How can a son learn to respect himself if his father doesn't respect himself? Respecting yourself must be taught, handed down each generation through good, strong families, through good, healthy culture. You're an innocent, Jacob. An innocent victim of a war. An innocent victim of a culture that tells you the white man is evil—that 'people of color' have more value because of their suffering. That is the wrong kind of logic. People who can avoid their own suffering have greater value than those who wallow in it."

He stopped and poured Jacob a glass of water from a crystal pitcher.

"You are a descendant of Abel through Seth, the very same Abel killed by his own brother. From the very beginning the forces of evil have wanted to destroy us, the white man, the true chosen people." He put a hand to his chin, as though this fact pained him. "But we have persisted, dominated, brought the world magnificent things, shared those things even—in India, in the Middle East, in America. We've done this because we knew our history, knew our place as superior beings in the world. These young men have found themselves here. Here they're reminded of their greatness, their potential. You can see it in their faces, can't you?"

Jacob thought about Ian's face, the toughness, the certainty. That's it, that's what Jacob had seen in Ian—certainty.

"Yes," Jacob said.

"You can be great, too, Jacob. You can glow with your own greatness. But you have to love yourself. Do you want to love yourself?"

He wanted his father to love him more than the dead Vietnamese woman, but he'd destroyed that possibility, he knew. He'd killed something his father loved and there was no going back from that.

"Yes," Jacob said. He really did, too. He was starved for it. Maybe if he loved himself his parents wouldn't matter anymore. None of the fuckin' kids at school, either.

The reverend leaned forward and took Jacob's hands in his, as though they were about to pray. "You're a strong young white man. You're the descendant of great warriors, of powerful thinkers. You are the descendant of the people who built this country. It's in your DNA. You must love yourself. You're a traitor to the race if you don't. You are beautiful, Jacob. You are perfect. You are exactly what God wanted in the world."

Jacob couldn't help it, his pussy-self started to tear up. The man smiled and then pulled him into a hug. It was a grandfatherly embrace, tender and warm, and Jacob swelled with the openness of the gesture.

"Yes," the reverend said. "Sometimes we have to be reminded."

He let go of Jacob and leaned back again in his chair.

"Now, why don't you like yourself?"

Sensing a test, Jacob said, "I don't know. I've been taught all the wrong things, I guess."

The reverend smiled, but he couldn't tell if he'd passed the test or not—or even if it was a test. All Jacob knew was that he wanted to please this man. He'd flown him up in an airplane for fuck's sake, shown him his secret compound, invited him into his office, told him he was beautiful. Before this moment, he couldn't ever imagine someone calling him beautiful. That was a word you used for girls, for something more precious than precious.

"We're victims of a slow genocide," the reverend said. "In ten years we'll be a minority in this country. But there's us. We're the last stand. We're trying to save our people. By saving them, you'll remind yourself of who you are. Most of us want to do something, be someone. This world teaches children to be a cog in the wheel of industry. But that industry doesn't work for us."

The reverend grabbed Jacob's hand again, held it like he was passing a blessing through their palms.

"These protests now in Santa Elena," the reverend said, "offer us a unique opportunity. We've chosen you, Jacob, to help save our people. Ian will speak to you more about this. For now, it makes me very happy to see you on this journey. You give me hope."

When Jacob stepped outside onto the deck, Aryanna was there, like she'd been waiting for him, like she couldn't wait to see him. "Come on," she said, grabbing onto his suspenders and pulling him close. "I want to show you something."

———

The road rattled the hell out of the Z. Rutted with runoff, patched with snow, the dirt road wound up into the eastern mountains, rising above the lake in switchbacks. The road crested and dipped down into a valley, the land more desert here, the lodgepole and ponderosa thinning out, piñon and scrub holding the land together now. The Z bottomed out, spun its tires in slushy snow, until Ben, realizing he was going to tear up the car, finally pulled onto a national forest trailhead turnoff and parked it.

He grabbed the pocket-sized writing pad and a pen he'd snatched from his truck, locked the Z, and found a deer trail running through the sagebrush. Ten minutes in, something buzzed the air; when he looked up a toy airplane climbed into the thin mountain air, rolled, and dove back toward him, zipping a low pass just thirty feet from where he stood. He crouched and walked the tree line until he saw a six-foot privacy fence, running at least fifty yards long. NO TRESPASSING signs were nailed to the fence, and a PROTECTED BY SMITH & WESSON sign graced the gate to the compound. Voices murmured beyond the fence, Lynyrd Skynyrd's "Sweet Home Alabama" scratched out of stereo speakers. Shitty taste in music. He came up in the shadow of a ponderosa pine and saw the cars in the driveway. Two jacked-up jeeps and a shit-brown Oldsmobile were parked in front of the barn. A couple of bikes—a Harley, a Suzuki—were kick-standed next to a shed. Three other cars were parked on the browned grass—a Volkswagen Bug, a Ford Mustang 5.0, and a beat-up Dodge Charger. He slid along the fence line and ducked it over to the cover of the ponderosa's massive trunk.

A faded-yellow aluminum warehouse sat thirty yards from the house, a rusted padlock bolted closed the sliding doors. He walked down the side of the building, out of view of the barbecuers, and found a side door. He turned the handle: locked. He pulled the bump key from his wallet, slid it in, found a rock, tapped the key once, and turned the lock open. There were three snowmobiles inside, an ATV, and an old John Deere tractor. Garden utensils were stacked in a corner, an old propeller, a few rusted ten-speeds, an old baby crib, and a couple of dusty computer screens but no computers. In the corner of the warehouse, something was stacked and covered with a tarp. He pulled it up and found a pile of cardboard boxes. Using his pocketknife, he slit open the packing tape. Inside, he found baggies of pills—white ones with numbers stamped into them. He prized open a bag at the tape and slipped a few out and put them into his pocket. Methamphetamines, he figured, but he'd get Lofland to test them.

He slid around the back of the warehouse. From there he

could read the plates of the two cycles and four of the other vehicles—all California tags except two: Idaho on a Jeep Wagoneer and Utah on an AMC Eagle.

The toy plane buzzed the roof of the house and cut a turn toward the backyard. He started jotting down the plate numbers—6MVB008, 4NQG703—and the makes and models. Up a ridge behind the house, two lines of dust floated across the piñon pines. The dust trails spun mini tornadoes along the ridgeline. Then he saw them, two souped-up jeep four-by-fours tearing down the hillside. They weren't running a trail, just ripping the land up, their jacked-up chassis bouncing on monster-truck-sized tires. If he'd had a sniper rifle, he'd have blown their fucking tires out and ended the carnage. They were racing each other, their engines redline screaming. The rear jeep pulled ahead and then swerved in front before they both hit the gravel driveway and slammed the brakes into two sliding parking jobs. The assholes hopped out of the doorless chassis, slapped hands, and strode into the house. Two more CA plates. He jotted down the numbers.

Then the side-yard door screeched open. He dove behind the nearest truck and made himself dirt. From behind the tire, he saw a girl pawing a kid. Jacob Clay, he realized after a second look. The toy plane pulled out of a steep dive and zipped above the parked cars. The girl spun the kid and shoved him up against the closed fence door. His hands were dumbly at his sides, like he was all confusion, while her fingers worked at his jeans button. She kissed him on the nape of the neck as she unzipped him, and Ben had to lie there, catatonic in the snow-wet dirt, the plane making invisible shapes in the sky, while she took care of things.

———

The lieutenant opened the door to the holding cell. Bao had been asleep, curled up on the stainless-steel bench. They'd brought him a pillow and a blanket late last night and exhaustion finally knocked him out. But it had been a fitful sleep, full of ugly dreams—the helicopter, always the helicopter spinning toward the Pacific, his daughter drowning in black water.

"I hope you were able to rest, Mr. Phan."

"A little."

"May I?" the lieutenant said, pointing to the empty side of the bench. It was strange, a policeman asking permission to sit in his own holding cell.

Bao didn't know how long he'd been in the cell. There were no windows, except for the twelve-by-twelve square in the door that led to a hallway with no windows. There was a stainless-steel toilet in the corner, a stainless-steel shelf fastened to the concrete wall. The number 3 painted in black on that wall. A single fluorescent light flickered above his head. It reminded him of being on a ship, the navy ship that took them to Guam. This was a space without time, where the sun didn't rise or set, where the earth stopped moving, for all he knew. It seemed to him he'd spent his whole life in prisons. The prison of superpowers and politics, the prison of war, the prison of refugee camps, the prison of endless work. He'd spent his whole life trying to get out of prisons, and now, here he was, the only prison he'd been locked in that was of his own making.

Bao nodded and the lieutenant sat, rigidly, his back perfectly straight, his hands on his knees. He was a man in control, a man who followed the rules given to him. He reminded Bao of a soldier.

"You're free to go," the lieutenant said, quietly. "You will not be charged." The lieutenant narrowed his eyes at Bao. "The mayor only asks that you help end the protests."

"Protests?" Bao didn't know there'd been protests, locked in this nowhere world.

"Your brother organized it. People are angry about your arrest. They're angry about your daughter's . . ." He paused. "Your daughter's murder, too." He was quiet a moment. "Now," the lieutenant went on, "I won't tell you what to do regarding the protests. You follow your own conscience. But I will not bring charges against you."

Bao almost thanked the man, yet he'd been locked in this cell for committing no crime while his daughter's killer was still free.

"He didn't do it, did he?" Bao said. "Lucas Clay?"

Hernandez looked at him, seeming to weigh his words. "I think Mr. Clay had the opposite motivation when it came to your daughter."

Bao looked at his hands a moment. Love. He—she—had been in love and all he had been able to see was theft, that his daughter was being stolen from him. In his anger, he'd never considered that she had been an adult who understood her own feelings. Lucas Clay had tried to make him see that when he came to the grocery asking for Linh's hand. *You don't think she can make her own decisions? Who do you think you raised, Bao?* He had defined her, Bao realized now; defined her to suit his needs. He had made her his reward for everything he'd lost, a trophy daughter for his pain. For a moment, he re-visioned the night in the living room when she had shared that writer's quote with him. He couldn't remember it exactly, but it was something about the way people define others, about how those definitions belong to the definers and not the ones being defined. At the time he thought she was talking about white people, the way they saw race before they saw the person. Now, he could see, she had been sending him a message, too. *I'm your daughter,* Cha, *but my life is not yours.*

"Do you know who killed Linh?" Bao said now, looking at Hernandez.

Hernandez's eyes stayed on Bao, but they didn't betray anything.

"It's the same people who left the dog, yes?" Bao said. Then a memory flashed in his mind: Lucas Clay's son, in the grocery the morning after the dog had been dropped in the alley. *He's married,* Jacob had spat at Linh. *Leave my dad alone.* He was a boy, but he had radiated a dangerous anger when Bao grabbed his wrist. "It's the boy," Bao said. "Lucas's son."

"I'm sorry," the lieutenant said, "but I can't share any investigative information with you."

Bao scoffed. He knew the way the Garden Grove police left the Vietnamese boys to shoot each other in the street, the way they never followed up on robbery investigations. The white cops stayed in the white neighborhoods and left the Vietnamese to their own devices, even though they paid their taxes. It was the reason he'd bought the Smith & Wesson in the first place.

"You know what I think, Mr. Hernandez?" Bao said, grief glowing into anger. "I think people like me don't get the same justice others do."

Bao could tell he had angered the detective. Hernandez's jaw tightened. He raised his shoulders a bit, but still there was compassion in his eyes.

"You're right," Hernandez said. "I know a little about that myself."

Bao suddenly wanted to take his words back. The policeman was a Mexican, and Bao knew well enough that they were forced to tread similar waters. As long as most policemen were white, justice would mostly be for whites.

"I have a job to do," Hernandez said. "And I promise you, Mr. Phan, I swear with everything I am—as a man, a father, an arm of the law—that I will find the people who did this, arrest them, and build a case that no jury can ignore."

Bao scrutinized the detective's face. He was a deadly serious man and Bao believed him, though he doubted the system, doubted the world in which the man cast such promises.

"But please, Mr. Phan, don't make me arrest you again. You're not the kind of person I want to put in prison. And I don't want to be sliding your body into the back of a coroner's van. I want you here, in this town, living."

Bao was astonished to hear it. No one had ever said such a

thing to him. No one had ever said *I want you here* to him. The nice people had said, *You're welcome here,* as though they were hosting a long sleepover. But he'd never heard anyone say that he—or his wife or Linh—were wanted.

"I have two daughters," the lieutenant said, his voice quiet now. "I can imagine your pain, and I hope never to experience it. It's what we fear the most, as parents."

He didn't try to negate Bao's pain, didn't utter empty platitudes, as though a few words could plaster up the hole in his heart.

"I don't know what you folks believe," the lieutenant said, "but I know the soul lives on somewhere. I don't go to church much, and I don't know where it goes, but I believe it."

Bao wanted to tell him that Linh had visited him, that Linh's soul had moved through his body the night after her death, but they weren't intimates, they weren't friends; he was just a man who held the key to Bao's cell.

"I have to believe it," Bao said. "But I'm selfish. And I want her here with me."

Chapter Seventeen

The next morning, Ben called over to Nick Talbot at the station.

"Officially, I shouldn't be working with you," Nick said.

"I know," Ben said. "But like you said, computers are the future of police work."

"All right," Nick said. "Hit me with it."

Ben wanted to know what he needed to set up a computer at home and Nick laid it all out—a Commodore 64 would be the cheapest way to go, a floppy disk drive, a modem with basic terminal software. He could get it all at Kmart. So Ben drove across town to the store, instructions in hand, tossed everything he needed in a basket, pushed his Mastercard near the limit, and cruised it all back home.

Yesterday, when he'd gotten back from Big Bear, he'd called in a favor from the facilities manager at the city impound lot, got them to tow his Chevy over to Sears for new tires. He'd called the plates at Big Bear in to Vanek, too, and filled him in on the compound in the mountains, the meth pills. Vanek was interested in the Idaho and Utah plates, said he was going to put in a call to his buddy at Alcohol, Tobacco, and Firearms. A whole new ballgame once it went interstate. So for now, a waiting game, but Ben didn't feel like waiting.

Back at his place, Ben hauled the boxes of computer stuff up to the barn. Gus whinnied when he saw Ben, Tin Man spun around in his stall and gave Ben his rear end, as though in preemptive protest at a ride. Ben gave them both a bucket of oats, and then cleared his desk of detritus. Thankfully, the computer came with twelve pages of directions explaining how to set everything up. He followed step-by-step, plugging various cords into various ports, and pretty soon the machine was ready to go. He thought computer guys were supposed to be some kind of geniuses, but this was about as easy as setting up a hi-fi stereo. He pushed the POWER button, the screen flashed a white line across the left side, and then the monitor came to life and a blue screen faced him. *COMMODORE 64 BASIC V2*, the screen read. Below that was gibberish about RAM and bytes and then READY and a flashing cursor.

Shit, what did he do now?

He called over to Nick again.

"You know," he said, "people get pretty good consulting fees doing this kind of stuff." Nick sighed. "Write this down."

Ben did. ATDT prompt. Prompt for phone number. Dial it in.

"Most likely the BBS is running on an eight-line modem, so you might not get in at first," Nick said. "The modem you have has an automatic redial, so you might just have to be patient. When you get the password and get in," Nick went on, "you can probably set up a guest account. You'll want to do that with a handle, some fake name. Don't be stupid and use your real name."

Ben got off the phone and followed Nick's directions. It took six redials before he got in, but there it was again, the welcome page staring back at him: WELCOME TRUE PATRIOTS TO LIBERTY STORM NET! And then the password prompt. He went with the first thing that came to mind: *Posse Comitatus*.

PASSWORD NOT VALID.

He typed in: *88*

PASSWORD NOT VALID.

1488

PASSWORD NOT VALID.

———

When they got back from the mountains last night, Ian had taken him into the Heritage Park Public Library, fired up one of their computers, and showed him how to get onto the bulletin board.

"Make sure none of these librarians are looking over your shoulder."

Now, during lunch, Jacob went to the school library and hopped on one of the computers. His home economics class from last year had taught the students how to use the Macintosh computers, but he didn't have one at home and he'd only used one a couple of times to type up stupid papers for class.

He typed in the password now and logged in: *TuffShitSoldier*.

"There will be a sign," Ian had said yesterday. "We don't know what it is yet, but we will. It'll be something obvious, but something only we understand."

The screen flashed and the messages came up. People swore to fight for their race. People railed at ZOG. Someone went off about Odin and Valhalla. Another had listed the names of enemies. A lot of it was the kind of stuff Ian had talked about— the white race was going to be wiped out. America would be a nation of Godless mud peoples. A lot of it coming from the reverend Wales's sermons, which were here for everyone to read. NATION IS RACE!, FOR WHOM IS THE U.S. RUN?, HOLOCAUST OR HOLOHOAX?, THE JEW IN REVIEW, BLACKS AND THE GODLY ARGUMENT FOR SLAVERY, THE VISIONARY FICTION OF ANDREW MACDONALD. Honestly, it was a whole lot of the same thing, like people just repeating to each other what they'd heard elsewhere, but there were a lot of them, and he was here, with them, together in this blue screen.

They needed him, Ian had said, when he told Jacob the plan. Reverend Wales needed him. "What signify a few lives lost in a century or two? The tree of liberty must be refreshed from time to time with the blood of patriots and tyrants. It is its natural manure."

It is its natural manure.

He liked that line, though he didn't really know what it meant, to be honest. But Thomas Jefferson had said it, according to Ian, and he wrote the Constitution and he'd had slaves. The other part was the important part, the stuff about the tree of liberty. War was a natural thing. Humans had been doing it since the moment they stood upright. That's what Ian had said, and, well, wasn't his dad proof? Wasn't the whole damn twentieth century proof of the naturalness of war? It was an honorable thing, too, if the cause was right. Ian had said all this to him last night on the drive back from the airport, but Jacob understood now that Ian was repeating what the reverend Wales had taught him.

Then a new message popped on the screen. TRIBULATION, it read.

A few seconds later another.

TRIBULATION.

Another.

And by the end of lunch, his stomach cramping with hunger, seven more TRIBULATIONS burned from the computer screen.

———

Rachel had a date tonight, so Ben and Emma were up on the horses. They picked a trail above Shady Canyon, the backyards of new homes a couple hundred yards down the ridgeline creeping up the hillside. Emma was up ahead of him, spinning Gus around another dried puddle, looking for animal tracks.

Earlier, Ben had spent hours typing in passwords, trying different combinations, but nothing worked. And now his mind was playing word codes, dialing number combinations. It seemed futile; the code could be anything, and he was feeling a little pissed about spending nearly six hundred dollars for a box with wires that, at the moment, seemed useless.

"Coyote," Emma said now. Sure enough, the paw tracks preserved in caked mud.

The snow and rain from the last big storm had pooled along the trail and then dried in cracked layers of mud. You could read the faunal history of the last two weeks in the dried earth—the upside-down heart shape of mule deer hooves, the large hind feet of the jackrabbit, the strangely human-like feet of a raccoon. The deep ruts of four-wheel-drive tires.

"Looks like dinner, too." He pointed to a squirrel carcass, the stomach eaten out, the stunned head of the animal and its tail still stitched to the spine.

"Gross."

He and Emma had been up in the hills for an hour, Ben cooling off after Arthur—say it with a pretentious PhD accent—opened the door at Rachel's when Ben drove over to pick up Emma. The professor was dressed in black tie, Rachel coming down the stairs a couple moments later, lighting it up in a silver dress. They were off to a social psychology department fundraiser at the university, something about a potential donor, blah, blah, blah. It made sense, really, that Rachel would be with a professor. She was an intellectual and Ben was a blue-collar street predator. They had been high school sweethearts, but he wasn't the same man he was then, and she wasn't the same woman. It stung a bit, like someone pressing on a bruise, but he shook the man's hand and watched him lay a maroon sweater across Rachel's shoulders that made her so stunning Ben was sure she'd win a million bucks from whatever rich jerk was throwing money around.

"Don't worry about him, Dad," Emma said now, both of them riding side by side up the hill.

"I'm fine."

"He's kind of a dweeb," she said. "Mom and I definitely *do not* have the same taste in men."

"Really, I'm fine," Ben said. "And I'm kind of taken."

Quiet a moment, the two of them swaying on the horses.

"How's the Lance situation?" They hadn't talked about it since it all blew up.

"It's all right," she said. "Still kind of sucks when I see him, but it's the right thing. He's sweet, but I couldn't keep having the same conversations, over and over—skateboards, radical tubes, Led Zeppelin lyrics." She twirled her hand in the air.

They loped up Turtle Ridge, passing its namesake jumble of boulders, and turned up East Fork toward the reservoir. A couple of Sea Stallions shook the air above their heads and rumbled down toward the huge hangars of Tustin Air Station. It was a warm evening, but another big Pacific storm was working its way down from the Aleutians, and the sun had been devoured by the high-altitude steel-gray clouds that preceded the storm. The soap-water light left everything flat-looking and he sort of enjoyed the sadness in the landscape. All those sunny Southern California days could be oppressive for someone who knew the shit in the world.

"Natasha knew the girl who was killed, right?" Emma said, out of nowhere.

"She did."

"That's gotta be rough."

"It is."

The reservoir was ahead, a man-made oval looking like a fallen flying saucer in the strange light.

"How'd you know?"

"Mom told me."

The horses trotted when they got a whiff of the water, Gus jumping into full canter when he was fifty yards away, Tin Man content to jog it out. Ahead of him, Gus dipped his nose into the water and Emma seemed to jump in the saddle.

"Oh, shit," he heard her say, and then she was off the horse, stepping away from something on the edge of the reservoir.

Ben kicked Tin Man into a canter, coming up the right side of

Gus, his head still dipped to the water, when he saw what had frightened Emma. Oh, shit, indeed.

———

After they discovered the bloodied shirt and sock, Ben and Emma had cantered the horses down into the nearest neighborhood, Casa Sol, and rode a greenbelt to Alta Plaza, where he called it in on a pay phone. They'd ridden back up to the scene together, too, Ben in full cop mode, Emma silent in a way he only recognized in retrospect, after Natasha got on the scene and Hernandez sent him packing and they got back to the house and she had finally broken into tears. He'd hugged her and then tried to feed her some chicken soup, but his heart was split in two—the father one here with her, trying to work through her trauma, and his cop one jonesing like an addict to be up there.

"How old was she?" she asked.

"Twenty-two."

"Just six years older than me."

From where they sat at the dining room table, they could see the light towers illuminating the crime scene just a half mile away. Rain had started to sheet down, and the ghostly hue from the spotlights unsettled even him. The scene was practically in their backyard, a fact Emma had pointed out at least three times.

"That's why those people are protesting, right? Linh's murder?"

She was sipping tea now.

"Yes. And other things they're tired of."

They would be taking a cast of the four-wheel-drive tires. Ian's Power Wagon, he was sure of it.

"What things?" she said.

He told her—about the dog, about the attack on the migrant workers, the graffiti, and the daily lesser evils.

"Em," Ben said. "I'm sorry you saw that today."

"It was just blood on a shirt," she said. "I've seen blood before."

Blood on a shirt and a sock. It was the sock that interested him the most. A long knee-high sock, a hole in the bottom where the duct tape had broken and the cue ball had fallen through. They'd be dragging the reservoir, trying to find the cue ball. But Ben didn't think it was there. It was on the beach. It would have broken through the fabric in the attack on Linh. The department had had crews down there, combing the sand, but they hadn't found anything.

"Yes," he said. "But not like this, right?"

His first inclination was to console Emma, to agree it was just blood on a shirt. But he couldn't bullshit her on this. Knowing where the blood came from, knowing what caused it to be spilled made a difference.

"I don't know," she said. "Maybe it's something I needed to see. You know, I go to school with some of their kids, but I've never really tried to get to know them. I mean, I've never been mean to them, like some kids, but I've just kind of stuck with my group. Isn't that weird?"

"It's not your fault this woman is dead."

She was quiet, chewing on something she didn't know how to articulate yet. *He* didn't really know how to articulate the thing she was trying give voice to. It was racism, sure, that was obvious with the white supremacists. But weren't the supremacists the terror arm of something more subtle, something more ingrained in the culture? Since the afternoon up in Westminster with Vanek, he had seen shit everywhere—a swastika scratched into a toilet stall, WETBACKS GO HOME! tagged onto a drainage ditch retaining wall, the bumper stickers on the backs of cars asking "Americans" to bring the flag with them when they left Westminster, little signals he hadn't paid much attention to; they were just part of the landscape, something he passed every day on the way to work, to the grocery store, to the taquería in the strip mall. Something he could ignore because he wasn't the object of the attacks. Race was always an underlying force when he worked the North Hollywood streets—the white cops coming in to patrol the mostly Latino neighborhoods, some of those cops openly racist, some of them using the badge to justify their violence against people they were charged to protect and serve, and the community's distrust of the cops, even the good ones. It had been exhausting, it had felt like a war, like they were an invading force. It was dawning on Ben that one of the reasons he left the LAPD and moved his family back to Santa Elena was so that he could pretend race wasn't an issue, so that he didn't have to feel like the enemy to the people he thought he was trying to protect. He didn't think, at the time, that moving back to Santa Elena made him culpable in a larger system and the purposeful denial that laid the foundation for that system.

"I don't know," she said. "I'm mostly happy here. I mean, you and Mom divorcing sucked, but this has been a good place to grow up. But I'm starting to think it's not always such a nice place, you know what I mean?"

He nodded. If you had a happy childhood, you grew up believing people were mostly good. He wanted that for her, wanted her to believe in the goodness of people. But he didn't want that belief to be forged out of ignorance, didn't want her to think all white people were nice just because they had been mostly nice to her.

"Most places are a combination of both. Nice and mean. It's human nature. It's in the DNA of people."

"But this is different, right?" she said. "It's not just a few jerks, you know?"

"It's a good thing to notice," he said. "You can change it, if you notice it."

———

Three hours later, Natasha drove up to the house. It was Ben's night with Emma, but he'd paged Rachel and she had called him back and they'd both agreed that it'd be good for Emma to get out of sight of the investigation lights and spend the night at her mother's condo. So Rachel cut her date short and Ben was alone when Natasha walked through the front door, her hair slicked back wet from working the scene, her eyes puffy and hollowed out. She kissed him softly on the lips when she came through the door and then they sat at the table in front of the window, watching the lights of the crime scene through the torrents.

"Type AB negative on the shirt," she said. "Linh's blood type. The rarest type."

He'd suspected it would be Linh's blood, and he figured she did, too, but it didn't change the gut punch of saying it out loud.

"Drink?" Ben said.

"No," she said. "Not right now." She stared out the window. "Bao and Ai drove up to County today. Begging me to release Linh's body."

This was tough on families, Ben knew. Their loved ones locked away in stainless-steel bins until the investigation was complete.

Natasha shook her head. "This job." She let out a long breath of air. "At least Bao's out of jail."

"There's a missing cue ball from the Rowans' pool table," Ben said. "I'm pretty sure it's down at the beach."

He glanced at the television and she did, too. He'd been watching the eleven o'clock news before she arrived—drive-by shootings in South Central, the War on Drugs, President Reagan giving an address on Soviet relations from Camp David. He'd turned down the volume when he saw her headlights coming up the drive, but he wanted to keep an eye on the weather. Now a reporter was standing in the driving rain, pointing to the Newport Beach surf driven by the storm and flooding Ocean Front Walk.

"This storm's going to churn things up down at Crystal Cove," she said.

"Yeah," he said. "Low tide's at six fifty-four in the morning."

"A trip to the beach then."

"A trip to the beach."

———

There was one thing Jacob was good at: destroying things. It was so easy. If people knew how fuckin' easy it was, they'd never sleep at night. He knew what it meant to have things destroyed—a person, a marriage, a family. It had frightened him when he was a dumb little kid, but when he started looking at his dad's 'Nam pics, really looked at them, took them into his head, that fear started to seem stupid. Things were made and things were destroyed. That's just how it was.

Jacob was in the garage now, a baggie full of gunpowder on the workbench, a length of lead pipe, two brass caps, a box of carpenter nails. *You put nails in there,* he remembered Ian saying, *you could do some real damage.* It was late, after midnight. He'd pretended to go to sleep. Around 10:30, his mom had come into his room, the first time in years—at least as far as he knew—and touched his cheek. Then he lay there for two hours, waiting for the lights to go out, waiting for the sound of the television coming from her room, which meant she was in bed passed out.

Wear gloves, Ian had said. *Latex. When you're finished, throw them away in a plastic bag, and set it out with the trash tomorrow. It's trash day. By tomorrow afternoon, it'll be lost in the dump.* The bombs weren't hard to make. It was just like the PVC bombs, except these were with a lead water pipe. They had given him the materials just before leaving the mountains, a plastic bag tied tight he wasn't supposed to open until he was home. *No questions,* Ian had said. *About anything. It's better that way.*

Now he soldered the brass cap onto one end of the pipe. It wasn't a big pipe, maybe two inches in diameter, about eight inches long. He mixed the gunpowder with the carpenter nails and poured the mixture into the pipe.

He didn't really understand The Tribulation, as Ian called it. Didn't really get the race war thing and how it watered the tree of liberty. *If one of them attacks us,* Ian had said, *white people will lose it. Doesn't matter if we attack first. That's when the war starts.* In the *Diaries,* man, they went full-on nuclear to purify the country, but that was just a book. They told him about Posse Comitatus, that's what the flags had been about, a group, something important to join. But he really didn't get that, either. But they had a plan—the reverend Wales had a plan—and Jacob was a part of it, a part of something important.

He topped off the pipe and packed it down with a tobacco pipe tamper. Then he worked on the screws to the engine of the radio-controlled plane, the same one he'd flown at the barbecue when Aryanna bumped her hip into him and said, "Hey flyboy," like he was some real cool dude. He'd read about how to make a controlled fuse in *Soldier of Fortune.* Inside, he found the solenoid to the toy engine and carefully worked it loose.

He didn't really understand how he fit into the plan. Yeah, he got what he was supposed to do tomorrow, but he didn't really know why this was the start of things. In the back of his mind, he wondered why they hadn't asked Ian to do it, thought again about the detective saying that Ian sold him out, that it had been Jacob's plan to kill the girl. *No questions.*

He could do this. He hated everything. It felt like an oil fire burning in his chest, a constantly fed fire that burned everything away. He knew the cops were watching his house. When the time came, he would jump the backyard fence, sneak through the neighbor's yard, and take the walkways through the housing tract to get out.

He attached the fuse to the solenoid coils. A fucking toy from Toys R Us, one push of the switch and boom. It was funny, in a way, a kid's toy to start a war.

Chapter Eighteen

The beach was torn all to hell when they got there. Dunes of sand, chunks of driftwood, coils of sea kelp, shoes, and water bottles. The storm was still pumping, pelts of rain, wind kicking up salt froth off the pounding waves. They split the beach in half, Natasha taking the south end and Ben walking the north.

Natasha combed the beach with a metal rake, Ben toeing away sand with his feet. He stomped around the firepit, which was now a water-logged mess of ash. He combed the dunes, dug a piece of driftwood into the eddies where detritus had gathered in pools of stagnant water. For three hours they walked the beach, the storm lashing their faces, their clothes soaked through. Three goddamned hours, all manner of human junk lodged in the sand. Fifteen more minutes and he was calling it. And then through the wail of wave and wind he heard Natasha calling his name. He turned to find her waving her arms at him, and he sprinted the thirty yards over to where she stood.

"Got it," she said. "I got it."

Jesus Christ, it was no bullshit—the white top of the cue ball sticking out of a puddle of water like a tiny skull.

After finding the cue ball, Ben and Natasha drove up to the Texaco station on PCH and Ben called Vanek from the phone booth. They met at Ben's place, in the barn, the cue ball in a ziplock on the desk near the computer. Ben and Natasha had stopped to pick up breakfast burritos on the way back, but no one was eating. Natasha was at the computer, going through Ben's case notes, trying passwords for the supremacists' bulletin board. Ben and Vanek were working at a folding card table Ben had set up. Vanek had run the license plates and was now laying out the names one by one, notebook paper for each with handwritten case history notes.

David Webber, armed robbery, Security Pacific Bank, St. George, Utah.

Gunnar Kelly, domestic abuse of wife—broken wrist and fractured orbital bone; assault with a deadly weapon—a beer bottle attack on a homosexual couple in Idaho Falls.

Michael Pruitt, shot the windows out of a Unitarian Universalist church in Phoenix, Arizona.

Winston Heimel, battery—curbed a black man in Anaheim, California, shattered his jaw and broke the man's larynx.

Every single one of them ex-prisoners, a litany of attacks, weapons charges, domestic abuse. Everyone except the reverend Wales, Paul and Ian Rowan, and the recruit, Jacob Clay, had a rap sheet.

Whitman Kavanaugh, vandalism, swastika burned into the front-yard grass of a Hispanic couple, Levittown, Pennsylvania.

Brian Pence, stabbed a Planned Parenthood physician outside a Salt Lake City clinic, claimed he was stopping the "genocide" of white babies.

Garrett Bolton, sexual assault, sodomized a black teenager with a broomstick, San Clemente, California.

One problem? No outstanding warrants. Like they'd all become model citizens once they left jail, which pretty much defied the universal law of ex-cons.

"I drove out to San Bernardino and checked real estate records," Vanek said. "Wales's place in Big Bear is owned by Promise14Ministries, LLC."

"So a promise to create a theocratic white ethno-state?" Ben said.

Vanek just cocked his head.

"What's the LLC?" Natasha asked, while she typed away.

"Limited liability company," Vanek said. "Wyoming started them in '77, but they haven't really caught on yet, apparently. Somehow shelters the owners from debts and court judgments. Since this is a 'ministry,' it's exempt from paying federal taxes, too."

"Pays to be a church."

"Here's the real kicker," Vanek said. "The owner of the LLC gets to remain anonymous."

"That's how Wales got off the grid," Ben said. "That's why no one's been able to find him for two years."

"Right," Vanek said. "I asked my accountant about this yesterday. He says it would be a good way to launder money, too."

"So if you're dealing methamphetamine," Ben said, "you could run the money through the ministry and it'd come out clean."

"Exactly," Vanek said.

"One of those names, Winston Heimel, was the owner of the meth house that burned," Ben said.

Vanek nodded. "I remembered that. He's one of these Idaho guys. I put in a call with my Alcohol, Tobacco, and Firearms connection, Agent Aidan Graham, and ran the names you got up in Big Bear through him. He pinged on this Heimel guy, said they were eyeing him for a drive-by hit on a couple of troopers up in Idaho. Says Heimel has connections to an Elias Girnt Klein, who's got a little compound of his own up in Jerome County, Idaho, the Church of Jesus Christ Christian."

"As opposed to Church of Jesus Christ Hindu?" Ben said.

Vanek smiled. "Wants to make it clear, apparently, that messianic Jews need not apply. This Elias Klein guy likes to be called reverend, too, it seems."

"Did we ever figure out what the fourteen stands for?" Natasha said.

Ben glanced over at her as she crossed something out on a piece of paper.

"No," Ben said. "We got the eighty-eight, but not the fourteen."

"Klein left California in the 1970s, to get away from the 'mongrels,'" Vanek continued, "and bought some cheap acreage up in the Rocky Mountain foothills of Idaho. Espouses the Northwest Territorial Imperative. He's got this idea that the Northwest is the natural place for people with Nordic blood to live."

God's country, Ben thought.

"Used to hold a yearly Aryan Nation Congress in Idaho, brought in supremacists from all over the country."

"Used to?" Natasha said from the desk.

"It took them awhile to figure out that if they all gathered in one place, it was easy for the FBI to watch them."

"Shooting fish in a barrel," Ben said.

"When they started using the internets, they could be connected and underground," Vanek said. "The feds had this Winston Heimel character living at the Idaho compound until a year ago. Then he dropped off the map."

"Seems stupid to have Heimel's name on the meth house," Ben said.

"Stupid for him," Vanek said, "but it keeps Wales and the LLC clean. Wales, like all these jerks, wants to create a white ethno-state, reclaim the country for the white race. He talked about it in his sermons, protecting Adamic people and all that." Vanek tossed a hand in the air. "Says Southern California was stolen from them."

"Rancho Santa Elena," Ben said. "A master-planned city for a master race."

"If they can just keep the Asians out," Natasha said.

"Yeah, and my DB, Walter Brennan, was getting in the way," Vanek said. "He was breaking Orion's near monopoly on real estate."

"Buying up commercial property"—Ben was nodding now—"when it was in the planning stage, before they even broke ground."

"We must protect the existence of Adamic peoples and a future for our children," Natasha whispered to herself.

"Then advertising in Little Saigon," Vanek said, "overcharging business owners who wanted to get their foot in the door."

They were quiet a moment, the air buzzing around them with the adrenaline of the pieces falling into place.

"So why didn't Paul Rowan register his Orion real estate company as an LLC?"

"Maybe your councilman isn't so smart," Vanek said.

"Yeah, probably," Ben said. "But what if this Promise14 LLC isn't just Wales but also this Elias Klein guy and other 'reverends' all over the country? An organized syndicate connected by this bulletin board?" He nodded toward Natasha and the Commodore 64. "Be smart to have unaffiliated tentacles out there working for you, expendable people."

"Right," Vanek said. "Tentacles you could cut off to preserve the body."

"Looked like barracks up in Big Bear," Ben said. "Had six trailers lined up, like some makeshift dorms."

"Get out of jail," Vanek said. "Halfway house in the mountains with reverend Wales waiting for you, then send you out into the world to do the dirty work."

"Fourteen words," Natasha said. "We must protect the existence of Adamic peoples and a future for our children." She counted each word out on her fingers as she said them. "That's fourteen words."

"Already tried the number," Ben said. "Maybe try spelling out the word?"

Natasha's fingers flew across the keyboard. "Nope."

"Ian Rowan has a record," Ben said to Vanek. "My lieutenant arrested him some years back, animal cruelty. Seems some friend of theirs purged the paperwork. Said he disappeared for a while, though. Off to some kind of Outward Bound thing."

"The church of Richard Wales," Vanek said. "Assemble an Aryan army."

"Maybe try *fourteen words*, the whole thing, typed out?" Ben said.

"And get this," Vanek said. "*Orion* is an acronym. Our race is our nation. These people like their acronyms, don't they?"

"Nope. Wait. *One, Four, W, O, R D, S,*" Natasha said while she typed it out. The screen flashed. "That's it. We're in."

———

Two days ago, as soon as he was released from jail, Bao had driven with Ai up to the coroner's office and pleaded with Natasha to release Linh's body. They wouldn't until the investigation was finished.

"I'm sorry," Natasha said, her voice quiet but firm. "I can't."

Bao understood why, he knew that Linh's body, after the autopsy, would not be hers anymore, but Natasha's refusal infuriated him. The law didn't care that Linh's consciousness needed to separate from her body, that cutting her flesh could splinter her soul, troubling it in the afterlife. They couldn't perform the Nhập Quan, the entering of the coffin; they couldn't carry Linh's body to the crematorium.

After Natasha's refusal, Bao had dropped Ai off at home and driven to Corona del Mar to Lucas Clay's insurance office. Closed, the blinds drawn. He then stopped at a shopping center on Pacific Coast Highway and scoured the white pages in a phone booth, looking for Lucas Clay's home address. There were thirteen Clays listed but no Lucas Clay, no Clays listed at all in Santa Elena. Burning with impotence, he then drove circles around Santa Elena, looking for the boy, hoping to see him coming out of a record store, wishing to find him pedaling a BMX bike down the sidewalk, burning to discover him riding a skateboard down a residential street. Bao didn't know what he'd do if he found Lucas's son—the police still had his revolver—but he was certain that the boy was Linh's killer and he was determined to face him. The compulsion pushed him to drive the streets of Santa Elena well past sunset until he heard Lieutenant Hernandez's voice in his head, *Don't make me arrest you again,* and he realized, then, that he was being cruel to Ai, leaving her abandoned at home once again in a house without Linh.

Today, he and Ai had received people of the community at the house. They had a picture of Linh on the mantel next to the Buddha, her eighteen-year-old face, braces still shining on her teeth. Giang and his family brought rice, Trai lit incense. They kept their front door open and people arrived, offering condolences, bowing to Linh's picture, and then they were gone and the house was theirs, empty and unalterably changed.

Now Ai was shut up in their room—the lights off, curtains drawn, the door closed, the ugly cheerful chirps of the television. Bao had cleaned the house, he'd fixed a broken shutter, he'd washed all the windows, so he went outside in the late-afternoon light and mowed the rain-wet lawn, making neat lines in the grass until all of it was cut, only to start over from the beginning and cut it again.

When he was finished, he stood there on the edge of his patch of grass, the lawnmower engine still running. The house, this little square of wood and windows, suddenly seemed useless. His grocery, Ai, his own limbs and the blood coursing through them, all of it, felt as insubstantial to him as the dry desert air. Then he remembered the protest.

Seconds later, he was on the kitchen phone, dialing Danh's number.

"Yes," his brother said. "Yes. Let's not let Linh die for noth-ing."

_____

Ben paged Hernandez and asked him to meet them outside city hall. Vanek drove back to Huntington Beach to put in a call to Agent Graham at the ATF to give him the lowdown on what they'd discovered. The parking lot around city hall was crammed with protestor cars when Ben and Natasha got there, and he had to park on a little patch of landscaped grass. The rally was not just Asians, but a large contingent of white folks, too. The rain had let up, just a drizzle now. Another storm was on the way, but that didn't seem to tamp down the turnout.

TRIBULATION. There had been at least two dozen messages on the bulletin board using that word. The rest was the ugly bullshit you'd expect, but suddenly, as of yesterday morning, TRIBULATION kept popping up. The period of war and famine and suffering before the second coming of Christ, Natasha had reminded them as they scrolled through the messages. Ben al-most laughed at the vaingloriousness of it, as though these white supremacists could summon the second coming. "Race war," Vanek had said. "They're talking about a race war."

Ben saw Emma at the rally, standing in a cluster of her high school friends, a sign raised over her head: a hand-drawn pic-ture of the Statue of Liberty. GIVE ME YOUR TIRED, YOUR POOR, YOUR HUDDLED MASSES.

He didn't like it, Emma being here, didn't like it at all. Espe-cially now, after what they'd just read on the board. But last night Rachel had decided to let Emma skip school so she could join the protest today.

"She's traumatized," Rachel had said on the phone. "This is her way of working through it. It's disgusting what happened to that woman."

"I don't like it."

"Ben," she said. "She's missing gym and Latin, a dead language. I'd be there if I didn't have to teach. This is something you can't be silent about. You should be proud of her."

He was proud of her, of course, but the rally, fed by Danh Phan's media addiction, was turning it into a circus. The local ACLU had gotten involved, students from the university—some who knew Linh and many who did not—waved signs between classes. The newspapers—*Los Angeles Times, Orange County Register*—were both covering Linh's death, the *Times* running the story front page: VIETNAMESE WOMAN FOUND MURDERED ON ORANGE COUNTY BEACH. *Vietnamese American*, Natasha said, when she read that headline.

Lance was there, too, with his crew of skateboarders. RACISM IS UNCOOL, read Lance's poster in shaky marker. Yeah, he liked the kid. The mayor was there, of course, talking to a news reporter. Some guy with a ponytail and a tie-dyed shirt stood at a music stand with the letters SEHS spray-painted on the back, shouting into a microphone about our responsibility to refugees, especially from an "immoral" war like Vietnam. There was even a makeshift kitchen, a Vietnamese woman serving soup out of a big silver saucepot. Uniforms had formed a perimeter around the protest, a cop every twenty feet or so. One was at the makeshift kitchen, the woman ladling soup into his Styrofoam bowl.

Ben scanned the crowd and found Hernandez walking toward them, up the hill to the parking lot.

"We got the weapon," Ben said to Hernandez once he reached them. He handed the lieutenant the ziplock bag with the cue ball inside, and Hernandez weighed it in his hands.

If the lieutenant was excited about it, he didn't show it. "Where'd you find it?"

"The beach. Not going to be any prints after churning around in the water," Ben said. "But there's a missing cue ball in Rowan's garage."

"Don't say anything about that until we get a warrant," Hernandez said. "We don't want to be hit with inadmissible."

"This concerned citizen will keep his lips zipped."

Then Ben told Hernandez about getting into the bulletin board and the chatter about The Tribulation.

"Sounds like an apocalyptic cult," the lieutenant said, his eyes scanning the crowd.

"There're five levels on this site," Ben said. "Each password-protected. We could only get into Level One."

Then Ben rattled off all the info he got from Vanek about the Idaho joint, told him about the connections to the reverend Wales in Big Bear, told him about the guys in from Utah, Pennsylvania. Floated the theory that the Brennan murder was in retaliation for leasing to Vietnamese and to cut off competition with Orion. That the attack on the Phans was to frighten them into selling their store. Linh because she was dating Jacob Clay's father. But as they talked, all three of them kept an eye on the protests, scanning the crowd. Any crowd made a cop nervous, but a crowd full of bereaved and angry people held a different kind of charge. And there were too many eyes on this now, emotions running too high.

Ben saw Bao, standing to the right of the podium. He was dressed in white pants and robe, his forehead wrapped in a white headband. He looked like a ghost standing there, his face ashen with grief, his head bowed—thinking, it seemed, or just trying to keep it together.

Ben told Hernandez about the Posse Comitatus group, about white genocide—Hernandez shot Ben an incredulous glance when he said that—about trying to start a race war.

"Lieutenant, we need to get Nick all-in on this," Ben said. "If they're using the board for planning, it's happening at a higher level than the one we were on."

The hippie introduced Bao. Shit, if Bao was going to speak, emotions would get incandescent. As soon as Bao was done speaking, he was going to get Emma out of here—whether she liked it or not.

People cheered for Bao, but he just stood there, his head

bowed, his eyes closed. Then Danh Phan, the master of cere-
monies, walked over, held Bao's hand, and helped him up the
stairs. It was hard not to be moved by the gesture, the intimate
expression of brotherly love, and it cast Danh in a new light for
Ben—not just an opportunistic politician, but a devoted sib-
ling, a man hurt by his niece's death. A leader of a grieving
community.

"I'm going down there," Natasha said, and short-stepped it
down the hill until she was standing next to Emma in the
crowd. Emma glanced at her and then briefly hugged her with
her right arm. Ben allowed himself a small smile about that.

Then Bao was standing in front of everyone, unfolding a
piece of paper across the music stand. "She would have graduated university in three months," he said. "She wanted to be a
professor of literature. American and world literature." He
paused and let that soak in. "She loved pizza, especially the
Hawaiian kind with pineapple. Her favorite team was the Lakers. She loved Magic Johnson." The crowd was stunned into
silence. "The first time we went to the San Diego Zoo, when
she was twelve, she cried when she saw the monkeys locked in
a cage. She had a foul mouth, especially when she was angry,
especially if she was angry with me."

A few people laughed, sadly. Natasha was already in tears.
Emma's sign was dangling at her side, her eyes locked on Bao.
For two weeks when she was seven, Linh refused to eat anything but McDonald's chicken nuggets with sweet-and-sour
sauce. A goal she made in an AYSO soccer play-off game. A
hamster she buried in the backyard, a flower planted above it.
The day she lost a tooth down in the brass tubes of the trom-
bone she was playing. Ben glanced around—even the cops were
riveted, it seemed, as Bao conjured his daughter back into
being in front of the crowd. The day she was born— Bao paused
there, seemingly unable to go on or unwilling to share with
these strangers his first moments together with his daughter in
the world. "She's now gone," Bao said, looking up at the crowd

now. "My daughter's murderers sent her on her way. Sent her home into the next life."

Then Bao glanced across the crowd, something to his right catching his attention. Ben followed Bao's eyes and saw someone standing in the shadow of a tree. The man was dressed in dark clothes, a hoodie pulled over his head. There was something in his hands, something square and small.

Bao yelled something in Vietnamese into the microphone and a few people, panicked suddenly, started to push themselves through the crowd.

"Got a bogey," Ben said to Hernandez as he started walking toward the man. Then he noticed the boots, the red laces. Shit. "Get people out of here," Ben said to Hernandez.

The lieutenant bolted toward the crowd, yelling, "Move. Everyone move."

The man was shaking the box in his hand now, an antenna, catching the afternoon light. Ben, dashing past a uniform, barked out an order to the cop to evacuate.

The man came out of the shadows now, dropped the remote control—that's what it was, a remote control. Jesus, could only mean one thing. Ben sprinted across the grass toward the man, who was now running toward a Styrofoam cooler that sat near the makeshift kitchen. Bao was sprinting, too, toward the man, as though he was determined to tackle him. *Shit, don't*, Ben thought. Run away. The man threw open the cooler top. The woman at the kitchen, the one ladling soup, turned to look at him and then started to run. The man pulled a lighter from his pocket now—Jesus, he wasn't going to get to him—stuck the flame down into the cooler—it happened so fast, so goddamned fast—turned and then started to sprint away. And then everything blasted white.

———

The world exploded into silence, Bao's body concussed backward, something hard and hot-wet slapping against his legs, everything erased. When his vision came back to him, Bao found himself crumpled on the cement, a mound of shredded flesh burning against his pant leg. He recognized it for what it was, but he couldn't piece together thoughts, the ability to think blasted out of him. He shook his head and saw a policeman, bent over another cop who lay twisted in a puddle of blood. The cop's calf had been blown from his body—and, Bao saw now, the black boot attached to the hot flesh lodged against his pant leg. The other policeman, the one bent over the body, was yelling to someone over his shoulder, but Bao heard nothing but ringing, like a bell had been gonged in his head.

Then someone's hot palm was on his back. He turned and Ai was there, a streak of blood creasing her forehead. She said something, but her lips only pantomimed sound. She lifted him by the armpits with a strength he didn't know she possessed, and his legs and then his feet reassembled themselves beneath his torso as she dragged him toward a patch of grass. Three others sat in various states of bewilderment, their faces white with shock, as though they, too, hadn't quite come back into the world.

On the grass, his mind started to piece the world together. At least three people bleeding on the ground, policemen bent over their bodies, panicked people running toward the parking lot. They had been bombed. Lucas Clay's son had bombed them, the image of the boy standing on the edge of the protest just moments before coming back to him. He had recognized the boy immediately, saw the remote control in his hand, and he had known, instantly, that he could only be there to do violence to them. Bao had been witness to the My Canh Café bombing in Saigon in 1965, buying cigarettes just down the street when the first of the two bombs exploded. He had run away at first, but then had run back toward the barge when he saw the people moaning in the street. He never thought he'd be witness to such a scene here, in California.

Then Bao saw her, Miss Natasha, crumpled on the cement, a young woman leaning over her, holding her hand and crying. Spurts of blood spilled onto the pavement from Miss Natasha's left thigh. It pumped out of the hole in her flesh, in the rhythm of her heartbeat. The young woman, a girl, really, silently pleaded with her, but Bao could see that Natasha's eyes were rolling back into her head.

Bao tore his belt from the loops and limped through the thrumming silence to Miss Natasha's side. The girl screamed at him when he got there, tears streaking her face. He touched her cheek briefly, trying to calm her, and then lifted Miss Natasha's leg, her blood washing his hands, and looped the belt around her upper thigh. He tightened the belt now, pulling it past the first and second holes, the blood slowing when he reached the third. Miss Natasha's head lolled back in the girl's arms, one eyelid open, that eye staring into the sky as though it saw everything. She was gone, he thought. *She's gone.*

———

Natasha was both in her body and out of it. Floating, yet somehow still down there with her physical self on the street, where Emma held her hand. What she felt toward Emma at that moment was beyond description, beyond the power of arranging twenty-six letters.

It was a strange feeling, this "floating," as though the *you* of yourself couldn't be located in any one place—neither contained within her flesh, fed by her blood, which was now pooling on the pavement, nor separate from it, either. Some kind of invisible tether moored her to her body, but she was above everything, watching the chaos play out like a rehearsed drama, some tragic play on a very small stage in which she used to have a role.

What she knew as herself existed, but it was uncontained by her bone and viscera, by the barrier of dermis and epidermis.

Here, suspended in a gauzy film, she wasn't flesh but wasn't immaterial, either; she was air, she was the oxygen that everyone breathed.

At a glance, she could measure her blood pooling on the cement: nearly three pints, a Class 3 hemorrhage. Her body would need a transfusion. Ambulances hadn't arrived, the hospital was five minutes away without traffic; she could do the math. But it didn't bother her, not at all. Leaving her body was, well, a miraculous feeling, like realizing your flesh was just a temporary container, a harsh preparatory school for your soul. Here, now, her real-self wanted nothing, felt a calm that was like breathing underwater.

Ben was lying on the grassy hill near where the bomb had exploded. He was moving, and she could tell, from here—feel it, really—that his body was intact. If she left him, though, she didn't know how he'd be. A brief flutter of regret passed through her, but then she thought of Emma. He would be fine because of Emma. She knew that everything he loved was contained in his daughter.

Three people had already passed out of their bodies—she hadn't seen their souls rise into the air, but she had felt them, whatever energy trapped in their skin and bone, released into oxygen. She felt them now, too—a policeman; Tuyen Ngo, the woman serving the pho to the protestors; and a young man from the university—electricity in the air, a warm current of passing life. They were gone, though, in a few seconds, gone into a place she could feel was near, but still on some other plane from her own. She looked down at herself, and Bao was there now, clasping a belt around her leg. She felt a slight pinch in her thigh, though when she looked down at this self, she saw nothing but a strange light—no legs, no torso, no arms or hands, nothing corporeal, nothing terrestrial.

The boy who exploded the bomb, his violence had violated him, too. That's what it felt like to her, like his violence was something that had possessed him—used him and blew him up. She felt his fear, his anger—two feelings that seemed suddenly profoundly silly to her. Those two feelings—emotional cousins, really—encapsulated the problem of the body. Once you had something that could be violated, you put barriers around yourself to protect it. She felt a shocking tenderness toward everyone below, including the boy. She understood how that sounded—how that would sound to everyone down there on the street, but she couldn't feel it any other way. Death: She'd lived near it for so long now, but she never truly understood it—except in the scientific, physical sense—and that lack of understanding had been her fear, too. Fear was such a void now it seemed to have never existed, like she could say what it was, etymologize it, but would be incapable of the paralyzing feeling ever again.

The boy was on his knees now. He was wounded, but it was a bloodless wound. He was concussed inside his body, she felt it, the blast wave bludgeoning his internal organs. His violence might be a gift to himself; if there was no hell, if love was his punishment. If she were still down there, with her body, she'd hate the boy—as everyone down there did, and rightly so—but that feeling was gone, too, like something purified by fire and blown into the stratosphere.

Now a white light shone in the corner of this molecular world, something above her and to the right, if directions mattered in this place. It looked like the sun, but both brighter and softer, as though that star was a portal to another space. It shone down on her—it wasn't warm or cold, but pulsated at body temperature. She felt someone pass in front of that sun, like a prisming of light, and then that light—*that someone*—was beside her. The air grew warmer, as though that prism of light had entered into her. And the light sat within her, that's the only way she could describe it. It sat within her, a pulsing thrum like the vibration of first light, and for a moment, a flashing second, she thought of Linh, the childhood Linh; small and new to the world.

Emma. She was Ben's first thought when the world came back to him. Emma. But he couldn't move, his muscles paralyzed, it seemed, his ears ringing with tinnitus. The man who exploded the bomb was just a few yards away, stumbling to get up. If Ben had his revolver and could make his arm work, he could pop him and be done with it—no affidavits, no arrests, no court dates, no juries. Ben could see his face now. It was the kid, Jacob Clay, looking impossibly young, his lips pressed together in pain. Beyond the boy, a car spun out of the parking lot— white, something domestic. It swerved into the street, throwing up smoke, and was gone. Something burned his skin through his pants and he slapped his hands down his legs, expecting to find nubs of flesh and bone. But they were both there, intact, as far as he could tell. Soup, he realized. The burning liquid was soup.

Six uniforms and Carolina streaked by him, running toward the bomber, their guns drawn. Carolina glanced at him, as if to make sure he wasn't a ghost, but she kept the chase.

Emma. Carolina would take care of Jacob Clay. Ben needed Emma. He found his legs and stumbled toward the carnage. The makeshift kitchen was obliterated, shards of plastic table, shredded tarp, hunks of chicken and broth wetting the ground. The soup woman splayed on the wet ground, her blood mixing with the broth. At least three were down near the kitchen, the stink of open flesh, the char of exploded gunpowder. His vision blurred in and out—a cop performing CPR on a student, his protest sign dropped in his own blood. He called Emma's name, but it resonated only inside his head. Emma.

Then he saw her. Oh, God. She was there, holding—no!— Natasha's head. Natasha's body lay twisted on the ground, as though dropped from the sky. Relief and terror seized him. Bao was next to Natasha, wrapping his belt around her thigh, a tourniquet, he realized, and then he saw the blood, Emma's bare left knee pressed into the pool. Oh, Jesus, no.

He stumbled across the grass and grabbed Emma by the shoulders, checked to make sure she was intact.

"Dad!" she said, her voice sounding ten feet deep. "Oh, God, Dad!"

Behind her, he saw Lance running toward his daughter.

"You okay?" Ben yelled at her, in case she was deaf, too.

"Dad, oh, no!" She was cradling Natasha's head, trying to keep it out of her own blood.

Then Lance was there, his hand on Emma's shoulder, pressing a relieved kiss on the part in her hair. The kid seemed suddenly brave, transfigured by his expression of raw emotion.

"Are you okay?" Ben said again. "Answer me."

She nodded, her eyes electrified with terror.

"Get her out of here," he yelled at Lance. "Get inside the station and wait there."

Ben gently slid his hand beneath Emma's, pried hers away, and Lance lifted his daughter to her feet. Natasha's head lolled as he cupped it in the palm of his hand, one of her eyes staring up at the sky. *No, you're not leaving. Not yet.*

He watched Bao cinch the belt around Natasha'a thigh, the blood slowing to a trickle. Then he lifted her up, so small, so light, as though she'd already left the earth. There were no ambulances yet, no emergency lights on El Rancho Road, just cops, leaning over bodies, doing the work of EMTs. Natasha needed blood. That was the only thing that would save her. He carried her across the landscaped hill, stumbled into the parking lot to his truck, secured her in the passenger seat, and gunned it for Hoag Hospital.

Natasha felt herself lifted, both this self and her corporeal self. She looked down and watched Ben hoist her to his chest, her blood slicking his shirt. She felt his fear, a transformer fire of it, and the light that had camped in her vibrated out of her body. She was in his arms yet still floating. *Ben,* she tried to telepath to him, *let go. It's okay.*

He carried her across the courtyard, people running in panic, Carolina and three other officers sprinting toward the boy. She watched this both from the incorporeal space she occupied and from Ben's arms, a discordant stereo perception that thrummed on the edge of pain—shocking to have the echo of that feeling back. *Ben, let me go,* she tried to telepath to him. *Please, let go.* But then she was strapped in his car. She heard him say, "If you die on me, I'm going to kill you."

Something glowed in her ethereal self with that.

He spun the tires out of the parking lot, and she watched her physical self be driven away from her ethereal self, the sun above her dimming, a dying star's last light warming her skin.

———

When Jacob came to, he saw the car Ian had stolen swerving into the street; Ian, he knew, was behind the wheel, blasting down El Rancho Road. The remote hadn't worked, he suddenly remembered. From the car, he had pushed and pushed the button but nothing happened. *Light it,* Ian had said, handing him a Bic and shoving him out the door. *Go light the fucker.*

Jacob managed to get to his feet now, but his legs wouldn't work right. His insides hurt like hell, like his organs had been pummeled with a crowbar. It felt like the bomb had exploded inside his gut. He was deaf, couldn't hear anything. He could see, though, could see what he'd done, the destruction he'd created. He didn't know what he'd expected, but holy shit! The cop was carrying a woman up the hill to the parking lot. Beyond him other cops were coming for him, their guns drawn. He'd blown the fucking world up. Look at it!

He tried to run but his legs felt like rag-doll limbs sewed to his body. They held him up but they felt like fabric legs, felt like he'd have to reach down and lift them. Then somehow he got one foot in front of the other, his whole chest exploding, his lungs like liquid, like he was underwater with his mouth wide open, sucking down ocean water. He wanted someone, but he didn't know who. His mother? His father? But he was running now, somehow, running on fabric legs. He was nearly to the street—he would stumble into traffic, try to get into the orange grove on the other side, but then where? Ian was in the car, speeding away from him, and he knew, as sure as shit he'd blown people to bits, that Ian wasn't coming back for him. Ian would be back on the plane, up to the mountains where the air was clean, the snow cold.

He ran, the street fifteen feet away, but then someone took his rag-doll legs out from under him and dug his cheek into the sidewalk cement. Another someone stabbed a knee into the small of his back. Something pummeled his face once and pummeled it again, *You fucker,* a man's voice said. Crack of knuckles against bone. *You motherfucker.* His arms were jerked behind his back, a palm pressed his skull into the cement, and then cold metal cut into his wrists. "If there's a hell," the motherfucker man said, "you're going to it."

Chapter Nineteen

"**C**ode blue," the trauma nurse yelled as she slammed Natasha's gurney into the swinging doors that led to emergency op. "Femoral hemorrhage, need four point six units, O negative, and get a—" The doors swung closed, the woman he loved swept into another world.

For a moment, he was paralyzed. He couldn't barge into the operating room and hold Natasha's hand, he had no legal authority to go after the white car, which he knew Ian was driving. He was useless and that uselessness amplified his terror. He'd almost lost Emma and was likely to lose Natasha, if he was reading the signs right. If Natasha didn't come out the other side of this, it was over for him, a big empty black hole blasted out of his center.

The world had a strange greenish tint to it, concussion most likely, his ears still rang with tinnitus—though the sonic world was coming back to him—but he wasn't seeing any damn doctor. He found a phone in the waiting room and called Rachel at her high school.

"She left for the day," the front office secretary said. "Some kind of emergency."

Emma must have called her. He was headed out to the parking lot, about to drive back to the station to check on his daughter, when the two other women in his life rushed through the hospital's automatic doors.

"Ben," Rachel said, her hand held out to him. "I'm so sorry."

He thought she'd take his hand, give it a reassuring squeeze, but even though he was slicked with Natasha's blood, she threw her arms around him and held him. Emma did, too, a broken family briefly together again in tragedy.

———

The evening news was on in the waiting room, Tom Brokaw drawling the shock of a series of racially motivated coordinated attacks.

Three dead, shooting with an assault rifle, Trinity AME Church, Salt Lake City.

Thirteen injured, firebombing, Al Sadiq Community Center, West Philadelphia.

Two dead, three injured, shooting, Alcohol, Tobacco, and Firearms field office, Spokane, Washington.

Emma and Rachel were with him in the waiting room, Emma to his left, his ex-wife in the chair to his right. Emma was wearing someone else's shirt; the picture of a guy with a surfboard silhouetted by a setting sun. LAGUNA BEACH in large script above it, as though she'd had her vacation interrupted. Something out of the station lost and found? From Lance?

They'd gotten a nurse to check Emma out, to make sure there wasn't anything they were missing. A miracle. She was fine, a small scratch on her left arm from some kind of projectile, lingering tinnitus, but otherwise she was okay—physically, at least. *It was Natasha that saved me,* Emma had said. *It was Natasha. She was right next to me.* And he kissed his daughter and held her.

Rachel convinced him to get looked at, too. His right eardrum was perforated, eardrops and three months to heal. A shard of a carpenter nail was lodged in his left shoulder, something he hadn't felt until the nurse, using some kind of forceps, pulled it from his skin. She checked his scalp and skull. He heard her suck in air as she pulled something from his hair.

"What is it?" he said.

She simply shook her head and dropped whatever it was in a stainless-steel sink.

The nurse left him then and he sat there alone behind a curtained-off corner of the emergency room, all manner of action swirling around him, urgency he tried to read for signs about Natasha. But they spoke a professional vernacular here, and except for a few phrases it was all Greek to him.

"Here," the nurse said, holding up a polo button-down. "Resident overnight bag."

She left him with a medical waste bag. He took off his shirt, washed himself with a paper towel and isopropyl alcohol, put on the resident's shirt, which was too small and stretched at the shoulders, slid his bloody shirt into the plastic bag, and carried Natasha's blood with him out to the waiting room where Rachel was sitting.

Three dead, seven injured, pipe-bombing, Rancho Santa Elena City Hall, Brokaw was saying. They showed scenes from city hall, twisted metal, scars of blood on the cement, shredded clothes.

"God," she said. "It looks like a war zone."

Natasha's blood mixed with others' on the cement at city hall, her blood in the bag at his feet, on the passenger seat of his truck, now her blood on the fucking television, like it was some macabre form of entertainment.

"It is," he said. "It is now."

"Ben," Rachel said. She looked at him, took his hand in hers and intertwined their fingers. He still knew her face better than anyone else's, though he hadn't studied it in a long time. Still knew how to read the emotions that floated to the surface of her eyes. He knew what she wanted to say right then, and he was pretty sure he wouldn't mind hearing it, but to her credit she kept the words locked away. He nodded, squeezed her hand, and they watched the television a few minutes like that, hostage to the images.

"I don't know what I'm going to do," he finally said, "if she doesn't make it."

"I know."

Then Emma came out of the bathroom where she'd gone to wash her face clean of tears, walked across the floor, glancing at her parents holding hands. She sat back down next to him, lassoed her arms around his waist, and rested her head against his shoulder.

"She's going to be okay, Dad," she said. "I know it."

He touched his palm to her cheek. Rachel got up and asked the nurse at the front desk to change the channel. The woman clicked the remote from the desk. *The Wonder Years. Jesus,* he thought. *Who the fuck had a childhood like that? Like drinking a bottomless milkshake.*

Nearly three hours later, the doctor emerged from the other-world of the operating room.

"She's stable," he said.

God, it felt like light spilled into his body. Rachel placed her hand on the small of his back, and then suddenly he was exhausted, his legs giving out. Rachel let out a little *Oh,* when he fell to the waiting room chair, and then all three of them were huddled around him. A nurse brought him water and he sat there breathing for a minute until his body reassembled itself.

"Whoever cinched her leg with that belt," Dr. Akoma said after they got him a cup of water, "saved her life."

Bao, Ben thought. Whatever future Ben had with Natasha, he owed it to Bao.

"We had some clotting problems," Dr. Akoma said. He ex-

plained that the cut was very jagged. Fusing the artery was difficult. "Not sure about that leg." He paused. "We'll keep an eye
on it."

She was alive. That's all that mattered. She was here, with
him still.

"She flatlined for at least eight minutes," the doctor said
now, sitting next to him. "We almost declared. But then she
was back."

He knew it, knew she'd been dead by the look in her one
opened eye. And he knew what the doctor was going to say
next.

"There may be some brain damage. We'll have to wait and
see."

"I need to see her."

"She's in recovery right now," he said. "When we get her in
ICU you can stick your head in—briefly."

Rachel and Emma went home just after midnight. They invited him to come back to the condo with them, have some
leftover lasagna, but he was staying here. He wandered down
to the cafeteria, tried to eat a chicken-fried steak, but it was
soggy with grease and it tasted like flesh. He sipped an orange
juice, worked through a hunk of string cheese, and then returned to the waiting room, thinking about Natasha losing a
leg, about her being brain-damaged. What would that mean for
them? The leg, no problem. But her mind? He loved everything
about her—her legs, her hips, her breasts, sure, her small
hands, her green eyes, and her slightly crooked smile. But it
was the way she saw the world clearly, the way she discerned
the right thing to do when others didn't even know something
was wrong. Without her mind, who would she be? Who would
he be in love with?

"Detective," someone said.

Ben turned and Hernandez was there, coffee in hand, looking like he'd just got off the battlefield—flecks of blood on his
lapel and the wrist of his shirt, another bull's-eye of blood on

his left knee. Hernandez sat down next to him and handed Ben the coffee. He smelled like gunpowder and sweat, a hint of soup and torn-open flesh, Old Spice to cover it all up.

"I hear she made it," he said.

"How'd you know?"

"Secret chief-of-police phone line. Heard about the other possibilities, too."

Ben nodded. "She's here. For now, I'll take that."

Hernandez dropped his right palm on Ben's knee, a fatherly gesture that caused a sudden ache for Ben's own father. He wanted his dad, like he was a frightened child—which, he'd come to think, we all were, always, forever, at least some part of us, frightened kids stumbling through life.

"I'm guessing you heard the other news?" Hernandez said.

"Yeah," Ben said. "Who'd we lose here?"

Ben was shocked by the national scale of the attacks, but right now he could only deal local. Even this morning, when they'd finally gotten into the board, Ben didn't have the foresight to imagine what had happened this afternoon. They were in a new world now, and he wouldn't underestimate them again.

"David Barnes. First year out of the academy." Hernandez paused. "Got a three-month-old. Engaged to marry his girlfriend in June."

Ben pressed the heels of his hands to his eyes and Hernandez told him the rest. Two others killed, the woman serving the soup, a college kid. Eleven in the hospital, two in critical condition. Pipe bomb packed with nails.

"If Mr. Phan hadn't seen the kid," Hernandez said, "if he hadn't told people to run, it could have been much worse."

Run, Ben realized. That's what Bao had yelled in Vietnamese from the podium. Ben guessed Hernandez was right. He'd only seen Jacob because Bao saw him first. Who knows how many more people would be dead—Emma among them?—if Bao hadn't understood immediately what was about to happen.

"Mayor was hit, too," Hernandez said. "Shrapnel in—well, his left buttocks."

Ben looked at the lieutenant to make sure he wasn't bullshitting him. Hernandez just raised his eyebrows.

"He'll survive, though. Already had a press conference from his hospital bed. The usual *This kind of thing doesn't happen here, please keep investing.*"

They were silent a few moments. A mom ran a kid in, a cut gashing his lip. A nurse stepped outside to have a cigarette, a couple huddled together on the other side of the waiting room.

"Don't know if the Clay kid's going to make it," Hernandez said. "We hauled him in, started coughing up blood. Looks internal."

"I don't care."

Hernandez looked at him. "His dad's a vet from the war. Carolina remembers Jacob from a couple of years ago. Got called on a domestic. Looked like Mr. Clay had used his wife's face as a punching bag. She wouldn't press charges, though. Carolina figures Jacob was getting it, too."

"How many kids get knocked around by their old man and don't go out and blow people up? Hell, my dad cuffed me a few times. Is the kid here, in this hospital?"

"You think I'm going to tell you that?"

Smart man. If he knew the room, Ben would want to take the elevator up and finish the boy off. Fucking bastard in the same hospital as Natasha. There was something unholy about that.

"Ian Rowan was feeding him poison," Hernandez said. "He's fifteen. You know how vulnerable a fifteen-year-old boy can be. That war," Hernandez said, as an aside. "Vietnam spread a sickness."

"You're not going to find any sympathy in me for that Clay kid. Not going to happen."

"I want the kid in jail so he has to live with what he did," Hernandez said.

"And if you don't have Ian in custody yet," Ben went on, "I might have to blow a hole in his head."

"Take a walk with me," Hernandez said.

They stepped out into the cold early-morning air, into the lit-up parking lot where Hernandez's unmarked was parked in an OFFICIAL VEHICLES ONLY spot. They got inside; the lieutenant turned on the car and fired up the heat, spits of rain spattering the windshield. Then he pulled a manila envelope from the back seat and set it on the dashboard in front of them. Ben opened it: his badge, his gun.

"You're a policeman," Hernandez said. "Not a vigilante. You swore an oath."

Yes, he fucking did. For a moment, he considered not picking up his badge and the revolver. Thought about leaving that oath on the dashboard. Thought it might be worth it to stay civilian and use his dad's old Remington to blow a couple of holes in these white supremacists.

But Ben grabbed his service revolver off the dashboard, slid it beneath his belt, and pulled the polo shirt over it. He pocketed his badge, too, a sworn cop again.

"Ian's on the run," Hernandez said. "Stolen Crown Victoria. White. APB already issued. A plane registered to Richard Wales took off from John Wayne Airport two and a half hours ago. Our esteemed councilman has disappeared, too, it seems."

"Paul Rowan's on the run?" Ben said. They didn't have anything solid on the councilman, just his son. "He's indicting himself by running."

"No one ever said he was smart."

Ben nodded. "They're flying up to Big Bear."

"I imagine they think they're safe up there," Hernandez said. "Something else. The ATF's on this now."

"Dammit." The feds. Alcohol, Tobacco, and Firearms. "We're off it?"

"Off the bombing," Hernandez said. "Got us completely

closed out since it's interstate, seems to be connected to these other attacks around the country. Seems they coordinated on the internets message boards. The Clay kid's going down with them, if he pulls through. If they get Ian, he's most likely just an accomplice—stole the car, drove Jacob Clay to plant the bomb, but didn't light the fuse. The federal agent in charge is Aidan Graham."

Vanek's connection, Ben remembered.

"The murder of Miss Phan is still ours, though," Hernandez said. "I want you bringing Ian in on that, I want him on murder. That's our case. None of this would have happened if we'd gotten this finished earlier. This is ours, you understand?"

"Yeah," Ben said. "I'm with you."

"And Detective Vanek's got his own warrant to serve, on the Brennan murder case," Hernandez said. "I called him. He's on his way down here now."

Ben nodded.

"This is his and yours," Hernandez said. "I wish I could ride with you both, but I've got three new murders to deal with— and a brand-new police widow to attend to."

Right. When the department is attacked, the chief of police couldn't go AWOL, even if it was to hunt a killer.

"Right now," Hernandez said, "ATF's got all their resources on the bombing. They know about the Big Bear compound, but they're waiting on more resources from the El Centro office. I want Ian arrested and brought up on charges for the murder of Miss Phan before the feds get to him. You got me?"

"Got you." Unfinished business.

An unmarked police cruiser pulled up and parked a few spaces down.

The lieutenant's Motorola rang. "Hernandez," the lieutenant said when he picked up. Ben could hear the voice on the other line but couldn't make out the words.

Detective Vanek got out of the cruiser and started toward them.

The lieutenant hung up the mobile. "Ian's brother Michael just showed up at the station," Hernandez said. "Seems he's got a few things to say."

"I'll be right behind you," Ben said. "But I gotta do something first."

When he got out of Hernandez's cruiser, Vanek was standing in front of him.

"How is she?" Vanek said, his face tight with worry.

Ben just shook his head once and said: "Alive."

———

Natasha had not been moved out of recovery yet.

"Got a piece of paper and a pen?" he asked the nurse.

The nurse found one in a drawer in the reception desk. *Remember, we're going to Hawaii next year,* he wrote. *You promised.* He thought of other things to say, things he'd wanted to say for some time now, but he wanted her next to him when he did. *Be right back.*

He folded up the paper and gave it to the nurse.

"Please," he said. "Can you make sure she gets this when she wakes up?"

———

The kid, Michael Rowan, looked like he hadn't slept in a month. Hernandez had made everything as comfortable for him as possible—the interview table turned toward the door instead of the wall, a plastic cup of water, a little air-conditioning. The kid wants to talk, let him know we're all ears.

Michael looked around, swallowed hard. The bruise on his right cheek had faded.

"I saw what he did on TV," Michael said. "A couple of guys from my school were hurt. I have science class with one of them."

"I think they'll be okay," Hernandez said. "The doctors are very good over there."

The kid nodded; he seemed in shock, like he couldn't quite believe anything—what his brother had done, how he came to be sitting in this room.

"What do you know about the bombing?" Ben asked.

"Nothing," the kid said, shaking his head. "Not the bombing, anyway."

"You know about Liberty Net?" Ben said.

"Yeah," the kid said. "I used to go on it, but Ian got me banned. I mean, my brother pretty much cut me off."

"Why?"

"I didn't have balls enough to be in his gang." His throat seemed to seize up and he gulped down half the cup of water. "I was there that night up in Huntington."

"The night they killed Mr. Brennan?"

"Oh, shit," he said, his face going white. "They killed him? I didn't know. I thought we were just going to beat him up, send a message, you know?"

"Sometimes things get out of hand," Hernandez said, putting his hand on the boy's shoulder. "I'm sure the prosecutor and the judge will understand." Hernandez was trying to comfort and terrify him at the same time, trying to get the kid to think they were the only thing keeping him from a lifetime in prison.

"*If* you help us out on this," Ben said.

The kid glanced at him.

"We were hopped up on speed," the kid said. "On the way up, Ian kept saying, *This is your night, bro.*"

"Do you mind if we record this?" Hernandez said, as nice as can be. The kid needed a lawyer, but they hadn't arrested him. He'd come to them. Ben found a tape recorder in the left-side drawer of his desk, set it on the interview table in front of the kid, and pressed RECORD.

"So it was your night," Hernandez said. "What did he mean by that?"

"To get in, to be a part of the posse, not just their busboy, not just their fucking servant."

"Posse Comitatus?"

He nodded. "He joined after he was sent away to Wales's place."

"Richard Wales? Up in Big Bear?"

"I don't know where," Michael said. "I just know that was the guy."

"So you had to spill some blood?"

"I was tweaking, man, so it's all like flashes in my brain, you know?" He paused, like the next part was difficult to tell. "So Clocker trips the lock on the back door, and Fisker and the twins drag the dude out of bed. He's still in his pajamas and all, confused like he's still dreaming.

"They get him down in the kitchen and he starts threatening to call the cops, points his finger at Ian. 'You don't scare me, you punks. You and your dad can't intimidate me.'"

"Your dad?"

"I don't know why he said that," the kid said.

"Did your dad order you guys to beat Brennan up?" Ben asked.

"I don't know. They don't tell me about that stuff. I know, though, my old man was pissed off about the Vietnamese moving in. Would rant about it over dinner, talk about my dead brother, about how he didn't die in the war so that we could become some new Vietnam. I mean, in my house they're chinks. Blacks are niggers, you know? Muds or niggers, depending on who you're talking with, my brother or my old man."

"So Mr. Brennan is in Ian's face, telling him he can't be intimidated by your father."

The kid was nodding, going back into the memory. "And Ian clocks him under the chin, one swing of the homey and the dude's jaw kind of swings on a hinge. But the fucker doesn't go down. He comes at Ian, gets his claws around Ian's neck. But there were six of us, and Fisker and the twins get in on it, the guy stumbling out onto the deck, before he goes down. They're pounding him, you know—with the homey socks, kicking him, too. At one point, Fisker's boot got caught on the guy's pajama button or something and the man grabbed Fisker's leg and wouldn't let go. Clocker stomped on his wrist then and the dude let out this muffled scream and he curled up into a ball."

The shred of red shoelace, Ben thought.

"'He's yours,' Ian says to me, but the guy sounds like he's choking now, like someone got a shot into his neck, and I really didn't want to, you know? Then Ian yells at me to kick him. I do, in the stomach, once, and I hear the air go out of him. I thought that would be enough. But no, Ian says, 'Kick him again.' And I did. 'Harder,' he says. And I did. 'Harder,' he says again."

The kid paused. "The guy looked up at me then. I mean, the look on his face." He stopped again. "His face. I can't explain it. It just, I don't know. But this guy was looking at me, like straight in the eye, and I thought, *He's a white dude, why we beating the shit out of him?*" The kid shook his head and took a sip of the water. "I stopped then. It just felt wrong, man. I told Ian that was enough.

"'You're saying no to *me*, Mikey? Me? He's a traitor. Kick him.'

"'He's had enough.'

"Ian looks around then, all the guys staring back at him, like they were wondering what he was going to do. I mean they were all there—Clocker, Fisker, the twins, all of them standing around. Someone laughed. Not sure who, but I knew I was fucked then.

"'You kick him,' Ian says, 'or I'm gonna beat the fucking shit out of you, too, race traitor.'" The kid ran his fingers through his hair. "You don't know him, man. It wasn't bullshit."

He pulled up his T-shirt to show a scar on the left side of his abdomen.

"Knife?" Ben asked.

"Screwdriver. I think something happened to him after our brother was killed. But I was like three then, so I don't know. Just how it is. Gotta be careful around Ian."

"So you kicked him?" Ben said.

"No, man," Michael said. "I told Ian he could go fuck himself. I didn't care if he beat the shit out of me, too. I wasn't going to thrash a white dude who did nothing to me."

The kid's almost-humanity pissed Ben off. Would he have done it if Brennan had been black or Mexican or Vietnamese? Would he have kicked the life out of him? Ben guessed he would have.

"Ian hit you?" Ben said.

"Just once," the kid said, rubbing the bruise now. "And then he spun around and cracked the dude in the skull with the homey. I ran then, down the beach. Stayed out all night down at Bolsa Chica Beach. Took a bus home the next morning, and that was it. I was out."

They gave the kid a minute, let the air settle with the memory.

"Do you know anything about the Phan murder?" Hernandez asked gently.

The kid was quiet a minute, grinding his jaw. Yeah, he knew something.

"He'll kill me. If he doesn't, one of the others will. I mean, look at what they did today."

"What if we can protect you?" Hernandez said, leaning over the table like he was the kid's best friend. "We've got a dilemma here. I understand you're scared, but I'm going to have to charge you with second-degree murder. I know you didn't want to do it. I know you were frightened. But you *were* there. You did kick the man."

The kid was openly weeping now.

"But Ian can't get you if he's in jail."

"Yes, he can," he said, looking at Hernandez then.

That was no bullshit. Guys behind bars ordered hits all the time.

"As long as they're around. You see what's going on, right? This isn't just about Ian or my dad. This is something bigger than that. You know what they do to race traitors?"

"What if we can get them all?" Hernandez said. "What if I said I can get you immunity? Keep you out of jail? If you tell me everything you know about the Phan murder. The prosecutor is an old friend of mine. I think he'll listen."

The kid's eyes bounced back and forth between Ben and Hernandez. The kid was fucked, and he knew it. What to do? You could see him thinking. Go the way of Abel or trust these cops?

"Will he get the gas chamber?" He sounded hopeful, like that screwdriver was still stabbed in his side and he wanted revenge.

"That's up to the prosecutor and the jury," Hernandez said.

Chapter Twenty

Halfway up the mountain, the snow fell heavy, the third big Aleutian storm to hit the basin in two weeks. Cars were pulled to the side of Highway 18, men down in the white slush strapping chains to their car tires. Ben's Chevy was locked in four-wheel drive and they plowed through the thickening cement, the whole world lost in white. They had two department-issue Remington riot shotguns—one in the back behind the driver's seat, the other in Vanek's hands resting across his lap, as though he was ready to shoot at any moment—three bags of shells, and their Smith & Wessons, locked and loaded with extra cartridges stuffed into their coat pockets. Ben had borrowed one of the department's M24 sniper rifles, too, scoped with AN/PVS-10 sights.

The plan? They'd park Ben's Chevy a half mile down National Forest Road 419, hike up the riverbed that ran alongside Wales's compound, stake out the place, and rendition Ian under cover of night. It wasn't much—the kind of plan Lieutenant Hernandez, in a saner moment, would not have condoned. At least Ben and Vanek were both wearing the new Kevlar vests, a quiet acknowledgment that this was likely to be a shoot-in/ shoot-out type of deal.

"Take Ian Rowan alive," Hernandez had said back at the station after they got the warrant for his arrest, "*if* you can." He'd put a lot of emphasis on that *if,* and Ben had the sense that there wouldn't be a whole lot of questions if they did, indeed, bring in a body. Judge Sullivan, presented with Michael's testimony this morning, couldn't pull off some legal mumbo-jumbo justification not to issue this time. Michael said he had seen Ian making the homey socks in the garage the night of Linh's murder, the cue ball slipped into one of them, the end wrapped in duct tape. He'd seen Ian throw the rake into the back of the truck, too. Michael had also been with the gang when they killed the dog. Ian had poisoned the steak and then tossed it over the wall into the backyard and they waited until the dog came stumbling out front, blood foaming at the mouth. They had coaxed it into the back of the Power Wagon and drove it out to the orange groves, the assholes trying to hold it down in the bed of the truck, the dog biting at Clocker's boots before it finally died. Ian cut the dog's throat, the kid had said, because he knew it'd freak people out.

The road ascended into steep switchbacks, the ridge to the right falling into white, the sky above spinning with windblown flakes. Whatever Vanek was feeling, he expressed it in silence—which Ben respected—and they sat in the cab listening to the highway patrol scanner for road closure alerts. Neither one of them was thinking straight about this, Ben knew that. There was a kind of insanity that came with hatred, and he, they, were feeling it now, a vengeful energy buzzing between them that bound Ben to Vanek—at least for now. If Vanek wanted to help Ben avenge Natasha's near murder, that was fine with Ben. Jesus, Vanek was practically sitting in a puddle of Natasha's blood. Two hours before, they'd tried to dab it up off the passenger seat, the two of them pressing towels to the upholstery. But there'd been a lot of it, and Ben had found a couple of blankets he kept for nights at the beach and laid them over the seat. When Vanek sat down in it, Ben swore the man had said a prayer—the detective's hands folded on his lap, his eyes closed, his lips moving in silence when Ben threw the truck into gear.

As he drove, Ben kept seeing Natasha's empty eye, staring into the deep beyond. She had been dead and then she came back to life, like some sort of miracle, if you believed in such things. But all he could think was *Those bastards killed her, that fucker Ian and his stupid recruit killed the woman I love*. And that mantra ran run-on sentences of rage in his mind all the way up the mountain—switchbacking it up to sixty-seven hundred feet, cutting a left onto 38 toward Fawnskin, drive-bying the airport to confirm that the Comanche was there, tied down in the gathering snow.

But the feds beat them to it. The ATF had roadblocked the forest service road at the turnoff at Highway 38, a circus of feds, local cops, and national and local news media standing around in front of the sawhorses. Apparently the El Centro resources had been ready to spring into action. One of the ATF heavies at the blockade tried to wave them off, but Ben flashed his warrant for arrest.

"This is ours now," the agent said.

"Call Graham," Vanek said, "and tell him Joseph Vanek is here."

The agent stepped away, spoke into his two-way, then came back and pulled a sawhorse aside for them to drive through.

"Friends in high places, huh?" the agent said with some disdain.

Ben had to hand it to the ATF. They came prepared—a half dozen ATV four-wheelers, a few snowmobiles, two four-wheel-drive explosives and fire investigation units, and so many four-by-four Fords it was like being on a dealer's lot. At least two dozen guys in ATF jackets stood around the field office with M16s hanging from their shoulders. If it'd been Ben, he would have gone for a sneak attack, but not the feds; it was a full-fledged paramilitary circus for them.

"Either Graham's planning to go to war," Ben said, "or he thinks he'll make them piss their pants and come out with their hands up."

Ben was parking the Chevy behind what seemed to be a small tank. It looked like the V-100 personnel carrier the LAPD used in the Pacoima raid Vanek had mentioned the day they met in Little Saigon. At least this place justified its use. The compound, looking like some kind of dilapidated concentration camp in the snow, sat fifty yards down the road, a gray curl of smoke rising from a chimney into the whiteness.

"Don't think these are the surrendering type," Vanek said. "And I don't like all the media out there. They should have kept this under wraps."

"This's a goddamned pressure cooker," Ben said.

The supremacists were cornered, but Graham was cornered, too, by this show of government power, by the news media two miles down the road.

"The endgame," Vanek said, "and it's just begun."

In Graham's defense, the attacks all over the US *were* headline news. Part of the federal government mandate was to keep things under control, or to at least look like they had things under control. Regardless, you could feel the tension even before they got out of the truck, and as soon as Graham shook their hands at the makeshift command post, Ben knew the ATFs were playing hot, too.

"You been watching your back?" Graham said to Vanek when they shook hands.

"It's a way of life," Vanek said.

The agent had a military buzz cut and wore aviator glasses.

"You better get the bomb disposal guys to check your mailbox," Graham said. "We don't need to lose another cop." Graham turned to Ben then. "They got one of yours, right?"

"Yeah," Ben said. "New kid out of the police academy."

"And a number of civilians," Vanek said.

"Goddamn. Took out two of ours up in Spokane." Graham shook his head and rapped the heel of his hand against the metal folding table. "Goddamn."

"What is the current situation?" Vanek said, in such a measured tone he suddenly seemed in charge.

The agent barked out a couple of orders to his officers and then gave Ben and Vanek the lowdown. Perimeter thirty yards out, from field office here to the creek wash on the east side of the property. Maybe on another assignment Graham was all professional calm, but on this one he was buzzing with urgency. A cop murdered was like losing a brother, even if you didn't know the uniform. His death could have been yours and that fear, that realization of vulnerability, always manifested in rage. Ben didn't blame him, but seeing the irrational in the eyes of the agent-in-charge embarrassed him; surely it had been the look in his own eyes on the drive up, that murderous human DNA calling out for revenge.

From here, Ben could see three skinheads on the porch of the house, rifles slung over their shoulders. Counted at least fifteen armed men, but it wasn't clear if that was an accurate number. Behind the slatted fence that barricaded the driveway stood two more men, though he couldn't see any firearms. Ben guessed that they were armed, and that the fifteen number was low.

Snipers on the southern and northern ridges of the canyon, Graham continued, but limited visibility with the heavy snow. No choppers, no eye-in-the-sky.

"So you're flying blind," Vanek said, glancing at Ben.

"You got shoot-on-sight orders?" Ben asked.

"No," Graham said, frustration in his voice. "Right now we're exercising a tax evasion warrant on Wales."

"That's it?" Ben said. Jesus.

"You got evidence I don't know about that proves Wales ordered all of these attacks?"

They didn't, but Ben suspected they'd find a computer setup much like the one in his barn if they got inside the compound. Ben suspected, too, that Wales was just one "reverend" in a larger conspiracy. That someone like him had to be pulling the strings in the other cities around the country. He doubted Wales was calling the shots in places like West Philly, and it made sense for Elias Klein's people up in Idaho to hit the Spokane target.

"We were sitting on the warrant while we tried to build conspiracy and domestic terrorism," Graham said. "But the attacks changed the calculus. Who you exercising murder on?"

"Ian Rowan," Vanek said.

"Both of us," Ben said. "On two different murders."

"Good," Graham said. "That gives us some leverage, should we need to go all-in here."

With murder warrants comes justification for force. With tax evasion? Public sympathy a little less robust for shooting off rounds. Probably be some sympathy for IRS dodgers.

"I was up here last week," Ben said. "There were a bunch of little kids."

"Snipers got visuals on six, at least."

Graham handed him a pair of binoculars. "Southwest bedroom."

Ben zoomed in, the snow coming harder now, the flakes huge in the scopes. Nothing, just a square of clean glass, and then a woman stepped into his vision, a baby cradled in her arms. She put her face up to the window, as though to peer through the snow to follow the siege surrounding her.

"Mother and infant," Ben said.

"Seven kids then. Trying to get a phone line in," Graham said, "see about negotiations."

They were going to have to wait them out or get those kids out before the shooting started.

"So we sit on our hands for now," Graham said, "and hit 'em with a few things tonight."

Man, they lit up the place like it was a Kennedy Space Center night launch—the spots reflecting off the freshly fallen snow, the falling flakes strobing through the air. But worse, they brought in huge speakers and hit the supremacists—and everyone else—with the recorded death screeches of rabbits being slaughtered.

"Jesus," Ben said to Vanek. "Who's the sicko who came up with this idea?"

They were in the truck, running the engine for the heat, the windows rolled up to tamp down the sound, at least to take the edge off of it.

"Sick tactics for a sick world," Vanek said.

They were quiet for a while, the horrible sound railing outside, the snow piling halfway up the windshield now.

"How're you holding up?" Vanek said.

So they were both sitting here, getting buried by snow, thinking about Natasha.

"I'm all right," Ben said, which was a lie.

"You love her," Vanek said. "I can tell."

"I do."

He was quiet a moment. "Good," he said finally. "That's good."

By sunrise, the snow was still falling, after a brief respite overnight, and according to the weather report on the radio, it wasn't going to let up for another thirty-six hours. At least two feet had fallen in the last twenty-four, and the ATF agents stood around in shin-high white stuff, their toes, if Ben's were any indication, wet and numb and pretty damn sick of plowing lines in the cold. Someone had apparently checked the white pages overnight, because when Ben and Vanek plowed over to the command post at 7:30, Graham was on a portable handheld calling into the house.

"Wales won't talk to any federal agent," Graham said, frustration already bubbling over. "Says we represent a hostile illegitimate government. Says he'll only talk to local cops."

So Ben called in five minutes later and identified himself.

"Yes, Officer Wade. We know who you are." His voice was quiet, calm. "Let us speak face-to-face, like men. Unarmed, of course."

"We'll have snipers on you."

"I understand."

Vanek protested the idea—said he didn't like Ben out there in the open like that, exposed—but Graham ran with it. Ben took off his dirty harry and set his rig on the folding table.

"Here," Vanek said, lifting up his pant leg and unstrapping an ankle holster with a nice little Beretta double-action fit snug inside. "For insurance."

Ben fitted it around his ankle and trudged out across the virgin snow, not knowing what the hell he was going to say to this "reverend." Knowing, only, that he needed to get those kids out of there. Knowing, too, he needed to keep his own shit under control, if he was going to do it.

"You came armed, Detective."

The reverend stood on the other side of the front gate, dressed only in a three-piece suit—no winter coat, no boots. Snowflakes stuck to his close-cropped hair and he smiled at Ben, as though he was enjoying the situation.

"I did," he said. Good guess or one of the supremacists had glasses on them. Ben nodded at the two men flanking him, each gripping a Remington Gamemaster hunting rifle. "You have your insurance, I have mine."

"Not a good start to us establishing trust."

Ben thought he caught a whiff of gasoline.

"I trust you won't shoot me," Ben said, "if I don't try to shoot you."

The reverend smiled. Something about the man reminded Ben of his grandfather—the dapper dress, the tie bar and vest, the clippered cut of his hair, the tufts of wiry gray on his earlobes. He was like something cut out of the 1940s, minus the fedora—a lie of American male wholesomeness.

"Fair enough," he said. "You see how the federal government overreacts. I'm wanted only because I refuse to pay taxes to that swamp in DC. I gave them my son, that was tax enough."

"Your son?"

"The Battle of Huế."

"I'm sure that was difficult."

"Good," he said, smiling. "You're smart, Detective. The first two steps in a hostage negotiation. Listen and establish empathy. It would be easier, however, for me to have a rapport with you if you weren't wearing that ankle pistol."

"Is this a hostage negotiation?"

"All are here of their own accord."

Ben glanced up at the southwest window. It was empty, just the reflected dishwasher light of the snowstorm staring back at him. Again, that hint of gasoline.

"So this is about your son?" Ben said. "Killing Brennan, killing a young woman, murdering policemen . . ."

"I'm wanted for tax evasion, Detective." His face was serious, as though he truly believed he hadn't ordered any murders, hadn't orchestrated executions.

". . . blowing up innocent people?"

"Original sin, Mr. Wade. None of us is innocent."

"How old was your son?"

The reverend smiled. "You used to work LAPD gangs, but you left. You moved down south."

"You've done your research."

"I have a special interest in Rancho Santa Elena."

"What kind of interest?"

"It's a pretty place, organized, safe," the reverend said. "You were sick of the brutality in North Hollywood. You were tired of the lack of regard for life."

Who wouldn't be?

"We don't want Santa Elena to become that, do we?"

Ben just looked at the man, that *we* getting under his skin.

"Everywhere they live," he said, "there's violence, there's drugs, there's raping, looting."

They. Ben remembered his *those people* with Hernandez in the bar the other day and felt a wave of shame that his thinking could ever be aligned with a man such as this one.

Wales rested his bare hand on a slat of the gate, his fingers pressing into the snow. A ring circled the fat of his ring finger, a blue shield set against a red background. Ben couldn't see the details, but he guessed it would be the cross and crown, the wolfsangel, the same symbol on the flag at the meth house. "Even the Asians. Some people think they're fine, but you see Little Saigon. The drugs, the gangs. You don't want to raise your little girl in a place like that."

"I'd appreciate it if you'd keep my daughter out of this conversation."

The reverend glanced at him and smiled.

"We're protecting civilization," he said. "Protecting it for you, for me, for our children, protecting what our forefathers built."

"Right," Ben said. "We must protect the existence of Adamic peoples and a future for our children."

The reverend glanced at him, something like fear flashing across his eyes, as though he couldn't believe Ben knew the secret phrase.

"The fourteen words," Ben said, nodding. "We know about the bulletin board, too. If you wanted to keep it secret, your enforcers shouldn't have shoved it down a murder victim's throat."

"Detective Wade," he said, seeming to get his composure back. "We're still in the rapport-building stage."

"So you use Paul Rowan's real estate company to redline minorities out and when that doesn't work, intimidation, and if that doesn't do it, violence."

"You'd be nervous, yes, if Emma was in school with a bunch of blacks? You'd worry the schools were falling apart? You'd worry they might find her attractive. You'd worry that *she* might find them attractive."

"Leave my daughter out of this." Ben's voice was tight now.

"You'd worry your property values would fall." He gave Ben a knowing look. "I know the fears of white people. Even the liberal ones, though they're less honest than most and hide what they feel inside, brainwashed by public schools and affirmative action into feeling guilty for their accomplishments."

Ben had had enough of this.

"I'm worried about the children you have here," Ben said.

"And so am I."

"The agent-in-charge," Ben said, "is feeling a lot of pressure to do something here. I'd wait you out, cut off your food, starve you out, but not this guy."

"The Jews in Washington want blood."

Jesus, it took everything he had not to punch this man in the mouth.

"I would like to ask you to let the children go."

"So we're into the influence stage?"

"The children have nothing to do with this."

"It's all about the children, the future of the race." The reverend laughed quietly. "As you so eloquently pointed out to me a few moments ago. I thought you were smart, Detective. I have no leverage, no protection if I offer you the children."

"You'll use them as human shields?"

"Officer," the reverend said. "If anything happens to these children it will be because of you and those ZOG agents."

"If you give up Ian Rowan," Ben said, a rising panic tightening in him, "that might take the pressure off a bit. Might convince them to pull back." He was just making shit up, had no idea if Graham would listen to him, even if he did bring Ian in. "This doesn't have to be inevitable."

"You are right," the reverend said. "It does not have to be. You've surrounded the house, you're trespassing on the property."

The property. "This isn't your place, right?" Ben said. "Whose is it? Who owns the LLC?"

The reverend smiled. "I'm just one of many preaching the gospel, Detective." He removed his arm from the fence post, brushed snow from his sleeve. "What happens here today is up to you. The road that led you here will also lead you away."

"You know it isn't going to work that way."

Wales smiled. "The tree of liberty, Detective, must be refreshed from time to time."

———

"With the blood of patriots and tyrants," Vanek said. "Thomas Jefferson."

"Look, this guy's a narcissist," Ben said. "He's a fucking cult leader. He's got no intention of negotiating."

It's all about the children, Ben remembered the reverend saying. That kind of man, one full of such self-reverence, wasn't going to give himself up; wasn't going to give anyone up.

Graham was pacing under the little tent, the full weight of his authority bearing down on him. He wanted to go all-in—a tank to bulldoze the front gate, concussion grenades, full-out assault with armed agents.

"Pull back," Vanek said. "Give them some space to breathe."

"If he's not coming now," Graham said, "he's not coming later. We can't just pack everything up and roll down the mountain."

"You can," Vanek said, that calm sound to his voice again. "Temporarily."

"He's killed three law enforcement officers, Detective."

"And nearly killed my girlfriend," Ben said. "Almost got my daughter, too. I want him as much as anyone. Maybe more."

Graham stood on the edge of the tent, facing the compound.

The snow was now coming in blowing squalls, and it was starting to feel like the world was being erased.

"All right, we'll smoke them out," Graham said quietly. "But I'll be damned if I'm pulling this operation."

And five minutes later the first canister of tear gas went arcing through the sky.

―――――

Five canisters made it over the fence, a sixth died just outside the gate, all of them sending up thick yellow smoke, billows of toxic piss-colored chloroacetophenone that would leave the supremacists gasping for air. Graham seemed to think they would come running out of the compound into the waiting arms of the ATF, but it was eerily silent. No cries, no staggering skinheads, just yellow clouds soiling the pure white air.

Then another billow of smoke whorled up from behind the house. This smoke was darker, black with burned petroleum. The gas.

"They're burning the place," Ben said to Vanek.

"Holy Christ," Vanek said.

Someone screamed, but still there was no movement, just the rush of smoke and then flames licking up the side of the house. Ben could smell it now, that fetid ammonia stink of burning methamphetamine fueling the fire. It spread so fast all they could do was stare in shock until the window in the southwest corner of the house shattered and there they were, the mother and the baby. The flames were eating up the side of the house now, brown smoke spilling out from the window, too. She held one hand to her mouth, the other gripped the baby to her chest.

"The V-100," Vanek yelled to Graham.

Graham bolted across the snowy ground, hollered something at the ATF standing near one of the tank's huge wheels. The agent climbed up into the cab of the armored vehicle, fired it up, and Graham, Vanek, and Ben, their weapons drawn, followed behind the personnel carrier as it battered down the front gate. The ATF driving the tank parked it just past the window, turning it sideways to give them cover from any barrage of bullets.

The woman was leaning out over the edge of the windowsill now, some thirty feet up in the house. The tear gas and smoke were spinning circles around them and Graham, swept up in a windblown swirl of both, went down to his knees, choking and gasping for air. The fire was raging now, fueled by the gas and meth, and Ben felt his eyelashes melt. Vanek was gasping, too, and Ben's throat started to seize up. He turned his face for a pocket of clean air, sucked it up, and pretended he was going deep under a crashing wave. He held his hands in the air, gestured for her to throw the child.

The woman was dangling the boy out the window, trying to close the gap between the baby and Ben's outstretched arms. Then a billow of smoke engulfed her, and she dropped the boy. He tumbled away from Ben, his little arms spinning in the smoky air. Ben leapt to catch him, snatched at the air and caught a leg, but the boy slipped through his grasp and slammed to the ground. Thank God for the wet grass, which must have softened the fall, because the boy was alive and wailing, his face streaked with mucusy tears. Wrapping the child in his arms, Ben looked up and saw flames shooting out the window, the wooden frame already melting into licks of fire.

Above the rush of the flames, Ben heard pops of gunfire. They made a run for it then, all of them stumbling out ahead of the tank until an agent yanked Ben behind an ATF Ford and they laid the screaming child across the back seat. Nothing seemed to be broken, at first glance, but part of the child's onesie had melted into the boy's shoulder and Ben scooped snow from the ground and pressed the coldness against the child's skin. "We need first aid," Ben said to the agent, who took off running toward the tent.

Ben glanced up through the windows of the truck. It was all

chaos—the compound engulfed in flames, the pop pop pop of gunshots, agents ducking for cover. But the shots didn't seem to be flying at them—no puffs of shot-up snow, no ricocheting off cars. The shooting was happening inside the house, Ben guessed. One big suicide for the true believers in the Aryan race.

"We gotta get this kid down the hill to the hospital," Ben said to Graham, who was pressing fists of snow to his burning eyes.

Graham called out to two agents, both of whom jumped in a four-by-four and spun it through the snow over to them. Ben dropped the kid in the arms of the agent in the passenger seat and they sped off down the forest service road toward town.

Vanek was standing next to Ben now, spitting gobs of mucus to the snow. He coughed once, stood up straight, and took in the inferno with Ben. Ben noticed the hair on the right side of Vanek's head had been singed to little rust-colored curls.

"God," Vanek said, his voice shaking a bit. "We've made martyrs out of them."

_____

But not everyone, it seemed, was ready to self-immolate. Three skinheads stumbled out from behind the house, one of them trailing a shirt full of flames. Two agents tackled the flame-thrower, and a throng of ATFs shoved the other two into the snow and cuffed them.

Then a snowmobile zoomed up the ridge twenty-five yards to the north of the house. Councilman Rowan was driving the machine, and Ian, slumped against his father's back, the bare puckered skin of third-degree burns shining red through his charred shirt. He bounced on the seat as though barely clinging to consciousness. Rowan powered the machine up the ridge, slipping between trees, clouds of freshly fallen snow taking flight again in his wake.

A four-wheel ATV was parked twenty feet away from where Ben stood.

"Radio down to Big Bear," Ben said to Vanek, "and tell them we got runners."

Ben stumbled to the ATV, fired it up, spun a U-turn, and blasted up the plowed trail left by the snowmobile. It was open forest—fallen trunks, jags of rock—for the first quarter mile, and then the path hit a snowmobile run. He could see them up ahead now, a billow of snow blowing into the trees. They had the advantage, the snowmobile easily slipping through the three feet of snow, while the ATV spun tires, fishtailed on turns. He had to slow to keep from flipping the machine, but he balanced it and kept chase, the billow of smoke growing smaller in the distance as they raced downhill.

Three minutes later, they hit Route 38. He had the advantage now. The road had been recently plowed and the ATV's tires raced easily over the icy cement. The shoulder of the road was now a five-foot mountain of plowed snow, and Rowan had to ride the highway, the snowmobile's skids throwing up sparks on the exposed pavement. A quarter mile up, Ben saw the flashing lights of the Big Bear police. Rowan saw them, too, and he took one of the mountains of snow, the machine lifting into the air briefly before dropping down on the other side. Ben couldn't see them now, the berm of snow cutting off his vision, but he could see the cloud rising in their wake. Rowan hadn't crashed it; he was still running.

Ben knew they were headed to the airport. He could see the small tower in the half-mile distance. He gunned the ATV, hoping to beat them there. Three Big Bear patrols zoomed down on his left and he spun a finger in the air and pointed south. They spun U-turns and soon were riding up his ass, sirens wailing.

But Rowan beat them to the tarmac. When Ben swung the ATV into the parking lot, the councilman was already dragging his son to the waiting Comanche, the door swung open, the pilot firing up the propeller. Ben got around the fence and gunned it past the tie-downs. Rowan seemed to be having a difficult time getting his injured son into the cabin and when

Ben got within fifty yards, he snatched his .38 out of his shoulder rig and fired off a round, hitting the councilman in the shoulder. The councilman rolled off the wing and slammed onto the tarmac. The pilot, witness to the shot, started rolling the plane down the taxiway before he could get the door closed, Ian slumped in the back seat, the small plane throwing up a blizzard of snow.

Ben was all-out now, the engine of the four-wheeler redlined. The plane made a left onto the runway, the pilot finally getting the door closed, and Ben was able to get out ahead of it, running the taxiway that paralleled the airstrip. How the fuck the plane was going to get enough speed in the thick snow to take off, Ben didn't know. But the pilot was giving it a shot and as he powered the engine up, Ben slammed the brakes on the ATV, stood up on the runners, and popped three shots off at the wheels as the Comanche roared past.

He thought he'd missed. Thought he was going to watch them rise into the white sky and fly away to who the hell knew where. Arizona? Mexico? But then, three-quarters of the way down, the plane swerved to the left, spinning circles across the runway. The ice and snow must have helped it along, because it didn't come to a stop, just kept whirlwinding snow until it spun right out onto the ice of the lake.

Ben kicked the ATV into gear again and gunned it as the Comanche finally came to rest on the open lake ice, the right wing of the plane folded into itself, the propeller warped into useless half circles. He slammed on the brakes at the edge, jumped off the machine, his .38 drawn. They were thirty yards away—Ben could see the pilot and Ian, stunned, it seemed, by the whirling dervish of a ride. Thirty yards of thin ice, and Ben stepped out onto it, his boots slipping beneath him. The pilot cracked the door, scrambled down the wing, and just as Ben was about to fire off a round, the ice broke beneath the plane and the whole mess fell into the water below.

Chapter Twenty-one

It would take them until the next morning to get divers up to the lake. Meanwhile the compound burned throughout the day. There was no way to get fire trucks up through the snow—even the four-wheel-drive quints couldn't plow up the forest service road—so the ATFs stood around and watched the place send up plumes of ash that landed on their caps and on the shoulders of their jackets. By evening a gray pall had coated the new snow—incinerated wood and insulation, electrical wires and human bodies—and the compound was a smoldering shell with spots of dying flame.

"Anybody else get out?" Ben said to Vanek after he ATV'd it back up to the compound.

"No," Vanek said, shaking his head.

When Ben had gotten back to Paul Rowan, the Big Bear police had already cuffed him and called in an ambulance. They'd left him lying in the snow, next to a splatter of his own blood. The bullet had torn a chunk out of his shoulder, but he'd live. Ben had directed the Big Bear Police Department to secure the crash site until the feds showed up and shut the whole airport down, then he headed back up, an irrational hope that some-one had got the other kids out.

"It went up too fast."

Jesus, Ben thought, *the apocalypse of Reverend Richard Potter Wales.* And there was nothing else to say, or do, really, except to stand and gawk at the spectacle of extremism taken to the ex-treme. Those kids would have been raised to hate, to stew in their own bile. Hating was no way to live. Yet children were children and they deserved a chance at life.

By early evening the storm had broken and soon news heli-copters were circling, shooting images of the destroyed com-pound into millions of homes in the basin—and into living rooms in the rest of the nation. Graham was sitting at the fold-ing table underneath the tent, writing something on a legal pad. His hand was pressed to his forehead, as though he knew he was screwed—he had pushed too fast, too hard—but was determined to spin his news conference in such a way as to save his ass. Ben didn't envy him and he wasn't going to defend him, either, but he felt a little sorry for the man. He'd fucked up, pushed the issue when he should have waited it out, and now dozens of people were dead, including children, because of his lack of patience. But he'd also put his life on the line when they were trying to save the kids. In Ben's book, that cut him a bit of a break.

Ben and Vanek then rode together down the hill, back into Big Bear City, and got a room at Honey Bear Lodge on the de-partment's dime. Ben called down to Hoag from the phone in the lobby while Vanek checked them in.

"Any change?" Vanek asked when Ben got back to the room.

"No." Natasha was still in a coma.

There wasn't much to do until morning, so they cleaned up, Ben dabbing Vaseline on the right side of his face where the skin was singed red, took their legal pads to the Grizzly Café, and quietly wrote out the narrative of the day's events, occasionally cross-checking their facts, while the day's spectacle played out on the television bolted to the wall in the corner of the café.

The business of things helped, but it had been a whole lotta death in the last few days and the pall of it hovered in the diner's air between them. Word was out about the kids, and talking heads on the news were already questioning the police and their tactics. They were only serving a tax evasion warrant. Ben knew that was coming. This was a case of federal overreach, according to one suit in the box, an implementation of flawed tactics. Vanek and Ben would have to hold their own presser to set the narrative straight about the warrants—though that would be a bit of a dance since they didn't want any ownership over the conflagration. Eyewitness News even flashed photos of Wales in his business suit, playing the role of Leave-It-to-Beaver businessman. Shot a few pics of the skinheads across the screen, too, boyish faces, clean-cut and smiling. No tats in those shots, no boots with laces the color of spilled blood. In the news's defense, they mentioned the Wales group's ties to other national groups, ones implicated in the series of attacks in other parts of the country. But there was a tone of shock to the broadcast, as though the reporters and the anchors couldn't quite wrap their heads around the idea that these nice-looking white people could do such terrible things.

The feds would most likely finish their investigation, maybe find concrete evidence to link Wales to the bombing at the protest in Santa Elena. Perhaps even piece together, with unequivocal evidence, what law enforcement already knew: that there was an interstate conspiracy of hate to terrorize and kill minorities. That would be tough, though; whoever was behind this hid behind the anonymity of that limited liability company, a formalized business of terror. And if Wales was running the bulletin boards, which Ben was sure he was, the computers with that evidence went up in the fire. Regardless, there wouldn't be any trial for Wales, and evidence meant shit without the confirmation of a trial conviction; that was part of a trial's social function, to publicly acknowledge a truth that would allow acceptance of the facts and the just necessity for punishment. The death of the suspects let a doubt loose in the world for those who chose to believe in the endless innocence of white men. Martyrs for sure, Ben thought. You could see the exposition to the story being laid out already. In a few days, the news would be flashing pictures of the children killed— murdered by their caretaker and not the police, but that wouldn't matter; the tragic death of white children would sear the public and the living would be blamed.

Suddenly, as though the producers had quickly grown bored with the spectacle, the newscast shifted to a yellow-taped crime scene in South Central. Vanek, who hadn't been watching the broadcast, his nose focused on his own narrative, looked up now and watched the screen. The victim's Air Jordans sticking out from under the white sheet, a pool of blood in the gutter. The crack cocaine wars, the daily carnage, the ritual evening spectacle shot into homes, and then a face, a black one—his kinked hair, the razor-notched eyebrows, the menace of his mugshot eyes staring directly into the café.

Vanek lifted his chin at the screen. "Took just five minutes," he said, shaking his head, "and the old bogeyman is back."

Yeah, Ben got it, in a place like Santa Elena, those pictures terrified people and their fear justified their beliefs. The man on the screen, though, was a killer, if the evidence was right, and got whatever he deserved—and *he* would get his trial. But Ben understood what Vanek was saying and he wasn't about to argue with the man on the very day a group of white folks self-immolated so they wouldn't have to live in the same town as a few minorities.

The county sheriff's divers got in at 7:00 the next morning, and Vanek and Ben stood on the edge of the lake and watched the men in wet suits and scuba gear go down under the ice. It didn't take them long—ten, fifteen minutes—to haul up the bodies of the pilot and Ian, each bloated and bleached with cold and stiff with rigor mortis. Ian was the last to be slung into the boat, his body frozen blue, his right arm, the one with the 1488 tattoo, rigored into a sort of wave, his curled fingers sticking up above the bow of the boat as the divers turned to bring it to shore.

—————

When he came to, Jacob was in a white room—white walls, white floors, a white ceiling punctuated with a white light. Something beeped to his left, a machine lit up with little green lights and digital numbers. A hospital, he realized. He was in a hospital. Something touched his left wrist and startled him. When he turned he found his father there, sitting on the edge of a chair.

"Stay calm," his father said. His voice was quiet, a whisper almost. "You have blast lung. There's nothing you can do, Jacob. Just stay calm."

Jacob felt it now, his insides wet feeling, swollen. When he breathed, it was like suffocating, like his mouth was open underwater.

"Am I going to die?" he said. It took all his energy to get the words out and he felt like he was breathing underwater again.

His father was silent a moment, staring into Jacob's eyes, as though trying to make an important decision.

"You might, son." His father's face was inches from his, water in his eyes. "You blew yourself up." He was quiet again, his eyes searching Jacob's. "You blew yourself up and three other . . ."

Jacob knew what he was going to say, could hear the other things he didn't say, too. Those three people he destroyed—and the woman his father loved. What Jacob remembered of that night was the aftermath—the woman's collapsed skull, her blood shining in the firelight; he'd done it, it was him, but he hadn't *seen* himself doing it. He'd closed his eyes, something black exploding in his mind, and swung, and swung. He'd helped Ian take her body out into the water on an old surfboard they found in one of the shacks, pushed her off beyond the waves, hoping her body would stay at sea. He remembered, now, what his father had said about what it felt like to kill people. *Like nothing*, he had said at the restaurant what felt like years ago. *It's what you feel afterward, when it's quiet again, when you know.* Jacob thought he understood that feeling now and he wanted to tell his dad, but the words stayed locked inside.

"I know," his father said, as though reading his mind. "You were angry. You hated me. I was the one you hated."

He did, but he had hated her, too, hated them, hated everyone—hated himself. Something felt like it was leaking inside him, and his forehead started to sweat.

"I'm sorry I wasn't a good father to you. The war got stuck inside me and I took it out on you and your mother. You deserved better than me."

Jacob couldn't breathe again, water sloshing his lungs. God, it hurt now, like there were little cuts up and down the inside of his torso. His father stroked his forehead and it helped. Jacob was still breathing in water, but his father's warm palm helped.

"You know what Buddhists believe about death?" his father said. "They believe in reincarnation, that people who die come back in another body to live another life. They believe the cycle of life and death and life again is a cycle of pain, that to be in a body is painful." His father's voice sounded a way he'd never heard before—sad but hopeful, too. "They believe every life should be used to be a better person, to strive for nirvana—which is a sort of Heaven. Not a place, but something else—an understanding of everything. If you've reached nirvana in life, you see a bright light when you die and you become one with everything."

He rubbed Jacob's hand now, and Jacob felt the warmth of it.

The water was deep in his mind, he felt it, the pressure, the weight of it. It was a falling, a slow sinking into sludge. Shoes squeaked the floor, then the door opened to the room.

"Oh, Jacob," his mother said, her voice quaking. "Everything's going to be all right." Then she was there on the opposite side of the bed, her hand stroking his shaved head. Her hand weighted him down, pushed him further into the sludge.

"I hope the universe is a Buddhist one," his dad whispered. "I hope that for you."

———

Monday morning, Ben, Lieutenant Hernandez, and Carolina led three teams of officers on raids of the homes where the rest of Ian's gang lived. When Vanek and Ben were up in Big Bear, Hernandez had compiled the evidence on the young men, secured arrest warrants, and now they were going in. Martin Fisker, nineteen. Raymond Benedict, aka Clocker, and the twins, Brett and Richard Powell—all twenty. Michael had laid it all out for Hernandez in an evening of interviews, trying to secure his immunity. Names, addresses, the overheard conversation between Ian and Jacob, the plan to ambush Linh in the university parking lot, a tutorial on making homey socks.

It had been an all-nighter—wrapping things up in Big Bear, the drive back to town, securing the warrants from Judge Sullivan, and the planning of the raids. A team of five for each arrest. Predawn. The lieutenant had even called the media, told the detectives reporters would be there waiting at the station when they hauled the men in. He wanted everyone to see these hometown products, wanted everyone to have to look closely at them.

There were no gunfights during the raids, nobody ran; they were young men, boys, really, sleeping in their bedrooms. Three of them still in their childhood homes.

When Ben and his team arrived at Raymond Benedict's home, they simply knocked, showed the warrant to Raymond's father, who read it saying, *No, not Ray.* Ben and two uniforms walked through the den, leaving Mr. Benedict to his disbelief. Guns drawn, they stalked down a short hallway to a bedroom with a NO TRESPASSING sign hanging on the door. Ben led the way, shouldering open the door, flipping on the lights, pointing his revolver at a lump curled up on the bottom bunk of a bunk bed.

They hauled him out of bed, all six foot three of him in his tighty-whiteys, a stupid child in a man's body. *I didn't do it, I swear,* he said. *It was Ian and that kid Jacob.* His mother screaming, his dad asking what this was about. When Ben got Raymond cuffed, he noticed the wallpaper, little toy planes flying through a puffy clouded sky. Pushed up against the wall was a desk with a computer on it, and hanging above that was a flag, the red background, the blue shield, the cross and wolfsangel. How the hell could these parents be so shocked? It was right there in front of them, on the wall, right next to the kiddie bunk bed.

It took until the afternoon to get the search warrant for the Rowans' house on Comet Street, the judge, it seemed, a bit hesitant to issue on one of the city's esteemed leaders. He and Hernandez went in with three uniforms, flashed the paper to Mrs. Rowan, who seemed to not understand what it meant.

"C'mon, Mom," Michael said, walking his mother out to the backyard to sit at the patio table. "Let's go watch the birds."

Michael didn't ask about his father or his brother, and Ben didn't offer anything. Someone from ATF likely alerted the family about yesterday's events, though the house didn't feel heavy with grief.

They started in the garage first, taking pictures of the pool table with the missing cue ball, printing the sticks, the handle on the fridge. They bagged copies of two books, *The Camp of the Saints* by Jean Raspail and a dog-eared copy of *The Turner Diaries* by William Pierce. Then they worked the house, tearing through the drawers of Paul Rowan's desk—tax audit notice from the

IRS, mortgage papers, medical bills for Mrs. Rowan, car loans, phone bills, and then, in the back of the left-side drawer, they found the missing files from Walter Brennan's house in Huntington Beach, the properties in Rancho Santa Elena outlined in red ink. In Ian's room, they found the computer—a Tandy TRS-80 with a modem and floppy disk drive—and hauled it all out for evidence.

And hanging on a hook above Ian's dresser like a mini memorial, they found an M1 army combat helmet, the words KILL 'EM ALL written in black Sharpie across the shell.

————

That evening, when Natasha woke, someone was there, asleep in the chair in the corner of the room. Her vision was blurry, the world reassembling itself, and she didn't recognize him at first. She watched him for a few minutes—his mouth flung open, a quiet snore ululating from his throat. She smiled. It was Ben, she realized, happy to hear his snoring again. She didn't wake him, just eyed him, the man, she thought, she might have come back into this world for.

This was the first time she'd seen the hospital room, but she knew it already—the dull whiteness of it, the faint iron taint of blood in the air, the burn of bleach. Until they'd given her morphine—which sent her into black sleep—she'd been witness to it all: the nurse performing CPR, Dr. Akoma trying to fuse her femoral artery, and then the doctor declaring her "gone." She had smiled at that, high above the OR table. She had wanted to wave at him and say, *I'm right here*. But that had felt mean to her, beneath her new status as disembodied—as, well, dead.

She had seen the boy, Jacob, arrive at the hospital, too. She didn't think he'd died, but she'd been with him somehow—in that other place. She knew he was near her in the hospital and she wanted to see him. In her body, the feeling didn't make sense to her. She wanted hatred, wanted that old feeling back like jonesing for a drug. But she tried to hold that disembodied feeling with her in her embodied self, knew it was something important she needed to keep.

Out the window, rows of orange trees spread beneath a desert blue sky. The place she'd been just a couple days before—if she could call it a place—was shapeless, it vibrated energy, but there was nothing to touch, nothing to see, not like "Heaven" at all—at least as it had been described to her, like some cloud palace above Mount Olympus. It had been a place of feeling, of calm—that's the best way to describe it, free feeling, but connected, too, as though she had been absorbed. That's it: She had felt absorbed. A pang of remorse gripped her body; she was back into the confused world, breathing in the place that had more questions than answers.

She watched Ben and she felt a shadow of that feeling she'd had when she was disembodied; it vibrated here, too—in her body, in the air between them—though more quietly. She *had* come back for him, but not only for him. She'd come back because, well, she didn't know why. She had come back because Bao Phan had belted a tourniquet around her thigh. An image of him flashed in her mind, his hands, flecked with blood, gently tightening the leather around her skin. Ben had gotten her to the hospital, but Bao was the one who saved her. The other reasons, the reasons why she chose not to let herself be absorbed, she'd have to sort out with this second chance at living.

She touched Ben now, the bone of his knee, one hinge of the miracle of the fragile human form, and he woke.

"Can I buy you a drink, Detective?" Her voice was rough from not being used, the words strange in her mouth.

He smiled, relief coloring his face.

"If you got the money, honey," he said, standing now to touch her face, "I got the time."

———

Ben stayed with her as much as he could. He'd go to the station, work on getting Linh's murder case in order, help Vanek by phone on the Brennan case, and then drive back to the hospital, to sit in the chair next to Natasha, who dozed in and out.

Natasha's last day in ICU, she sent Ben off with a note for Bao. It was simply a folded-over piece of hospital stationery. *Thank you,* she had written in an unsteady hand. He drove across town to the Phans' place, knocked on the door, and handed Bao the note. When Bao read it, he simply nodded, folded the paper back up, and slid it into his shirt pocket.

"From me, too, Bao," Ben said. "From me, too."

Bao nodded his acknowledgment and then Ben headed back to the hospital.

He didn't tell Natasha about the raid in Big Bear until she was out of ICU and into a room with a view toward the ocean.

"The children, too?" she asked.

"Yes," he said. "We saved one, a baby boy."

She stared at him a moment then looked away. He took her hand then and she held it to her chest.

"What about Jacob?"

"I don't know," he said.

"Please find out."

He flashed his badge at reception, got referred to an ICU doctor, who walked him through the kid's chart. Blast lung, internal bleeding, critical condition, prognosis grave. Couldn't say he felt bad about it. He went back and told her and all she said was *Thank you.*

The next day, she ate, she drank, color coming back into her skin. When she first woke from the coma, she hadn't looked entirely there, as though some part of her was still in the otherworld. But now her eyes were green again, her skin once again browned by the sun. So far there had been no complications with her leg. Damn miracle.

"I want to see Jacob," she said.

"Unless you want to finish him off," Ben said, "what the hell do you want to see him for?"

"Ben, something happened to me, when I was gone. I can't explain it to you, I can barely explain it to myself. But I need to know about him."

He didn't get it. What the hell did she want with him? The kid almost killed her, killed Linh, a young woman she loved, bombed three others into oblivion. As far as Ben was concerned, the kid was a terrorist, fifteen years old or not. Seemed to him the kid got what he deserved.

She let out a sigh. "That boy hates because he's frightened. He's been walking around in the dark most of his life. I know something that he doesn't know. I need to tell him." She looked at Ben hard, in a way he had never seen. "Do this for me."

He flashed his badge again, got sent again to ICU where, at first, there seemed to be some confusion. The kid wasn't on the list, wasn't in ICU. Maybe he'd stabilized, was going to live. One of the nurses told him to wait, she wanted to check something. She disappeared for a few minutes, then came back and said, "Deceased. At 5:17 this morning. Graveyard shift transferred the body to the morgue."

He expected to feel something, but the news just sat flat in him.

When he got back to her room and told her, she was silent a moment. He wasn't able to read her feelings; something about her had become opaque.

"Take me to him."

Ben rolled her down to the morgue in a wheelchair he'd found in the hallway outside her room. The nurses objected, saying she wasn't well enough to be moved yet. Ben showed them his badge—the magic ticket—and said it was police business. He had to do this two more times, to get off the floor, and then to convince the skeptical morgue manager in the basement.

When they got into the refrigerator, the boy was near the front, laid out on a gurney, three hours dead, but the color still in his skin.

"Give me some time," she said, and wheeled herself over to the boy.

Ben stood in the corner of the morgue, his coat lapel pulled up against the cold, and watched her grab the boy's pale hand. The kid reminded Ben of Lance for a moment, the boy's body in transition to manhood, that in-between place of confusion. It made him think of the kids up in LA, children caught up in violence they couldn't control. But no, forget that. Those kids were screwed—by the system, by the crack epidemic, by a whole country that didn't give a damn about them. This kid lived in Rancho Santa Elena, this kid went to good schools, everything in this country made to privilege him. His violence was born out of some other sickness, some cancer living in the body of white America.

Natasha leaned close to the boy, his shaved head clipper-nicked, his face the alabaster hue of bloodless capillaries. She was talking to the boy, he could tell, her head bowed to his ear, the occasional gesture that accompanies words. It was like she was blessing him. Ben stood there and watched her, her lips moving, like she was imparting all the wisdom in the universe to the dead boy. And he stood there for another twenty minutes, at least, watching the woman he loved share an intimacy with her almost-killer. The kid was dead. That was it. That's wisdom for you: Kill and be killed. Yeah, that was wisdom he knew as gospel.

———

The next day, sitting outside of the hospital in his cruiser, Ben put in a call to Vanek.

Ben had been building the Brennan case with Vanek, told the detective he'd let him know when Natasha came out of the coma. He'd kept it secret, though, these first days, wanted to keep her to himself. Finally, his conscience got the better of him.

"If it's all right with you," Vanek said, "I'd like to see her."

Ben wanted to say no, but Vanek was a good cop. Seemed like a pretty good man, too. And Natasha could make up her own mind about who she wanted to see. What did they have, after all, if he felt he had to guard it?

"Don't think it's my place to give permission," he said. "She's in room seven-oh-seven."

Ben was still sitting there in the parking lot fifteen minutes later when Vanek pulled up. When the detective walked through the front door of the hospital, Ben checked his watch, 10:13, hopeful Vanek would be striding back out the door real soon.

———

She had been dozing when Detective Vanek knocked on her door and nudged it open. She felt an uncomplicated joy as soon as she realized who it was—his three-piece suit, his slicked-back hair, like a man out of another time.

"Come here." She held out her hand. He strode across the room, the spice of aftershave preceding him, sat on the chair next to her bed, and took her hand. "You told me to be careful with those people," she said. "You were right."

"I wish I'd been wrong," he said, his brown eyes on her, like he was looking through her somehow.

She smiled. "It's okay. I'm okay." She felt his wedding ring, and she turned his hand over, ran her finger over it. "Your wife's in a good place."

"I know," he said, his eyes welling with emotion. "I have faith in that."

"I've never really believed that until now."

She wanted to tell him what had happened to her when she was dead, but it felt beyond words. She thought, too, that somehow he already knew. There was something old-soul about Detective Vanek, as though he'd already lived three lives.

"It's a helpful thing to believe," he said. Vanek glanced out the window, and then looked back at her. "What I wanted to tell you the other day"—he hesitated a moment—"is that you remind me of her, of Deborah."

She wasn't sure how to think about what he was saying.

"It's been strange," he said, "to feel the same thing again with another person." He laughed. "And I barely know you."

"Sometimes you just know people."

He nodded and covered up her hand with both of his.

"Ben's a good man."

She smiled. "I know."

"He's outside in his cruiser," Vanek said. "Waiting for me to come out."

She laughed.

"He doesn't think I noticed."

He smiled and then bowed his head until his forehead was resting on the back of her hand. And they sat there for three minutes, maybe more, holding hands, his forehead resting on her knuckles, until he squeezed her palm once, let go, and walked out of the room.

———

Bao was surprised to find the temple full of people, spilling out into the courtyard of the industrial park. Mostly it was people from the Vietnamese community, but there were others, too—Miss Natasha, just released from the hospital, Detective Benjamin Wade, the police lieutenant, and complete strangers—white people who had protested, others who had simply heard about the story on the news. Some of them came up to him, shook his hand, and said things: *I'm so sorry for your loss* or *I feel terrible about this. This isn't who we are. You're welcome here.* He was happy that they were here to honor Linh, but he couldn't absorb their need to express their sense of guilt, not now at least, so he simply smiled and nodded to them and then retreated to stand next to the casket. Linh's body was inside, wrapped in white cloth, a white handkerchief placed over her face.

Outside, the police had erected barriers to keep the press away from the funeral. Since the bombings, their home phone had exploded with calls from reporters asking for interviews, news vans had been camped out in front of the house, reporters calling out questions whenever Bao or Ai stepped outside. Danh told Bao that some of the news articles about the bombing were calling Bao a hero. He didn't feel like a hero and he ignored all requests for interviews until, finally, Lieutenant Hernandez had shut it all down, pushing the news vans and cameras and reporters outside the entrance to their housing tract so they could plan the funeral in private.

The community was chanting now, Bao, Ai, Danh and his family dressed in white, too, standing next to the coffin. The rest of the community was dressed in black, many of them holding white lotus flowers, their voices, too, lifting Linh up to the next life. Early in the chants, he imagined his daughter at her wedding. It had been a longtime fantasy for him, her wedding day, here, in California. He would walk her down the aisle, pass her off to a handsome young Vietnamese man— second generation, though, a citizen, no wounded refugees, no one holding on to the old things. Ai would cry, a face full of tears—of love, of triumph. They would dance all night, eat from a five-foot-tall cake, shower the newlyweds with money, and watch them drive off in a limousine to their honeymoon in Hawaii, halfway across the Pacific to Vietnam, knowing they would be back here to California to offer them grandchildren.

But he was holding on to her now, when he was supposed to be letting her go. She had another life to live, with other people. An hour into the chants, he moved into another place, one of light somewhere high in the consciousness of his closed eyes, a place inside his head that felt vast. Linh was there and would always be there, as long as he lived, and maybe, if she lived another life, they would somehow cross paths again—in their grocery, by chance at a restaurant, maybe sitting on a beach watching the waves—not knowing each other, but feeling something pass between them.

Or maybe she had somehow reached nirvana, maybe she had extinguished the three fires inside herself—passion, aversion, ignorance—and had come to that place where the body wasn't needed anymore. Maybe she'd come back to him in thunderclouds or desert wind; in the waves pulled by the moon, or in the oxygen he breathed. Maybe that's how it would be, as easy as breathing her in.

And he chanted. They chanted.

———

A couple of weeks later, Ben was a witness in the preliminary hearing for *State of California versus Rowan*. When Ben and Vanek put together the murder case and charged Paul Rowan with second-degree murder for the killing of Walter Brennan, the feds gave him up to local control. The ATF only had him on evading arrest and reckless endangerment in the chase in Big Bear, and their case was complicated by a whole lot of bad press about their tactics.

It had been a long two weeks—Ben and Vanek, working with Hernandez, making sure their case was airtight, Natasha convalescing at his place, a physical therapist visiting every couple of days to get her leg strong again. After Linh's funeral, Natasha had insisted that they attend the funerals of the three people killed in the bombing—David Barnes, the police recruit; Liam Ross, a UC student who had been in Linh's literature program; and Tuyen Ngo, the mother of three who had been serving soup at the protest. The funerals exhausted Natasha—all that unnecessary loss and its radiating pain—and after each she collapsed in bed for the rest of the day, her body still weak from the violence done to it. It would be a long recovery, it seemed, but he could have been mourning her at a funeral this week, too. The one spot of hope? The boy who had been thrown from the burning window was in foster care at OC4Kids and up for adoption. Natasha had asked about him and Ben had called up to social services. The kid wouldn't remember his mother or father, an erasure that perhaps could save him. Maybe the kid would get adopted, have a chance at a normal life not filled with hate.

The Superior Court of California was up in Orange, just down the street from the coroner's office. Paul Rowan sat alone at the defendant's table, dressed in a dark-blue suit, arm in a sling, a ream of paper in front of him. Mrs. Rowan and Michael sat a row behind him, dressed in their Sunday best.

"You're representing yourself?" the judge said.

"Yes I am, sir."

The judge glared at him a moment. Ben smiled to himself. These decisions, born out of ego, stupidity, or both, rarely went well for the defendant.

The judge, apparently feeling generous, advised Paul Rowan of his rights as legal representation, knowledge any practicing attorney would have had as he walked into the courtroom. *You have a right to peremptory challenges, the right to make evidentiary objections, the right to cross-examine witnesses.* Rowan sat and listened, took a few notes, but it wasn't clear if the man actually understood what the judge was saying. Watching him sitting there alone at the big wooden table, it struck Ben how small he looked, so lost in his own sense of genetic superiority that he was blind to his mediocrity. So bound to his hatred, he had been willing to sacrifice a son—and a family—for it. It struck Ben then that racism—the violent kind Rowan traded in and the kind that lived beneath the surface of places like Rancho Santa Elena—was a sort of suicide. Like Wales and the stupid zealots up in Big Bear, Ben was starting to think a whole lot of white people in this country would be willing to burn it all down, democracy, America, the whole damn thing, to maintain the fantasy of their superiority. The small man sitting in front of the judge was easy to hate; white people who thought themselves good folks could point a finger at him to assuage their own guilty conscience, but the ugliness ran much deeper than that. How he would change that, he didn't know yet, but he didn't want to pretend anymore that he was innocent of it. That kind of pretending, when you knew it was a lie, was a stone in your heart.

The prosecutor laid out his case, basically the same narrative Ben and Vanek had spent weeks putting together, which boiled down to: Paul Rowan ordered his son to attack Walter Brennan in retaliation for leasing Brennan's property to Asian tenants. After fifteen minutes, the prosecutor called Ben to the witness stand to lay out the evidence: his son Michael's testimony—Michael looked at his feet while Ben spoke—the autopsy report, the homey socks, the methamphetamine, the connection to Wales, the evidence at the house on Comet Street.

About halfway through the questioning a man walked into the courtroom and sat down in the back. Ben watched him a moment—he was late, his suit was a slick slim cut, he was wearing a straight black tie, a white pocket handkerchief, glasses. He looked like a geeky member of the Rat Pack.

"Does the defense wish to cross-examine?"

"Yes, Your Honor," Rowan said, standing up and nervously glancing at his wife behind him.

He stopped then, noticing, it seemed, the man at the back of the room. Ben swore he saw Rowan visibly shake, like he'd been hit with a zap of electricity. Ben looked at the man in the back of the room again. He sat there, his legs crossed at the knee, impassive eyes looking straight ahead.

"Mr. Rowan," the judge said, "do you wish to cross-examine the witness?"

Even the dullest defense attorney would go after Ben over Michael's taped testimony—the kid had been frightened and he and Hernandez had put the screws to him in their taped interview. His plea deal gave him motivation, too, to implicate his brother and by extension their father. But Rowan stood there, sweat gathering at his temples. He glanced at the man

again and then looked at his family, as though some dire understanding had jolted his consciousness.

"I plead nolo contendere," Rowan said.

The judge, as astonished as everyone else in the room, said,
"You suddenly wish to plead no contest?"

"Yes," Rowan said, the word nearly catching in his throat.

"You understand, that in the eyes of this court, your sentencing will be commensurate with a guilty plea?"

Rowan was quiet a few moments. The judge sounded tough
and maybe he *would* throw the book at him a month or two
later at sentencing, but something about the way he'd taken his
time to explain the law to Rowan a few minutes earlier made
Ben doubt it. Fifteen-to-life was the sentencing guideline, and
Ben imagined Rowan's punishment would fall on the light side
of that range.

"I do," Rowan finally said.

The man in the back suddenly stood up and walked out of
the courtroom, not even glancing at Rowan, apparently satis-
fied with the outcome. Yeah, no trial, no talking.

As soon as the judge banged his gavel and called out a sentencing date, Ben ran through the courtroom, bolted down the
steps of the courthouse and into the parking lot, but the man
was nowhere to be found. When he got to his cruiser, parked in
an official spot next to two other police cars, an envelope was
slipped beneath the driver's side windshield wiper. Inside,
folded perfectly into thirds, was a typed note: *Race traitor*, it
read. *We're watching you.*

Acknowledgments

I didn't know it at the time, but the inspiration for *The Recruit* came at a dinner in the Philadelphia suburbs with the Vietnamese American writer Monique Truong. Monique had visited Villanova University for our literary festival, and talking at the restaurant following her reading, we realized that we had a surprising almost-connection. When I was five years old, I was living in a house that was just five minutes away from the now-closed Marine Corps Air Station El Toro runway, where Monique, seven at the time, and her family landed as refugees from the Vietnam War. It's an obvious thing, I guess, but something hit me that night thinking about the brief physical proximity of our childhoods, and yet the extreme differences in our circumstances at that time. I was struck, too, about how little I knew about the history of the war, even as it happened right next door to my childhood home. I mean, I knew the history in a vague sort of way, but I do not recall having ever learned about it in high school or college. As a child, the war was a sort of ancient history to me, but that night in 2011 I was sitting next to someone, a contemporary of mine, at a nice restaurant in the wealthy Main Line suburbs, whose life had been radically altered by it. Seven years later, when I was struggling to write Bao Phan's sections, I contacted Monique and she told me about the University of California, Irvine's *Viet Stories: Vietnamese American Oral History Project,* which was an invaluable resource to me when I knew my imagination was failing to do justice to the refugee experience. I'm grateful to Monique, and to all those powerful and often poignant first-person narratives in UCI's archive.

In the 1980s, that war was not so distant as I thought, of course, and it was always a shadow hanging over my childhood. One of my earliest memories with my father is watching the war broadcast live on the evening news after he came home from work. Our neighbor across the street had fought in the infantry in Vietnam and suffered PTSD, though they didn't call it that at the time. His two sons bore the brunt of his anguish, suffering beatings when their father was gripped by flashbacks. His youngest son later started making pipe bombs, blowing holes in his backyard, and once, accompanied by me, blowing up an outdoor picnic bench at our elementary school. The war radiated trauma in that house, and though I lost touch with them years ago, I think about the two brothers often and hope they are well wherever they are in the world.

Jan Herman's *The Lucky Few: The Fall of Saigon and the Rescue Mission of the USS* Kirk helped me to imagine the harrowing escape from Saigon as the city fell in April 1975. The tales of heroism—of both the South Vietnamese army officers who managed to get their families out of Saigon on military helicopters, and the American navy sailors who helped to land those aircraft on a ship too small for the mission—are astonishing to read.

I didn't discover Kathleen Belew's *Bring the War Home: The White Power Movement and Paramilitary America* until late in the writing of this novel, but it helped to clarify for me what I was trying to dramatize in *The Recruit:* that the aftermath of the Vietnam War sparked a new white supremacy movement, one that coalesced in the 1980s around the fledgling internet and ultimately found legitimacy as a mainstream political movement in the presidency of Donald Trump. In later drafts of the novel, I turned to Belew's book to help me make sure I kept my fiction grounded (mostly) in reality.

I cannot thank my editor, Kate Medina, enough. Her wisdom, her guidance, her editorial brilliance, and above all, her patience (I'm a slow and sloppy writer) is more than any author can hope for. To Noa Shapiro, who kept everything running smoothly, even during a pandemic. Thanks, too, to Gina Centrello for her continued support of my work. And all my gratitude to the Random House team who helped shepherd this book into the world: Andy Ward, Avideh Bashirrad, Barbara Fillon, Madison Dettlinger, Michael Hoak, Maria Braeckel, Susan Corcoran, Karen Fink, Rebecca Berlant, Benjamin Dreyer, Sandra Sjursen, Kelly Chian, Caroline Cunningham, and Carlos Beltrán.

As always, I'm so grateful for my agent, Dorian Karchmar, who took me on years ago when I had almost nothing worth reading and stuck with me until I did. I will always be thankful.

I'm indebted to the dean's office of the College of Liberal Arts and Sciences at Villanova, which granted me a research leave in the fall of 2017 when I was at a critical juncture in the first draft of this novel. To the English department: I'm proud to be working among such dedicated scholars and educators. And a shout-out to my students, who remind me on a regular basis how truly rewarding teaching can be. Keep writing!

Big thanks to my friend retired LAPD homicide detective and Villanova grad Robert Jakucs, who was always willing to educate me when my limited investigative procedural knowledge failed.

I didn't have a computer when I was growing up in the 1980s and remain, to this day, mostly computer illiterate, so a couple of hallelujahs to my friend—the man with all the tools—Nick DiPatri, and to George Talbot for the "nerd talk" about early internet bulletin board systems that helped me pretend I knew what I was talking about in this book.

My good friends Janet Baker, Dawn Roth, and Craig Rutter all read various iterations of the book at important times during its development. Their encouragement helped me to keep going when all I really wanted to do was drink IPAs and play guitar.

All my love to my fantastically talented, kind, and thoughtful children, Nathaniel and Adeline, who put up with being ignored while I type away in the attic. I'm beyond proud and so lucky to be your father.

Last but always first, my love, my gratitude, my respect, and my awe for my wonderful Miriam. None of this life without you.

ABOUT THE TYPE

This book is set in Iowan Old Style. Designed by noted sign painter John Downer in 1991 and modeled after the types cut by Nicolas Jenson and Francesco Griffo in fifteenth-century Italy, it is a very readable typeface—sturdy-looking, open, and unfussy.